The House of Cobwebs
and Other Stories

by

George Gissing

The Echo Library 2007

Published by

The Echo Library

Echo Library
131 High St.
Teddington
Middlesex TW11 8HH

www.echo-library.com

Please report serious faults in the text to complaints@echo-library.com

ISBN 1-40681-004-5

CONTENTS

THE WORK OF GEORGE GISSING

AN INTRODUCTORY SURVEY

> 'Les gens tout à fait heureux, forts et bien portants, sont-ils préparés comme il faut pour comprendre, pénétrer, exprimer la vie, notre vie si tourmentée et si courte?'
>
> MAUPASSANT.

In England during the sixties and seventies of last century the world of books was dominated by one Gargantuan type of fiction. The terms book and novel became almost synonymous in houses which were not Puritan, yet where books and reading, in the era of few and unfree libraries, were strictly circumscribed. George Gissing was no exception to this rule. The English novel was at the summit of its reputation during his boyish days. As a lad of eight or nine he remembered the parts of *Our Mutual Friend* coming to the house, and could recall the smile of welcome with which they were infallibly received. In the dining-room at home was a handsomely framed picture which he regarded with an almost idolatrous veneration. It was an engraved portrait of Charles Dickens. Some of the best work of George Eliot, Reade, and Trollope was yet to make its appearance; Meredith and Hardy were still the treasured possession of the few; the reigning models during the period of Gissing's adolescence were probably Dickens and Trollope, and the numerous satellites of these great stars, prominent among them Wilkie Collins, William Black, and Besant and Rice.

Of the cluster of novelists who emerged from this school of ideas, the two who will attract most attention in the future were clouded and obscured for the greater period of their working lives. Unobserved, they received, and made their own preparations for utilising, the legacy of the mid-Victorian novel—moral thesis, plot, underplot, set characters, descriptive machinery, landscape colouring, copious phraseology, Herculean proportions, and the rest of the cumbrous and grandiose paraphernalia of *Chuzzlewit, Pendennis*, and *Middlemarch*. But they received the legacy in a totally different spirit. Mark Rutherford, after a very brief experiment, put all these elaborate properties and conventions reverently aside. Cleverer and more docile, George Gissing for the most part accepted them; he put his slender frame into the ponderous collar of the author of the *Mill on the Floss*, and nearly collapsed in wind and limb in the heart-breaking attempt to adjust himself to such an heroic type of harness.

The distinctive qualities of Gissing at the time of his setting forth were a scholarly style, rather fastidious and academic in its restraint, and the personal discontent, slightly morbid, of a self-conscious student who finds himself in the position of a sensitive woman in a crowd. His attitude through life was that of a man who, having set out on his career with the understanding that a second-class ticket is to be provided, allows himself to be unceremoniously hustled into the rough and tumble of a noisy third. Circumstances made him revolt against an anonymous start in life for a refined and educated man under such conditions. They also made him prolific. He shrank from the restraints and humiliations to which the poor and shabbily dressed private tutor is exposed—

revealed to us with a persuasive terseness in the pages of *The Unclassed, New Grub Street, Ryecroft,* and the story of *Topham's Chance.* Writing fiction in a garret for a sum sufficient to keep body and soul together for the six months following payment was at any rate better than this. The result was a long series of highly finished novels, written in a style and from a point of view which will always render them dear to the studious and the book-centred. Upon the larger external rings of the book-reading multitude it is not probable that Gissing will ever succeed in impressing himself. There is an absence of transcendental quality about his work, a failure in humour, a remoteness from actual life, a deficiency in awe and mystery, a shortcoming in emotional power, finally, a lack of the dramatic faculty, not indeed indispensable to a novelist, but almost indispensable as an ingredient in great novels of this particular genre.[1] In temperament and vitality he is palpably inferior to the masters (Dickens, Thackeray, Hugo, Balzac) whom he reverenced with such a cordial admiration and envy. A 'low vitality' may account for what has been referred to as the 'nervous exhaustion' of his style. It were useless to pretend that Gissing belongs of right to the 'first series' of English Men of Letters. But if debarred by his limitations from a resounding or popular success, he will remain exceptionally dear to the heart of the recluse, who thinks that the scholar does well to cherish a grievance against the vulgar world beyond the cloister; and dearer still, perhaps, to a certain number of enthusiasts who began reading George Gissing as a college night-course; who closed *Thyrza* and *Demos* as dawn was breaking through the elms in some Oxford quadrangle, and who have pursued his work patiently ever since in a somewhat toilsome and broken ascent, secure always of suave writing and conscientious workmanship, of an individual prose cadence and a genuine vein of Penseroso:—

'Thus, Night, oft see me in thy pale career...
Where brooding Darkness spreads his jealous wings,
And the night-raven sings.'

Yet by the larger, or, at any rate, the intermediate public, it is a fact that Gissing has never been quite fairly estimated. He loses immensely if you estimate him either by a single book, as is commonly done, or by his work as a whole, in the perspective of which, owing to the lack of critical instruction, one or two books of rather inferior quality have obtruded themselves unduly. This brief survey of the Gissing country is designed to enable the reader to judge the novelist by eight or nine of his best books. If we can select these aright, we feel sure that he will end by placing the work of George Gissing upon a considerably higher level than he has hitherto done.

The time has not yet come to write the history of his career—fuliginous in

---

[1] The same kind of limitations would have to be postulated in estimating the brothers De Goncourt, who, falling short of the first magnitude, have yet a fully recognised position upon the stellar atlas.

not a few of its earlier phases, gathering serenity towards its close,—finding a soul of goodness in things evil. This only pretends to be a chronological and, quite incidentally, a critical survey of George Gissing's chief works. And comparatively short as his working life proved to be—hampered for ten years by the sternest poverty, and for nearly ten more by the sad, illusive optimism of the poitrinaire—the task of the mere surveyor is no light or perfunctory one. Artistic as his temperament undoubtedly was, and conscientious as his writing appears down to its minutest detail, Gissing yet managed to turn out rather more than a novel per annum. The desire to excel acted as a spur which conquered his congenital inclination to dreamy historical reverie. The reward which he propounded to himself remained steadfast from boyhood; it was a kind of *Childe Harold* pilgrimage to the lands of antique story—

'Whither Albano's scarce divided waves
Shine from a sister valley;—and afar
The Tiber winds, and the broad ocean laves
The Latian coast where sprang the Epic War.'

Twenty-six years have elapsed since the appearance of his first book in 1880, and in that time just twenty-six books have been issued bearing his signature. His industry was worthy of an Anthony Trollope, and cost his employers barely a tithe of the amount claimed by the writer of *The Last Chronicle of Barset*. He was not much over twenty-two when his first novel appeared.[2] It was entitled *Workers in the Dawn*, and is distinguished by the fact that the author writes himself George Robert Gissing; afterwards he saw fit to follow the example of George Robert Borrow, and in all subsequent productions assumes the style of 'George Gissing.' The book begins in this fashion: 'Walk with me, reader, into Whitecross Street. It is Saturday night'; and it is what it here seems, a decidedly crude and immature performance. Gissing was encumbered at every step by the giant's robe of mid-Victorian fiction. Intellectual giants, Dickens and Thackeray, were equally gigantic spendthrifts. They worked in a state of fervid heat above a glowing furnace, into which they flung lavish masses of unshaped metal, caring little for immediate effect or minute dexterity of stroke, but knowing full well that the emotional energy of their temperaments was capable of fusing the most intractable material, and that in the end they would produce their great, downright effect. Their spirits rose and fell, but the case was desperate, copy had to be despatched for the current serial. Good and bad had to make up the tale against time, and revelling in the very exuberance and excess

---

[2] Three vols. 8vo, 1880 (Remington). It was noticed at some length in the *Athenoeum* of June 12th, in which the author's philosophic outlook is condemned as a dangerous compound of Schopenhauer, Comte, and Shelley. It is somewhat doubtful if he ever made more for a book than the £250 he got for *New Grub Street*. £200, we believe, was advanced on *The Nether World*, but this proved anything but a prosperous speculation from the publisher's point of view, and £150 was refused for *Born in Exile*.

of their humour, the novelists invariably triumphed.

To the Ercles vein of these Titans of fiction, Gissing was a complete stranger. To the pale and fastidious recluse and anchorite, their tone of genial remonstrance with the world and its ways was totally alien. He knew nothing of the world to start with beyond the den of the student. His second book, as he himself described it in the preface to a second edition, was the work of a very young man who dealt in a romantic spirit with the gloomier facts of life. Its title, *The Unclassed*,[3] excited a little curiosity, but the author was careful to explain that he had not in view the *déclassés* but rather those persons who live in a limbo external to society, and refuse the statistic badge. The central figure Osmond Waymark is of course Gissing himself. Like his creator, raving at intervals under the vile restraints of Philistine surroundings and with no money for dissipation, Osmond gives up teaching to pursue the literary vocation. A girl named Ida Starr idealises him, and is helped thereby to a purer life. In the four years' interval between this somewhat hurried work and his still earlier attempt the young author seems to have gone through a bewildering change of employments. We hear of a clerkship in Liverpool, a searing experience in America (described with but little deviation in *New Grub Street*), a gas-fitting episode in Boston, private tutorships, and cramming engagements in 'the poisonous air of working London.' Internal evidence alone is quite sufficient to indicate that the man out of whose brain such bitter experiences of the educated poor were wrung had learnt in suffering what he taught—in his novels. His start in literature was made under conditions that might have appalled the bravest, and for years his steps were dogged by hunger and many-shaped hardships. He lived in cellars and garrets. 'Many a time,' he writes, 'seated in just such a garret (as that in the frontispiece to *Little Dorrit*) I saw the sunshine flood the table in front of me, and the thought of that book rose up before me.' He ate his meals in places that would have offered a way-wearied tramp occasion for criticism. 'His breakfast consisted often of a slice of bread and a drink of water. Four and sixpence a week paid for his lodging. A meal that cost more than sixpence was a feast.' Once he tells us with a thrill of reminiscent ecstasy how he found sixpence in the street! The ordinary comforts of modern life were unattainable luxuries. Once when a newly posted notice in the lavatory at the British Museum warned readers that the basins were to be used (in official phrase) 'for casual ablutions only,' he was abashed at the thought of his own complete dependence upon the facilities of the place. Justly might the author call this a tragi-comical incident. Often in happier times he had brooding memories of the familiar old horrors—the foggy and gas-lit labyrinth of Soho—shop windows containing puddings and pies kept hot by steam rising through perforated metal—a young novelist of 'two-and-twenty or thereabouts' standing before the display, raging with hunger, unable to purchase even one pennyworth of food. And this is no

[3] Three vols., 1884, dedicated to M.C.R. In one volume 'revised,' 1895 (preface dated October 1895).

fancy picture,[4] but a true story of what Gissing had sufficient elasticity of humour to call 'a pretty stern apprenticeship.' The sense of it enables us to understand to the full that semi-ironical and bitter, yet not wholly unamused passage, in *Ryecroft*:—

> 'Is there at this moment any boy of twenty, fairly educated, but without means, without help, with nothing but the glow in his brain and steadfast courage in his heart, who sits in a London garret and writes for dear life? There must be, I suppose; yet all that I have read and heard of late years about young writers, shows them in a very different aspect. No garretteers, these novelists and journalists awaiting their promotion. They eat—and entertain their critics—at fashionable restaurants, they are seen in expensive seats at the theatre; they inhabit handsome flats—photographed for an illustrated paper on the first excuse. At the worst, they belong to a reputable club, and have garments which permit them to attend a garden party or an evening "at home" without attracting unpleasant notice. Many biographical sketches have I read during the last decade, making personal introduction of young Mr. This or young Miss That, whose book was—as the sweet language of the day will have it—"booming"; but never one in which there was a hint of stern struggles, of the pinched stomach and frozen fingers.'

In his later years it was customary for him to inquire of a new author 'Has he starved'? He need have been under no apprehension. There is still a God's plenty of attics in Grub Street, tenanted by genuine artists, idealists and poets, amply sufficient to justify the lamentable conclusion of old Anthony à Wood in his life of George Peele. 'For so it is and always hath been, that most poets die poor, and consequently obscurely, and a hard matter it is to trace them to their graves.' Amid all these miseries, Gissing upheld his ideal. During 1886-7 he began really to *write* and the first great advance is shown in *Isabel Clarendon*.[5] No book, perhaps, that he ever wrote is so rich as this in autobiographical indices. In the melancholy Kingcote we get more than a passing phase or a momentary glimpse at one side of the young author. A long succession of Kingcote's traits are obvious self-revelations. At the beginning he symbolically prefers the old road with the crumbling sign-post, to the new. Kingcote is a literary sensitive. The most ordinary transaction with uneducated ('that is uncivilised') people made him uncomfortable. Mean and hateful people by their suggestions made life hideous. He lacks the courage of the ordinary man. Though under thirty he is abashed by youth. He is sentimental and hungry for feminine sympathy, yet he realises that the woman who may with safety be taken in marriage by a poor

---

[4] Who but Gissing could describe a heroine as exhibiting in her countenance 'habitual nourishment on good and plenteous food'?

[5] *Isabel Clarendon.* By George Gissing. In two volumes, 1886 (Chapman and Hall). In reviewing this work the *Academy* expressed astonishment at the mature style of the writer—of whom it admitted it had not yet come across the name.

man, given to intellectual pursuits, is extremely difficult of discovery. Consequently he lives in solitude; he is tyrannised by moods, dominated by temperament. His intellect is in abeyance. He shuns the present—the historical past seems alone to concern him. Yet he abjures his own past. The ghost of his former self affected him with horror. Identity even he denies. 'How can one be responsible for the thoughts and acts of the being who bore his name years ago?' He has no consciousness of his youth—no sympathy with children. In him is to be discerned 'his father's intellectual and emotional qualities, together with a certain stiffness of moral attitude derived from his mother.' He reveals already a wonderful palate for pure literary flavour. His prejudices are intense, their character being determined by the refinement and idealism of his nature. All this is profoundly significant, knowing as we do that this was produced when Gissing's worldly prosperity was at its nadir. He was living at the time, like his own Harold Biffen, in absolute solitude, a frequenter of pawnbroker's shops and a stern connoisseur of pure dripping, pease pudding ('magnificent pennyworths at a shop in Cleveland Street, of a very rich quality indeed'), faggots and saveloys. The stamp of affluence in those days was the possession of a basin. The rich man thus secured the gravy which the poor man, who relied on a paper wrapper for his pease pudding, had to give away. The image recurred to his mind when, in later days, he discussed champagne vintages with his publisher, or was consulted as to the management of butlers by the wife of a popular prelate. With what a sincere recollection of this time he enjoins his readers (after Dr. Johnson) to abstain from Poverty. 'Poverty is the great secluder.' 'London is a wilderness abounding in anchorites.' Gissing was sustained amid all these miseries by two passionate idealisms, one of the intellect, the other of the emotions. The first was ancient Greece and Rome—and he incarnated this passion in the picturesque figure of Julian Casti (in *The Unclassed*), toiling hard to purchase a Gibbon, savouring its grand epic roll, converting its driest detail into poetry by means of his enthusiasm, and selecting Stilicho as a hero of drama or romance (a premonition here of *Veranilda*). The second or heart's idol was Charles Dickens—Dickens as writer, Dickens as the hero of a past England, Dickens as humorist, Dickens as leader of men, above all, Dickens as friend of the poor, the outcast, the pale little sempstress and the downtrodden Smike.

In the summer of 1870, Gissing remembered with a pious fidelity of detail the famous drawing of the 'Empty Chair' being framed and hung up 'in the school-room, at home'[6] (Wakefield).

---

[6] Of Gissing's early impressions, the best connected account, I think, is to be gleaned from the concluding chapters of *The Whirlpool*; but this may be reinforced (and to some extent corrected, or, here and there cancelled) by passages in *Burn in Exile* (vol. i.) and in *Ryecroft*. The material there supplied is confirmatory in the best sense of the detail contributed by Mr. Wells to the cancelled preface of *Veranilda*, touching the 'schoolboy, obsessed by a consuming passion for learning, at the Quaker's boarding-school at Alderley. He had come thither from Wakefield at the age of thirteen—after the death of his father, who was, in a double sense, the cardinal formative influence in his life. The tones of his father's voice, his father's gestures, never departed from him; when he read

'Not without awe did I see the picture of the room which was now tenantless: I remember too, a curiosity which led me to look closely at the writing-table and the objects upon it, at the comfortable round-backed chair, at the book-shelves behind. I began to ask myself how books were written and how the men lived who wrote them. It is my last glimpse of childhood. Six months later there was an empty chair in my own home, and the tenor of my life was broken.

'Seven years after this I found myself amid the streets of London and had to find the means of keeping myself alive. What I chiefly thought of was that now at length I could go hither or thither in London'simmensity seeking for the places which had been made known to me by Dickens.

'One day in the city I found myself at the entrance to Bevis Marks! I had just been making an application in reply to some advertisement—of course, fruitlessly; but what was that disappointment compared with the discovery of Bevis Marks! Here dwelt Mr. Brass and Sally and the Marchioness. Up and down the little street, this side and that, I went gazing and dreaming. No press of busy folk disturbed me; the place was quiet; it looked no doubt much the same as when Dickens knew it. I am not sure that I had any dinner that day; but, if not, I daresay I did not mind it very much.'

The broad flood under Thames bridges spoke to him in the very tones of 'the master.' He breathed Guppy's London particular, the wind was the black easter that pierced the diaphragm of Scrooge's clerk.

'We bookish people have our connotations for the life we do not live. In time I came to see London with my own eyes, but how much better when I saw it with those of Dickens!'

Tired and discouraged, badly nourished, badly housed—working under conditions little favourable to play of the fancy or intentness of the mind—then was the time, Gissing found, to take down Forster and read—read about Charles Dickens.

'Merely as the narrative of a wonderfully active, zealous, and successful life, this book scarce has its equal; almost any reader must find it exhilarating; but to me it yielded such special sustenance as in those days I could not have found elsewhere, and

---

aloud, particularly if it was poetry he read, his father returned in him. He could draw in those days with great skill and vigour—it will seem significant to many that he was particularly fascinated by Hogarth's work, and that he copied and imitated it; and his father's well-stocked library, and his father's encouragement, had quickened his imagination and given it its enduring bias for literary activity.' Like Defoe, Smollett, Sterne, Borrow, Dickens, Eliot, 'G.C.' is, half involuntarily, almost unconsciously autobiographic.

lacking which I should, perhaps, have failed by the way. I am not referring to Dickens's swift triumph, to his resounding fame and high prosperity; these things are cheery to read about, especially when shown in a light so human, with the accompaniment of so much geniality and mirth. No; the pages which invigorated me are those where we see Dickens at work, alone at his writing-table, absorbed in the task of the story-teller. Constantly he makes known to Forster how his story is getting on, speaks in detail of difficulties, rejoices over spells of happy labour; and what splendid sincerity in it all! If this work of his was not worth doing, why, nothing was. A troublesome letter has arrived by the morning's post and threatens to spoil the day; but he takes a few turns up and down the room, shakes off the worry, and sits down to write for hours and hours. He is at the sea-side, his desk at a sunny bay window overlooking the shore, and there all the morning he writes with gusto, ever and again bursting into laughter at his own thoughts.'[7]

The influence of Dickens clearly predominated when Gissing wrote his next novel and first really notable and artistic book, *Thyrza*.[8] The figure which irradiates this story is evidently designed in the school of Dickens: it might almost be a pastel after some more highly finished work by Daudet. But Daudet is a more relentless observer than Gissing, and to find a parallel to this particular effect I think we must go back a little farther to the heroic age of the *grisette* and the tearful *Manchon de Francine* of Henri Murger. *Thyrza*, at any rate, is a most exquisite picture in half-tones of grey and purple of a little Madonna of the slums; she is in reality the *belle fleur d'un fumier* of which he speaks in the epigraph of the *Nether World*. The *fumier* in question is Lambeth Walk, of which we have a Saturday night scene, worthy of the author of *L'Assommoir* and *Le Ventre de Paris* in his most perceptive mood. In this inferno, amongst the pungent odours, musty smells and 'acrid exhalations from the shops where fried fish and potatoes hissed in boiling grease,' blossomed a pure white lily, as radiant amid mean surroundings as Gemma in the poor Frankfort confectioner's shop of Turgenev's *Eaux Printanières*. The pale and rather languid charm of her face and figure are sufficiently portrayed without any set description. What could be more

---

[7] See a deeply interesting paper on Dickens by 'G.G.' in the New York *Critic*, Jan. 1902. Much of this is avowed autobiography.

[8] *Thyrza: A Novel* (3 vols., 1887). In later life we are told that Gissing affected to despise this book as 'a piece of boyish idealism.' But he was always greatly pleased by any praise of this 'study of two sisters, where poverty for once is rainbow-tinted by love.' My impression is that it was written before *Demos*, but was longer in finding a publisher; it had to wait until the way was prepared by its coarser and more vigorous workfellow. A friend writes: 'I well remember the appearance of the MS. Gissing wrote then on thin foreign paper in a small, thin handwriting, without correction. It was before the days of typewriting, and the MS. of a three-volume novel was so compressed that one could literally put it in one's pocket without the slightest inconvenience.' The name is from Byron's *Elegy on Thyrza*.

delicate than the intimation of the foregone 'good-night' between the sisters, or the scene of Lyddy plaiting Thyrza's hair? The delineation of the upper middle class culture by which this exquisite flower of maidenhood is first caressed and transplanted, then slighted and left to wither, is not so satisfactory. Of the upper middle class, indeed, at that time, Gissing had very few means of observation. But this defect, common to all his early novels, is more than compensated by the intensely pathetic figure of Gilbert Grail, the tender-souled, book-worshipping factory hand raised for a moment to the prospect of intellectual life and then hurled down by the caprice of circumstance to the unrelenting round of manual toil at the soap and candle factory. Dickens would have given a touch of the grotesque to Grail's gentle but ungainly character; but at the end he would infallibly have rewarded him as Tom Pinch and Dominie Sampson were rewarded. Not so George Gissing. His sympathy is fully as real as that of Dickens. But his fidelity to fact is greater. Of the Christmas charity prescribed by Dickens, and of the untainted pathos to which he too rarely attained, there is an abundance in *Thyrza*. But what amazes the chronological student of Gissing's work is the magnificent quality of some of the writing, a quality of which he had as yet given no very definite promise. Take the following passage, for example:—

'A street organ began to play in front of a public-house close by. Grail drew near; there were children forming a dance, and he stood to watch them.

Do you know that music of the obscure ways, to which children dance? Not if you have only heard it ground to your ears' affliction beneath your windows in the square. To hear it aright you must stand in the darkness of such a by-street as this, and for the moment be at one with those who dwell around, in the blear-eyed houses, in the dim burrows of poverty, in the unmapped haunts of the semi-human. Then you will know the significance of that vulgar clanging of melody; a pathos of which you did not dream will touch you, and therein the secret of hidden London will be half revealed. The life of men who toil without hope, yet with the hunger of an unshaped desire; of women in whom the sweetness of their sex is perishing under labour and misery; the laugh, the song of the girl who strives to enjoy her year or two of youthful vigour, knowing the darkness of the years to come; the careless defiance of the youth who feels his blood and revolts against the lot which would tame it; all that is purely human in these darkened multitudes speaks to you as you listen. It is the half-conscious striving of a nature which knows not what it would attain, which deforms a true thought by gross expression, which clutches at the beautiful and soils it with foul hands.

The children were dirty and ragged, several of them barefooted, nearly all bare-headed, but they danced with noisy merriment. One there was, a little girl, on crutches; incapable of taking a partner, she stumped round and round, circling upon the pavement, till giddiness came upon her and she had to fall back and lean against the wall, laughing aloud at her weakness. Gilbert stepped up to her, and put a penny into her hand; then, before she had recovered from her surprise, passed onwards.'—(p. 111.)

This superb piece of imaginative prose, of which Shorthouse himself might have been proud,[9] is recalled by an answering note in *Ryecroft*, in which he says, 'I owe many a page to the street-organs.'

And, where the pathos has to be distilled from dialogue, I doubt if the author of *Jack* himself could have written anything more restrainedly touching or in a finer taste than this:—

'Laughing with kindly mirth, the old man drew on his woollen gloves and took up his hat and the violin-bag. Then he offered to say good-bye.

"But you're forgetting your top-coat, grandad," said Lydia.

"I didn't come in it, my dear."

"What's that, then? I'm sure *we* don't wear such things."

She pointed to a chair, on which Thyrza had just artfully spread the gift. Mr. Boddy looked in a puzzled way; had he really come in his coat and forgotten it? He drew nearer.

"That's no coat o' mine, Lyddy," he said.

Thyrza broke into a laugh.

"Why, whose is it, then?" she exclaimed. "Don't play tricks, grandad; put it on at once!"

"Now come, come; you're keeping Mary waiting," said Lydia, catching up the coat and holding it ready.

Then Mr. Boddy understood. He looked from Lydia to Thyrza with dimmed eyes.

"I've a good mind never to speak to either of you again," he said in a tremulous voice. "As if you hadn't need enough of your money! Lyddy, Lyddy! And you're as bad, Thyrza, a grownup woman like you; you ought to teach your sister better. Why, there; it's no good; I don't know what to say to you. Now what do you think of this, Mary?"

Lydia still held up the coat, and at length persuaded the old man to don it. The effect upon his appearance was remarkable; conscious of it, he held himself more upright and stumped to the little square of looking-glass to try and regard himself. Here he furtively brushed a hand over his eyes.

"I'm ready, Mary, my dear; I'm ready! It's no good saying anything to girls like these. Good-bye, Lyddy; good-bye, Thyrza.

---

[9] I am thinking, in particular, of the old vielle-player's conversation in chap. xxiii. of *John Inglesant*; of the exquisite passage on old dance music—its inexpressible pathos—in chap. xxv.

May you have a happy Christmas, children! This isn't the first as you've made a happy one for me."—(p. 117.)

The anonymously published *Demos* (1886) can hardly be described as a typical product of George Gissing's mind and art. In it he subdued himself rather to the level of such popular producers as Besant and Rice, and went out of his way to procure melodramatic suspense, an ingredient far from congenial to his normal artistic temper. But the end justified the means. The novel found favour in the eyes of the author of *The Lost Sir Massingberd*, and Gissing for the first time in his life found himself the possessor of a full purse, with fifty 'jingling, tingling, golden, minted quid' in it. Its possession brought with it the realisation of a paramount desire, the desire for Greece and Italy which had become for him, as it had once been with Goethe, a scarce endurable suffering. The sickness of longing had wellnigh given way to despair, when 'there came into my hands a sum of money (such a poor little sum) for a book I had written. It was early autumn. I chanced to hear some one speak of Naples—and only death would have held me back.'[10]

The main plot of *Demos* is concerned with Richard Mutimer, a young socialist whose vital force, both mental and physical, is well above the average, corrupted by accession to a fortune, marrying a refined wife, losing his money in consequence of the discovery of an unsuspected will, and dragging his wife down with him,—down to *la misère* in its most brutal and humiliating shape. Happy endings and the Gissing of this period are so ill-assorted, that the 'reconciliations' at the close of both this novel and the next are to be regarded with considerable suspicion. The 'gentlefolk' in the book are the merest marionettes, but there are descriptive passages of first-rate vigour, and the voice of wisdom is heard from the lips of an early Greek choregus in the figure of an old parson called Mr. Wyvern. As the mouthpiece of his creator's pet hobbies parson Wyvern rolls out long homilies conceived in the spirit of Emerson's 'compensation,' and denounces the cruelty of educating the poor and making no after-provision for their intellectual needs with a sombre enthusiasm and a periodicity of style almost worthy of Dr. Johnson.[11]

---

[10] See *Emancipated*, chaps. iv.-xii.; *New Grub Street*, chap, xxvii.; *Ryecroft*, Autumn xix.; the short, not superior, novel called *Sleeping Fires*, 1895, chap. i. 'An encounter on the Kerameikos'; *The Albany*, Christmas 1904, p. 27; and *Monthly Review*, vol. xvi. 'He went straight by sea to the land of his dreams—Italy. It was still happily before the enterprise of touring agencies had fobbed the idea of Italian travel of its last vestiges of magic. He spent as much time as he could afford about the Bay of Naples, and then came on with a rejoicing heart to Rome—Rome, whose topography had been with him since boyhood, beside whose stately history the confused tumult of the contemporary newspapers seemed to him no more than a noisy, unmeaning persecution of the mind. Afterwards he went to Athens.'

[11] An impressive specimen of his eloquence was cited by me in an article in the *Daily Mail Year Book* (1906, p. 2). A riper study of a somewhat similar character is given in old Mr. Lashmar in *Our Friend the Charlatan*. (See his sermon on the blasphemy which would have us pretend that our civilisation obeys the spirit of Christianity, in chap, xviii.). For a

After *Demos*, Gissing returned in 1888 to the more sentimental and idealistic palette which he had employed for *Thyrza*. Renewed recollections of Tibullus and of Theocritus may have served to give his work a more idyllic tinge. But there were much nearer sources of inspiration for *A Life's Morning*. There must be many novels inspired by a youthful enthusiasm for *Richard Feverel*, and this I should take to be one of them. Apart from the idyllic purity of its tone, and its sincere idolatry of youthful love, the caressing grace of the language which describes the spiritualised beauty of Emily Hood and the exquisite charm of her slender hands, and the silvery radiance imparted to the whole scene of the proposal in the summer-house (in chapter iii., 'Lyrical'), give to this most unequal and imperfect book a certain crepuscular fascination of its own. Passages in it, certainly, are not undeserving that fine description of a style *si tendre qu'il pousse le bonheur à pleurer*. Emily's father, Mr. Hood, is an essentially pathetic figure, almost grotesquely true to life. 'I should like to see London before I die,' he says to his daughter. 'Somehow I have never managed to get so far.... There's one thing that I wish especially to see, and that is Holborn Viaduct. It must be a wonderful piece of engineering; I remember thinking it out at the time it was constructed. Of course you have seen it?' The vulgar but not wholly inhuman Cartwright interior, where the parlour is resolved into a perpetual matrimonial committee, would seem to be the outcome of genuine observation. Dagworthy is obviously padded with the author's substitute for melodrama, while the rich and cultivated Mr. Athel is palpably imitated from Meredith. The following tirade (spoken by the young man to his mistress) is Gissing pure. 'Think of the sunny spaces in the world's history, in each of which one could linger for ever. Athens at her fairest, Rome at her grandest, the glorious savagery of Merovingian Courts, the kingdom of Frederick II., the Moors in Spain, the magic of Renaissance Italy—to become a citizen of any one age means a lifetime of endeavour. It is easy to fill one's head with names and years, but that only sharpens my hunger.' In one form or another it recurs in practically every novel.[12] Certain of the later portions of this book, especially the chapter entitled 'Her Path in Shadow' are delineated through a kind of mystical haze, suggestive of some of the work of Puvis de Chavannes. The concluding chapters, taken as a whole, indicate with tolerable accuracy Gissing's affinities as a writer, and the pedigree of the type of novel by which he is best known. It derives from Xavier de Maistre and St. Pierre to *La Nouvelle Héloïse*,—nay, might one not almost say from the *pays du tendre* of *La Princesse de Clèves* itself. Semi-

---

criticism of *Demos* and *Thyrza* in juxtaposition with Besant's *Children of Gibeon*, see Miss Sichel on 'Philanthropic Novelists' (*Murray's Magazine*, iii. 506-518). Gissing saw deeper than to 'cease his music on a merry chord.'

[12] Sometimes, however, as in *The Whirlpool* (1897) with a very significant change of intonation:—'And that History which he loved to read—what was it but the lurid record of woes unutterable! How could he find pleasure in keeping his eyes fixed on century after century of ever-repeated torment—war, pestilence, tyranny; the stake, the dungeon; tortures of infinite device, cruelties inconceivable?'—(p. 326.)

sentimental theories as to the relations of the sexes, the dangers of indiscriminate education, the corruptions of wretchedness and poverty in large towns, the neglect of literature and classical learning, and the grievances of scholarly refinement in a world in which Greek iambic and Latin hexameter count for nothing,—such form the staple of his theses and tirades! His approximation at times to the confines of French realistic art is of the most accidental or incidental kind. For Gissing is at heart, in his bones as the vulgar say, a thorough moralist and sentimentalist, an honest, true-born, downright ineradicable Englishman. Intellectually his own life was, and continued to the last to be, romantic to an extent that few lives are. Pessimistic he may at times appear, but this is almost entirely on the surface. For he was never in the least blasé or ennuyé. He had the pathetic treasure of the humble and downcast and unkindly entreated—unquenchable hope. He has no objectivity. His point of view is almost entirely personal. It is not the *lacrimae rerum*, but the *lacrimae dierum suorum*, that makes his pages often so forlorn. His laments are all uttered by the waters of Babylon in a strange land. His nostalgia in the land of exile, estranged from every refinement, was greatly enhanced by the fact that he could not get on with ordinary men, but exhibited almost to the last a practical incapacity, a curious inability to do the sane and secure thing. As Mr. Wells puts it:—

> 'It is not that he was a careless man, he was a most careful one; it is not that he was a morally lax man, he was almost morbidly the reverse. Neither was he morose or eccentric in his motives or bearing; he was genial, conversational, and well-meaning. But he had some sort of blindness towards his fellow-men, so that he never entirely grasped the spirit of everyday life, so that he, who was so copiously intelligent in the things of the study, misunderstood, blundered, was nervously diffident, and wilful and spasmodic in common affairs, in employment and buying and selling, and the normal conflicts of intercourse. He did not know what would offend, and he did not know what would please. He irritated others and thwarted himself. He had no social nerve.'

Does not Gissing himself sum it up admirably, upon the lips of Mr. Widdowson in *The Odd Women*: 'Life has always been full of worrying problems for me. I can't take things in the simple way that comes natural to other men.' 'Not as other men are': more intellectual than most, fully as responsive to kind and genial instincts, yet bound at every turn to pinch and screw—an involuntary ascetic. Such is the essential burden of Gissing's long-drawn lament. Only accidentally can it be described as his mission to preach 'the desolation of modern life,' or in the gracious phrase of De Goncourt, *fouiller les entrailles de la vie*. Of the confident, self-supporting realism of *Esther Waters*, for instance, how little is there in any of his work, even in that most gloomily photographic portion of it which we are now to describe?

During the next four years, 1889-1892, Gissing produced four novels, and three of these perhaps are his best efforts in prose fiction. *The Nether World* of 1889 is certainly in some respects his strongest work, *la letra con sangre*, in which the ruddy drops of anguish remembered in a state of comparative tranquillity are most powerfully expressed. *The Emancipated*, of 1890, is with equal certainty, a *réchauffé* and the least successful of various attempts to give utterance to his enthusiasm for the *valor antica*—'the glory that was Greece and the grandeur that was Rome.' *New Grub Street*, (1891) is the most constructive and perhaps the most successful of all his works; while *Born in Exile* (1892) is a key-book as regards the development of the author's character, a *clavis* of primary value to his future biographer, whoever he may be. The *Nether World* contains Gissing's most convincing indictment of Poverty; and it also expresses his sense of revolt against the ugliness and cruelty which is propagated like a foul weed by the barbarous life of our reeking slums. Hunger and Want show Religion and Virtue the door with scant politeness in this terrible book. The material had been in his possession for some time, and in part it had been used before in earlier work. It was now utilised with a masterly hand, and the result goes some way, perhaps, to justify the well-meant but erratic comparisons that have been made between Gissing and such writers as Zola, Maupassant and the projector of the *Comédie Humaine*. The savage luck which dogs Kirkwood and Jane, and the worse than savage—the inhuman—cruelty of Clem Peckover, who has been compared to the Madame Cibot of Balzac's *Le Cousin Pons*, render the book an intensely gloomy one; it ends on a note of poignant misery, which gives a certain colour for once to the oft-repeated charge of morbidity and pessimism. Gissing understood the theory of compensation, but was unable to exhibit it in action. He elevates the cult of refinement to such a pitch that the consolations of temperament, of habit, and of humdrum ideals which are common to the coarsest of mankind, appear to elude his observation. He does not represent men as worse than they are; but he represents them less brave. No social stratum is probably quite so dull as he colours it. There is usually a streak of illusion or a flash of hope somewhere on the horizon. Hence a somewhat one-sided view of life, perfectly true as representing the grievance of the poet Cinna in the hands of the mob, but too severely monochrome for a serious indictment of a huge stratum of our common humanity. As in *Thyrza*, the sombreness of the ground generates some magnificent pieces of descriptive writing.

'Hours yet before the fireworks begin. Never mind; here by good luck we find seats where we can watch the throng passing and repassing. It is a great review of the people. On the whole, how respectable they are, how sober, how deadly dull! See how worn-out the poor girls are becoming, how they gape, what listless eyes most of them have! The stoop in the shoulders so universal among them merely means over-toil in the workroom. Not one in a thousand shows the elements of taste in dress; vulgarity and worse glares in all but every costume. Observe the middle-aged women; it would be small surprise that their good looks had vanished, but whence comes it they are animal, repulsive, absolutely vicious in ugliness? Mark the men in their turn; four in every six have visages so deformed by ill-health that they excite disgust; their hair is cut down to within half an inch of the scalp; their legs are twisted out of shape by evil conditions of life from birth upwards. Whenever a youth and a girl come along arm-in-arm, how flagrantly shows the man's coarseness! They are pretty, so many of these girls, delicate of feature, graceful did but their slavery allow them natural development; and the heart sinks as one sees them side by side with the men who are to be their husbands.

On the terraces dancing has commenced; the players of violins, concertinas, and penny whistles do a brisk trade among the groups eager for a rough-and-tumble valse; so do the pickpockets. Vigorous and varied is the jollity that occupies the external galleries, filling now in expectation of the fireworks; indescribable the mingled tumult that roars heavenwards. Girls linked by the half-dozen arm-in-arm leap along with shrieks like grotesque maenads; a rougher horseplay finds favour among the youths, occasionally leading to fisticuffs. Thick voices bellow in fragmentary chorus; from every side comes the yell, the cat-call, the ear-rending whistle; and as the bass, the never-ceasing accompaniment, sounds the myriad-footed tramp, tramp along the wooden flooring. A fight, a scene of bestial drunkenness, a tender whispering between two lovers, proceed concurrently in a space of five square yards. Above them glimmers the dawn of starlight.'—(pp. 109-11.)

From the delineation of this profoundly depressing milieu, by the aid of which, if the fate of London and Liverpool were to-morrow as that of Herculaneum and Pompeii, we should be able to reconstruct the gutters of our Imperial cities (little changed in essentials since the days of Domitian), Gissing turned his sketch-book to the scenery of rural England. He makes no attempt at the rich colouring of Kingsley or Blackmore, but, as page after page of *Ryecroft* testifies twelve years later, he is a perfect master of the *aquarelle*.

'The distance is about five miles, and, until Danbury Hill is reached, the countryside has no point of interest to distinguish it from any other representative bit of rural Essex. It is merely one of those quiet corners of flat, homely England, where man and beast seem on good terms with each other, where all green things grow in abundance, where from of old tilth and pasture-land are humbly observant of seasons and alternations, where the brown roads are familiar only with the tread of the labourer, with the light wheel of the farmer's gig, or the rumbling of the solid wain. By the roadside you pass occasionally a mantled pool, where perchance ducks or geese are enjoying themselves; and at times there is a pleasant glimpse of farmyard, with stacks and barns and stables. All things as simple as could be, but beautiful on this summer afternoon, and priceless when one has come forth from the streets of Clerkenwell.

* * * * *

'Danbury Hill, rising thick-wooded to the village church, which is visible for miles around, with stretches of heath about its lower slopes, with its far prospects over the sunny country, was the pleasant end of a pleasant drive.'—(*The Nether World*, pp. 164-165.)

The first part of this description is quite masterly—worthy, I am inclined to say, of Flaubert. But unless you are familiar with the quiet, undemonstrative nature of the scenery described, you can hardly estimate the perfect justice of the sentiment and phrasing with which Gissing succeeds in enveloping it.

Gissing now turned to the submerged tenth of literature, and in describing it he managed to combine a problem or thesis with just the amount of characterisation and plotting sanctioned by the novel convention of the day. The convention may have been better than we think, for *New Grub Street* is certainly its author's most effective work. The characters are numerous, actual, and alive. The plot is moderately good, and lingers in the memory with some obstinacy. The problem is more open to criticism, and it has indeed been criticised from more points of view than one.

'In *New Grub Street*,' says one of his critics,[13] 'Mr. Gissing has endeavoured to depict the shady side of literary life in an age dominated by the commercial spirit. On the whole, it is in its realism perhaps the least convincing of his novels, whilst being undeniably the most depressing. It is not that Gissing's picture of poverty in the literary profession is wanting in the elements of truth, although even in that profession there is even more eccentricity than the author leads us to suppose in the social position and evil plight of such men as Edwin Reardon and Harold Biffen. But the contrast between Edwin Reardon, the conscientious artist loving his art and working for its sake, and Jasper Milvain, the man of letters, who prospers simply because he is also a man of business, which is the main feature of the book and the principal support of its theme, strikes one throughout as strained to the point of unreality. In the first place, it seems almost impossible that a man of Milvain's mind and instincts should have deliberately chosen literature as the occupation of his life; with money and success as his only aim he would surely have become a stockbroker or a moneylender. In the second place, Edwin Reardon's dire failure, with his rapid descent into extreme poverty, is clearly traceable not so much to a truly artistic temperament in conflict with the commercial spirit, as to mental and moral weakness, which could not but have a baneful influence upon his work.'

This criticism does not seem to me a just one at all, and I dissent from it completely. In the first place, the book is not nearly so depressing as *The Nether World*, and is much farther removed from the strain of French and Russian pessimism which had begun to engage the author's study when he was writing *Thyrza*. There are dozens of examples to prove that Milvain's success is a

---

[13] F. Dolman in *National Review*, vol. xxx.; cf. *ibid.*, vol. xliv.

perfectly normal process, and the reason for his selecting the journalistic career is the obvious one that he has no money to begin stock-broking, still less money-lending. In the third place, the mental and moral shortcomings of Reardon are by no means dissembled by the author. He is, as the careful student of the novels will perceive, a greatly strengthened and improved rifacimento of Kingcote, while Amy Reardon is a better observed Isabel, regarded from a slightly different point of view. Jasper Milvain is, to my thinking, a perfectly fair portrait of an ambitious publicist or journalist of the day—destined by determination, skill, energy, and social ambition to become an editor of a successful journal or review, and to lead the life of central London. Possessing a keen and active mind, expression on paper is his handle; he has no love of letters as letters at all. But his outlook upon the situation is just enough. Reardon has barely any outlook at all. He is a man with a delicate but shallow vein of literary capacity, who never did more than tremble upon the verge of success, and hardly, if at all, went beyond promise. He was unlucky in marrying Amy, a rather heartless woman, whose ambition was far in excess of her insight, for economic position Reardon had none. He writes books to please a small group. The books fail to please. Jasper in the main is right—there is only a precarious place for any creative litterateur between the genius and the swarm of ephemera or journalists. A man writes either to please the hour or to produce something to last, relatively a long time, several generations—what we call 'permanent.' The intermediate position is necessarily insecure. It is not really wanted. What is lost by society when one of these mediocre masterpieces is overlooked? A sensation, a single ray in a sunset, missed by a small literary coterie! The circle is perhaps eclectic. It may seem hard that good work is overwhelmed in the cataract of production, while relatively bad, garish work is rewarded. But so it must be. 'The growing flood of literature swamps every thing but works of primary genius.' Good taste is valuable, especially when it takes the form of good criticism. The best critics of contemporary books (and these are by no means identical with the best critics of the past and its work) are those who settle intuitively upon the writing that is going to appeal more largely to a future generation, when the attraction of novelty and topicality has subsided. The same work is done by great men. They anticipate lines of action; philosophers generally follow (Machiavelli's theories the practice of Louis XI., Nietzsche's that of Napoleon I.). The critic recognises the tentative steps of genius in letters. The work of fine delicacy and reserve, the work that follows, lacking the real originality, is liable to neglect, and *may* become the victim of ill-luck, unfair influence, or other extraneous factors. Yet on the whole, so numerous are the publics of to-day, there never, perhaps, was a time when supreme genius or even supreme talent was so sure of recognition. Those who rail against these conditions, as Gissing seems here to have done, are actuated consciously or unconsciously by a personal or sectional disappointment. It is akin to the crocodile lament of the publisher that good modern literature is neglected by the public, or the impressionist's lament about the great unpaid greatness of the great unknown—the exclusively literary view of literary rewards. Literature must be governed by over-mastering impulse or directed at profit.

But *New Grub Street* is rich in memorable characters and situations to an extent unusual in Gissing; Biffen in his garret—a piece of genre almost worthy of Dickens; Reardon the sterile plotter, listening in despair to the neighbouring workhouse clock of St. Mary-le-bone; the matutinal interview between Alfred Yule and the threadbare surgeon, a vignette worthy of Smollett. Alfred Yule, the worn-out veteran, whose literary ideals are those of the eighteenth century, is a most extraordinary study of an *arriéré*—certainly one of the most crusted and individual personalities Gissing ever portrayed. He never wrote with such a virile pen: phrase after phrase bites and snaps with a singular crispness and energy; material used before is now brought to a finer literary issue. It is by far the most tenacious of Gissing's novels. It shows that on the more conventional lines of fictitious intrigue, acting as cement, and in the interplay of emphasised characters, Gissing could, if he liked, excel. (It recalls Anatole France's *Le Lys Rouge*, showing that he, too, the scholar and intellectual *par excellence*, could an he would produce patterns in plain and fancy adultery with the best.) Whelpdale's adventures in Troy, U.S.A., where he lived for five days on pea-nuts, are evidently semi-autobiographical. It is in his narrative that we first made the acquaintance of the American phrase now so familiar about literary productions going off like hot cakes. The reminiscences of Athens are typical of a lifelong obsession—to find an outlet later on in *Veranilda*. On literary *réclame*, he says much that is true—if not the whole truth, in the apophthegm for instance, 'You have to become famous before you can secure the attention which would give fame.' Biffen, it is true, is a somewhat fantastic figure of an idealist, but Gissing cherished this grotesque exfoliation from a headline by Dickens—and later in his career we shall find him reproducing one of Biffen's ideals with a singular fidelity.

'Picture a woman of middle age, wrapped at all times in dirty rags (not to be called clothing), obese, grimy, with dishevelled black hair, and hands so scarred, so deformed by labour and neglect, as to be scarcely human. She had the darkest and fiercest eyes I ever saw. Between her and her mistress went on an unceasing quarrel; they quarrelled in my room, in the corridor, and, as I knew by their shrill voices, in places remote; yet I am sure they did not dislike each other, and probably neither of them ever thought of parting. Unexpectedly, one evening, this woman entered, stood by the bedside, and began to talk with such fierce energy, with such flashing of her black eyes, and such distortion of her features, that I could only suppose that she was attacking me for the trouble I caused her. A minute or two passed before I could even hit the drift of her furious speech; she was always the most difficult of the natives to understand, and in rage she became quite unintelligible. Little by little, by dint of questioning, I got at what she meant. There had been *guai*, worse than usual; the mistress had reviled her unendurably for some fault or other, and was it not hard that she should be used like this after having *tanto, tanto lavorato*! In fact, she was appealing for my sympathy, not abusing me at all. When she went on to say that she was alone in the world, that all her kith and kin were *freddi morti* (stone dead), a pathos in her aspect and her words took hold upon me; it was much as if some heavy-laden beast of burden had suddenly found tongue and protested in the rude beginnings of articulate utterance against its hard lot. If only we could have learnt in intimate detail the life of this domestic serf[14]! How interesting and how sordidly picturesque against the background of romantic landscape, of scenic history! I looked long into her sallow, wrinkled face, trying to imagine the thoughts that ruled its expression. In some measure my efforts at kindly speech succeeded, and her "Ah, Cristo!" as she turned to go away, was not without a touch of solace.'

In 1892 Gissing was already beginning to try and discard his down look, his lugubrious self-pity, his lamentable cadence. He found some alleviation from self-torment in *David Copperfield*, and he determined to borrow a feather from 'the master's' pinion—in other words, to place an autobiographical novel to his credit. The result was *Born in Exile* (1892), one of the last of the three-volume novels,—by no means one of the worst. A Hedonist of academic type, repelled by a vulgar intonation, Gissing himself is manifestly the man in exile. Travel, fair women and college life, the Savile club, and Great Malvern or the Cornish coast, music in Paris or Vienna—this of course was the natural milieu for such a man. Instead of which our poor scholar (with Homer and Shakespeare and Pausanias piled upon his one small deal table) had to encounter the life of the shabby recluse in London lodgings—synonymous for him, as passage after passage in his books recounts, with incompetence and vulgarity in every form, at best 'an ailing lachrymose slut incapable of effort,' more often sheer foulness and dishonesty, 'by lying, slandering, quarrelling, by drunkenness, by brutal vice, by all abominations that distinguish the lodging-letter of the metropolis.' No book exhibits more naïvely the extravagant value which Gissing put upon the mere externals of refinement. The following scathing vignette of his unrefined younger brother by the hero, Godfrey Peak, shows the ferocity with which this feeling could manifest itself against a human being who lacked the elements of scholastic learning (the brother in question had failed to give the date of the Norman Conquest):—

'He saw much company and all of low intellectual order; he had purchased a bicycle and regarded it as a source of distinction, or means of displaying himself before shopkeepers' daughters; he believed himself a moderate tenor and sang verses of sentimental imbecility; he took in several weekly papers of unpromising title for the chief purpose of deciphering cryptograms, in which pursuit he

---

[14] Here is a more fully prepared expression of the very essence of Biffen's artistic ideal.—*By the Ionian Sea*, chap. x.

had singular success. Add to these characteristics a penchant for cheap jewellery, and Oliver Peak stands confessed.'

The story of the book is revealed in Peak's laconic ambition, 'A plebeian, I aim at marrying a lady.' It is a little curious, some may think, that this motive so skilfully used by so many novelists to whose work Gissing's has affinity, from Rousseau and Stendhal (*Rouge et Noire*) to Cherbuliez (*Secret du Précepteur*) and Bourget (*Le Disciple*), had not already attracted him, but the explanation is perhaps in part indicated in a finely written story towards the close of this present volume.[15] The white, maidenish and silk-haired fairness of Sidwell, and Peak's irresistible passion for the type of beauty suggested, is revealed to us with all Gissing's wonderful skill in shadowing forth feminine types of lovelihood. Suggestive too of his oncoming passion for Devonshire and Western England are strains of exquisite landscape music scattered at random through these pages. More significant still, however, is the developing faculty for personal satire, pointing to a vastly riper human experience. Peak was uncertain, says the author, with that faint ironical touch which became almost habitual to him, 'as to the limits of modern latitudinarianism until he met Chilvers,' the sleek, clerical advocate of 'Less St. Paul and more Darwin, less of Luther and more of Herbert Spencer':—

> 'The discovery of such fantastic liberality in a man whom he could not but dislike and contemn gave him no pleasure, but at least it disposed him to amusement rather than antagonism. Chilvers's pronunciation and phraseology were distinguished by such original affectation that it was impossible not to find entertainment in listening to him. Though his voice was naturally shrill and piping, he managed to speak in head notes which had a ring of robust utterance. The sound of his words was intended to correspond with their virile warmth of meaning. In the same way he had cultivated a habit of the muscles which conveyed an impression that he was devoted to athletic sports. His arms occasionally swung as if brandishing dumb-bells, his chest now and then spread itself to the uttermost, and his head was often thrown back in an attitude suggesting self-defence.'

Of Gissing's first year or so at Owens, after leaving Lindow Grove School at Alderley,[16] we get a few hints in these pages. Like his 'lonely cerebrate' hero, Gissing himself, at school and college, 'worked insanely.' Walked much alone, shunned companionship rather than sought it, worked as he walked, and was marked down as a 'pot-hunter.' He 'worked while he ate, he cut down his sleep, and for him the penalty came, not in a palpable, definable illness, but in an abrupt, incongruous reaction and collapse.' With rage he looked back on these insensate years of study which had weakened him just when he should have been carefully fortifying his constitution.

---

[15] See page 260.
[16] With an exhibition gained when he was not yet fifteen.

The year of this autobiographical record[17] marked the commencement of Gissing's reclamation from that worst form of literary slavery—the chain-gang. For he had been virtually chained to the desk, perpetually working, imprisoned in a London lodging, owing to the literal lack of the means of locomotion.[18] His most strenuous work, wrung from him in dismal darkness and wrestling of spirit, was now achieved. Yet it seems to me both ungrateful and unfair to say, as has frequently been done, that his subsequent work was consistently inferior. In his earlier years, like Reardon, he had destroyed whole books—books he had to sit down to when his imagination was tired and his fancy suffering from deadly fatigue. His corrections in the days of *New Grub Street* provoked not infrequent, though anxiously deprecated, remonstrance from his publisher's reader. Now he wrote with more assurance and less exhaustive care, but also with a perfected experience. A portion of his material, it is true, had been fairly used up, and he had henceforth to turn to analyse the sufferings of well-to-do lower middle-class families, people who had 'neither inherited refinement nor acquired it, neither proletarian nor gentlefolk, consumed with a disease of vulgar pretentiousness, inflated with the miasma of democracy.' Of these classes it is possible that he knew less, and consequently lacked the sureness of touch and the fresh draughtsmanship which comes from ample knowledge, and that he had, consequently, to have increasing resort to books and to invention, to hypothesis and theory.[19] On the other hand, his power of satirical writing was continually expanding and developing, and some of his very best prose is contained in four of these later books: *In the Year of Jubilee* (1894), *Charles Dickens* (1898), *By the Ionian Sea* (1901), and *The Private Papers of Henry Ryecroft* (1903); not far below any of which must be rated four others, *The Odd Women* (1893), *Eve's Ransom* (1895), *The Whirlpool* (1897), and *Will Warburton* (1905), to which may be

---

[17] Followed in 1897 by *The Whirlpool* (see p. xvi), and in 1899 and 1903 by two books containing a like infusion of autobiographical experience, *The Crown of Life*, technically admirable in chosen passages, but sadly lacking in the freshness of first-hand, and *The Private Papers of Henry Ryecroft*, one of the rightest and ripest of all his productions.

[18] 'I hardly knew what it was to travel by omnibus. I have walked London streets for twelve and fifteen hours together without even a thought of saving my legs or my time, by paying for waftage. Being poor as poor can be, there were certain things I had to renounce, and this was one of them.'—*Ryecroft*. For earlier scenes see *Monthly Review*, xvi., and *Owens College Union Mag.*, Jan. 1904, pp. 80-81.

[19] 'He knew the narrowly religious, the mental barrenness of the poor dissenters, the people of the slums that he observed so carefully, and many of those on the borders of the Bohemia of which he at least was an initiate, and he was soaked and stained, as he might himself have said, with the dull drabs of the lower middle class that he hated. But of those above he knew little.... He did not know the upper middle classes, which are as difficult every whit as those beneath them, and take as much time and labour and experience and observation to learn.'—'The Exile of George Gissing,' *Albany*, Christmas 1904. In later life he lost sympathy with the 'nether world.' Asked to write a magazine article on a typical 'workman's budget,' he wrote that he no longer took an interest in the 'condition of the poor question.'

added the two collections of short stories.

Few, if any, of Gissing's books exhibit more mental vigour than *In the Year of Jubilee*. This is shown less, it may be, in his attempted solution of the marriage problem (is marriage a failure?) by means of the suggestion that middle class married people should imitate the rich and see as little of each other as possible, than in the terse and amusing characterisations and the powerfully thought-out descriptions. The precision which his pen had acquired is well illustrated by the following description, not unworthy of Thomas Hardy, of a new neighbourhood.

'Great elms, the pride of generations passed away, fell before the speculative axe, or were left standing in mournful isolation to please a speculative architect; bits of wayside hedge still shivered in fog and wind, amid hoardings variegated with placards and scaffoldings black against the sky. The very earth had lost its wholesome odour; trampled into mire, fouled with builders' refuse and the noisome drift from adjacent streets, it sent forth, under the sooty rain, a smell of corruption, of all the town's uncleanliness. On this rising locality had been bestowed the title of "Park." Mrs. Morgan was decided in her choice of a dwelling here by the euphonious address, Merton Avenue, Something-or-other Park.'

Zola's wonderful skill in the animation of crowds has often been commented upon, but it is more than doubtful if he ever achieved anything superior to Gissing's marvellous incarnation of the jubilee night mob in chapter seven. More formidable, as illustrating the venom which the author's whole nature had secreted against a perfectly recognisable type of modern woman, is the acrid description of Ada, Beatrice, and Fanny French.

'They spoke a peculiar tongue, the product of sham education and a mock refinement grafted upon a stock of robust vulgarity. One and all would have been moved to indignant surprise if accused of ignorance or defective breeding. Ada had frequented an "establishment for young ladies" up to the close of her seventeenth year: the other two had pursued culture at a still more pretentious institute until they were eighteen. All could "play the piano"; all declared—and believed—that they "knew French." Beatrice had "done" Political Economy; Fanny had "been through" Inorganic Chemistry and Botany. The truth was, of course, that their minds, characters, propensities, had remained absolutely proof against such educational influence as had been brought to bear upon them. That they used a finer accent than their servants, signified only that they had grown up amid falsities, and were enabled, by the help of money, to dwell above-stairs, instead of with their spiritual kindred below.'

The evils of indiscriminate education and the follies of our grotesque examination system were one of Gissing's favourite topics of denunciation in later years, as evidenced in this characteristic passage in his later manner in this same book:—

> 'She talked only of the "exam," of her chances in this or that "paper," of the likelihood that this or that question would be "set." Her brain was becoming a mere receptacle for dates and definitions, vocabularies and rules syntactic, for thrice-boiled essence of history, ragged scraps of science, quotations at fifth hand, and all the heterogeneous rubbish of a "crammer's" shop. When away from her books, she carried scraps of paper, with jottings to be committed to memory. Beside her plate at meals lay formulae and tabulations. She went to bed with a manual, and got up with a compendium.'

The conclusion of this book and its predecessor, *The Odd Women*,[20] marks the conclusion of these elaborated problem studies. The inferno of London poverty, social analysis and autobiographical reminiscence, had now alike been pretty extensively drawn upon by Gissing. With different degrees of success he had succeeded in providing every one of his theses with something in the nature of a jack-in-the-box plot which the public loved and he despised. There remained to him three alternatives: to experiment beyond the limits of the novel; to essay a lighter vein of fiction; or thirdly, to repeat himself and refashion old material within its limits. Necessity left him very little option. He adopted all three alternatives. His best success in the third department was achieved in *Eve's Ransom* (1895). Burrowing back into a projection of himself in relation with a not impossible she, Gissing here creates a false, fair, and fleeting beauty of a very palpable charm. A growing sense of her power to fascinate steadily raises Eve's standard of the minimum of luxury to which she is entitled. And in the course of this evolution, in the vain attempt to win beauty by gratitude and humility, the timid Hilliard, who seeks to propitiate his charmer by ransoming her from a base liaison and supporting her in luxury for a season in Paris, is thrown off like an old glove when a richer *parti* declares himself. The subtlety of the portraiture and the economy of the author's sympathy for his hero impart a subacid flavour of peculiar delicacy to the book, which would occupy a high place in the repertoire

---

[20] *The Odd Women* (1893, new edition, 1894) is a rather sordid and depressing survey of the life-histories of certain orphaned daughters of a typical Gissing doctor—grave, benign, amiably diffident, terribly afraid of life. 'From the contact of coarse actualities his nature shrank.' After his death one daughter, a fancy-goods shop assistant (no wages), is carried off by consumption; a second drowns herself in a bath at a charitable institution; another takes to drink; and the portraits of the survivors, their petty, incurable maladies, their utter uselessness, their round shoulders and 'very short legs,' pimples, and scraggy necks—are as implacable and unsparing as a Maupassant could wish. From the deplorable insight with which he describes the nerveless, underfed, compulsory optimism of these poor in spirit and poor in hope Gissing might almost have been an 'odd woman' himself. In this book and *The Paying Guest* (1895) he seemed to take a savage delight in depicting the small, stiff, isolated, costly, unsatisfied pretentiousness and plentiful lack of imagination which cripples suburbia so cruelly.— See *Saturday Review*, 13 Apr. 1896; and see also *ib.*, 19 Jan. 1895.

of any lesser artist. It well exhibits the conflict between an exaggerated contempt for, and an extreme susceptibility to, the charm of women which has cried havoc and let loose the dogs of strife upon so many able men. In *The Whirlpool* of 1897, in which he shows us a number of human floats spinning round the vortex of social London,[21] Gissing brings a melodramatic plot of a kind disused since the days of *Demos* to bear upon the exhausting lives and illusive pleasures of the rich and cultured middle class. There is some admirable writing in the book, and symptoms of a change of tone (the old inclination to whine, for instance, is scarcely perceptible) suggestive of a new era in the work of the novelist— relatively mature in many respects as he now manifestly was. Further progress in one of two directions seemed indicated: the first leading towards the career of a successful society novelist 'of circulating fame, spirally crescent,' the second towards the frame of mind that created *Ryecroft*. The second fortunately prevailed. In the meantime, in accordance with a supreme law of his being, his spirit craved that refreshment which Gissing found in revisiting Italy. 'I want,' he cried, 'to see the ruins of Rome: I want to see the Tiber, the Clitumnus, the Aufidus, the Alban Hills, Lake Trasimenus! It is strange how these old times have taken hold of me. The mere names in Roman history make my blood warm.' Of him the saying of Michelet was perpetually true: 'J'ai passé à côté du monde, et j'ai pris l'histoire pour la vie.' His guide-books in Italy, through which he journeyed in 1897 (*en prince* as compared with his former visit, now that his revenue had risen steadily to between three and four hundred a year), were Gibbon, his *semper eadem*, Lenormant (*la Grande-Grèce*), and Cassiodorus, of whose epistles, the foundation of the material of *Veranilda*, he now began to make a special study. The dirt, the poverty, the rancid oil, and the inequable climate of Calabria must have been a trial and something of a disappointment to him. But physical discomfort and even sickness was whelmed by the old and overmastering enthusiasm, which combined with his hatred of modernity and consumed Gissing as by fire. The sensuous and the emotional sides of his experience are blended with the most subtle artistry in his *By the Ionian Sea*, a short volume of impressions, unsurpassable in its kind, from which we cannot refrain two characteristic extracts:—

'At Cotrone the tone of the dining-room was decidedly morose. One man—he seemed to be a sort of clerk—came only to quarrel. I am convinced that he ordered things which he knew that the people could not cook, just for the sake of reviling their handiwork when it

---

[21] The whirlpool in which people just nod or shout to each other as they spin round and round. The heroine tries to escape, but is drawn back again and again, and nearly submerges her whole environment by her wild clutches. Satire is lavished upon misdirected education (28), the sluttishness of London landladies, self-adoring Art on a pedestal (256), the delegation of children to underlings, sham religiosity (229), the pampered conscience of a diffident student, and the *mensonge* of modern woman (300), typified by the ruddled cast-off of Redgrave, who plays first, in her shrivelled paint, as procuress, and then, in her naked hideousness, as blackmailer.

was presented. Therewith he spent incredibly small sums; after growling and remonstrating and eating for more than an hour, his bill would amount to seventy or eighty centesimi, wine included. Every day he threatened to withdraw his custom; every day he sent for the landlady, pointed out to her how vilely he was treated, and asked how she could expect him to recommend the Concordia to his acquaintances. On one occasion I saw him push away a plate of something, plant his elbows on the table, and hide his face in his hands; thus he sat for ten minutes, an image of indignant misery, and when at length his countenance was again visible, it showed traces of tears.'—(pp. 102-3.)

The unconscious paganism that lingered in tradition, the half-obscured names of the sites celebrated in classic story, and the spectacle of the white oxen drawing the rustic carts of Virgil's time—these things roused in him such an echo as *Chevy Chase* roused in the noble Sidney, and made him shout with joy. A pensive vein of contemporary reflection enriches the book with passages such as this:—

'All the faults of the Italian people are whelmed in forgiveness as soon as their music sounds under the Italian sky. One remembers all they have suffered, all they have achieved in spite of wrong. Brute races have flung themselves, one after another, upon this sweet and glorious land; conquest and slavery, from age to age, have been the people's lot. Tread where one will, the soil has been drenched with blood. An immemorial woe sounds even through the lilting notes of Italian gaiety. It is a country, wearied and regretful, looking ever backward to the things of old.'—(p. 130.)

The *Ionian Sea* did not make its appearance until 1901, but while he was actually in Italy, at Siena, he wrote the greater part of one of his very finest performances; the study of *Charles Dickens*, of which he corrected the proofs 'at a little town in Calabria.' It is an insufficient tribute to Gissing to say that his study of Dickens is by far the best extant. I have even heard it maintained that it is better in its way than any single volume in the 'Man of Letters'; and Mr. Chesterton, who speaks from ample knowledge on this point, speaks of the best of all Dickens's critics, 'a man of genius, Mr. George Gissing.' While fully and frankly recognising the master's defects in view of the artistic conscience of a later generation, the writer recognises to the full those transcendent qualities which place him next to Sir Walter Scott as the second greatest figure in a century of great fiction. In defiance of the terrible, and to some critics damning, fact that Dickens entirely changed the plan of *Martin Chuzzlewit* in deference to the popular criticism expressed by the sudden fall in the circulation of that serial, he shows in what a fundamental sense the author was 'a literary artist if ever there was one,' and he triumphantly refutes the rash daub of unapplied criticism represented by the parrot cry of 'caricature' as levelled against Dickens's humorous portraits. Among the many notable features of this veritable *chef-d'oeuvre* of under 250 pages is the sense it conveys of the superb gusto of

Dickens's actual living and breathing and being, the vindication achieved of two ordinarily rather maligned novels, *The Old Curiosity Shop* and *Little Dorrit*, and the insight shown into Dickens's portraiture of women, more particularly those of the shrill-voiced and nagging or whining variety, the 'better halves' of Weller, Varden, Snagsby and Joe Gargery, not to speak of the Miggs, the Gummidge, and the M'Stinger. Like Mr. Swinburne and other true men, he regards Mrs. Gamp as representing the quintessence of literary art wielded by genius. Try (he urges with a fine curiosity) 'to imagine Sarah Gamp as a young girl'! But it is unfair to separate a phrase from a context in which every syllable is precious, reasonable, thrice distilled and sweet to the palate as Hybla honey.[22]

Henceforth Gissing spent an increasing portion of his time abroad, and it was from St. Honorè en Morvan, for instance, that he dated the preface of *Our Friend the Charlatan* in 1901. As with *Denzil Quarrier* (1892) and *The Town Traveller* (1898) this was one of the books which Gissing sometimes went the length of asking the admirers of his earlier romances 'not to read.' With its prefatory note, indeed, its cheap illustrations, and its rather mechanical intrigue, it seems as far removed from such a book as *A Life's Morning* as it is possible for a novel by the same author to be. It was in the South of France, in the neighbourhood of Biarritz, amid scenes such as that described in the thirty-seventh chapter of *Will Warburton*, or still further south, that he wrote the greater part of his last three books, the novel just mentioned, which is probably his best essay in the lighter ironical vein to which his later years inclined,[23] *Veranilda*, a romance of the time of Theodoric the Goth, written in solemn fulfilment of a vow of his youth, and *The Private Papers of Henry Ryecroft*, which to my mind remains a legacy for Time to take account of as the faithful tribute of one of the truest artists of the generation he served.

In *Veranilda* (1904) are combined conscientious workmanship, a pure style of finest quality, and archaeology, for all I know to the contrary, worthy of Becker or Boni. Sir Walter himself could never in reason have dared to aspire to such a fortunate conjuncture of talent, grace, and historic accuracy. He possessed only that profound knowledge of human nature, that moulding humour and quick sense of dialogue, that live, human, and local interest in matters antiquarian, that statesmanlike insight into the pith and marrow of the historic past, which makes one of Scott's historical novels what it is—the envy of artists, the delight of young and old, the despair of formal historians.

---

[22] A revised edition (the date of Dickens's birth is wrongly given in the first) was issued in 1902, with topographical illustrations by F.G. Kitton. Gissing's introduction to *Nickleby* for the Rochester edition appeared in 1900, and his abridgement of Forster's *Life* (an excellent piece of work) in 1903 [1902]. The first collection of short stories, twenty-nine in number, entitled *Human Odds and Ends*, was published in 1898. It is justly described by the writer of the most interesting 'Recollections of George Gissing' in the *Gentleman's Magazine*, February 1906, as 'that very remarkable collection.'

[23] It also contains one of the most beautiful descriptions ever penned of the visit of a tired town-dweller to a modest rural home, with all its suggestion of trim gardening, fresh country scents, indigenous food, and homely simplicity.—*Will Warburton*, chap. ix.

Veranilda is without a doubt a splendid piece of work; Gissing wrote it with every bit of the care that his old friend Biffen expended upon *Mr. Bailey, grocer.* He worked slowly, patiently, affectionately, scrupulously. Each sentence was as good as he could make it, harmonious to the ear, with words of precious meaning skilfully set; and he believed in it with the illusion so indispensable to an artist's wellbeing and continuance in good work. It represented for him what *Salammbô* did to Flaubert. But he could not allow himself six years to write a book as Flaubert did. *Salammbô,* after all, was a magnificent failure, and *Veranilda,*—well, it must be confessed, sadly but surely, that *Veranilda* was a failure too. Far otherwise was it with *Ryecroft,* which represents, as it were, the *summa* of Gissing's habitual meditation, aesthetic feeling and sombre emotional experience. Not that it is a pessimistic work,—quite the contrary, it represents the mellowing influences, the increase of faith in simple, unsophisticated English girlhood and womanhood, in domestic pursuits, in innocent children, in rural homeliness and honest Wessex landscape, which began to operate about 1896, and is seen so unmistakably in the closing scenes of *The Whirlpool.* Three chief strains are subtly interblended in the composition. First that of a nature book, full of air, foliage and landscape—that English landscape art of Linnell and De Wint and Foster, for which he repeatedly expresses such a passionate tendre,[24] refreshed by 'blasts from the channel, with raining scud and spume of mist breaking upon the hills' in which he seems to crystallise the very essence of a Western winter. Secondly, a paean half of praise and half of regret for the vanishing England, passing so rapidly even as he writes into 'a new England which tries so hard to be unlike the old.' A deeper and richer note of thankfulness, mixed as it must be with anxiety, for the good old ways of English life (as lamented by Mr. Poorgrass and Mark Clark[25]), old English simplicity, and old English fare—the fine prodigality of the English platter, has never been raised. God grant that the leaven may work! And thirdly there is a deeply brooding strain of saddening yet softened autobiographical reminiscence, over which is thrown a light veil of literary appreciation and topical comment. Here is a typical *cadenza,* rising to a swell at one point (suggestive for the moment of Raleigh's famous apostrophe), and then most gently falling, in a manner not wholly unworthy, I venture to think, of Webster and Sir Thomas Browne, of both of which authors there is internal evidence that Gissing made some study.

> 'I always turn out of my way to walk through a country churchyard; these rural resting-places are as attractive to me as a town cemetery is repugnant. I read the names upon the stones and find a deep solace in thinking that for all these the fret and the fear of life are over. There comes to me no touch of sadness; whether it be a little child or an aged man, I have the same sense of happy

---

[24] 'I love and honour even the least of English landscape painters.'—*Ryecroft.*
[25] 'But what with the parsons and clerks and school-people and serious tea-parties, the merry old ways of good life have gone to the dogs—upon my carcass, they have!'—*Far from the Madding Crowd.*

accomplishment; the end having come, and with it the eternal peace, what matter if it came late or soon? There is no such gratulation as *Hic jacet*. There is no such dignity as that of death. In the path trodden by the noblest of mankind these have followed; that which of all who live is the utmost thing demanded, these have achieved. I cannot sorrow for them, but the thought of their vanished life moves me to a brotherly tenderness. The dead amid this leafy silence seem to whisper encouragement to him whose fate yet lingers: As we are, so shalt thou be; and behold our quiet!'—(p. 183.)

And in this deeply moving and beautiful passage we get a foretaste, it may be, of the euthanasia, following a brief summer of St. Martin, for which the scarred and troublous portions of Gissing's earlier life had served as a preparation. Some there are, no doubt, to whom it will seem no extravagance in closing these private pages to use the author's own words, of a more potent Enchanter: 'As I close the book, love and reverence possess me.'

* * * * *

Whatever the critics may determine as to the merit of the stories in the present volume, there can be no question as to the interest they derive from their connection with what had gone before. Thus *Topham's Chance* is manifestly the outcome of material pondered as early as 1884. *The Lodger in Maze Pond* develops in a most suggestive fashion certain problems discussed in 1894. Miss Rodney is a re-incarnation of Rhoda Nunn and Constance Bride. *Christopherson* is a delicious expansion of a mood indicated in *Ryecroft* (Spring xii.), and *A Capitalist* indicates the growing interest in the business side of practical life, the dawn of which is seen in *The Town Traveller* and in the discussion of Dickens's potentialities as a capitalist. The very artichokes in *The House of Cobwebs* (which, like the kindly hand that raised them, alas! fell a victim to the first frost of the season) are suggestive of a charming passage detailing the retired author's experience as a gardener. What Dr. Furnivall might call the 'backward reach' of every one of these stories will render their perusal delightful to those cultivated readers of Gissing, of whom there are by no means a few, to whom every fragment of his suave and delicate workmanship 'repressed yet full of power, vivid though sombre in colouring,' has a technical interest and charm. Nor will they search in vain for Gissing's incorrigible mannerisms, his haunting insistence upon the note of 'Dort wo du nicht bist ist das Glück,' his tricks of the brush in portraiture, his characteristic epithets, the *dusking* twilight, the *decently ignoble* penury, the *not ignoble* ambition, the *not wholly base* riot of the senses in early manhood. In my own opinion we have here in *The Scrupulous Father*, and to a less degree, perhaps, in the first and last of these stories, and in *A Poor Gentleman* and *Christopherson*, perfectly characteristic and quite admirable specimens of Gissing's own genre, and later, unstudied, but always finished prose style.

* * * * *

But a few words remain to be said, and these, in part at any rate, in recapitulation. In the old race, of which Dickens and Thackeray were representative, a successful determination to rise upon the broad back of popularity coincided with a growing conviction that the evil in the world was steadily diminishing. Like healthy schoolboys who have worked their way up to the sixth form, they imagined that the bullying of which they had had to complain was become pretty much a thing of the past. In Gissing the misery inherent in the sharp contrasts of modern life was a far more deeply ingrained conviction. He cared little for the remedial aspect of the question. His idea was to analyse this misery as an artist and to express it to the world.

One of the most impressive elements in the resulting novels is the witness they bear to prolonged and intense suffering, the suffering of a proud, reserved, and over-sensitive mind brought into constant contact with the coarse and brutal facts of life. The creator of Mr. Biffen suffers all the torture of the fastidious, the delicately honourable, the scrupulously high-minded in daily contact with persons of blunt feelings, low ideals, and base instincts. 'Human cattle, the herd that feed and breed, with them it was well; but the few born to a desire for ever unattainable, the gentle spirits who from their prisoning circumstance looked up and afar, how the heart ached to think of them!' The natural bent of Gissing's talent was towards poetry and classical antiquity. His mind had considerable natural affinity with that of Tennyson.[26] He was passionately fond of old literature, of the study of metre and of historical reverie. The subtle curiosities of Anatole France are just of the kind that would have appealed irresistibly to him. His delight in psychological complexity and feats of style are not seldom reminiscent of Paul Bourget. His life would have gained immeasurably by a transference to less pinched and pitiful surroundings: but it is more than doubtful whether his work would have done so.

The compulsion of the twin monsters Bread and Cheese forced him to write novels the scene of which was laid in the one milieu he had thoroughly observed, that of either utterly hideous or shabby genteel squalor in London. He gradually obtained a rare mastery in the delineation of his unlovely *mise en scène*. He gradually created a small public who read eagerly everything that came from his pen, despite his economy of material (even of ideas), and despite the repetition to which a natural tendency was increased by compulsory over-production. In all his best books we have evidence of the savage and ironical delight with which he depicted to the shadow of a hair the sordid and vulgar elements by which he had been so cruelly depressed. The aesthetic observer who wanted material for a picture of the blank desolation and ugliness of modern city life could find no better substratum than in the works of George Gissing. Many of his descriptions of typical London scenes in Lambeth Walk, Clerkenwell, or Judd Street, for instance, are the work of a detached, remorseless, photographic

---

[26] In a young lady's album I unexpectedly came across the line from *Maud*, 'Be mine a philosopher's life in the quiet woodland ways,' with the signature, following the quotation marks, 'George Gissing.' The borrowed aspiration was transparently sincere. 'Tennyson he worshipped' (see *Odd Women*, chap. i.). The contemporary novelist he liked most was Alphonse Daudet.

artist realising that ugly sordidness of daily life to which the ordinary observer becomes in the course of time as completely habituated as he does to the smoke-laden air. To a cognate sentiment of revolt I attribute that excessive deference to scholarship and refinement which leads him in so many novels to treat these desirable attributes as if they were ends and objects of life in themselves. It has also misled him but too often into depicting a world of suicides, ignoring or overlooking a secret hobby, or passion, or chimaera which is the one thing that renders existence endurable to so many of the waifs and strays of life. He takes existence sadly—too sadly, it may well be; but his drabs and greys provide an atmosphere that is almost inseparable to some of us from our gaunt London streets. In Farringdon Road, for example, I look up instinctively to the expressionless upper windows where Mr. Luckworth Crewe spreads his baits for intending advertisers. A tram ride through Clerkenwell and its leagues of dreary, inhospitable brickwork will take you through the heart of a region where Clem Peckover, Pennyloaf Candy, and Totty Nancarrow are multiplied rather than varied since they were first depicted by George Gissing. As for the British Museum, it is peopled to this day by characters from *New Grub Street*.

There may be a perceptible lack of virility, a fluctuating vagueness of outline about the characterisation of some of his men. In his treatment of crowds, in his description of a mob, personified as 'some huge beast purring to itself in stupid contentment,' he can have few rivals. In tracing the influence of women over his heroes he evinces no common subtlety; it is here probably that he is at his best. The *odor di femmina*, to use a phrase of Don Giovanni's, is a marked characteristic of his books. Of the kisses—

> 'by hopeless fancy feigned
> On lips that are for others'—

there are indeed many to be discovered hidden away between these pages. And the beautiful verse has a fine parallel in the prose of one of Gissing's later novels. 'Some girl, of delicate instinct, of purpose sweet and pure, wasting her unloved life in toil and want and indignity; some man, whose youth and courage strove against a mean environment, whose eyes grew haggard in the vain search for a companion promised in his dreams; they lived, these two, parted perchance only by the wall of neighbour houses, yet all huge London was between them, and their hands would never touch.' The dream of fair women which occupies the mood of Piers Otway in the opening passage of the same novel, was evidently no remotely conceived fancy. Its realisation, in ideal love, represents the author's *Crown of Life*. The wise man who said that Beautiful Woman[27] was a heaven to the eye, a hell to the soul, and a purgatory to the purse of man, could

---

[27] With unconscious recollection, it may be, of Pope's notable phrase in regard to Shakespeare, he speaks in his last novel of woman appearing at times as 'a force of Nature rather than an individual being' (*Will Warburton*, p. 275).

hardly find a more copious field of illustration than in the fiction of George Gissing.

Gissing was a sedulous artist; some of his books, it is true, are very hurried productions, finished in haste for the market with no great amount either of inspiration or artistic confidence about them. But little slovenly work will be found bearing his name, for he was a thoroughly trained writer; a suave and seductive workmanship had become a second nature to him, and there was always a flavour of scholarly, subacid and quasi-ironical modernity about his style. There is little doubt that his quality as a stylist was better adapted to the studies of modern London life, on its seamier side, which he had observed at first hand, than to stories of the conventional dramatic structure which he too often felt himself bound to adopt. In these his failure to grapple with a big objective, or to rise to some prosperous situation, is often painfully marked. A master of explanation and description rather than of animated narrative or sparkling dialogue, he lacked the wit and humour, the brilliance and energy of a consummate style which might have enabled him to compete with the great scenic masters in fiction, or with craftsmen such as Hardy or Stevenson, or with incomparable wits and conversationalists such as Meredith. It is true, again, that his London-street novels lack certain artistic elements of beauty (though here and there occur glints of rainy or sunset townscape in a half-tone, consummately handled and eminently impressive); and his intense sincerity cannot wholly atone for this loss. Where, however, a quiet refinement and delicacy of style is needed as in those sane and suggestive, atmospheric, critical or introspective studies, such as *By the Ionian Sea*, the unrivalled presentment of *Charles Dickens*, and that gentle masterpiece of softened autobiography, *The Private Papers of Henry Ryecroft* (its resignation and autumnal calm, its finer note of wistfulness and wide human compassion, fully deserve comparison with the priceless work of Silvio Pellico) in which he indulged himself during the last and increasingly prosperous years of his life, then Gissing's style is discovered to be a charmed instrument. That he will *sup late*, our Gissing, we are quite content to believe. But that a place is reserved for him, of that at any rate we are reasonably confident. The three books just named, in conjunction with his short stories and his *New Grub Street* (not to mention *Thyrza* or *The Nether World*), will suffice to ensure him a devout and admiring group of followers for a very long time to come; they accentuate profoundly the feeling of vivid regret and almost personal loss which not a few of his more assiduous readers experienced upon the sad news of his premature death at St. Jean de Luz on the 28th December 1903, at the early age of forty-six.

ACTON,
February 1906.

A CHRONOLOGICAL RECORD

1880. Workers in the Dawn.
1884. The Unclassed.
1886. Isabel Clarendon.
1886. Demos.
1887. Thyrza.
1888. A Life's Morning.
1889. The Nether World.
1890. The Emancipated.
1891. New Grub Street.
1892. Born in Exile.
1892. Denzil Quarrier.
1893. The Odd Women.
1894. In the Year of Jubilee.
1895. The Paying Guest.
1895. Sleeping Fires.
1895. Eve's Ransom.
1897. The Whirlpool.
1898. Human Odds and Ends: Stories and Sketches.
1898. The Town Traveller.
1898. Charles Dickens: a Critical Study.
1899. The Crown of Life.
1901. Our Friend the Charlatan.
1901. By the Ionian Sea. Notes of a Ramble in Southern Italy.
1903. Forster's Life of Dickens—Abridgement.
1903. The Private Papers of Henry Ryecroft.
1904. Veranilda: a Romance.
1905. Will Warburton: a Romance of Real Life.
1906. The House of Cobwebs, and other Stories.

[Of notices and reviews of George Gissing other than those mentioned in the foregoing notes the following is a selection:—*Times*, 29 Dec. 1903; *Guardian*, 6 Jan. 1904; *Outlook*, 2 Jan. 1904; *Sphere*, 9 Jan. 1904; *Athenaeum*, 2 and 16 Jan. 1904; *Academy*, 9 Jan. 1904 (pp. 40 and 46); New York *Nation*, 11 June 1903 (an adverse but interesting paper on the anti-social side of Gissing); *The Bookman* (New York), vol. xviii.; *Independent Review*, Feb. 1904; *Fortnightly Review*, Feb. 1904; *Contemporary Review*, Aug. 1897; C.F.G. Masterman's *In Peril of Change*, 1905, pp. 68-73; *Atlantic Monthly*, xciii. 280; *Upton Letters*, 1905, p. 206.]

THE HOUSE OF COBWEBS

IT was five o'clock on a June morning. The dirty-buff blind of the lodging-house bedroom shone like cloth of gold as the sun's unclouded rays poured through it, transforming all they illumined, so that things poor and mean seemed to share in the triumphant glory of new-born day. In the bed lay a young man who had already been awake for an hour. He kept stirring uneasily, but with no intention of trying to sleep again. His eyes followed the slow movement of the sunshine on the wall-paper, and noted, as they never had done before, the details of the flower pattern, which represented no flower wherewith botanists are acquainted, yet, in this summer light, turned the thoughts to garden and field and hedgerow. The young man had a troubled mind, and his thoughts ran thus:—

'I must have three months at least, and how am I to live?... Fifteen shillings a week—not quite that, if I spread my money out. Can one live on fifteen shillings a week—rent, food, washing?... I shall have to leave these lodgings at once. They're not luxurious, but I can't live here under twenty-five, that's clear.... Three months to finish my book. It's good; I'm hanged if it isn't! This time I shall find a publisher. All I have to do is to stick at my work and keep my mind easy.... Lucky that it's summer; I don't need fires. Any corner would do for me where I can be quiet and see the sun.... Wonder whether some cottager in Surrey would house and feed me for fifteen shillings a week?... No use lying here. Better get up and see how things look after an hour's walk.'

So the young man arose and clad himself, and went out into the shining street. His name was Goldthorpe. His years were not yet three-and-twenty. Since the age of legal independence he had been living alone in London, solitary and poor, very proud of a wholehearted devotion to the career of authorship. As soon as he slipped out of the stuffy house, the live air, perfumed with freshness from meadows and hills afar, made his blood pulse joyously. He was at the age of hope, and something within him, which did not represent mere youthful illusion, supported his courage in the face of calculations such as would have damped sober experience. With boyish step, so light and springy that it seemed anxious to run and leap, he took his way through a suburb south of Thames, and pushed on towards the first rising of the Surrey hills. And as he walked resolve strengthened itself in his heart. Somehow or other he would live independently through the next three months. If the worst came to the worst, he could earn bread as clerk or labourer, but as long as his money lasted he would pursue his purpose, and that alone. He sang to himself in this gallant determination, happy as if some one had left him a fortune.

In an ascending road, quiet and tree-shadowed, where the dwellings on either side were for the most part old and small, though here and there a brand-new edifice on a larger scale showed that the neighbourhood was undergoing change such as in our time destroys the picturesque in all London suburbs, the cheery dreamer chanced to turn his eyes upon a spot of desolation which aroused his curiosity and set his fancy at work. Before him stood three deserted houses, a little row once tenanted by middle-class folk, but now for some time unoccupied and unrepaired. They were of brick, but the fronts had a stucco facing cut into imitation of ashlar, and weathered to the sombrest grey. The windows of the ground floor and of that above, and the fanlights above the doors, were boarded up, a guard against unlicensed intrusion; the top story had not been thought to stand in need of this protection, and a few panes were broken. On these dead frontages could be traced the marks of climbing plants, which once hung their leaves about each doorway; dry fragments of the old stem still adhered to the stucco. What had been the narrow strip of fore-garden, railed from the pavement, was now a little wilderness of coarse grass, docks, nettles, and degenerate shrubs. The paint on the doors had lost all colour, and much of it was blistered off; the three knockers had disappeared, leaving indications of rough removal, as if—which was probably the case—they had fallen a prey to marauders. Standing full in the brilliant sunshine, this spectacle of abandonment seemed sadder, yet less ugly, than it would have looked under a gloomy sky. Goldthorpe began to weave stories about its musty squalor. He crossed the road to make a nearer inspection; and as he stood gazing at the dishonoured thresholds, at the stained and cracked boarding of the blind windows, at the rusty paling and the broken gates, there sounded from somewhere near a thin, shaky strain of music, the notes of a concertina played with uncertain hand. The sound seemed to come from within the houses, yet how could that be? Assuredly no one lived under these crazy roofs. The musician was playing 'Home, Sweet Home,' and as Goldthorpe listened it seemed to him that the sound was not stationary. Indeed, it moved; it became more distant, then again the notes sounded more distinctly, and now as if the player were in the open air. Perhaps he was at the back of the houses?

On either side ran a narrow passage, which parted the spot of desolation from inhabited dwellings. Exploring one of these, Goldthorpe found that there lay in the rear a tract of gardens. Each of the three lifeless houses had its garden of about twenty yards long. The bordering wall along the passage allowed a man of average height to peer over it, and Goldthorpe searched with curious eye the piece of ground which was nearest to him. Many a year must have gone by since any gardening was done here. Once upon a time the useful and ornamental had both been represented in this modest space; now, flowers and vegetables, such of them as survived in the struggle for existence, mingled together, and all alike were threatened by a wild, rank growth of grasses and weeds, which had obliterated the beds, hidden the paths, and made of the whole garden plot a green jungle. But Goldthorpe gave only a glance at this still life; his interest was engrossed by a human figure, seated on a campstool near the back wall of the house, and holding a concertina, whence, at this moment, in slow, melancholy strain, 'Home, Sweet Home' began to wheeze forth. The player was a middle-aged man, dressed like a decent clerk or shopkeeper, his head shaded with an old straw hat rather too large for him, and on his feet—one of which swung as he sat with legs crossed—a pair of still more ancient slippers, also too large. With head aside, and eyes looking upward, he seemed to listen in a mild ecstasy to the notes of his instrument. He had a round face of much simplicity and good-nature, semicircular eyebrows, pursed little mouth with abortive moustache, and short thin beard fringing the chinless lower jaw. Having observed this unimposing person for a minute or two, himself unseen, Goldthorpe surveyed the rear of the building, anxious to discover any sign of its still serving as human habitation; but nothing spoke of tenancy. The windows on this side were not boarded, and only a few panes were broken; but the chief point of contrast with the desolate front was made by a Virginia creeper, which grew luxuriantly up to the eaves, hiding every sign of decay save those dim, dusty apertures which seemed to deny all possibility of life within. And yet, on looking steadily, did he not discern something at one of the windows on the top story—something like a curtain or a blind? And had not that same window the appearance of having been more recently cleaned than the others? He could not be sure; perhaps he only fancied these things. With neck aching from the strained position in which he had made his survey over the wall, the young man turned away. In the same moment 'Home, Sweet Home' came to an end, and, but for the cry of a milkman, the early-morning silence was undisturbed.

Goldthorpe pursued his walk, thinking of what he had seen, and wondering what it all meant. On his way back he made a point of again passing the deserted houses, and again he peered over the wall of the passage. The man was still there, but no longer seated with the concertina; wearing a round felt hat instead of the straw, he stood almost knee-deep in vegetation, and appeared to be examining the various growths about him. Presently he moved forward, and, with head still bent, approached the lower end of the garden, where, in a wall higher than that over which Goldthorpe made his espial, there was a wooden door. This the man opened with a key, and, having passed out, could be heard to turn a lock behind him. A minute more, and this short, respectable figure came into sight at the end of the passage. Goldthorpe could not resist the opportunity thus offered. Affecting to turn a look of interest towards the nearest roof, he waited until the stranger was about to pass him, then, with civil greeting, ventured upon a question.

'Can you tell me how these houses come to be in this neglected state?'

The stranger smiled; a soft, modest, deferential smile such as became his countenance, and spoke in a corresponding voice, which had a vaguely provincial accent.

'No wonder it surprises you, sir. I should be surprised myself. It comes of quarrels and lawsuits.'

'So I supposed. Do you know who the property belongs to?'

'Well, yes, sir. The fact is—it belongs to me.'

The avowal was made apologetically, and yet with a certain timid pride. Goldthorpe exhibited all the interest he felt. An idea had suddenly sprung up in his mind; he met the stranger's look, and spoke with the easy good-humour natural to him.

'It seems a great pity that houses should be standing empty like that. Are they quite uninhabitable? Couldn't one camp here during this fine summer weather? To tell you the truth, I'm looking for a room—as cheap a room as I can get. Could you let me one for the next three months?'

The stranger was astonished. He regarded the young man with an uneasy smile.

'You are joking, sir.'

'Not a bit of it. Is the thing quite impossible? Are all the rooms in too bad a state?'

'I won't say *that*,' replied the other cautiously, still eyeing his interlocutor with surprised glances. 'The upper rooms are really not so bad—that is to say, from a humble point of view. I—I have been looking at them just now. You really mean, sir—?'

'I'm quite in earnest, I assure you,' cried Goldthorpe cheerily. 'You see I'm tolerably well dressed still, but I've precious little money, and I want to eke out the little I've got for about three months. I'm writing a book. I think I shall manage to sell it when it's done, but it'll take me about three months yet. I don't care what sort of place I live in, so long as it's quiet. Couldn't we come to terms?'

The listener's visage seemed to grow rounder in progressive astonishment; his eyes declared an emotion akin to awe; his little mouth shaped itself as if about to whistle.

'A book, sir? You are writing a book? You are a literary man?'

'Well, a beginner. I have poverty on my side, you see.'

'Why, it's like Dr. Johnson!' cried the other, his face glowing with interest. 'It's like Chatterton!—though I'm sure I hope you won't end like him, sir. It's like Goldsmith!—indeed it is!'

'I've got half Oliver's name, at all events,' laughed the young man. 'Mine is Goldthorpe.'

'You don't say so, sir! What a strange coincidence! Mine, sir, is Spicer. I—I don't know whether you'd care to come into my garden? We might talk there—'

In a minute or two they were standing amid the green jungle, which Goldthorpe viewed with delight. He declared it the most picturesque garden he had ever seen.

'Why, there are potatoes growing there. And what are those things? Jerusalem artichokes? And look at that magnificent thistle; I never saw a finer thistle in my life! And poppies—and marigolds—and broad-beans—and isn't that lettuce?'

Mr. Spicer was red with gratification.

'I feel that something might be done with the garden, sir,' he said. 'The fact is, sir, I've only lately come into this property, and I'm sorry to say it'll only be mine for a little more than a year—a year from next midsummer day, sir. There's the explanation of what you see. It's leasehold property, and the lease is just coming to its end. Five years ago, sir, an uncle of mine inherited the property from his brother. The houses were then in a very bad state, and only one of them let, and there had been lawsuits going on for a long time between the leaseholder and the ground-landlord—I can't quite understand these matters, they're not at all in my line, sir; but at all events there were quarrels and lawsuits, and I'm told one of the tenants was somehow mixed up in it. The fact is, my uncle wasn't a very well-to-do man, and perhaps he didn't feel able to repair the houses, especially as the lease was drawing to its end. Would you like to go in and have a look round?'

They entered by the back door, which admitted them to a little wash-house. The window was over-spun with cobwebs, thick, hoary; each corner of the ceiling was cobweb-packed; long, dusty filaments depended along the walls. Notwithstanding, Goldthorpe noticed that the house had a water-supply; the sink was wet, the tap above it looked new. This confirmed a suspicion in his mind, but he made no remark. They passed into the kitchen. Here again the work of the spider showed thick on every hand. The window, however, though uncleaned for years, had recently been opened; one knew that by the torn and ragged condition of the webs where the sashes joined. And lo! on the window-sill stood a plate, a cup and saucer, a knife, a fork, a spoon—all of them manifestly new-washed. Goldthorpe affected not to see these objects; he averted his face to hide an involuntary smile.

'I must light a candle,' said Mr. Spicer. 'The staircase is quite dark.'

A candle stood ready, with a box of matches, on the rusty cooking-stove. No fire had burned in the grate for many a long day; of that the visitor assured himself. Save the objects on the window-sill, no evidence of human occupation was discoverable. Having struck a light, Mr. Spicer advanced. In the front passage, on the stairs, on the landing, every angle and every projection had its drapery of cobwebs. The stuffy, musty air smelt of cobwebs; so, at all events, did Goldthorpe explain to himself a peculiar odour which he seemed never to have smelt. It was the same in the two rooms on the first floor. Through the boarded windows of that in front penetrated a few thin rays from the golden sky; they gleamed upon dust and web, on faded, torn wall-paper and a fireplace in ruins.

'I shouldn't recommend you to take either of *these* rooms,' said Mr. Spicer, looking nervously at his companion. 'They really can't be called attractive.'

'Those on the top are healthier, no doubt,' was the young man's reply. 'I noticed that some of the window-glass is broken. That must have been good for airing.'

Mr. Spicer grew more and more nervous. He opened his little round mouth, very much like a fish gasping, but seemed unable to speak. Silently he led the way to the top story, still amid cobwebs; the atmosphere was certainly purer up here, and when they entered the first room they found themselves all at once in such a flood of glorious sunshine that Goldthorpe shouted with delight.

'Ah, I could live here! Would it cost much to have panes put in? An old woman with a broom would do the rest.' He added in a moment, 'But the back windows are not broken, I think?'

'No—I think not—I—no—'

Mr. Spicer gasped and stammered. He stood holding the candle (its light invisible) so that the grease dripped steadily on his trousers.

'Let's have a look at the other,' cried Goldthorpe. 'It gets the afternoon sun, no doubt. And one would have a view of the garden.'

'Stop, sir!' broke from his companion, who was red and perspiring. 'There's something I should like to tell you before you go into that room. I—it—the fact is, sir, that—temporarily—I am occupying it myself.'

'Oh, I beg your pardon, Mr. Spicer!'

'Not at all, sir! Don't mention it, sir. I have a reason—it seemed to me—I've merely put in a bed and a table, sir, that's all—a temporary arrangement.'

'Yes, yes; I quite understand. What could be more sensible? If the house were mine, I should do the same. What's the good of owning a house, and making no use of it?'

Great was Mr. Spicer's satisfaction.

'See what it is, sir,' he exclaimed, 'to have to do with a literary man! You are large-minded, sir; you see things from an intellectual point of view. I can't tell you how it gratifies me, sir, to have made your acquaintance. Let us go into the back room.'

With nervous boldness he threw the door open. Goldthorpe, advancing respectfully, saw that Mr. Spicer had not exaggerated the simplicity of his arrangements. In a certain measure the room had been cleaned, but along the angle of walls and ceiling there still clung a good many cobwebs, and the state of the paper was deplorable. A blind hung at the window, but the floor had no carpet. In one corner stood a little camp bed, neatly made for the day; a table and a chair, of the cheapest species, occupied the middle of the floor, and on the hearth was an oil cooking-stove.

'It's wonderful how little one really wants,' remarked Mr. Spicer, 'at all events in weather such as this. I find that I get along here very well indeed. The only expense I had was for the water-supply. And really, sir, when one comes to think of it, the situation is pleasant. If one doesn't mind loneliness—and it happens that I don't. I have my books, sir—'

He opened the door of a cupboard containing several shelves. The first thing Goldthorpe's eye fell upon was the concertina; he saw also sundry articles of clothing, neatly disposed, a little crockery, and, ranged on the two top shelves, some thirty volumes, all of venerable aspect.

'Literature, sir,' pursued Mr. Spicer modestly, 'has always been my comfort. I haven't had very much time for reading, but my motto, sir, has been *nulla dies sine linea.*'

It appeared from his pronunciation that Mr. Spicer was no classical scholar, but he uttered the Latin words with infinite gusto, and timidly watched their effect upon the listener.

'This is delightful,' cried Mr. Goldthorpe. 'Will you let me have the front room? I could work here splendidly—splendidly! What rent do you ask, Mr. Spicer?'

'Why really, sir, to tell you the truth I don't know what to say. Of course the windows must be seen to. The fact is, sir, if you felt disposed to do that at your own expense, and—and to have the room cleaned, and—and, let us say, to bear half the water-rate whilst you are here, why, really, I hardly feel justified in asking anything more.'

It was Goldthorpe's turn to be embarrassed, for, little as he was prepared to pay, he did not like to accept a stranger's generosity. They discussed the matter in detail, with the result that for the arrangement which Mr. Spicer had proposed there was substituted a weekly rent of two shillings, the lease extending over a period of three months. Goldthorpe was to live quite independently, asking nothing in the way of domestic service; moreover, he was requested to introduce no other person to the house, even as casual visitor. These conditions Mr. Spicer set forth, in a commercial hand, on a sheet of notepaper, and the agreement was solemnly signed by both contracting parties.

On the way home to breakfast Goldthorpe reviewed his position now that he had taken this decisive step. It was plain that he must furnish his room with the articles which Mr. Spicer found indispensable, and this outlay, be as economical as he might, would tell upon the little capital which was to support him for three months. Indeed, when all had been done, and he found himself, four days later, dwelling on the top story of the house of cobwebs, a simple computation informed him that his total expenditure, after payment of rent, must not exceed fifteenpence a day. What matter? He was in the highest spirits, full of energy and hope. His landlord had been kind and helpful in all sorts of ways, helping him to clean the room, to remove his property from the old lodgings, to make purchases at the lowest possible rate, to establish himself as comfortably as circumstances permitted. And when, on the first morning of his tenancy, he was awakened by a brilliant sun, the young man had a sensation of comfort and satisfaction quite new in his experience; for he was really at home; the bed he slept on, the table he ate at and wrote upon, were his own possessions; he thought with pity of his lodging-house life, and felt a joyous assurance that here he would do better work than ever before.

In less than a week Mr. Spicer and he were so friendly that they began to eat together, taking it in turns to prepare the meal. Now and then they walked in company, and every evening they sat smoking (very cheap tobacco) in the wild garden. Little by little Mr. Spicer revealed the facts of his history. He had begun life, in a midland town, as a chemist's errand-boy, and by steady perseverance, with a little pecuniary help from relatives, had at length risen to the position of chemist's assistant. For five-and-twenty years he practised such rigid economy that, having no one but himself to provide for, he began to foresee a possibility of passing his old age elsewhere than in the workhouse. Then befell the death of his uncle, which was to have important consequences for him. Mr. Spicer told the story of this exciting moment late one evening, when, kept indoors by rain, the companions sat together upstairs, one on each side of the rusty and empty fireplace.

'All my life, Mr. Goldthorpe, I've thought what a delightful thing it must be to have a house of one's own. I mean, really of one's own; not only a rented house, but one in which you could live and die, feeling that no one had a right to turn you out. Often and often I've dreamt of it, and tried to imagine what the feeling would be like. Not a large, fine house—oh dear, no! I didn't care how small it might be; indeed, the smaller the better for a man of my sort. Well, then, you can imagine how it came upon me when I heard—But let me tell you first that I hadn't seen my uncle for fifteen years or more. I had always thought him a well-to-do man, and I knew he wasn't married, but the truth is, it never came into my head that he might leave me something. Picture me, Mr. Goldthorpe— you have imagination, sir—standing behind the counter and thinking about nothing but business, when in comes a young gentleman—I see him now—and asks for Mr. Spicer. "Spicer is my name, sir," I said. "And you are the nephew," were his next words, "of the late Mr. Isaac Spicer, of Clapham, London?" That shook me, sir, I assure you it did, but I hope I behaved decently. The young gentleman went on to tell me that my uncle had left no will, and that I was believed to be his next-of-kin, and that if so, I inherited all his property, the principal part of which was three houses in London. Now try and think, Mr. Goldthorpe, what sort of state I was in after hearing that. You're an intellectual man, and you can enter into another's mind. Three houses! Well, sir, you know what houses those were. I came up to London at once (it was last autumn), and I saw my uncle's lawyer, and he told me all about the property, and I saw it for myself. Ah, Mr. Goldthorpe! If ever a man suffered a bitter disappointment, sir!'

He ended on a little laugh, as if excusing himself for making so much of his story, and sat for a moment with head bowed.

'Fate played you a nasty trick there,' said Goldthorpe. 'A knavish trick.'

'One felt almost justified in using strong language, sir—though I always avoid it on principle. However, I must tell you that the houses weren't all. Luckily there was a little money as well, and, putting it with my own savings, sir, I found it would yield me an income. When I say an income, I mean, of course, for a man in my position. Even when I have to go into lodgings, when my houses become the property of the ground-landlord—to my mind, Mr. Goldthorpe, a very great injustice, but I don't set myself up against the law of the land—I shall just be able to live. And that's no small blessing, sir, as I think you'll agree.'

'Rather! It's the height of human felicity, Mr. Spicer. I envy you vastly.'

'Well, sir, I'm rather disposed to look at it in that light myself. My nature is not discontented, Mr. Goldthorpe. But, sir, if you could have seen me when the lawyer began to explain about the houses! I was absolutely ignorant of the leasehold system; and at first I really couldn't understand. The lawyer thought me a fool, I fear, sir. And when I came down here and saw the houses themselves! I'm afraid, Mr. Goldthorpe, I'm really afraid, sir, I was weak enough to shed a tear.'

They were sitting by the light of a very small lamp, which did not tend to cheerfulness.

'Come,' cried Goldthorpe, 'after all, the houses are yours for a twelvemonth. Why shouldn't we both live on here all the time? It'll be a little breezy in winter, but we could have the fireplaces knocked into shape, and keep up good fires. When I've sold my book I'll pay a higher rent, Mr. Spicer. I like the old house, upon my word I do! Come, let us have a tune before we go to bed.'

Smiling and happy, Mr. Spicer fetched from the cupboard his concertina, and after the usual apology for what he called his 'imperfect mastery of the instrument,' sat down to play 'Home, Sweet Home.' He had played it for years, and evidently would never improve in his execution. After 'Home, Sweet Home' came 'The Bluebells of Scotland,' after that 'Annie Laurie'; and Mr. Spicer's repertory was at an end. He talked of learning new pieces, but there was not the slightest hope of this achievement.

Mr. Spicer's mental development had ceased more than twenty years ago, when, after extreme efforts, he had attained the qualification of chemist's assistant. Since then the world had stood still with him. Though a true lover of books, he knew nothing of any that had been published during his own lifetime. His father, though very poor, had possessed a little collection of volumes, the very same which now stood in Mr. Spicer's cupboard. The authors represented in this library were either English classics or obscure writers of the early part of the nineteenth century. Knowing these books very thoroughly, Mr. Spicer sometimes indulged in a quotation which would have puzzled even the erudite. His favourite poet was Cowper, whose moral sentiments greatly soothed him. He spoke of Byron like some contemporary who, whilst admitting his lordship's genius, felt an abhorrence of his life. He judged literature solely from the moral point of view, and was incapable of understanding any other. Of fiction he had read very little indeed, for it was not regarded with favour by his parents. Scott was hardly more than a name to him. And though he avowed acquaintance with one or two works of Dickens, he spoke of them with an uneasy smile, as if in some doubt as to their tendency. With these intellectual characteristics, Mr. Spicer naturally found it difficult to appreciate the attitude of his literary friend, a young man whose brain thrilled in response to modern ideas, and who regarded himself as the destined leader of a new school of fiction. Not indiscreet, Goldthorpe soon became aware that he had better talk as little as possible of the work which absorbed his energies. He had enough liberality and sense of humour to understand and enjoy his landlord's conversation, and the simple goodness of the man inspired him with no little respect. Thus they got along together remarkably well. Mr. Spicer never ceased to feel himself honoured by the presence under his roof of one who—as he was wont to say—wielded the pen. The tradition of Grub Street was for him a living fact. He thought of all authors as struggling with poverty, and continued to cite eighteenth-century examples by way of encouraging Goldthorpe and animating his zeal. Whilst the young man was at work Mr. Spicer moved about the house with soundless footsteps. When invited into his tenant's room he had a reverential demeanour, and the sight of manuscript on the bare deal table caused him to subdue his voice.

The weeks went by, and Goldthorpe's novel steadily progressed. In London he had only two or three acquaintances, and from them he held aloof, lest necessity or temptation should lead to his spending money which he could not spare. The few letters which he received were addressed to a post-office—impossible to shock the nerves of a postman by requesting him to deliver correspondence at this dead house, of which the front door had not been opened for years. The weather was perfect; a great deal of sunshine, but as yet no oppressive heat, even in the chambers under the roof. Towards the end of June Mr. Spicer began to amuse himself with a little gardening. He had discovered in the coal-hole an ancient fork, with one prong broken and the others rusting away. This implement served him in his slow, meditative attack on that part of the jungle which seemed to offer least resistance. He would work for a quarter of an hour, then, resting on his fork, contemplate the tangled mass of vegetation which he had succeeded in tearing up.

'Our aim should be,' he said gravely, when Goldthorpe came to observe his progress, 'to clear the soil round about those vegetables and flowers which seem worth preserving. These broad-beans, for instance—they seem to be a very fine sort. And the Jerusalem artichokes. I've been making inquiry about the artichokes, and I'm told they are not ready to eat till the autumn. The first frost is said to improve them. They're fine plants—very fine plants.'

Already the garden had supplied them with occasional food, but they had to confess that, for the most part, these wild vegetables lacked savour. The artichokes, now shooting up into a leafy grove, were the great hope of the future. It would be deplorable to quit the house before this tuber came to maturity.

'The worst of it is,' remarked Mr. Spicer one day, when he was perspiring freely, 'that I can't help thinking of how different it would be if this garden was really my own. The fact is, Mr. Goldthorpe, I can't put much heart into the work; no, I can't. The more I reflect, the more indignant I become. Really now, Mr. Goldthorpe, speaking as an intellectual man, as a man of imagination, could anything be more cruelly unjust than this leasehold system? I assure you, it keeps me awake at night; it really does.'

The tenor of his conversation proved that Mr. Spicer had no intention of leaving the house until he was legally obliged to do so. More than once he had an interview with his late uncle's solicitor, and each time he came back with melancholy brow. All the details of the story were now familiar to him; he knew all about the lawsuits which had ruined the property. Whenever he spoke of the ground-landlord, known to him only by name, it was with a severity such as he never permitted himself on any other subject. The ground-landlord was, to his mind, an embodiment of social injustice.

'Never in my life, Mr. Goldthorpe, did I grudge any payment of money as I grudge the ground-rent of these houses. I feel it as robbery, sir, as sheer robbery, though the sum is so small. When, in my ignorance, the matter was first explained to me, I wondered why my uncle had continued to pay this rent, the houses being of no profit to him. But now I understand, Mr. Goldthorpe; the sense of possession is very sweet. Property's property, even when it's leasehold and in ruins. I grudge the ground-rent bitterly, but I feel, sir, that I couldn't bear to lose my houses until the fatal moment, when lose them I must.'

In August the thermometer began to mark high degrees. Goldthorpe found it necessary to dispense with coat and waistcoat when he was working, and at times a treacherous languor whispered to him of the delights of idleness. After one particularly hot day, he and his landlord smoked together in the dusking garden, both unusually silent. Mr. Spicer's eye dwelt upon the great heap of weeds which was resulting from his labour; an odour somewhat too poignant arose from it upon the close air. Goldthorpe, who had been rather headachy all day, was trying to think into perfect clearness the last chapters of his book, and found it difficult.

'You know,' he said all at once, with an impatient movement, 'we ought to be at the seaside.'

'The seaside?' echoed his companion, in surprise. 'Ah, it's a long time since I saw the sea, Mr. Goldthorpe. Why, it must be—yes, it is at least twenty years.'

'Really? I've been there every year of my life till this. One gets into the way of thinking of luxuries as necessities. I tell you what it is. If I sell my book as soon as it's done, we'll have a few days somewhere on the south coast together.'

Mr. Spicer betrayed uneasiness.

'I should like it much,' he murmured, 'but I fear, Mr. Goldthorpe, I greatly fear I can't afford it.'

'Oh, but I mean that you shall go with me as my guest! But for you, Mr. Spicer, I might never have got my book written at all.'

'I feel it an honour, sir, I assure you, to have a literary man in my house,' was the genial reply. 'And you think the *work* will soon be finished, sir?'

Mr. Spicer always spoke of his tenant's novel as 'the work'—which on his lips had a very large and respectful sound.

'About a fortnight more,' answered Goldthorpe with grave intensity.

The heat continued. As he lay awake before getting up, eager to finish his book, yet dreading the torrid temperature of his room, which made the brain sluggish and the hand slow, Goldthorpe saw how two or three energetic spiders had begun to spin webs once more at the corners of the ceiling; now and then he heard the long buzzing of a fly entangled in one of these webs. The same thing was happening in Mr. Spicer's chamber. It did not seem worth while to brush the new webs away.

'When you come to think of it, sir,' said the landlord, 'it's the spiders who are the real owners of these houses. When I go away, they'll be pulled down; they're not fit for human habitation. Only the spiders are really at home here, and the fact is, sir, I don't feel I have the right to disturb them. As a man of imagination, Mr. Goldthorpe, you'll understand my thoughts!'

Only with a great effort was the novel finished. Goldthorpe had lost his appetite (not, perhaps, altogether a disadvantage), and he could not sleep; a slight fever seemed to be constantly upon him. But this work was a question of life and death to him, and he brought it to an end only a few days after the term he had set himself. The complete manuscript was exhibited to Mr. Spicer, who expressed his profound sense of the privilege. Then, without delay, Goldthorpe took it to the publishing house in which he had most hope.

The young author could now do nothing but wait, and, under the circumstances, waiting meant torture. His money was all but exhausted; if he could not speedily sell the book, his position would be that of a mere pauper.

Supported thus long by the artist's enthusiasm, he fell into despondency, saw the dark side of things. To be sure, his mother (a widow in narrow circumstances) had written pressing him to take a holiday 'at home,' but he dreaded the thought of going penniless to his mother's house, and there, perchance, receiving bad news about his book. An ugly feature of the situation was that he continued to feel anything but well; indeed, he felt sure that he was getting worse. At night he suffered severely; sleep had almost forsaken him. Hour after hour he lay listening to mysterious noises, strange crackings and creakings through the desolate house; sometimes he imagined the sound of footsteps in the bare rooms below; even hushed voices, from he knew not where, chilled his blood at midnight. Since crumbs had begun to lie about, mice were common; they scampered as if in revelry above the ceiling, and under the floor, and within the walls. Goldthorpe began to dislike this strange abode. He felt that under any circumstances it would be impossible for him to dwell here much longer.

When his last coin was spent, and he had no choice but to pawn or sell something for a few days' subsistence, the manuscript came back upon his hands. It had been judged—declined.

That morning he felt seriously unwell. After making known the catastrophe to Mr. Spicer—who was stricken voiceless—he stood silent for a minute or two, then said with quiet resolve:

'It's all up. I've no money, and I feel as if I were going to have an illness. I must say good-bye to you, old friend.'

'Mr. Goldthorpe!' exclaimed the other solemnly; 'I entreat you, sir, to do nothing rash! Take heart, sir! Think of Samuel Johnson, think of Goldsmith—'

'The extent of my rashness, Mr. Spicer, will be to raise enough money on my watch to get down into Derbyshire. I must go home. If I don't, you'll have the pleasant job of taking me to a hospital.'

Mr. Spicer insisted on lending him the small sum he needed. An hour or two later they were at St. Pancras Station, and before sunset Goldthorpe had found harbourage under his mother's roof. There he lay ill for more than a month, and convalescent for as long again. His doctor declared that he must have been living in some very unhealthy place, but the young man preferred to explain his illness by overwork. It seemed to him sheer ingratitude to throw blame on Mr. Spicer's house, where he had been so contented and worked so well until the hot days of latter August. Mr. Spicer himself wrote kind and odd little letters, giving an account of the garden, and earnestly hoping that his literary friend would be back in London to taste the Jerusalem artichokes. But Christmas came and went, and Goldthorpe was still at his mother's house.

Meanwhile the manuscript had gone from publisher to publisher, and at length, on a day in January—date ever memorable in Goldthorpe's life—there arrived a short letter in which a certain firm dryly intimated their approval of the story offered them, and their willingness to purchase the copyright for a sum of fifty pounds. The next morning the triumphant author travelled to London. For two or three days a violent gale had been blowing, with much damage throughout the country; on his journey Goldthorpe saw many great trees lying prostrate, beaten, as though scornfully, by the cold rain which now descended in torrents. Arrived in town, he went to the house where he had lodged in the time of comparative prosperity, and there was lucky enough to find his old rooms vacant. On the morrow he called upon the gracious publishers, and after that, under a sky now become more gentle, he took his way towards the abode of Mr. Spicer.

Eager to communicate the joyous news, glad in the prospect of seeing his simple-hearted friend, he went at a great pace up the ascending road. There were the three houses, looking drearier than ever in a faint gleam of winter sunshine. There were his old windows. But—what had happened to the roof? He stood in astonishment and apprehension, for, just above the room where he had dwelt, the roof was an utter wreck, showing a great hole, as if something had fallen upon it with crushing weight. As indeed was the case; evidently the chimney-stack had come down, and doubtless in the recent gale. Seized with anxiety on Mr. Spicer's account, he ran round to the back of the garden and tried the door; but it was locked as usual. He strained to peer over the garden wall, but could discover nothing that threw light on his friend's fate; he noticed, however, a great grove of dead, brown artichoke stems, seven or eight feet high. Looking up at the back windows, he shouted Mr. Spicer's name; it was useless. Then, in serious alarm, he betook himself to the house on the other side of the passage, knocked at the door, and asked of the woman who presented herself whether anything was known of a gentleman who dwelt where the chimney-stack had just fallen. News was at once forthcoming; the event had obviously caused no small local excitement. It was two days since the falling of the chimney, which happened towards evening, when the gale blew its hardest. Mr. Spicer was at that moment sitting before the fire, and only by a miracle had he escaped destruction, for an immense weight of material came down through the rotten roof, and even broke a good deal of the flooring. Had the occupant been anywhere but close by the fireplace, he must have been crushed to a mummy; as it was, only a few bricks struck him, inflicting severe bruises on back and arms. But the shock had been serious. When his shouts from the window at length attracted attention and brought help, the poor man had to be carried downstairs, and in a thoroughly helpless state was removed to the nearest hospital.

'Which room was he in?' inquired Goldthorpe. 'Back or front?'

'In the front room. The back wasn't touched.'

Musing on Mr. Spicer's bad luck—for it seemed as if he had changed from the back to the front room just in order that the chimney might fall on him—Goldthorpe hastened away to the hospital. He could not be admitted to-day, but heard that his friend was doing very well; on the morrow he would be allowed to see him.

So at the visitors' hour Goldthorpe returned. Entering the long accident ward, he searched anxiously for the familiar face, and caught sight of it just as it began to beam recognition. Mr. Spicer was sitting up in bed; he looked pale and meagre, but not seriously ill; his voice quivered with delight as he greeted the young man.

'I heard of your inquiring for me yesterday, Mr. Goldthorpe, and I've hardly been able to live for impatience to see you. How are you, sir? How are you? And what news about the *work*, sir?'

'We'll talk about that presently, Mr. Spicer. Tell me all about your accident. How came you to be in the front room?'

'Ah, sir,' replied the patient, with a little shake of the head, 'that indeed was singular. Only a few days before, I had made a removal from my room into yours. I call it yours, sir, for I always thought of it as yours; but thank heaven you were not there. Only a few days before. I took that step, Mr. Goldthorpe, for two reasons: first, because water was coming through the roof at the back in rather unpleasant quantities, and secondly, because I hoped to get a little morning sun in the front. The fact is, sir, my room had been just a little depressing. Ah, Mr. Goldthorpe, if you knew how I have missed you, sir! But the *work*—what news of the *work*?'

Smiling as though carelessly, the author made known his good fortune. For a quarter of an hour Mr. Spicer could talk of nothing else.

'This has completed my cure!' he kept repeating. 'The work was composed under my roof, my own roof, sir! Did I not tell you to take heart?'

'And where are you going to live?' asked Goldthorpe presently. 'You can't go back to the old house.'

'Alas! no, sir. All my life I have dreamt of the joy of owning a house. You know how the dream was realised, Mr. Goldthorpe, and you see what has come of it at last. Probably it is a chastisement for overweening desires, sir. I should have remembered my position, and kept my wishes within bounds. But, Mr. Goldthorpe, I shall continue to cultivate the garden, sir. I shall put in spring lettuces, and radishes, and mustard and cress. The property is mine till midsummer day. You shall eat a lettuce of my growing, Mr. Goldthorpe; I am bent on that. And how I grieve that you were not with me at the time of the artichokes—just at the moment when they were touched by the first frost!'

'Ah! They were really good, Mr. Spicer?'

'Sir, they seemed good to *me*, very good. Just at the moment of the first frost!'

A CAPITALIST

AMONG the men whom I saw occasionally at the little club in Mortimer Street,—and nowhere else,—was one who drew my attention before I had learnt his name or knew anything about him. Of middle age, in the fullness of health and vigour, but slenderly built; his face rather shrewd than intellectual, interesting rather than pleasing; always dressed as the season's mode dictated, but without dandyism; assuredly he belonged to the money-spending, and probably to the money-getting, world. At first sight of him I remember resenting his cap-à-pie perfection; it struck me as bad form—here in Mortimer Street, among fellows of the pen and the palette.

'Oh,' said Harvey Munden, 'he's afraid of being taken for one of us. He buys pictures. Not a bad sort, I believe, if it weren't for his snobbishness.'

'His name?'

'Ireton. Has a house in Fitzjohn Avenue, and a high-trotting wife.'

Six months later I recalled this description of Mrs. Ireton. She was the talk of the town, the heroine of the newest divorce case. By that time I had got to know her husband; perhaps once a fortnight we chatted at the club, and I found him an agreeable acquaintance. Before the Divorce Court flashed a light of scandal upon his home, I felt that there was more in him than could be discovered in casual gossip; I wished to know him better. Something of shyness marked his manner, and like all shy men he sometimes appeared arrogant. He had a habit of twisting his moustache nervously and of throwing quick glances in every direction as he talked; if he found some one's eye upon him, he pulled himself together and sat for a moment as if before a photographer. One easily perceived that he was not a man of liberal education; he had rather too much of the 'society' accent; his pronunciation of foreign names told a tale. But I thought him good-hearted, and when the penny-a-liners began to busy themselves with his affairs, I felt sorry for him.

Nothing to his dishonour came out in the trial. He and his interesting spouse had evidently lived a cat-and-dog life throughout the three years of their marriage, but the counthercharges brought against him broke down completely. It was abundantly proved that he had *not* kept a harem somewhere near Leicester Square; that he had *not* thrown a decanter at Mrs. Ireton. She, on the other hand, left the court with tattered reputation. Ireton got his release, and the weekly papers applauded.

But in Mortimer Street we saw him no more. Some one said that he had gone to live in Paris; some one else reported that he had purchased an estate in Bucks. Presently he was forgotten.

Some three years went by, and I was spending the autumn at a village by the New Forest. One day I came upon a man kneeling under a hedge, examining some object on the ground,—fern or flower, or perhaps insect. His costume showed that he was no native of the locality; I took him for a stray townsman, probably a naturalist. He wore a straw hat and a rough summer suit; a wallet hung from his shoulder. The sound of my steps on crackling wood caused him to turn and look at me. After a moment's hesitation I recognised Ireton.

And he knew me; he smiled, as I had often seen him smile, with a sort of embarrassment. We greeted each other.

'Look here,' he said at once, when the handshaking was over, 'can you tell me what this little flower is?'

I stooped, but was unable to give him the information he desired.

'You don't go in for that kind of thing?'

'Well, no.'

'I'm having a turn at it. I want to know the flowers and ferns. I have a book at my lodgings, and I look the things up when I get home.'

His wallet contained a number of specimens; he plucked up the little plant by the root, and stowed it away. I watched him with curiosity. Perhaps I had seen only his public side; perhaps even then he was capable of dressing roughly, and of rambling for his pleasure among fields and wood. But such a possibility had never occurred to me. I wondered whether his brilliant wife had given him a disgust for the ways of town. If so, he was a more interesting man than I had supposed.

'Where are you staying?' he asked, after a glance this way and that.

I named the village, two miles away.

'Working?'

'Idling merely.'

In a few minutes he overcame his reserve and began to talk of the things which he knew interested me. We discussed the books of the past season, the exhibitions, the new men in letters and art. Ireton said that he had been living at a wayside inn for about a week; he thought of moving on, and, as I had nothing to do, suppose he came over for a few days to the village where I was camped? I welcomed the proposal.

'There's an inn, I dare say? I like the little inns in this part of the country. Dirty, of course, and the cooking hideous; but it's pleasant for a change. I like to be awoke by the cock crowing, and to see the grubby little window when I open my eyes.'

I began to suspect that he had come down in the world. Could his prosperity have been due to Mrs. Treton? Had she carried off the money? He might affect a liking for simple things when grandeur was no longer in his reach. Yet I remembered that he had undoubtedly been botanising before he knew of my approach, and such a form of pastime seemed to prove him sincere.

By chance I witnessed his arrival the next morning. He drove up in a farmer's trap, his luggage a couple of large Gladstone-bags. That day and the next we spent many hours together. His vanity, though not outgrown, was in abeyance; he talked with easy frankness, yet never of what I much desired to know, his own history and present position. It was his intellect that he revealed to me. I gathered that he had given much time to study during the past three years, and incidentally it came out that he had been living abroad; his improved pronunciation of the names of French artists was very noticeable. At his age— not less than forty-five—this advance argued no common mental resources.

Whether he had suffered much, I could not determine; at present he seemed light-hearted enough.

Certainly there was no affectation in his pursuit of botany; again and again I saw him glow with genuine delight when he had identified a plant. After all, this might be in keeping with his character, for even in the old days he had never exhibited—at all events to me—a taste for the ignobler luxuries, and he had seemed to me a very clean-minded man. I never knew any one who refrained so absolutely from allusion, good or bad, to his friends or acquaintances. He might have stood utterly alone in the world, a simple spectator of civilisation.

At length I ventured upon a question.

'You never see any of the Mortimer Street men?'

'No,' he answered carelessly, 'I haven't come in their way lately, somehow.'

That evening our ramble led us into an enclosure where game was preserved. We had lost our way, and Ireton, scornful of objections, struck across country, making for a small plantation which he thought he remembered. Here, among the trees, we were suddenly face to face with an old gentleman of distinguished bearing, who regarded us sternly.

'Is it necessary,' he said, 'to tell you that you are trespassing?'

The tone was severe, but not offensive. I saw my companion draw himself to his full height.

'Not at all necessary,' he answered, in a voice that surprised me, it was so nearly insolent. 'We are making our way to the road as quickly as possible.'

'Then be so good as to take the turning to the right when you reach the field,' said our admonisher coldly. And he turned his back upon us.

I looked at Ireton. To my astonishment he was pallid, the lines of his countenance indicating fiercest wrath. He marched on in silence till we had reached the field.

'The fellow took us for cheap-trippers, I suppose,' then burst from his lips.

'Not very likely.'

'Then why the devil did he speak like that?'

The grave reproof had exasperated him; he was flushed and his hands trembled. I observed him with the utmost interest, and it became clear from the angry words he poured forth that he could not endure to be supposed anything but a gentleman at large. Here was the old characteristic; it had merely been dormant. I tried to laugh him out of his irritation, but soon saw that the attempt was dangerous. On the way home he talked very little; the encounter in the wood had thoroughly upset him.

Next morning he came into my room with a laugh that I did not like; he seated himself stiffly, looked at me from beneath his knitted brows, and said in an aggressive tone:

'I have got to know all about that impudent old fellow.'

'Indeed? Who is he?'

'A poverty-stricken squire, with an old house and a few acres—the remnants of a large estate gambled away by his father. I know him by name, and I'm quite sure that he knows me. If I had offered him my card, as I thought of doing, I dare say his tone would have changed.'

This pettishness amused me so much that I pretended to be a little sore myself.

'His poverty, I suppose, has spoilt his temper.'

'No doubt,—I can understand that,' he added, with a smile. 'But I don't allow people to treat me like a tramp. I shall go up and see him this afternoon.'

'And insist on an apology?'

'Oh, there'll be no need of insisting. The fellow has several unmarried daughters.'

It seemed to me that my companion was bent on showing his worst side. I returned to my old thoughts of him; he was snobbish, insolent, generally detestable; but a man to be studied, and I let him talk as he would.

The reduced squire was Mr. Humphrey Armitage, of Brackley Hall. For my own part, the demeanour of this gentleman had seemed perfectly adapted to the occasion; we were strangers plunging through his preserves, and his tone to us had nothing improper; it was we who owed an apology. In point of breeding, I felt sure that Ireton could not compare with Mr. Armitage for a moment, and it seemed to me vastly improbable that the invader of Brackley Hall would meet with the kind of reception he anticipated.

I saw Ireton when he set out to pay his call. His Gladstone-bags had provided him with the costume of Piccadilly; from shining hat to patent-leather shoes, he was immaculate. Seeing that he had to walk more than a mile, that the month was September, and that he could not pretend to have come straight from town, this apparel struck me as not a little inappropriate; I could only suppose that the man had no social tact.

At seven in the evening he again sought me. His urban glories were exchanged for the ordinary attire, but I at once read in his face that he had suffered no humiliation.

'Come and dine with me at the inn,' he exclaimed cordially; 'if one may use such a word as *dine* under the circumstances.'

'With pleasure.'

'To-morrow I dine with the Armitages.'

He regarded me with an air of infinite satisfaction. Surprised, I held my peace. 'It was as I foresaw. The old fellow welcomed me with open arms. His daughters gave me tea. I had really a very pleasant time.'

I mused and wondered.

'You didn't expect it; I can see that.'

'You told me that Mr. Armitage would recognise your name,' I answered evasively.

'Precisely. Not long ago I gave him, through an agent, a very handsome price for some pictures he had to sell.'

Again he looked at me, watching the effect of his words.

'Of course,' he continued, 'there were ample apologies for his treatment of us yesterday. By the bye, I take it for granted you don't carry a dress-suit in your bag?'

'Heaven forbid!'

'To be sure—pray don't misunderstand me. I meant that you had expressly told me of your avoidance of all such formalities. Therefore you will be glad that I excused you from dining at the Hall.'

For a moment I felt uncomfortable, but after all I *was* glad not to have the trouble of refusing on my own account.

'Thanks,' I said, 'you did the right thing.'

We walked over to the inn, and sat down at a rude but not unsatisfying table. After dinner, Ireton proposed that we should smoke in the garden. 'It's quiet, and we can talk.' The sun had just set; the sky was magnificent with afterglow. Ireton's hint about privacy led me to hope that he was going to talk more confidentially than hitherto, and I soon found that I was not mistaken.

'Do you know,' he began, calling me by my name, 'I fancy you have been criticising me—yes, I know you have. You think I made an ass of myself about that affair in the wood. Well, I have no doubt I did. Now that it has turned out pleasantly, I can see and admit that there was nothing to make a fuss about.'

I smiled.

'Very well. Now, you're a writer. You like to get at the souls of men. Suppose I show you a bit of mine.'

He had drunk freely of the potent ale, and was now sipping a strong tumbler of hot whisky. Possibly this accounted in some measure for his communicativeness.

'Up to the age of five-and-twenty I was clerk in a drug warehouse. To this day even the faintest smell of drugs makes my heart sink. If I can help it, I never go into a chemist's shop. I was getting a pound a week, and I not only lived on it, but kept up a decent appearance. I always had a good suit of clothes for Sundays and holidays—made at a tailor's in Holborn. Since he disappeared I've never been able to find any one who fitted me so well. I paid six-and-six a week for a top bedroom in a street near Gray's Inn Road. Did you suppose I had gone through the mill?'

I made no answer, and, after looking at me for a moment, Ireton resumed:

'Those were damned days! It wasn't the want of good food and good lodgings that troubled me most,—but the feeling that I was everybody's inferior. There's no need to tell you how I was brought up; I was led to expect better things, that's enough. I never got used to being ordered about. When I was told to do this or that, I answered with a silent curse,—and I wonder it didn't come out sometimes. That's my nature. If I had been born the son of a duke, I couldn't have resented a subordinate position more fiercely than I did. And I used to rack my brain with schemes for getting out of it. Many a night I have lain awake for hours, trying to hit on some way of earning my living independently. I planned elaborate forgeries. I read criminal cases in the newspapers to get a hint that I might work upon. Well, that only means that I had exhausted all the honest attempts, and found them all no good. I was in despair, that's all.'

He finished his whisky and shouted to the landlord, who presently brought him another glass.

'What's that bird making the strange noise?'

'A night-jar, I think.'

'Nice to be sitting here, isn't it? I had rather be here than in the swellest London club. Well, I was going to tell you how I got out of that beastly life. You know, I'm really a very quiet fellow. I like simple things; but all my life, till just lately, I never had a chance of enjoying them; of living as I chose. The one thing I can't stand is to feel that I am looked down upon. That makes a madman of me.'

He drank, and struck a match to relight his pipe.

'One Saturday afternoon I went to an exhibition in Coventry Street. The pictures were for sale, and admission was free. I have always been fond of water-colours; at that time it was one of my ambitions to possess a really good bit of landscape in water-colour but, of course, I knew that the prices were beyond me. Well, I walked through the gallery, and there was one thing that caught my fancy; I kept going back to it again and again. It was a bit of sea-coast by Ewart Merry,—do you know him? He died years ago; his pictures fetch a fairly good price now. As I was looking at it, the fellow who managed the show came up with a man and woman to talk about another picture near me; he tried his hardest to persuade them to buy, but they wouldn't, and I dare say it disturbed his temper. Seeing him stand there alone, I stepped up to him, and asked the price of the water-colour. He just gave a look at me, and said, "Too much money for you."

'Now, you must remember that I was in my best clothes, and I certainly didn't look like a penniless clerk. If the fellow had struck a blow at me, I couldn't have been more astonished than I was by that answer. Astonishment was the first feeling, and it lasted about a second; then my heart gave a great leap, and began to beat violently, and for a moment I couldn't see anything, and I felt hot and cold by turns. I can remember this as well as if it happened yesterday; I must have gone through it in memory many thousands of times.'

I observed his face, and saw that even now he suffered from the recollection.

'When he had spoken, the blackguard turned away. I couldn't move, and the wonder is that I didn't swallow his insult, and sneak out of the place,—I was so accustomed, you see, to repress myself. But of a sudden something took hold of me, and pushed me forward,—it really didn't seem to be my own will. I said, "Wait a minute"; and the man turned round. Then I stood looking him in the eyes. "Are you here," I said, "to sell pictures, or to insult people who come to buy?" I must have spoken in a voice he didn't expect; he couldn't answer, and stared at me. "I asked you the price of that water-colour, and you will be good enough to answer me civilly." Those were my very words. They came without thinking, and afterwards I felt satisfied with myself when I remembered them. It wouldn't have been unnatural if I had sworn at him, but this was the turning-point of my life, and I behaved in a way that surprised myself. At last he replied, "The price is forty guineas," and he was going off again, but I stopped him. "I will buy it. Take my name and address." "When will it be paid for?" he asked. "On Monday."

'I followed him to the table, and he entered my name and address in a book. Then I looked straight at him again. "Now, you understand," I said, "that that picture is mine, and I shall either come or send for it about one o'clock on Monday. If I hadn't wanted it specially, you would have lost a sale by your impertinence." And I marched out of the room.

'But I was in a fearful state. I didn't know where I was going,—I walked straight on, street after street, and just missed being run over half a dozen times. Perspiration dripped from me. The only thing I knew was that I had triumphed over a damned brute who had insulted me. I had stopped his mouth; he believed he had made a stupid mistake; he could never have imagined that a fellow without a sovereign in the world was speaking to him like that. If I had knocked him down the satisfaction would have been very slight in comparison.'

The gloom of nightfall had come upon us, and I could no longer see his face distinctly, but his voice told me that he still savoured that triumph. He spoke with exultant passion. I was beginning to understand Ireton.

'Isn't the story interesting?' he asked, after a pause.

'Very. Pray go on.'

'Well, you mustn't suppose that it was a mere bit of crazy bravado. I knew how I was going to get the money—the forty guineas. And as soon as I could command myself, I went to do the business.

'A fellow-clerk in the drug warehouse had been badly in want of money not long before that, and I knew he had borrowed twenty pounds from a loan office, paying it back week by week, with heavy interest, out of his screw, poor devil. I could do the same. I went straight off to the lender. It was a fellow called Crowther; he lived in Dean Street, Soho; in a window on the ground floor there was a card with "Sums from One pound to a Hundred lent at short notice." I was lucky enough to find him at home; we did our business in a little back room, where there was a desk and a couple of chairs, and nothing else but dirt. I expected to find an oldish man, but he seemed about my own age, and on the whole I didn't dislike the look of him,—a rather handsome young fellow, fairly well dressed, with a taking sort of smile. I began by telling him where I was employed, and mentioned my fellow-clerk, whom he knew. That made him quite cheerful; he offered me a drink, and we got on very well. But he thought forty guineas a big sum; would I tell him what I wanted it for? No, I wouldn't do that. Well, how long would it take me to pay it back? Could I pay a pound a week? No, I couldn't. He began to shake his head and to look at me thoughtfully. Then he asked no end of questions, to find out who I was and what people I had belonging to me, and what my chances were. Then he made me have another drink, and at last I was persuaded into telling him the whole story. First of all he stared, and then he laughed; I never saw a man laugh more heartily. At last he said, "Why didn't you tell me you had value in hand? See here, I'll look at that picture on Monday morning, and I shouldn't wonder if we can do business." This alarmed me,—I was afraid he might get talking to the picture-dealer. But he promised not to say a word about me.

'On Sunday I sent a note to the warehouse, saying that I should not be able to come to business till Monday afternoon. It was the first time I had ever done such a thing, and I knew I could invent some story to excuse myself. Most of that day I spent in bed; I didn't feel myself, yet it was still a great satisfaction to me that I had got the better of that brute. On Monday at twelve I kept the appointment in Dean Street. Crowther hadn't come in, and I sat for a few minutes quaking. When he turned up, he was quite cheerful. "Look here!" he said, "will you sell me that picture for thirty pounds?" "What then?" I asked. "Why, then you can pay me another thirty pounds, and I'll give you twelve months to do it in. You shall have your forty guineas at once." I tried to reflect, but I was too agitated. However, I saw that to pay thirty pounds in a year meant that I must live on about eight shillings a week. "I don't know how I'm to do it," I said. He looked at me. "Well, I won't be hard on you. Look here, you shall pay me six bob a week till the thirty quid's made up. Now, you can do *that?*" Yes I could do that, and I agreed. In another ten minutes our business was settled,— my signature was so shaky that I might safely have disowned it afterwards. Then we had a drink at a neighbouring pub, and we walked together towards Coventry Street. Crowther was to wait for me near the picture-dealer's.

'I entered with a bold step, promising myself pleasure in a new triumph over the brute. But he wasn't there. I saw only an under-strapper. I had no time to lose, for I must be at business by two o'clock. I paid the money—notes and gold—and took away the picture under my arm. Of course, it had been removed from the frame in which I first saw it, and the assistant wrapped it up for me in brown paper. At the street corner I surrendered it to Crowther. "Come and see me after business to-morrow," he said, "I should like to have a bit more talk with you."

'So I had come out of it gloriously. I cared nothing about losing the picture, and I didn't grieve over the six shillings a week that I should have to pay for the next two years. If I went into that gallery again, I should be treated respectfully—that was sufficient.'

He laughed, and for a minute or two we sat silent. From the inn sounded rustic voices; the village worthies were gathered for their evening conversation.

'That's the best part of my story,' said Ireton at length. 'What followed is commonplace. Still, you might like to hear how I bridged the gulf, from fourteen shillings a week to the position I now hold. Well, I got very intimate with Crowther, and found him really a very decent fellow. He had a good many irons in the fire. Besides his loan office, which paid much better than you would imagine, he had a turf commission agency, which brought him in a good deal of money, and shortly after I met him he became part proprietor of a club in Soho. He very soon talked to me in the frankest way of all his doings; I think he was glad to be on friendly terms with me simply because I was better educated and could behave decently. I don't think he ever did anything illegal, and he had plenty of good feeling,—but that didn't prevent him from squeezing eighty per cent, or so out of many a poor devil who had borrowed to save himself or his family from starvation. That was all business; he drew the sharpest distinctions between business and private relations, and was very ignorant. I never knew a man so superstitious. Every day he consulted signs and omens. For instance, to decide whether the day was to be lucky for him—in betting and so on—he would stand at a street corner and count the number of white horses that passed in five minutes; if he had made up his mind on an even number, and an even number passed, then he felt safe in following his impulses for the day; if the number were odd, he would do little or no speculation. When he was going to play cards for money, he would find a beggar and give him something, even if he had to walk a great distance to do it. He often used to visit an Italian who kept fortune-telling canaries, and he always followed the advice he got. It put him out desperately if he saw the new moon through glass, or over his left shoulder. There was no end to his superstitions, and, whether by reason of them or in spite of them, he certainly prospered. When he died, ten or twelve years ago, he left fifteen thousand pounds.

'I have to thank him for my own good luck. "Look here," he said to me, "it's only duffers that go on quill-driving at a quid a week. A fellow like you ought to be doing better." "Show me the way," I said. And I was ready to do whatever he told me. I had a furious hunger for money; the adventure in Coventry Street had thoroughly unsettled me, and I would have turned burglar rather than go on much longer as a wretched slave, looked down upon by everybody, and exposed to insult at every corner. I dreamed of money-making, and woke up feverish with determination. At last Crowther gave me a few jobs to do for him in my off-time. They weren't very nice jobs, and I shouldn't like to explain them to you; but they brought me in half a sovereign now and then. I began to get an insight into the baser modes of filling one's pocket. Then something happened; my mother died, and I became the owner of a house at Notting Hill of fifty pounds rental. I talked over my situation with Crowther, and he advised me, as it turned out, thoroughly well. I was to raise money on this house,—not to sell it,—and take shares in a new music-hall which Crowther was connected with. There's no reason why I shouldn't tell you; it was the Marlborough. I did take shares, and at the end of the second twelve months I was drawing a dividend of sixty per cent. I have never drawn less than thirty, and the year before last we touched seventy-five. At present I am a shareholder in three other halls,—and they don't do badly.

'I suppose it isn't only good luck; no doubt I have a sort of talent for money-making, but I never knew it before I met Crowther. By just opening my eyes to the fact that money could be earned in other ways than at the regular kinds of employment, he gave me a start, and I went ahead. There isn't a man in the world has suffered more than I have for want of money, and no one ever worked with a fiercer resolve to get out of the hell of contemptible poverty. It would fill a book, the history of my money-making. The first big sum I ever was possessed of came to me at the age of two-and-thirty, when I sold a proprietary club (the one Crowther had a share in and which I had ultimately got into my own hands) for nine thousand pounds; but I owed about half of this. I went on and on, and I got into society; *that* came through the Marlborough,—a good story, but I mustn't tell it. At last I married—a rich woman.'

He paused, and I thought, but was not quite sure, that I heard him sigh.

'We won't talk about that either. I shall not marry a rich woman again, that's all. In fact, I don't care for such people; my best friends, real friends, are all more or less strugglers, and perhaps there's no harm in saying that it gives me pleasure to help them when I've a chance. I like to buy a picture of a poor devil artist. I like to smoke my pipe with good fellows who never go out of their way for money's sake. All the same, it's a good thing to be well off. But for that, now, I couldn't make the acquaintance of such people as these at Brackley Hall. I more than half like them. Old Armitage is a gentleman, and looks back upon generations of gentlemen, his ancestors. Ah! you can't buy that! And his daughters are devilish nice girls, with sweet soft voices. I'm glad the old fellow met us yesterday.'

It was now dark; I looked up and saw the stars brightening. We sat for another quarter of an hour, each busy with his own thoughts, then rose and parted for the night.

A week later, when I returned to London, Ireton was still living at the little inn, and a letter I received from him at the beginning of October told me he had just left. 'The country was exquisite that last week,' he wrote;—and it struck me that 'exquisite' was a word he must have caught from some one else's lips.

I heard from him again in the following January. He wrote from the Isle of Wight, and informed me that in the spring he was to be married to Miss Ethel Armitage, second daughter of Humphrey Armitage, Esq., of Brackley Hall.

CHRISTOPHERSON

IT was twenty years ago, and on an evening in May. All day long there had been sunshine. Owing, doubtless, to the incident I am about to relate, the light and warmth of that long-vanished day live with me still; I can see the great white clouds that moved across the strip of sky before my window, and feel again the spring languor which troubled my solitary work in the heart of London.

Only at sunset did I leave the house. There was an unwonted sweetness in the air; the long vistas of newly lit lamps made a golden glow under the dusking flush of the sky. With no purpose but to rest and breathe, I wandered for half an hour, and found myself at length where Great Portland Street opens into Marylebone Road. Over the way, in the shadow of Trinity Church, was an old bookshop, well known to me: the gas-jet shining upon the stall with its rows of volumes drew me across. I began turning over pages, and—invariable consequence—fingering what money I had in my pocket. A certain book overcame me; I stepped into the little shop to pay for it.

While standing at the stall, I had been vaguely aware of some one beside me, a man who also was looking over the books; as I came out again with my purchase, this stranger gazed at me intently, with a half-smile of peculiar interest. He seemed about to say something. I walked slowly away; the man moved in the same direction. Just in front of the church he made a quick movement to my side, and spoke.

'Pray excuse me, sir—don't misunderstand me—I only wished to ask whether you have noticed the name written on the flyleaf of the book you have just bought?'

The respectful nervousness of his voice naturally made me suppose at first that the man was going to beg; but he seemed no ordinary mendicant. I judged him to be about sixty years of age; his long, thin hair and straggling beard were grizzled, and a somewhat rheumy eye looked out from his bloodless, hollowed countenance; he was very shabbily clad, yet as a fallen gentleman, and indeed his accent made it clear to what class he originally belonged. The expression with which he regarded me had so much intelligence, so much good-nature, and at the same time such a pathetic diffidence, that I could not but answer him in the friendliest way. I had not seen the name on the flyleaf, but at once I opened the book, and by the light of a gas-lamp read, inscribed in a very fine hand, 'W. R. Christopherson, 1849.'

'It is my name,' said the stranger, in a subdued and uncertain voice.

'Indeed? The book used to belong to you?'

'It belonged to me.' He laughed oddly, a tremulous little crow of a laugh, at the same time stroking his head, as if to deprecate disbelief. 'You never heard of the sale of the Christopherson library? To be sure, you were too young; it was in 1860. I have often come across books with my name in them on the stalls— often. I had happened to notice this just before you came up, and when I saw you look at it, I was curious to see whether you would buy it. Pray excuse the freedom I am taking. Lovers of books—don't you think—?'

The broken question was completed by his look, and when I said that I quite understood and agreed with him he crowed his little laugh.

'Have you a large library?' he inquired, eyeing me wistfully.

'Oh dear, no. Only a few hundred volumes. Too many for one who has no house of his own.'

He smiled good-naturedly, bent his head, and murmured just audibly:

'My catalogue numbered 24,718.'

I was growing curious and interested. Venturing no more direct questions, I asked whether, at the time he spoke of, he lived in London.

'If you have five minutes to spare,' was the timid reply, 'I will show you my house. I mean'—again the little crowing laugh—'the house which *was* mine.'

Willingly I walked on with him. He led me a short distance up the road skirting Regent's Park, and paused at length before a house in an imposing terrace.

'There,' he whispered, 'I used to live. The window to the right of the door—that was my library. Ah!'

And he heaved a deep sigh.

'A misfortune befell you,' I said, also in a subdued voice.

'The result of my own folly. I had enough for my needs, but thought I needed more. I let myself be drawn into business—I, who knew nothing of such things—and there came the black day—the black day.'

We turned to retrace our steps, and walking slowly, with heads bent, came in silence again to the church.

'I wonder whether you have bought any other of my books?' asked Christopherson, with his gentle smile, when we had paused as if for leave-taking.

I replied that I did not remember to have come across his name before; then, on an impulse, asked whether he would care to have the book I carried in my hand; if so, with pleasure I would give it him. No sooner were the words spoken than I saw the delight they caused the hearer. He hesitated, murmured reluctance, but soon gratefully accepted my offer, and flushed with joy as he took the volume.

'I still have a few books,' he said, under his breath, as if he spoke of something he was ashamed to make known. 'But it is very rarely indeed that I can add to them. I feel I have not thanked you half enough.'

We shook hands and parted.

My lodging at that time was in Camden Town. One afternoon, perhaps a fortnight later, I had walked for an hour or two, and on my way back I stopped at a bookstall in the High Street. Some one came up to my side; I looked, and recognised Christopherson. Our greeting was like that of old friends.

'I have seen you several times lately,' said the broken gentleman, who looked shabbier than before in the broad daylight, 'but I—I didn't like to speak. I live not far from here.'

'Why, so do I,' and I added, without much thinking what I said, 'do you live alone?'

'Alone? oh no. With my wife.'

There was a curious embarrassment in his tone. His eyes were cast down and his head moved uneasily.

We began to talk of the books on the stall, and turning away together continued our conversation. Christopherson was not only a well-bred but a very intelligent and even learned man. On his giving some proof of erudition (with the excessive modesty which characterised him), I asked whether he wrote. No, he had never written anything—never; he was only a bookworm, he said. Thereupon he crowed faintly and took his leave.

It was not long before we again met by chance. We came face to face at a street corner in my neighbourhood, and I was struck by a change in him. He looked older; a profound melancholy darkened his countenance; the hand he gave me was limp, and his pleasure at our meeting found only a faint expression.

'I am going away,' he said in reply to my inquiring look. 'I am leaving London.'

'For good?'

'I fear so, and yet'—he made an obvious effort—'I am glad of it. My wife's health has not been very good lately. She has need of country air. Yes, I am glad we have decided to go away—very glad—very glad indeed!'

He spoke with an automatic sort of emphasis, his eyes wandering, and his hands twitching nervously. I was on the point of asking what part of the country he had chosen for his retreat, when he abruptly added:

'I live just over there. Will you let me show you my books?'

Of course I gladly accepted the invitation, and a couple of minutes' walk brought us to a house in a decent street where most of the ground-floor windows showed a card announcing lodgings. As we paused at the door, my companion seemed to hesitate, to regret having invited me.

'I'm really afraid it isn't worth your while,' he said timidly. 'The fact is, I haven't space to show my books properly.'

I put aside the objection, and we entered. With anxious courtesy Christopherson led me up the narrow staircase to the second-floor landing, and threw open a door. On the threshold I stood astonished. The room was a small one, and would in any case have only just sufficed for homely comfort, used as it evidently was for all daytime purposes; but certainly a third of the entire space was occupied by a solid mass of books, volumes stacked several rows deep against two of the walls and almost up to the ceiling. A round table and two or three chairs were the only furniture—there was no room, indeed, for more. The window being shut, and the sunshine glowing upon it, an intolerable stuffiness oppressed the air. Never had I been made so uncomfortable by the odour of printed paper and bindings.

'But,' I exclaimed, 'you said you had only a *few* books! There must be five times as many here as I have.'

'I forget the exact number,' murmured Christopherson, in great agitation. 'You see, I can't arrange them properly. I have a few more in—in the other room.'

He led me across the landing, opened another door, and showed me a little bedroom. Here the encumberment was less remarkable, but one wall had completely disappeared behind volumes, and the bookishness of the air made it a disgusting thought that two persons occupied this chamber every night.

We returned to the sitting-room, Christopherson began picking out books from the solid mass to show me. Talking nervously, brokenly, with now and then a deep sigh or a crow of laughter, he gave me a little light on his history. I learnt that he had occupied these lodgings for the last eight years; that he had been twice married; that the only child he had had, a daughter by his first wife, had died long ago in childhood; and lastly—this came in a burst of confidence, with a very pleasant smile—that his second wife had been his daughter's governess. I listened with keen interest, and hoped to learn still more of the circumstances of this singular household.

'In the country,' I remarked, 'you will no doubt have shelf room?'

At once his countenance fell; he turned upon me a woebegone eye. Just as I was about to speak again sounds from within the house caught my attention; there was a heavy foot on the stairs, and a loud voice, which seemed familiar to me.

'Ah!' exclaimed Christopherson with a start, 'here comes some one who is going to help me in the removal of the books. Come in, Mr. Pomfret, come in!'

The door opened, and there appeared a tall, wiry fellow, whose sandy hair, light blue eyes, jutting jawbones, and large mouth made a picture suggestive of small refinement but of vigorous and wholesome manhood. No wonder I had seemed to recognise his voice. Though we only saw each other by chance at long intervals, Pomfret and I were old acquaintances.

'Hallo!' he roared out, 'I didn't know you knew Mr. Christopherson.'

'I'm just as much surprised to find that *you* know him!' was my reply.

The old book-lover gazed at us in nervous astonishment, then shook hands with the newcomer, who greeted him bluffly, yet respectfully. Pomfret spoke with a strong Yorkshire accent, and had all the angularity of demeanour which marks the typical Yorkshireman. He came to announce that everything had been settled for the packing and transporting of Mr. Christopherson's library; it remained only to decide the day.

'There's no hurry,' exclaimed Christopherson. 'There's really no hurry. I'm greatly obliged to you, Mr. Pomfret, for all the trouble you are taking. We'll settle the date in a day or two—a day or two.'

With a good-humoured nod Pomfret moved to take his leave. Our eyes met; we left the house together. Out in the street again I took a deep breath of the summer air, which seemed sweet as in a meadow after that stifling room. My companion evidently had a like sensation, for he looked up to the sky and broadened out his shoulders.

'Eh, but it's a grand day! I'd give something for a walk on Ilkley Moors.'

As the best substitute within our reach we agreed to walk across Regent's Park together. Pomfret's business took him in that direction, and I was glad of a talk about Christopherson. I learnt that the old book-lover's landlady was Pomfret's aunt. Christopherson's story of affluence and ruin was quite true.

Ruin complete, for at the age of forty he had been obliged to earn his living as a clerk or something of the kind. About five years later came his second marriage.

'You know Mrs. Christopherson?' asked Pomfret.

'No! I wish I did. Why?'

'Because she's the sort of woman it does you good to know, that's all. She's a lady—*my* idea of a lady. Christopherson's a gentleman too, there's no denying it; if he wasn't, I think I should have punched his head before now. Oh, I know 'em well! why, I lived in the house there with 'em for several years. She's a lady to the end of her little finger, and how her husband can 'a borne to see her living the life she has, it's more than I can understand. By—! I'd have turned burglar, if I could 'a found no other way of keeping her in comfort.'

'She works for her living, then?'

'Ay, and for his too. No, not teaching; she's in a shop in Tottenham Court Road; has what they call a good place, and earns thirty shillings a week. It's all they have, but Christopherson buys books out of it.'

'But has he never done anything since their marriage?'

'He did for the first few years, I believe, but he had an illness, and that was the end of it. Since then he's only loafed. He goes to all the book-sales, and spends the rest of his time sniffing about the second-hand shops. She? Oh, she'd never say a word! Wait till you've seen her.'

'Well, but,' I asked, 'what has happened. How is it they're leaving London?'

'Ay, I'll tell you; I was coming to that. Mrs. Christopherson has relatives well off—a fat and selfish lot, as far as I can make out—never lifted a finger to help her until now. One of them's a Mrs. Keeting, the widow of some City porpoise, I'm told. Well, this woman has a home down in Norfolk. She never lives there, but a son of hers goes there to fish and shoot now and then. Well, this is what Mrs. Christopherson tells my aunt, Mrs. Keeting has offered to let her and her husband live down yonder, rent free, and their food provided. She's to be housekeeper, in fact, and keep the place ready for any one who goes down.'

'Christopherson, *I* can see, would rather stay where he is.'

'Why, of course, he doesn't know how he'll live without the bookshops. But he's glad for all that, on his wife's account. And it's none too soon, I can tell you. The poor woman couldn't go on much longer; my aunt says she's just about ready to drop, and sometimes, I know, she looks terribly bad. Of course, she won't own it, not she; she isn't one of the complaining sort. But she talks now and then about the country—the places where she used to live. I've heard her, and it gives me a notion of what she's gone through all these years. I saw her a week ago, just when she had Mrs. Keeting's offer, and I tell you I scarcely knew who it was! You never saw such a change in any one in your life! Her face was like that of a girl of seventeen. And her laugh—you should have heard her laugh!'

'Is she much younger than her husband?' I asked.

'Twenty years at least. She's about forty, I think.' I mused for a few moments.

'After all, it isn't an unhappy marriage?'

'Unhappy?' cried Pomfret. 'Why, there's never been a disagreeable word between them, that I'll warrant. Once Christopherson gets over the change, they'll have nothing more in the world to ask for. He'll potter over his books—'

'You mean to tell me,' I interrupted, 'that those books have all been bought out of his wife's thirty shillings a week?'

'No, no. To begin with, he kept a few out of his old library. Then, when he was earning his own living, he bought a great many. He told me once that he's often lived on sixpence a day to have money for books. A rum old owl; but for all that he's a gentleman, and you can't help liking him. I shall be sorry when he's out of reach.'

For my own part, I wished nothing better than to hear of Christopherson's departure. The story I had heard made me uncomfortable. It was good to think of that poor woman rescued at last from her life of toil, and in these days of midsummer free to enjoy the country she loved. A touch of envy mingled, I confess, with my thought of Christopherson, who henceforth had not a care in the world, and without reproach might delight in his hoarded volumes. One could not imagine that he would suffer seriously by the removal of his old haunts. I promised myself to call on him in a day or two. By choosing Sunday, I might perhaps be lucky enough to see his wife.

And on Sunday afternoon I was on the point of setting forth to pay this visit, when in came Pomfret. He wore a surly look, and kicked clumsily against the furniture as he crossed the room. His appearance was a surprise, for, though I had given him my address, I did not in the least expect that he would come to see me; a certain pride, I suppose, characteristic of his rugged strain, having always made him shy of such intimacy.

'Did you ever hear the like of *that*!' he shouted, half angrily. 'It's all over. They're not going! And all because of those blamed books!'

And spluttering and growling, he made known what he had just learnt at his aunt's home. On the previous afternoon the Christophersons had been surprised by a visit from their relatives and would-be benefactress, Mrs. Keeting. Never before had that lady called upon them; she came, no doubt (this could only be conjectured), to speak with them of their approaching removal. The close of the conversation (a very brief one) was overheard by the landlady, for Mrs. Keeting spoke loudly as she descended the stairs. 'Impossible! Quite impossible! I couldn't think of it! How could you dream for a moment that I would let you fill my house with musty old books? Most unhealthy! I never knew anything so extraordinary in my life, never!' And so she went out to her carriage, and was driven away. And the landlady, presently having occasion to go upstairs, was aware of a dead silence in the room where the Christophersons were sitting. She knocked—prepared with some excuse—and found the couple side by side, smiling sadly. At once they told her the truth. Mrs. Keeting had come because of a letter in which Mrs. Christopherson had mentioned the fact that her husband had a good many books, and hoped he might be permitted to remove them to the house in Norfolk. She came to see the library—with the result already heard. They had the choice between sacrificing the books and losing what their relative offered.

'Christopherson refused?' I let fall.

'I suppose his wife saw that it was too much for him. At all events, they'd agreed to keep the books and lose the house. And there's an end of it. I haven't been so riled about anything for a long time!'

Meantime I had been reflecting. It was easy for me to understand Christopherson's state of mind, and without knowing Mrs. Keeting, I saw that she must be a person whose benefactions would be a good deal of a burden. After all, was Mrs. Christopherson so very unhappy? Was she not the kind of woman who lived by sacrifice—one who had far rather lead a life disagreeable to herself than change it at the cost of discomfort to her husband? This view of the matter irritated Pomfret, and he broke into objurgations, directed partly against Mrs. Keeting, partly against Christopherson. It was an 'infernal shame,' that was all he could say. And after all, I rather inclined to his opinion.

When two or three days had passed, curiosity drew me towards the Christophersons' dwelling. Walking along the opposite side of the street, I looked up at their window, and there was the face of the old bibliophile. Evidently he was standing at the window in idleness, perhaps in trouble. At once he beckoned to me; but before I could knock at the house-door he had descended, and came out.

'May I walk a little way with you?' he asked.

There was worry on his features. For some moments we went on in silence.

'So you have changed your mind about leaving London?' I said, as if carelessly.

'You have heard from Mr. Pomfret? Well—yes, yes—I think we shall stay where we are—for the present.'

Never have I seen a man more painfully embarrassed. He walked with head bent, shoulders stooping; and shuffled, indeed, rather than walked. Even so might a man bear himself who felt guilty of some peculiar meanness.

Presently words broke from him.

'To tell you the truth, there's a difficulty about the books.' He glanced furtively at me, and I saw he was trembling in all his nerves. 'As you see, my circumstances are not brilliant.' He half-choked himself with a crow. 'The fact is we were offered a house in the country, on certain conditions, by a relative of Mrs. Christopherson; and, unfortunately, it turned out that my library is regarded as an objection—a fatal objection. We have quite reconciled ourselves to staying where we are.'

I could not help asking, without emphasis, whether Mrs. Christopherson would have cared for life in the country. But no sooner were the words out of my mouth than I regretted them, so evidently did they hit my companion in a tender place.

'I think she would have liked it,' he answered, with a strangely pathetic look at me, as if he entreated my forbearance.

'But,' I suggested, 'couldn't you make some arrangements about the books? Couldn't you take a room for them in another house, for instance?'

Christopherson's face was sufficient answer; it reminded me of his pennilessness. 'We think no more about it,' he said. 'The matter is settled—quite settled.'

There was no pursuing the subject. At the next parting of the ways we took leave of each other.

I think it was not more than a week later when I received a postcard from Pomfret. He wrote: 'Just as I expected. Mrs. C. seriously ill.' That was all.

Mrs. C. could, of course, only mean Mrs. Christopherson. I mused over the message—it took hold of my imagination, wrought upon my feelings; and that afternoon I again walked along the interesting street.

There was no face at the window. After a little hesitation I decided to call at the house and speak with Pomfret's aunt. It was she who opened the door to me.

We had never seen each other, but when I mentioned my name and said I was anxious to have news of Mrs. Christopherson, she led me into a sitting-room, and began to talk confidentially.

She was a good-natured Yorkshirewoman, very unlike the common London landlady. 'Yes, Mrs. Christopherson had been taken ill two days ago. It began with a long fainting fit. She had a feverish, sleepless night; the doctor was sent for; and he had her removed out of the stuffy, book-cumbered bedroom into another chamber, which luckily happened to be vacant. There she lay utterly weak and worn, all but voiceless, able only to smile at her husband, who never moved from the bedside day or night. He, too,' said the landlady, 'would soon break down: he looked like a ghost, and seemed "half-crazed."'

'What,' I asked, 'could be the cause of this illness?'

The good woman gave me an odd look, shook her head, and murmured that the reason was not far to seek.

'Did she think,' I asked, 'that disappointment might have something to do with it?'

Why, of course she did. For a long time the poor lady had been all but at the end of her strength, and *this* came as a blow beneath which she sank.

'Your nephew and I have talked about it,' I said. 'He thinks that Mr. Christopherson didn't understand what a sacrifice he asked his wife to make.'

'I think so too,' was the reply. 'But he begins to see it now, I can tell you. He says nothing but.'

There was a tap at the door, and a hurried tremulous voice begged the landlady to go upstairs.

'What is it, sir?' she asked.

'I'm afraid she's worse,' said Christopherson, turning his haggard face to me with startled recognition. 'Do come up at once, please.'

Without a word to me he disappeared with the landlady. I could not go away; for some ten minutes I fidgeted about the little room, listening to every sound in the house. Then came a footfall on the stairs, and the landlady rejoined me.

'It's nothing,' she said. 'I almost think she might drop off to sleep, if she's left quiet. He worries her, poor man, sitting there and asking her every two minutes how she feels. I've persuaded him to go to his room, and I think it might do him good if you went and had a bit o' talk with him.'

I mounted at once to the second-floor sitting-room, and found Christopherson sunk upon a chair, his head falling forwards, the image of despairing misery. As I approached he staggered to his feet. He took my hand in a shrinking, shamefaced way, and could not raise his eyes. I uttered a few words of encouragement, but they had the opposite effect to that designed.

'Don't tell me that,' he moaned, half resentfully. 'She's dying—she's dying— say what they will, I know it.'

'Have you a good doctor?'

'I think so—but it's too late—it's too late.'

As he dropped to his chair again I sat down by him. The silence of a minute or two was broken by a thunderous rat-tat at the house-door. Christopherson leapt to his feet, rushed from the room; I, half fearing that he had gone mad, followed to the head of the stairs.

In a moment he came up again, limp and wretched as before.

'It was the postman,' he muttered. 'I am expecting a letter.'

Conversation seeming impossible, I shaped a phrase preliminary to withdrawal; but Christopherson would not let me go.

'I should like to tell you,' he began, looking at me like a dog under punishment, 'that I have done all I could. As soon as my wife fell ill, and when I saw—I had only begun to think of it in that way—how she felt the disappointment, I went at once to Mrs. Keeting's house to tell her that I would sell the books. But she was out of town. I wrote to her—I said I regretted my folly—I entreated her to forgive me and to renew her kind offer. There has been plenty of time for a reply, but she doesn't answer.'

He had in his hand what I saw was a bookseller's catalogue, just delivered by the postman. Mechanically he tore off the wrapper and even glanced over the first page. Then, as if conscience stabbed him, he flung the thing violently away.

'The chance has gone!' he exclaimed, taking a hurried step or two along the little strip of floor left free by the mountain of books. 'Of course she said she would rather stay in London! Of course she said what she knew would please me! When—when did she ever say anything else! And I was cruel enough—base enough—to let her make the sacrifice!' He waved his arms frantically. 'Didn't I know what it cost her? Couldn't I see in her face how her heart leapt at the hope of going to live in the country! I knew what she was suffering; I *knew* it, I tell you! And, like a selfish coward, I let her suffer—I let her drop down and die— die!'

'Any hour,' I said, 'may bring you the reply from Mrs. Keeting. Of course it will be favourable, and the good news—'

'Too late, I have killed her! That woman won't write. She's one of the vulgar rich, and we offended her pride; and such as she never forgive.'

He sat down for a moment, but started up again in an agony of mental suffering.

'She is dying—and there, there, that's what has killed her!' He gesticulated wildly towards the books. 'I have sold her life for those. Oh!—oh!'

With this cry he seized half a dozen volumes, and, before I could understand what he was about, he had flung up the window-sash, and cast the books into the street. Another batch followed; I heard the thud upon the pavement. Then I caught him by the arm, held him fast, begged him to control himself.

'They shall all go!' he cried. 'I loathe the sight of them. They have killed my dear wife!'

He said it sobbing, and at the last words tears streamed from his eyes. I had no difficulty now in restraining him. He met my look with a gaze of infinite pathos, and talked on while he wept.

'If you knew what she has been to me! When she married me I was a ruined man twenty years older. I have given her nothing but toil and care. You shall know everything—for years and years I have lived on the earnings of her labour. Worse than that, I have starved and stinted her to buy books. Oh, the shame of it! The wickedness of it! It was my vice—the vice that enslaved me just as if it had been drinking or gambling. I couldn't resist the temptation—though every day I cried shame upon myself and swore to overcome it. She never blamed me; never a word—nay, not a look—of a reproach. I lived in idleness. I never tried to save her that daily toil at the shop. Do you know that she worked in a shop?—She, with her knowledge and her refinement leading such a life as that! Think that I have passed the shop a thousand times, coming home with a book in my hands! I had the heart to pass, and to think of her there! Oh! Oh!'

Some one was knocking at the door. I went to open, and saw the landlady, her face set in astonishment, and her arms full of books.

'It's all right,' I whispered. 'Put them down on the floor there; don't bring them in. An accident.'

Christopherson stood behind me; his look asked what he durst not speak. I said it was nothing, and by degrees brought him into a calmer state. Luckily, the doctor came before I went away, and he was able to report a slight improvement. The patient had slept a little and seemed likely to sleep again. Christopherson asked me to come again before long—there was no one else, he said, who cared anything about him—and I promised to call the next day.

I did so, early in the afternoon. Christopherson must have watched for my coming: before I could raise the knocker the door flew open, and his face gleamed such a greeting as astonished me. He grasped my hand in both his.

'The letter has come! We are to have the house.'

'And how is Mrs. Christopherson?'

'Better, much better, Heaven be thanked! She slept almost from the time when you left yesterday afternoon till early this morning. The letter came by the first post, and I told her—not the whole truth,' he added, under his breath. 'She thinks I am to be allowed to take the books with me; and if you could have seen her smile of contentment. But they will all be sold and carried away before she knows about it; and when she sees that I don't care a snap of the fingers!'

He had turned into the sitting-room on the ground floor. Walking about excitedly, Christopherson gloried in the sacrifice he had made. Already a letter was despatched to a bookseller, who would buy the whole library as it stood. But would he not keep a few volumes? I asked. Surely there could be no objection to a few shelves of books; and how would he live without them? At first he declared vehemently that not a volume should be kept—he never wished to see a book again as long as he lived. But Mrs. Christopherson? I urged. Would she not be glad of something to read now and then? At this he grew pensive. We discussed the matter, and it was arranged that a box should be packed with select volumes and taken down into Norfolk together with the rest of their luggage. Not even Mrs. Keeting could object to this, and I strongly advised him to take her permission for granted.

And so it was done. By discreet management the piled volumes were stowed in bags, carried downstairs, emptied into a cart, and conveyed away, so quietly that the sick woman was aware of nothing. In telling me about it, Christopherson crowed as I had never heard him; but methought his eye avoided that part of the floor which had formerly been hidden, and in the course of our conversation he now and then became absent, with head bowed. Of the joy he felt in his wife's recovery there could, however, be no doubt. The crisis through which he had passed had made him, in appearance, a yet older man; when he declared his happiness tears came into his eyes, and his head shook with a senile tremor.

Before they left London, I saw Mrs. Christopherson—a pale, thin, slightly made woman, who had never been what is called good-looking, but her face, if ever face did so, declared a brave and loyal spirit. She was not joyous, she was not sad; but in her eyes, as I looked at them again and again, I read the profound thankfulness of one to whom fate has granted her soul's desire.

HUMPLEBEE

THE school was assembled for evening prayers, some threescore boys representing for the most part the well-to-do middle class of a manufacturing county. At either end of the room glowed a pleasant fire, for it was February and the weather had turned to frost.

Silence reigned, but on all the young faces turned to where the headmaster sat at his desk appeared an unwonted expression, an eager expectancy, as though something out of the familiar routine were about to happen. When the master's voice at length sounded, he did not read from the book before him; gravely, slowly, he began to speak of an event which had that day stirred the little community with profound emotion.

'Two of our number are this evening absent. Happily, most happily, absent but for a short time; in our prayers we shall render thanks to the good Providence which has saved us from a terrible calamity. I do not desire to dwell upon the circumstance that one of these boys, Chadwick, had committed worse than an imprudence in venturing upon the Long Pond; it was in disregard of my injunction; I had distinctly made it known that the ice was still unsafe. We will speak no more of that. All we can think of at present is the fact that Chadwick was on the point of losing his life; that in all human probability he would have been drowned, but for the help heroically afforded him by one of his schoolfellows. I say heroically, and I am sure I do not exaggerate; in the absence of Humplebee I may declare that he nobly perilled his own life to save that of another. It was a splendid bit of courage, a fine example of pluck and promptitude and vigour. We have all cause this night to be proud of Humplebee.'

The solemn voice paused. There was an instant's profound silence. Then, from somewhere amid the rows of listeners, sounded a clear, boyish note.

'Sir, may we give three cheers for Humplebee?'

'You may.'

The threescore leapt to their feet, and volleys of cheering made the schoolroom echo. Then the master raised his hand, the tumult subsided, and after a few moments of agitated silence, prayers began.

Next morning there appeared as usual at his desk a short, thin, red-headed boy of sixteen, whose plain, freckled face denoted good-humour and a certain intelligence, but would never have drawn attention amongst the livelier and comelier physiognomies grouped about him. This was Humplebee. Hitherto he had been an insignificant member of the school, one of those boys who excel neither at games nor at lessons, of whom nothing is expected, and rarely, if ever, get into trouble, and who are liked in a rather contemptuous way. Of a sudden he shone glorious; all tongues were busy with him, all eyes regarded him, every one wished for the honour of his friendship. Humplebee looked uncomfortable. He had the sniffy beginnings of a cold, the result of yesterday's struggle in icy water, and his usual diffident and monosyllabic inclination were intensified by the position in which he found himself. Clappings on the shoulder from bigger boys who had been wont to joke about his name made him flush nervously; to be addressed as 'Humpy,' or 'Beetle,' or 'Buz,' even though in a new tone, seemed to gratify him as little as before. It was plain that Humplebee would much have liked to be left alone. He stuck as closely as possible to his desk, and out of school-time tried to steal apart from the throng.

But an ordeal awaited him. Early in the afternoon there arrived, from a great town not far away, a well-dressed and high-complexioned man, whose every look and accent declared commercial importance. This was Mr. Chadwick, father of the boy who had all but been drowned. He and the headmaster held private talk, and presently they sent for Humplebee. Merely to enter the 'study' was at any time Humplebee's dread; to do so under the present circumstances cost him anguish of spirit.

'Ha! here he is!' exclaimed Mr. Chadwick, in the voice of bluff geniality which seemed to him appropriate. 'Humplebee, let me shake hands with you! Humplebee, I am proud to make your acquaintance; prouder still to thank you, to thank you, my boy!'

The lad was painfully overcome; his hands quivered, he stood like one convicted of disgraceful behaviour.

'I think you have heard of me, Humplebee. Leonard has no doubt spoken to you of his father. Perhaps my name has reached you in other ways?'

'Yes, sir,' faltered the boy.

'You mean that you know me as a public man?' urged Mr. Chadwick, whose eyes glimmered a hungry vanity.

'Yes, sir,' whispered Humplebee.

'Ha! I see you already take an intelligent interest in things beyond school. They tell me you are sixteen, Humplebee. Come, now; what are your ideas about the future? I don't mean'—Mr. Chadwick rolled a laugh—'about the future of mankind, or even the future of the English race; you and I may perhaps discuss such questions a few years hence. In the meantime, what are your personal ambitions? In brief, what would you like to be, Humplebee?'

Under the eye of his master and of the commercial potentate, Humplebee stood voiceless; he gasped once or twice like an expiring fish.

'Courage, my boy, courage!' cried Mr. Chadwick. 'Your father, I believe, destines you for commerce. Is that your own wish? Speak freely. Speak as though I were a friend you have known all your life.'

'I should like to please my father, sir,' jerked from the boy's lips.

'Good! Admirable! That's the spirit I like, Humplebee. Then you have no marked predilection? That was what I wanted to discover—well, well, we shall see. Meanwhile, Humplebee, get on with your arithmetic. You are good at arithmetic, I am sure?'

'Not very, sir.'

'Come, come, that's your modesty. But I like you none the worse for it, Humplebee. Well, well, get on with your work, my boy, and we shall see, we shall see.'

Therewith, to his vast relief, Humplebee found himself dismissed. Later in the day he received a summons to the bedroom where Mr. Chadwick's son was being carefully nursed. Leonard Chadwick, about the same age as his rescuer, had never deigned to pay much attention to Humplebee, whom he regarded as stupid and plebeian; but the boy's character was marked by a generous impulsiveness, which came out strongly in the present circumstances.

'Hallo, Humpy!' he cried, raising himself up when the other entered. 'So you pulled me out of that hole! Shake hands, Buzzy, old fellow! You've had a talk with my governor, haven't you? What do you think of him?'

Humplebee muttered something incoherent.

'My governor's going to make your fortune, Humpy!' cried Leonard. 'He told me so, and when he says a thing he means it. He's going to start you in business when you leave school; most likely you'll go into his own office. How will you like that, Humpy? My governor thinks no end of you; says you're a brick, and so you are. I shan't forget that you pulled me out of that hole, old chap. We shall be friends all our lives, you know. Tell me what you thought of my governor?'

When he was on his legs again, Leonard continued to treat Humplebee with grateful, if somewhat condescending, friendliness. In the talks they had together the great man's son continually expatiated upon his preserver's brilliant prospects. Beyond possibility of doubt Humplebee would some day be a rich man; Mr. Chadwick had said so, and whatever he purposed came to pass. To all this Humplebee listened in a dogged sort of way, now and then smiling, but seldom making verbal answer. In school he was not quite the same boy as before his exploit; he seemed duller, less attentive, and at times even incurred reproaches for work ill done—previously a thing unknown. When the holidays came, no boy was so glad as Humplebee; his heart sang within him as he turned his back upon the school and began the journey homeward.

That home was in the town illuminated by Mr. Chadwick's commercial and municipal brilliance; over a small draper's shop in one of the outskirt streets stood the name of Humplebee the draper. About sixty years of age, he had known plenty of misfortune and sorrows, with scant admixture of happiness. Nowadays things were somewhat better with him; by dint of severe economy he had put aside two or three hundred pounds, and he was able, moreover, to give his son (an only child) what is called a sound education. In the limited rooms above the shop there might have been a measure of quiet content and hopefulness, but for Mrs. Humplebee. She, considerably younger than her husband, fretted against their narrow circumstances, and grudged the money that was being spent—wasted, she called it—on the boy Harry.

From his father Harry never heard talk of pecuniary troubles, but the mother lost no opportunity of letting him know that they were poor, miserably poor; and adding, that if he did not work hard at school he was simply a cold-hearted criminal, and robbed his parents of their bread.

But during the last month or two a change had come upon the household. One day the draper received a visit from the great Mr. Chadwick, who told a wonderful story of Harry's heroism, and made proposals sounding so nobly generous that Mr. Humplebee was overcome with gratitude.

Harry, as his father knew, had no vocation for the shop; to get him a place in a manufacturer's office seemed the best thing that could be aimed at, and here was Mr. Chadwick talking of easy book-keeping, quick advancement, and all manner of vaguely splendid possibilities in the future. The draper's joy proved Mrs. Humplebee's opportunity. She put forward a project which had of late been constantly on her mind and on her lips, to wit, that they should transfer their business into larger premises, and give themselves a chance of prosperity. Humplebee need no longer hesitate. He had his little capital to meet the first expenses, and if need arose there need not be the slightest doubt that Mr. Chadwick would assist him. A kind gentleman Mr. Chadwick! Had he not expressly desired to see Harry's mother, and had he not assured her in every way possible of his debt and gratitude he felt towards all who bore the name of Humplebee? The draper, if he neglected his opportunity, would be an idiot—a mere idiot.

So, when the boy came home for his holidays he found two momentous things decided; first, that he should forthwith enter Mr. Chadwick's office; secondly, that the little shop should be abandoned and a new one taken in a better neighbourhood.

Now Harry Humplebee had in his soul a secret desire and a secret abhorrence. Ever since he could read his delight had been in books of natural history; beasts, birds, and fishes possessed his imagination, and for nothing else in the intellectual world did he really care. With poor resources he had learned a great deal of his beloved subjects. Whenever he could get away into the fields he was happy; to lie still for hours watching some wild thing, noting its features and its ways, seemed to him perfect enjoyment. His treasure was a collection, locked in a cupboard at home, of eggs, skeletons, butterflies, beetles, and I know not what. His father regarded all this as harmless amusement, his mother contemptuously tolerated it or, in worse humour, condemned it as waste of time. When at school the boy had frequent opportunities of pursuing his study, for he was in mid country and could wander as he liked on free afternoons; but neither the headmaster nor his assistant thought it worth while to pay heed to Humplebee's predilection. True, it had been noticed more than once that in writing an 'essay' he showed unusual observation of natural things; this, however, did not strike his educators as a matter of any importance; it was not their business to discover what Humplebee could do, and wished to do, but to make him do things they regarded as desirable. Humplebee was marked for commerce; he must study compound interest, and be strong at discount. Yet the boy loathed every such mental effort, and the name of 'business' made him sick at heart.

How he longed to unbosom himself to his father! And in the first week of his holiday he had a chance of doing so, a wonderful chance, such as had never entered his dreams. The town possessed a museum of Natural History, where, of course, Harry had often spent leisure hours. Half a year ago a happy chance had brought him into conversation with the curator, who could not but be struck by the lad's intelligence, and who took an interest in him. Now they met again; they had one or two long talks, with the result that, on a Sunday afternoon, the curator of the museum took the trouble to call upon Mr. Humplebee, to speak with him about his son. At the museum was wanted a lad with a taste for natural history, to perform at first certain easy duties, with the prospect of further advancement here or elsewhere. It seemed to the curator that Harry was the very boy for the place; would Mr. Humplebee like to consider this suggestion? Now, if it had been made to him half a year ago, such an offer would have seemed to Mr. Humplebee well worth consideration, and he knew that Harry would have heard of it with delight; as it was, he could not entertain the thought for a moment.

Impossible to run the risk of offending Mr. Chadwick; moreover, who could hesitate between the modest possibilities of the museum and such a career as waited the lad under the protection of his powerful friend? With nervous haste the draper explained how matters stood, excused himself, and begged that not another word on the subject might be spoken in his son's hearing.

Harry Humplebee knew what he had lost; the curator, in talk with him, had already thrown out his suggestion; at their next meeting he discreetly made known to the boy that other counsels must prevail. For the first time Harry felt a vehement impulse, prompting him to speak on his own behalf, to assert and to plead for his own desires. But courage failed him. He heard his father loud in praise of Mr. Chadwick, intent upon the gratitude and respect due to that admirable man. He knew how his mother would exclaim at the mere hint of disinclination to enter the great man's office. And so he held his peace, though it cost him bitterness of heart and even secret tears. A long, long time passed before he could bring himself to enter again the museum doors.

He sat on a stool in Mr. Chadwick's office, a clerk at a trifling salary. Everything, his father reminded him, must have a beginning; let him work well and his progress would be rapid. Two years passed and he was in much the same position; his salary had increased by one half, but his work remained the same, mechanical, dreary, hateful to him in its monotony. Meanwhile his father's venture in the new premises had led to great embarrassments; business did not thrive; the day came when Mr. Humplebee, trembling and shamefaced, felt himself drawn to beg help of his son's so-called benefactor. He came away from the interview with empty hands. Worse than that, he had heard things about Harry which darkened his mind with a new anxiety.

'I greatly fear,' said Mr. Chadwick, 'that your son must seek a place in some other office. It's a painful thing; I wish I could have kept him; but the fact of the matter is that he shows utter incapacity. I have no fault to find with him otherwise; a good lad; in a smaller place of business he might do well enough. But he's altogether below the mark in an office such as *mine*. Don't distress yourself, Mr. Humplebee, I beg, I shall make it my care to inquire for suitable openings; you shall hear from me—you shall hear from me. Pray consider that your son is under notice to leave this day month. As for the—other matter of which you spoke, I can only repeat that the truest kindness is only to refuse assistance. I assure you it is. The circumstances forbid it. Clearly, what you have to do is to call together your creditors, and arrive at an understanding. It is my principle never to try to prop up a hopeless concern such as yours evidently is. Good day to you, Mr. Humplebee; good day.'

A year later several things had happened. Mr. Humplebee was dead; his penniless widow had gone to live in another town on the charity of poor relatives, and Harry Humplebee sat in another office, drawing the salary at which he had begun under Mr. Chadwick, his home a wretched bedroom in the house of working-folk.

It did not appear to the lad that he had suffered any injustice. He knew his own inaptitude for the higher kind of office work, and he had expected his dismissal by Mr. Chadwick long before it came. What he did resent, and profoundly, was Mr. Chadwick's refusal to aid his father in that last death-grapple with ruinous circumstance. At the worst moment Harry wrote a letter to Leonard Chadwick, whom he had never seen since he left school. He told in simple terms the position of his family, and, without a word of justifying reminiscence, asked his schoolfellow to help them if he could. To this letter a reply came from London. Leonard Chadwick wrote briefly and hurriedly, but in good-natured terms; he was really very sorry indeed that he could do so little; the fact was, just now he stood on anything but good terms with his father, who kept him abominably short of cash. He enclosed five pounds, and, if possible, would soon send more.

'Don't suppose I have forgotten what I owe you. As soon as ever I find myself in an independent position you shall have substantial proof of my enduring gratitude. Keep me informed of your address.'

Humplebee made no second application, and Leonard Chadwick did not again break silence.

The years flowed on. At five-and-twenty Humplebee toiled in the same office, but he could congratulate himself on a certain progress; by dogged resolve he had acquired something like efficiency in the duties of a commercial clerk, and the salary he now earned allowed him to contribute to the support of his mother. More or less reconciled to the day's labour, he had resumed in leisure hours his favourite study; a free library supplied him with useful books, and whenever it was possible he went his way into the fields, searching, collecting, observing. But his life had another interest, which threatened rivalry to this intellectual pursuit. Humplebee had set eyes upon the maiden destined to be his heart's desire; she was the daughter of a fellow-clerk, a man who had grown grey in service of the ledger; timidly he sought to win her kindness, as yet scarce daring to hope, dreaming only of some happy change of position which might encourage him to speak. The girl was as timid as himself; she had a face of homely prettiness, a mind uncultured but sympathetic; absorbed in domestic cares, with few acquaintances, she led the simplest of lives, and would have been all but content to live on in gentle hope for a score of years. The two were beginning to understand each other, for their silence was more eloquent than their speech.

One summer day—the last day of his brief holiday—Humplebee was returning by train from a visit to his mother. Alone in a third-class carriage, seeming to read a newspaper, but in truth dreaming of a face he hoped to see in a few hours, he suddenly found himself jerked out of his seat, flung violently forward, bumped on the floor, and last of all rolled into a sort of bundle, he knew not where. Recovering from a daze, he said to himself, 'Why, this is an accident—a collision!' Then he tried to unroll himself, and in the effort found that one of his arms was useless; more than that, it pained him horribly. He stood up and tottered on to the seat. Then the carriage-door opened, and a voice shouted—

'Anybody hurt here?'

'I think my arm is broken,' answered Humplebee.

Two men helped him to alight. The train had stopped just outside a small station; on a cross line in front of the engine lay a goods truck smashed to pieces; people were rushing about with cries and gesticulations.

'Yes, the arm is broken,' remarked one of the men who had assisted Humplebee. 'It looks as if you were the only passenger injured.' That proved, indeed, to be the case; no one else had suffered more than a jolt or a bruise. The crowd clustered about this hero of the broken arm, expressing sympathy and offering suggestions. Among them was a well-dressed young man, rather good-looking and of lively demeanour, who seemed to enjoy the excitement; he, after gazing fixedly at the pain-stricken face, exclaimed in a voice of wonder—

'By jove! it's Humplebee!'

The sufferer turned towards him who spoke; his eyes brightened, for he recognised the face of Leonard Chadwick. Neither one nor the other had greatly altered during the past ten years; they presented exactly the same contrast of personal characteristic as when they were at school together. With vehement friendliness Chadwick at once took upon himself the care of the injured clerk. He shouted for a cab, he found out where the nearest doctor lived; in a quarter of an hour he had his friend under the doctor's roof. When the fracture had been set and bandaged, they travelled on together to their native town, only a few miles distant, Humplebee knowing for the first time in his life the luxury of a first-class compartment. On their way Chadwick talked exuberantly. He was delighted at this meeting; why, one of his purposes in coming north had been to search out Humplebee, whom he had so long scandalously neglected.

'The fact is, I've been going through queer times myself. The governor and I can't get along together; we quarrelled years ago, there's not much chance of our making it up. I've no doubt that was the real reason of his dismissing you from his office—a mean thing! The governor's a fine old boy, but he has his nasty side. He's very tight about money, and I—well, I'm a bit too much the other way, no doubt. He's kept me in low water, confound him! But I'm independent of him now. I'll tell you all about it to-morrow, you'll feel better able to talk. Expect me at eleven in the morning.'

Through a night of physical suffering Humplebee was supported by a new hope. Chadwick the son, warm-hearted and generous, made a strong contrast with Chadwick the father, pompous and insincere. When the young man spoke of his abiding gratitude there was no possibility of distrusting him, his voice rang true, and his handsome features wore a delightful frankness. Punctual to his appointment, Leonard appeared next morning. He entered the poor lodging as if it had been a luxurious residence, talked suavely and gaily with the landlady, who was tending her invalid, and, when alone with his old schoolfellow, launched into a detailed account of a great enterprise in which he was concerned. Not long ago he had become acquainted with one Geldershaw, a man somewhat older than himself, personally most attractive, and very keen in business. Geldershaw had just been appointed London representative of a great manufacturing firm in Germany. It was a most profitable undertaking, and, out of pure friendship, he had offered a share in the business to Leonard Chadwick.

'Of course, I put money into it. The fact is, I have dropped in for a few thousands from a good old aunt, who has been awfully kind to me since the governor and I fell out. I couldn't possibly have found a better investment, it means eight or nine per cent, my boy, at the very least! And look here, Humplebee, of course you can keep books?'

'Yes, I can,' answered the listener conscientiously.

'Then, old fellow, a first-rate place is open to you. We want some one we can thoroughly trust; you're the very man Geldershaw had in his eye. Would you mind telling me what screw you get at present?'

'Two pounds ten a week.'

'Ha, ha!' laughed Chadwick exultantly. 'With us you shall begin at double the figure, and I'll see to it that you have a rise after the first year. What's more, Humplebee, as soon as we get fairly going, I promise you a share in the business. Don't say a word, old boy! My governor treated you abominably. I've been in your debt for ten years or so, as you know very well, and often enough I've felt deucedly ashamed of myself. Five pounds a week to begin with, and a certainty of a comfortable interest in a thriving affair! Come, now, is it agreed?'

Humplebee forgot his pain; he felt ready to jump out of bed and travel straightway to London.

'And you know,' pursued Chadwick, when they had shaken hands warmly, 'that you have a claim for damages on the railway company. Leave that to me; I'll put the thing in train at once, through my own solicitor. You shall pocket a substantial sum, my boy! Well, I'm afraid I must be off; I've got my hands full of business. Quite a new thing for me to have something serious to do; I enjoy it! If I can't see you again before I go back to town, you shall hear from me in a day or two. Here's my London address. Chuck up your place here at once, so as to be ready for us as soon as your arm's all right. Geldershaw shall write you a formal engagement.'

Happily his broken arm was the left. Humplebee could use his right hand, and did so, very soon after Chadwick's departure, to send an account of all that had befallen him to his friend Mary Bowes. It was the first time he had written to her. His letter was couched in terms of studious respect, with many apologies for the liberty he took. Of the accident he made light—a few days would see him re-established—but he dwelt with some emphasis upon the meeting with Leonard Chadwick, and what had resulted from it.

'I did him a good turn once, when we were at school together. He is a good, warm-hearted fellow, and has sought this opportunity of showing that he remembered the old time.'

Thus did Humplebee refer to the great event of his boyhood. Having despatched the letter, he waited feverishly for Miss Bowes' reply; but days passed, and still he waited in vain. Agitation delayed his recovery; he was suffering as he had never suffered in his life, when there came a letter from London, signed with the name of Geldershaw, repeating in formal terms the offer made to him by Leonard Chadwick, and requesting his immediate acceptance or refusal. This plucked him out of his despondent state, and spurred him to action. With the help of his landlady he dressed himself, and, having concealed his bandaged arm as well as possible, drove in a cab to Miss Bowes' dwelling. The hour being before noon, he was almost sure to find Mary at home, and alone. Trembling with bodily weakness and the conflict of emotions, he rang the door bell. To his consternation there appeared Mary's father.

'Hallo! Humplebee!' cried Mr. Bowes, surprised but friendly. 'Why, I was just going to write to you. Mary has had scarlet fever. I've been so busy these last ten days, I couldn't even inquire after you. Of course, I saw about your smash in the newspaper; how are you getting on?'

The man with the bandaged arm could not utter a word. Horror-stricken he stared at Mr. Bowes, who had begun to express a doubt whether it would be prudent for him to enter the house.

Mary is convalescent; the anxiety's all over, but—'

Humplebee suddenly seized the speaker's hand, and in confused words expressed vehement joy. They talked for a few minutes, parted with cordiality, and Humplebee went home again to recover from his excitement.

A note from his employers had replied in terms of decent condolence to the message by which he explained his enforced absence. To-day he wrote to the principal, announcing his intention of resigning his post in their office. The response, delivered within a few hours, was admirably brief and to the point. Mr. Humplebee's place had, of course, been already taken temporarily by another clerk; it would have been held open for him, but, in view of his decision, the firm had merely to request that he would acknowledge the cheque enclosed in payment of his salary up to date. Not without some shaking of the hand did Humplebee pen this receipt; for a moment something seemed to come between him and the daylight, and a heaviness oppressed his inner man. But already he had despatched to London his formal acceptance of the post at five pounds a week, and in thinking of it his heart grew joyous. Two hundred and sixty pounds a year! It was beyond the hope of his most fantastic day-dreams. He was a made man, secure for ever against fears and worries. He was a man of substance, and need no longer shrink from making known the hope which ruled his life.

A second letter was written to Mary Bowes; but not till many copies had been made was it at length despatched. The writer declared that he looked for no reply until Mary was quite herself again; he begged only that she would reflect, meanwhile, upon what he had said, reflect with all her indulgence, all her native goodness and gentleness. And, indeed, there elapsed nearly a fortnight before the answer came; and to Humplebee it seemed an endless succession of tormenting days. Then—

Humplebee behaved like one distracted. His landlady in good earnest thought he had gone crazy, and was only reassured when he revealed to her what had happened. Mary Bowes was to be his wife! They must wait for a year and a half; Mary could not leave her father quite alone, but in a year and a half Mr. Bowes, who was an oldish man, would be able to retire on the modest fruit of his economies, and all three could live together in London. 'What,' cried Humplebee, 'was eighteen months? It would allow him to save enough out of his noble salary to start housekeeping with something more than comfort. Blessed be the name of Chadwick!'

When his arm was once more sound, and Mary's health quite recovered, they met. In their long, long talk Humplebee was led to tell the story of that winter day when he saved Leonard Chadwick's life; he related, too, all that had ensued upon his acquaintance with the great Mr. Chadwick, memories which would never lose all their bitterness. Mary was moved to tears, and her tears were dried by indignation. But they agreed that Leonard, after all, made some atonement for his father's heartless behaviour. Humplebee showed a letter that had come from young Chadwick a day or two ago; every line spoke generosity of spirit. 'When,' he asked, 'might they expect their new bookkeeper. They were in full swing; business promised magnificently. As yet, they had only a temporary office, but Geldershaw was in treaty for fine premises in the city. The sooner Humplebee arrived the better; fortune awaited him.'

It was decided that he should leave for London in two days.

The next evening he came to spend an hour or two with Mary and her father. On entering the room he at once observed something strange in the looks with which he was greeted. Mary had a pale, miserable air, and could hardly speak. Mr. Bowes, after looking at him fixedly for a moment, exclaimed—

'Have you seen to-day's paper?'

'I've been too busy,' he replied. 'What has happened?'

'Isn't your London man called Geldershaw?'

'Yes,' murmured Humplebee, with a sinking of the heart.

'Well, the police are after him; he has bolted. It's a long-firm swindle that he's been up to. You know what that means? Obtaining goods on false credit, and raising money on them. What's more, young Chadwick is arrested; he came before the magistrates yesterday, charged with being an accomplice. Here it is; read it for yourself.'

Humplebee dropped into a chair. When his eyes undazzled, he read the full report which Mr. Bowes had summarised. It was the death-blow of his hopes.

'Leonard Chadwick has been a victim, not a swindler,' sounded from him in a feeble voice. 'You see, he says that Geldershaw has robbed him of all his money—that he is ruined.'

'He *says* so,' remarked Mr. Bowes with angry irony.

'I believe him,' said Humplebee. His eyes sought Mary's. The girl regarded him steadily, and she spoke in a low firm voice—'I, too, believe him.'

'Whether or no,' said Mr. Bowes, thrusting his hands into his pockets, 'the upshot of it is, Humplebee, that you've lost a good place through trusting him. I had my doubts; but you were in a hurry, and didn't ask advice. If this had happened a week later, the police would have laid hands on you as well.'

'So there's something to be thankful for, at all events,' said Mary.

Again Humplebee met her eyes. He saw that she would not forsake him.

He had to begin life over again—that was all.

THE SCRUPULOUS FATHER

IT was market day in the little town; at one o'clock a rustic company besieged the table of the Greyhound, lured by savoury odours and the frothing of amber ale. Apart from three frequenters of the ordinary, in a small room prepared for overflow, sat two persons of a different stamp—a middle-aged man, bald, meagre, unimpressive, but wholly respectable in bearing and apparel, and a girl, evidently his daughter, who had the look of the latter twenties, her plain dress harmonising with a subdued charm of feature and a timidity of manner not ungraceful. Whilst waiting for their meal they conversed in an undertone; their brief remarks and ejaculations told of a long morning's ramble from the seaside resort some miles away; in their quiet fashion they seemed to have enjoyed themselves, and dinner at an inn evidently struck them as something of an escapade. Rather awkwardly the girl arranged a handful of wild flowers which she had gathered, and put them for refreshment into a tumbler of water; when a woman entered with viands, silence fell upon the two; after hesitations and mutual glances, they began to eat with nervous appetite.

Scarcely was their modest confidence restored, when in the doorway sounded a virile voice, gaily humming, and they became aware of a tall young man, red-headed, anything but handsome, flushed and perspiring from the sunny road; his open jacket showed a blue cotton shirt without waistcoat, in his hand was a shabby straw hat, and thick dust covered his boots. One would have judged him a tourist of the noisier class, and his rather loud 'Good morning!' as he entered the room seemed a serious menace to privacy; on the other hand, the rapid buttoning of his coat, and the quiet choice of a seat as far as possible from the two guests whom his arrival disturbed, indicated a certain tact. His greeting had met with the merest murmur of reply; their eyes on their plates, father and daughter resolutely disregarded him; yet he ventured to speak again.

'They're busy here to-day. Not a seat to be had in the other room.'

It was apologetic in intention, and not rudely spoken. After a moment's delay the bald, respectable man made a curt response.

'This room is public, I believe.'

The intruder held his peace. But more than once he glanced at the girl, and after each furtive scrutiny his plain visage manifested some disturbance, a troubled thoughtfulness. His one look at the mute parent was from beneath contemptuous eyebrows.

Very soon another guest appeared, a massive agricultural man, who descended upon a creaking chair and growled a remark about the hot weather. With him the red-haired pedestrian struck into talk. Their topic was beer. Uncommonly good, they agreed, the local brew, and each called for a second pint. What, they asked in concert, would England be without her ale? Shame on the base traffickers who enfeebled or poisoned this noble liquor! And how cool it was—ah! The right sort of cellar! He of the red hair hinted at a third pewter.

These two were still but midway in their stout attack on meat and drink, when father and daughter, having exchanged a few whispers, rose to depart.

After leaving the room, the girl remembered that she had left her flowers behind; she durst not return for them, and, knowing her father would dislike to do so, said nothing about the matter.

'A pity!' exclaimed Mr. Whiston (that was his respectable name) as they strolled away. 'It looked at first as if we should have such a nice quiet dinner.'

'I enjoyed it all the same,' replied his companion, whose name was Rose.

'That abominable habit of drinking!' added Mr. Whiston austerely. He himself had quaffed water, as always. 'Their ale, indeed! See the coarse, gross creatures it produces!'

He shuddered. Rose, however, seemed less consentient than usual. Her eyes were on the ground; her lips were closed with a certain firmness. When she spoke, it was on quite another subject.

They were Londoners. Mr. Whiston held the position of draughtsman in the office of a geographical publisher; though his income was small, he had always practised a rigid economy, and the possession of a modest private capital put him beyond fear of reverses. Profoundly conscious of social limits, he felt it a subject for gratitude that there was nothing to be ashamed of in his calling, which he might fairly regard as a profession, and he nursed this sense of respectability as much on his daughter's behalf as on his own. Rose was an only child; her mother had been dead for years; her kinsfolk on both sides laid claim to the title of gentlefolk, but supported it on the narrowest margin of independence. The girl had grown up in an atmosphere unfavourable to mental development, but she had received a fairly good education, and nature had dowered her with intelligence. A sense of her father's conscientiousness and of his true affection forbade her to criticise openly the principles on which he had directed her life; hence a habit of solitary meditation, which half fostered, yet half opposed, the gentle diffidence of Rose's character.

Mr. Whiston shrank from society, ceaselessly afraid of receiving less than his due; privately, meanwhile, he deplored the narrowness of the social opportunities granted to his daughter, and was for ever forming schemes for her advantage—schemes which never passed beyond the stage of nervous speculation. They inhabited a little house in a western suburb, a house illumined with every domestic virtue; but scarcely a dozen persons crossed the threshold within a twelvemonth. Rose's two or three friends were, like herself, mistrustful of the world. One of them had lately married after a very long engagement, and Rose still trembled from the excitement of that occasion, still debated fearfully with herself on the bride's chances of happiness. Her own marriage was an event so inconceivable that merely to glance at the thought appeared half immodest and wholly irrational.

Every winter Mr. Whiston talked of new places which he and Rose would visit when the holidays came round; every summer he shrank from the thought of adventurous novelty, and ended by proposing a return to the same western seaside-town, to the familiar lodgings. The climate suited neither him nor his daughter, who both needed physical as well as moral bracing; but they only thought of this on finding themselves at home again, with another long year of monotony before them. And it was so good to feel welcome, respected; to receive the smiling reverences of tradesfolk; to talk with just a little well-bred condescension, sure that it would be appreciated. Mr. Whiston savoured these things, and Rose in this respect was not wholly unlike him.

To-day was the last of their vacation. The weather had been magnificent throughout; Rose's cheeks were more than touched by the sun, greatly to the advantage of her unpretending comeliness. She was a typical English maiden, rather tall, shapely rather than graceful, her head generally bent, her movements always betraying the diffidence of solitary habit. The lips were her finest feature, their perfect outline indicating sweetness without feebleness of character. Such a girl is at her best towards the stroke of thirty. Rose had begun to know herself; she needed only opportunity to act upon her knowledge.

A train would take them back to the seaside. At the railway station Rose seated herself on a shaded part of the platform, whilst her father, who was exceedingly short of sight, peered over publications on the bookstall. Rather tired after her walk, the girl was dreamily tracing a pattern with the point of her parasol, when some one advanced and stood immediately in front of her. Startled, she looked up, and recognised the red-haired stranger of the inn.

'You left these flowers in a glass of water on the table. I hope I'm not doing a rude thing in asking whether they were left by accident.'

He had the flowers in his hand, their stems carefully protected by a piece of paper. For a moment Rose was incapable of replying; she looked at the speaker; she felt her cheeks burn; in utter embarrassment she said she knew not what.

'Oh!—thank you! I forgot them. It's very kind.'

Her hand touched his as she took the bouquet from him. Without another word the man turned and strode away.

Mr. Whiston had seen nothing of this. When he approached, Rose held up the flowers with a laugh.

'Wasn't it kind? I forgot them, you know, and some one from the inn came looking for me.'

'Very good of them, very,' replied her father graciously. 'A very nice inn, that. We'll go again—some day. One likes to encourage such civility; it's rare nowadays.'

He of the red hair travelled by the same train, though not in the same carriage. Rose caught sight of him at the seaside station. She was vexed with herself for having so scantily acknowledged his kindness; it seemed to her that she had not really thanked him at all; how absurd, at her age, to be incapable of common self-command! At the same time she kept thinking of her father's phrase, 'coarse, gross creatures,' and it vexed her even more than her own ill behaviour. The stranger was certainly not coarse, far from gross. Even his talk about beer (she remembered every word of it) had been amusing rather than offensive. Was he a 'gentleman'? The question agitated her; it involved so technical a definition, and she felt so doubtful as to the reply. Beyond doubt he had acted in a gentlemanly way; but his voice lacked something. Coarse? Gross? No, no, no! Really, her father was very severe, not to say uncharitable. But perhaps he was thinking of the heavy agricultural man; oh, he must have been!

Of a sudden she felt very weary. At the lodgings she sat down in her bedroom, and gazed through the open window at the sea. A sense of discouragement, hitherto almost unknown, had fallen upon her; it spoilt the blue sky and the soft horizon. She thought rather drearily of the townward journey to-morrow, of her home in the suburbs, of the endless monotony that awaited her. The flowers lay on her lap; she smelt them, dreamed over them. And then—strange incongruity—she thought of beer!

Between tea and supper she and her father rested on the beach. Mr. Whiston was reading. Rose pretended to turn the leaves of a book. Of a sudden, as unexpectedly to herself as to her companion, she broke silence.

'Don't you think, father, that we are too much afraid of talking with strangers?'

'Too much afraid?'

Mr. Whiston was puzzled. He had forgotten all about the incident at the dinner-table.

'I mean—what harm is there in having a little conversation when one is away from home? At the inn to-day, you know, I can't help thinking we were rather—perhaps a little too silent.'

'My dear Rose, did you want to talk about beer?'

She reddened, but answered all the more emphatically.

'Of course not. But, when the first gentleman came in, wouldn't it have been natural to exchange a few friendly words? I'm sure he wouldn't have talked of beer to *us*?'

'The *gentleman*? I saw no gentleman, my dear. I suppose he was a small clerk, or something of the sort, and he had no business whatever to address us.'

'Oh, but he only said good morning, and apologised for sitting at our table. He needn't have apologised at all.'

'Precisely. That is just what I mean,' said Mr. Whiston with self-satisfaction. 'My dear Rose, if I had been alone, I might perhaps have talked a little, but with you it was impossible. One cannot be too careful. A man like that will take all sorts of liberties. One has to keep such people at a distance.'

A moment's pause, then Rose spoke with unusual decision—

'I feel quite sure, father, that he would not have taken liberties. It seems to me that he knew quite well how to behave himself.'

Mr. Whiston grew still more puzzled. He closed his book to meditate this new problem.

'One has to lay down rules,' fell from him at length, sententiously. 'Our position, Rose, as I have often explained, is a delicate one. A lady in circumstances such as yours cannot exercise too much caution. Your natural associates are in the world of wealth; unhappily, I cannot make you wealthy. We have to guard our self-respect, my dear child. Really, it is not *safe* to talk with strangers—least of all at an inn. And you have only to remember that disgusting conversation about beer!'

Rose said no more. Her father pondered a little, felt that he had delivered his soul, and resumed the book.

The next morning they were early at the station to secure good places for the long journey to London. Up to almost the last moment it seemed that they would have a carriage to themselves. Then the door suddenly opened, a bag was flung on to the seat, and after it came a hot, panting man, a red-haired man, recognised immediately by both the travellers.

'I thought I'd missed it!' ejaculated the intruder merrily.

Mr. Whiston turned his head away, disgust transforming his countenance. Rose sat motionless, her eyes cast down. And the stranger mopped his forehead in silence.

He glanced at her; he glanced again and again; and Rose was aware of every look. It did not occur to her to feel offended. On the contrary, she fell into a mood of tremulous pleasure, enhanced by every turn of the stranger's eyes in her direction. At him she did not look, yet she saw him. Was it a coarse face? she asked herself. Plain, perhaps, but decidedly not vulgar. The red hair, she thought, was not disagreeably red; she didn't dislike that shade of colour. He was humming a tune; it seemed to be his habit, and it argued healthy cheerfulness. Meanwhile Mr. Whiston sat stiffly in his corner, staring at the landscape, a model of respectable muteness.

At the first stop another man entered. This time, unmistakably, a commercial traveller. At once a dialogue sprang up between him and Rufus. The traveller complained that all the smoking compartments were full.

'Why,' exclaimed Rufus, with a laugh, 'that reminds me that I wanted a smoke. I never thought about it till now; jumped in here in a hurry.'

The traveller's 'line' was tobacco; they talked tobacco—Rufus with much gusto. Presently the conversation took a wider scope.

'I envy you,' cried Rufus, 'always travelling about. I'm in a beastly office, and get only a fortnight off once a year. I enjoy it, I can tell you! Time's up today, worse luck! I've a good mind to emigrate. Can you give me a tip about the colonies?'

He talked of how he had spent his holiday. Rose missed not a word, and her blood pulsed in sympathy with the joy of freedom which he expressed. She did not mind his occasional slang; the tone was manly and right-hearted; it evinced a certain simplicity of feeling by no means common in men, whether gentle or other. At a certain moment the girl was impelled to steal a glimpse of his face. After all, was it really so plain? The features seemed to her to have a certain refinement which she had not noticed before.

'I'm going to try for a smoker,' said the man of commerce, as the train slackened into a busy station.

Rufus hesitated. His eye wandered.

'I think I shall stay where I am,' he ended by saying.

In that same moment, for the first time, Rose met his glance. She saw that his eyes did not at once avert themselves; they had a singular expression, a smile which pleaded pardon for its audacity. And Rose, even whilst turning away, smiled in response.

The train stopped. The commercial traveller alighted. Rose, leaning towards her father, whispered that she was thirsty; would he get her a glass of milk or of lemonade? Though little disposed to rush on such errands, Mr. Whiston had no choice but to comply; he sped at once for the refreshment-room.

And Rose knew what would happen; she knew perfectly. Sitting rigid, her eyes on vacancy, she felt the approach of the young man, who for the moment was alone with her. She saw him at her side: she heard his voice.

'I can't help it. I want to speak to you. May I?'

Rose faltered a reply.

'It was so kind to bring the flowers. I didn't thank you properly.'

'It's now or never,' pursued the young man in rapid, excited tones. 'Will you let me tell you my name? Will you tell me yours?'

Rose's silence consented. The daring Rufus rent a page from a pocket-book, scribbled his name and address, gave it to Rose. He rent out another page, offered it to Rose with the pencil, and in a moment had secured the precious scrap of paper in his pocket. Scarce was the transaction completed when a stranger jumped in. The young man bounded to his own corner, just in time to see the return of Mr. Whiston, glass in hand.

During the rest of the journey Rose was in the strangest state of mind. She did not feel in the least ashamed of herself. It seemed to her that what had happened was wholly natural and simple. The extraordinary thing was that she must sit silent and with cold countenance at the distance of a few feet from a person with whom she ardently desired to converse. Sudden illumination had wholly changed the aspect of life. She seemed to be playing a part in a grotesque comedy rather than living in a world of grave realities. Her father's dignified silence struck her as intolerably absurd. She could have burst into laughter; at moments she was indignant, irritated, tremulous with the spirit of revolt. She detected a glance of frigid superiority with which Mr. Whiston chanced to survey the other occupants of the compartment. It amazed her. Never had she seen her father in such an alien light. He bent forward and addressed to her some commonplace remark; she barely deigned a reply. Her views of conduct, of character, had undergone an abrupt and extraordinary change. Having justified without shadow of argument her own incredible proceeding, she judged everything and everybody by some new standard, mysteriously attained. She was no longer the Rose Whiston of yesterday. Her old self seemed an object of compassion. She felt an unspeakable happiness, and at the same time an encroaching fear.

The fear predominated; when she grew aware of the streets of London looming on either hand it became a torment, an anguish. Small-folded, crushed within her palm, the piece of paper with its still unread inscription seemed to burn her. Once, twice, thrice she met the look of her friend. He smiled cheerily, bravely, with evident purpose of encouragement. She knew his face better than that of any oldest acquaintance; she saw in it a manly beauty. Only by a great effort of self-control could she refrain from turning aside to unfold and read what he had written. The train slackened speed, stopped. Yes, it was London.

She must arise and go. Once more their eyes met. Then, without recollection of any interval, she was on the Metropolitan Railway, moving towards her suburban home.

A severe headache sent her early to bed. Beneath her pillow lay a scrap of paper with a name and address she was not likely to forget. And through the night of broken slumbers Rose suffered a martyrdom. No more self-glorification! All her courage gone, all her new vitality! She saw herself with the old eyes, and was shame-stricken to the very heart.

Whose the fault? Towards dawn she argued it with the bitterness of misery. What a life was hers in this little world of choking respectabilities! Forbidden this, forbidden that; permitted—the pride of ladyhood. And she was not a lady, after all. What lady would have permitted herself to exchange names and addresses with a strange man in a railway carriage—furtively, too, escaping her father's observation? If not a lady, what *was* she? It meant the utter failure of her breeding and education. The sole end for which she had lived was frustrate. A common, vulgar young woman—well mated, doubtless, with an impudent clerk, whose noisy talk was of beer and tobacco!

This arrested her. Stung to the defence of her friend, who, clerk though he might be, was neither impudent nor vulgar, she found herself driven back upon self-respect. The battle went on for hours; it exhausted her; it undid all the good effects of sun and sea, and left her flaccid, pale.

'I'm afraid the journey yesterday was too much for you,' remarked Mr. Whiston, after observing her as she sat mute the next evening.

'I shall soon recover,' Rose answered coldly.

The father meditated with some uneasiness. He had not forgotten Rose's singular expression of opinion after their dinner at the inn. His affection made him sensitive to changes in the girl's demeanour. Next summer they must really find a more bracing resort. Yes, yes; clearly Rose needed bracing. But she was always better when the cool days came round.

On the morrow it was his daughter's turn to feel anxious. Mr. Whiston all at once wore a face of indignant severity. He was absent-minded; he sat at table with scarce a word; he had little nervous movements, and subdued mutterings as of wrath. This continued on a second day, and Rose began to suffer an intolerable agitation. She could not help connecting her father's strange behaviour with the secret which tormented her heart.

Had something happened? Had her friend seen Mr. Whiston, or written to him?

She had awaited with tremors every arrival of the post. It was probable— more than probable—that *he* would write to her; but as yet no letter came. A week passed, and no letter came. Her father was himself again; plainly she had mistaken the cause of his perturbation. Ten days, and no letter came.

It was Saturday afternoon. Mr. Whiston reached home at tea-time. The first glance showed his daughter that trouble and anger once more beset him. She trembled, and all but wept, for suspense had overwrought her nerves.

'I find myself obliged to speak to you on a very disagreeable subject'—thus began Mr. Whiston over the tea-cups—'a very unpleasant subject indeed. My one consolation is that it will probably settle a little argument we had down at the seaside.'

As his habit was when expressing grave opinions (and Mr. Whiston seldom expressed any other), he made a long pause and ran his fingers through his thin beard. The delay irritated Rose to the last point of endurance.

'The fact is,' he proceeded at length, 'a week ago I received a most extraordinary letter—the most impudent letter I ever read in my life. It came from that noisy, beer-drinking man who intruded upon us at the inn—you remember. He began by explaining who he was, and—if you can believe it—had the impertinence to say that he wished to make my acquaintance! An amazing letter! Naturally, I left it unanswered—the only dignified thing to do. But the fellow wrote again, asking if I had received his proposal. I now replied, briefly and severely, asking him, first, how he came to know my name; secondly, what reason I had given him for supposing that I desired to meet him again. His answer to this was even more outrageous than the first offence. He bluntly informed me that in order to discover my name and address he had followed us home that day from Paddington Station! As if this was not bad enough, he went on to—really, Rose, I feel I must apologise to you, but the fact is I seem to have no choice but to tell you what he said. The fellow tells me, really, that he wants to know *me* only that he may come to know *you!* My first idea was to go with this letter to the police. I am not sure that I shan't do so even yet; most certainly I shall if he writes again. The man may be crazy—he may be dangerous. Who knows but he may come lurking about the house? I felt obliged to warn you of this unpleasant possibility.'

Rose was stirring her tea; also she was smiling. She continued to stir and to smile, without consciousness of either performance.

'You make light of it?' exclaimed her father solemnly.

'O father, of course I am sorry you have had this annoyance.'

So little was there of manifest sorrow in the girl's tone and countenance that Mr. Whiston gazed at her rather indignantly. His pregnant pause gave birth to one of those admonitory axioms which had hitherto ruled his daughter's life.

'My dear, I advise you never to trifle with questions of propriety. Could there possibly be a better illustration of what I have so often said—that in self-defence we are bound to keep strangers at a distance?'

'Father'

Rose began firmly, but her voice failed.

'You were going to say, Rose?'

She took her courage in both hands.

'Will you allow me to see the letters?'

'Certainly. There can be no objection to that.'

He drew from his pocket the three envelopes, held them to his daughter. With shaking hand Rose unfolded the first letter; it was written in clear commercial character, and was signed 'Charles James Burroughs.' When she had read all, the girl said quietly—

'Are you quite sure, father, that these letters are impertinent?'

Mr. Whiston stopped in the act of finger-combing his beard.

'What doubt can there be of it?'

'They seem to me,' proceeded Rose nervously, 'to be very respectful and very honest.'

'My dear, you astound me! Is it respectful to force one's acquaintance upon an unwilling stranger? I really don't understand you. Where is your sense of propriety, Rose? A vulgar, noisy fellow, who talks of beer and tobacco—a petty clerk! And he has the audacity to write to me that he wants to—to make friends with my daughter! Respectful? Honest? Really!'

When Mr. Whiston became sufficiently agitated to lose his decorous gravity, he began to splutter, and at such moments he was not impressive. Rose kept her eyes cast down. She felt her strength once more, the strength of a wholly reasonable and half-passionate revolt against that tyrannous propriety which Mr. Whiston worshipped.

'Father—'

'Well, my dear?'

'There is only one thing I dislike in these letters—and that is a falsehood.'

'I don't understand.'

Rose was flushing. Her nerves grew tense; she had wrought herself to a simple audacity which overcame small embarrassments.

'Mr. Burroughs says that he followed us home from Paddington to discover our address. That is not true. He asked me for my name and address in the train, and gave me his.'

The father gasped.

'He *asked*—? You *gave*—?'

'It was whilst you were away in the refreshment-room,' proceeded the girl, with singular self-control, in a voice almost matter-of-fact. 'I ought to tell you, at the same time, that it was Mr. Burroughs who brought me the flowers from the inn, when I forgot them. You didn't see him give them to me in the station.'

The father stared.

'But, Rose, what does all this mean? You—you overwhelm me! Go on, please. What next?'

'Nothing, father.'

And of a sudden the girl was so beset with confusing emotions that she hurriedly quitted her chair and vanished from the room.

Before Mr. Whiston returned to his geographical drawing on Monday morning, he had held long conversations with Rose, and still longer with himself. Not easily could he perceive the justice of his daughter's quarrel with propriety; many days were to pass, indeed, before he would consent to do more than make inquiries about Charles James Burroughs, and to permit that aggressive young man to give a fuller account of himself in writing. It was by silence that Rose prevailed. Having defended herself against the charge of immodesty, she declined to urge her own inclination or the rights of Mr. Burroughs; her mute patience did not lack its effect with the scrupulous but tender parent.

'I am willing to admit, my dear,' said Mr. Whiston one evening, *à propos* of nothing at all, 'that the falsehood in that young man's letter gave proof of a certain delicacy.'

'Thank you, father,' replied Rose, very quietly and simply.

It was next morning that the father posted a formal, proper, self-respecting note of invitation, which bore results.

A POOR GENTLEMAN

IT was in the drawing-room, after dinner. Mrs. Charman, the large and kindly hostess, sank into a chair beside her little friend Mrs. Loring, and sighed a question.

'How do you like Mr. Tymperley?'

'Very nice. Just a little peculiar.'

'Oh, he *is* peculiar! Quite original. I wanted to tell you about him before we went down, but there wasn't time. Such a very old friend of ours. My dear husband and he were at school together—Harrovians. The sweetest, the most affectionate character! Too good for this world, I'm afraid; he takes everything so seriously. I shall never forget his grief at my poor husband's death.—I'm telling Mrs. Loring about Mr. Tymperley, Ada.'

She addressed her married daughter, a quiet young woman who reproduced Mrs. Charman's good-natured countenance, with something more of intelligence, the reflective serenity of a higher type.

'I'm sorry to see him looking so far from well,' remarked Mrs. Weare, in reply.

'He never had any colour, you know, and his life... But I must tell you,' she resumed to Mrs. Loring. 'He's a bachelor, in comfortable circumstances, and—would you believe it?—he lives quite alone in one of the distressing parts of London. Where is it, Ada?'

'A poor street in Islington.'

'Yes. There he lives, I'm afraid in shocking lodgings—it must be, *so* unhealthy—just to become acquainted with the life of poor people, and be helpful to them. Isn't it heroic? He seems to have given up his whole life to it. One never meets him anywhere; I think ours is the only house where he's seen. A noble life! He never talks about it. I'm sure you would never have suspected such a thing from his conversation at dinner?'

'Not for a moment,' answered Mrs. Loring, astonished. 'He wasn't very gossipy—I gathered that his chief interests were fretwork and foreign politics.'

Mrs. Weare laughed. 'The very man! When I was a little girl he used to make all sorts of pretty things for me with his fret-saw; and when I grew old enough, he instructed me in the balance of Power. It's possible, mamma, that he writes leading articles. We should never hear of it.'

'My dear, anything is possible with Mr. Tymperley. And such a change, this, after his country life. He had a beautiful little house near ours, in Berkshire. I really can't help thinking that my husband's death caused him to leave it. He was so attached to Mr. Charman! When my husband died, and we left Berkshire, we altogether lost sight of him—oh, for a couple of years. Then I met him by chance in London. Ada thinks there must have been some sentimental trouble.'

'Dear mamma,' interposed the daughter, 'it was you, not I, who suggested that.'

'Was it? Well, perhaps it was. One can't help seeing that he has gone through something. Of course it may be only pity for the poor souls he gives his life to. A wonderful man!'

When masculine voices sounded at the drawing-room door, Mrs. Loring looked curiously for the eccentric gentleman. He entered last of all. A man of more than middle height, but much bowed in the shoulders; thin, ungraceful, with an irresolute step and a shy demeanour; his pale-grey eyes, very soft in expression, looked timidly this way and that from beneath brows nervously bent, and a self-obliterating smile wavered upon his lips. His hair had begun to thin and to turn grey, but he had a heavy moustache, which would better have sorted with sterner lineaments. As he walked—or sidled—into the room, his hands kept shutting and opening, with rather ludicrous effect. Something which was not exactly shabbiness, but a lack of lustre, of finish, singled him among the group of men; looking closer, one saw that his black suit belonged to a fashion some years old. His linen was irreproachable, but he wore no sort of jewellery, one little black stud showing on his front, and, at the cuffs, solitaires of the same simple description.

He drifted into a corner, and there would have sat alone, seemingly at peace, had not Mrs. Weare presently moved to a seat beside him.

'I hope you won't be staying in town through August, Mr. Tymperley?'

'No!—Oh no!—Oh no, I think not!'

'But you seem uncertain. Do forgive me if I say that I'm sure you need a change. Really, you know, you are *not* looking quite the thing. Now, can't I persuade you to join us at Lucerne? My husband would be so pleased— delighted to talk with you about the state of Europe. Give us a fortnight—do!'

'My dear Mrs. Weare, you are kindness itself! I am deeply grateful. I can't easily express my sense of your most friendly thoughtfulness. But, the truth is, I am half engaged to other friends. Indeed, I think I may almost say that I have practically...yes, indeed, it amounts to that.'

He spoke in a thinly fluting voice, with a preciseness of enunciation akin to the more feebly clerical, and with smiles which became almost lachrymose in their expressiveness as he dropped from phrase to phrase of embarrassed circumlocution. And his long bony hands writhed together till the knuckles were white.

'Well, so long as you *are* going away. I'm so afraid lest your conscientiousness should go too far. You won't benefit anybody, you know, by making yourself ill.'

'Obviously not!—Ha, ha!—I assure you that fact is patent to me. Health is a primary consideration. Nothing more detrimental to one's usefulness than an impaired... Oh, to be sure, to be sure!'

'There's the strain upon your sympathies. That must affect one's health, quite apart from an unhealthy atmosphere.'

'But Islington is not unhealthy, my dear Mrs. Weare! Believe me, the air has often quite a tonic quality. We are so high, you must remember. If only we could subdue in some degree the noxious exhalations of domestic and industrial chimneys!—Oh, I assure you, Islington has every natural feature of salubrity.'

Before the close of the evening there was a little music, which Mr.

Tymperley seemed much to enjoy. He let his head fall back, and stared upwards; remaining rapt in that posture for some moments after the music ceased, and at length recovering himself with a sigh.

When he left the house, he donned an overcoat considerably too thick for the season, and bestowed in the pockets his patent-leather shoes. His hat was a hard felt, high in the crown. He grasped an ill-folded umbrella, and set forth at a brisk walk, as if for the neighbouring station. But the railway was not his goal, nor yet the omnibus. Through the ambrosial night he walked and walked, at the steady pace of one accustomed to pedestrian exercise: from Notting Hill Gate to the Marble Arch; from the Marble Arch to New Oxford Street; thence by Theobald's Road to Pentonville, and up, and up, until he attained the heights of his own salubrious quarter. Long after midnight he entered a narrow byway, which the pale moon showed to be decent, though not inviting. He admitted himself with a latchkey to a little house which smelt of glue, lit a candle-end which he found in his pocket, and ascended two flights of stairs to a back bedroom, its size eight feet by seven and a half. A few minutes more, and he lay sound asleep.

Waking at eight o'clock—he knew the time by a bell that clanged in the neighbourhood—Mr. Tymperley clad himself with nervous haste. On opening his door, he found lying outside a tray, with the materials of a breakfast reduced to its lowest terms: half a pint of milk, bread, butter. At nine o'clock he went downstairs, tapped civilly at the door of the front parlour, and by an untuned voice was bidden enter. The room was occupied by an oldish man and a girl, addressing themselves to the day's work of plain bookbinding.

'Good morning to you, sir,' said Mr. Tymperley, bending his head. 'Good morning, Miss Suggs. Bright! Sunny! How it cheers one!'

He stood rubbing his hands, as one might on a morning of sharp frost. The bookbinder, with a dry nod for greeting, forthwith set Mr. Tymperley a task, to which that gentleman zealously applied himself. He was learning the elementary processes of the art. He worked with patience, and some show of natural aptitude, all through the working hours of the day.

To this pass had things come with Mr. Tymperley, a gentleman of Berkshire, once living in comfort and modest dignity on the fruit of sound investments. Schooled at Harrow, a graduate of Cambridge, he had meditated the choice of a profession until it seemed, on the whole, too late to profess anything at all; and, as there was no need of such exertion, he settled himself to a life of innocent idleness, hard by the country-house of his wealthy and influential friend, Mr. Charman. Softly the years flowed by. His thoughts turned once or twice to marriage, but a profound diffidence withheld him from the initial step; in the end, he knew himself born for bachelorhood, and with that estate was content. Well for him had he seen as clearly the delusiveness of other temptations! In an evil moment he listened to Mr. Charman, whose familiar talk was of speculation, of companies, of shining percentages. Not on his own account was Mr. Tymperley lured: he had enough and to spare; but he thought of his sister, married to an unsuccessful provincial barrister, and of her six children, whom it would be pleasant to help, like the opulent uncle of fiction, at their entering upon the world. In Mr. Charman he put blind faith, with the result that one morning he found himself shivering on the edge of ruin; the touch of confirmatory news, and over he went.

No one was aware of it but Mr. Charman himself and he, a few days later, lay sick unto death. Mr. Charman's own estate suffered inappreciably from what to his friend meant sheer disaster. And Mr. Tymperley breathed not a word to the widow; spoke not a word to any one at all, except the lawyer, who quietly wound up his affairs, and the sister whose children must needs go without avuncular aid. During the absence of his friendly neighbours after Mr. Charman's death, he quietly disappeared.

The poor gentleman was then close upon forty years old. There remained to him a capital which he durst not expend; invested, it bore him an income upon which a labourer could scarce have subsisted. The only possible place of residence—because the only sure place of hiding—was London, and to London Mr. Tymperley betook himself. Not at once did he learn the art of combating starvation with minim resources. During his initiatory trials he was once brought so low, by hunger and humiliation, that he swallowed something of his pride, and wrote to a certain acquaintance, asking counsel and indirect help. But only a man in Mr. Tymperley's position learns how vain is well-meaning advice, and how impotent is social influence. Had he begged for money, he would have received, no doubt, a cheque, with words of compassion; but Mr. Tymperley could never bring himself to that.

He tried to make profit of his former amusement, fretwork, and to a certain extent succeeded, earning in six months half a sovereign. But the prospect of adding one pound a year to his starveling dividends did not greatly exhilarate him.

All this time he was of course living in absolute solitude. Poverty is the great secluder—unless one belongs to the rank which is born to it; a sensitive man who no longer finds himself on equal terms with his natural associates, shrinks into loneliness, and learns with some surprise how very willing people are to forget his existence. London is a wilderness abounding in anchorites—voluntary or constrained. As he wandered about the streets and parks, or killed time in museums and galleries (where nothing had to be paid), Mr. Tymperley often recognised brethren in seclusion; he understood the furtive glance which met his own, he read the peaked visage, marked with understanding sympathy the shabby-genteel apparel. No interchange of confidences between these lurking mortals; they would like to speak, but pride holds them aloof; each goes on his silent and unfriended way, until, by good luck, he finds himself in hospital or workhouse, when at length the tongue is loosed, and the sore heart pours forth its reproach of the world.

Strange knowledge comes to a man in this position. He learns wondrous economies, and will feel a sort of pride in his ultimate discovery of how little money is needed to support life. In his old days Mr. Tymperley would have laid it down as an axiom that 'one' cannot live on less than such-and-such an income; he found that 'a man' can live on a few coppers a day. He became aware of the prices of things to eat, and was taught the relative virtues of nutriment. Perforce a vegetarian, he found that a vegetable diet was good for his health, and delivered to himself many a scornful speech on the habits of the carnivorous multitude. He of necessity abjured alcohols, and straightway longed to utter his testimony on a teetotal platform. These were his satisfactions. They compensate astonishingly for the loss of many kinds of self-esteem.

But it happened one day that, as he was in the act of drawing his poor little quarterly salvage at the Bank of England, a lady saw him and knew him. It was Mr. Charman's widow.

'Why, Mr. Tymperley, what *has* become of you all this time? Why have I never heard from you? Is it true, as some one told me, that you have been living abroad?'

So utterly was he disconcerted, that in a mechanical way he echoed the lady's last word: 'Abroad.'

'But why didn't you write to us?' pursued Mrs. Charman, leaving him no time to say more. 'How very unkind! Why did you go away without a word? My daughter says that we must have unconsciously offended you in some way. Do explain! Surely there can't have been anything'

'My dear Mrs. Charman, it is I alone who am to blame. I...the explanation is difficult; it involves a multiplicity of detail. I beg you to interpret my unjustifiable behaviour as—as pure idiosyncrasy.'

'Oh, you must come and see me. You know that Ada's married? Yes, nearly a year ago. How glad she will be to see you again. So often she has spoken of you. When can you dine? To-morrow?'

'With pleasure—with great pleasure.'

'Delightful!'

She gave her address, and they parted.

Now, a proof that Mr. Tymperley had never lost all hope of restitution to his native world lay in the fact of his having carefully preserved an evening-suit, with the appropriate patent-leather shoes. Many a time had he been sorely tempted to sell these seeming superfluities; more than once, towards the end of his pinched quarter, the suit had been pledged for a few shillings; but to part with the supreme symbol of respectability would have meant despair—a state of mind alien to Mr. Tymperley's passive fortitude. His jewellery, even watch and chain, had long since gone: such gauds are not indispensable to a gentleman's outfit. He now congratulated himself on his prudence, for the meeting with Mrs. Charman had delighted as much as it embarrassed him, and the prospect of an evening in society made his heart glow. He hastened home; he examined his garb of ceremony with anxious care, and found no glaring defect in it. A shirt, a collar, a necktie must needs be purchased; happily he had the means. But how explain himself? Could he confess his place of abode, his startling poverty? To do so would be to make an appeal to the compassion of his old friends, and from that he shrank in horror. A gentleman will not, if-it can possibly be avoided, reveal circumstances likely to cause pain. Must he, then, tell or imply a falsehood. The whole truth involved a reproach of Mrs. Charman's husband—a thought he could not bear.

The next evening found him still worrying over this dilemma. He reached Mrs. Charman's house without having come to any decision. In the drawing-room three persons awaited him: the hostess, with her daughter and son-in-law, Mr. and Mrs. Weare. The cordiality of his reception moved him all but to tears; overcome by many emotions, he lost his head. He talked at random; and the result was so strange a piece of fiction, that no sooner had he evolved it than he stood aghast at himself.

It came in reply to the natural question where he was residing.

'At present'—he smiled fatuously—'I inhabit a bed-sitting-room in a little street up at Islington.'

Dead silence followed. Eyes of wonder were fixed upon him. But for those eyes, who knows what confession Mr. Tymperley might have made? As it was...

'I said, Mrs. Charman, that I had to confess to an eccentricity. I hope it won't shock you. To be brief, I have devoted my poor energies to social work. I live among the poor, and as one of them, to obtain knowledge that cannot be otherwise procured.'

'Oh, how noble!' exclaimed the hostess.

The poor gentleman's conscience smote him terribly. He could say no more. To spare his delicacy, his friends turned the conversation. Then or afterwards, it never occurred to them to doubt the truth of what he had said. Mrs. Charman had seen him transacting business at the Bank of England, a place not suggestive of poverty; and he had always passed for a man somewhat original in his views and ways. Thus was Mr. Tymperley committed to a singular piece of deception, a fraud which could not easily be discovered, and which injured only its perpetrator.

Since then about a year had elapsed. Mr. Tymperley had seen his friends perhaps half a dozen times, his enjoyment of their society pathetically intense, but troubled by any slightest allusion to his mode of life. It had come to be understood that he made it a matter of principle to hide his light under a bushel, so he seldom had to take a new step in positive falsehood. Of course he regretted ceaselessly the original deceit, for Mrs. Charman, a wealthy woman, might very well have assisted him to some not undignified mode of earning his living. As it was, he had hit upon the idea of making himself a bookbinder, a craft somewhat to his taste. For some months he had lodged in the bookbinder's house; one day courage came to him, and he entered into a compact with his landlord, whereby he was to pay for instruction by a certain period of unremunerated work after he became proficient. That stage was now approaching. On the whole, he felt much happier than in the time of brooding idleness. He looked forward to the day when he would have a little more money in his pocket, and no longer dread the last fortnight of each quarter, with its supperless nights.

Mrs. Weare's invitation to Lucerne cost him pangs. Lucerne! Surely it was in some former state of existence that he had taken delightful holidays as a matter of course. He thought of the many lovely places he knew, and so many dream-landscapes; the London streets made them infinitely remote, utterly unreal. His three years of gloom and hardship were longer than all the life of placid contentment that came before. Lucerne! A man of more vigorous temper would have been maddened at the thought; but Mr. Tymperley nursed it all day long, his emotions only expressing themselves in a little sigh or a sadly wistful smile.

Having dined so well yesterday, he felt it his duty to expend less than usual on to-day's meals. About eight o'clock in the evening, after a meditative stroll in the air which he had so praised, he entered the shop where he was wont to make his modest purchases. A fat woman behind the counter nodded familiarly to him, with a grin at another customer. Mr. Tymperley bowed, as was his courteous habit.

'Oblige me,' he said, 'with one new-laid egg, and a small, crisp lettuce.'

'Only one to-night, eh?' said the woman.

'Thank you, only one,' he replied, as if speaking in a drawing-room. 'Forgive me if I express a hope that it will be, in the strict sense of the word, new-laid. The last, I fancy, had got into that box by some oversight—pardonable in the press of business.'

'They're always the same,' said the fat shopkeeper. 'We don't make no mistakes of that kind.'

'Ah! Forgive me! Perhaps I imagined—'

Egg and lettuce were carefully deposited in a little handbag he carried, and he returned home. An hour later, when his meal was finished, and he sat on a straight-backed chair meditating in the twilight, a rap sounded at his door, and a letter was handed to him. So rarely did a letter arrive for Mr. Tymperley that his hand shook as he examined the envelope. On opening it, the first thing he saw was a cheque. This excited him still more; he unfolded the written sheet with agitation. It came from Mrs. Weare, who wrote thus:—

> 'MY DEAR MR. TYMPERLEY,—After our talk last evening, I could not help thinking of you and your beautiful life of self-sacrifice. I contrasted the lot of these poor people with my own, which, one cannot but feel, is so undeservedly blest and so rich in enjoyments. As a result of these thoughts, I feel impelled to send you a little contribution to your good work—a sort of thank-offering at the moment of setting off for a happy holiday. Divide the money, please, among two or three of your most deserving pensioners; or, if you see fit, give it all to one. I cling to the hope that we may see you at Lucerne.—With very kind regards.

The cheque was for five pounds. Mr. Tymperley held it up by the window, and gazed at it. By his present standards of value five pounds seemed a very large sum. Think of what one could do with it! His boots—which had been twice repaired—would not decently serve him much longer. His trousers were in the last stage of presentability. The hat he wore (how carefully tended!) was the same in which he had come to London three years ago. He stood in need, verily, of a new equipment from head to foot; and in Islington five pounds would more than cover the whole expense. When, pray, was he likely to have such a sum at his free disposal?

He sighed deeply, and stared about him in the dusk.

The cheque was crossed. For the first time in his life Mr. Tymperley perceived that the crossing of a cheque may occasion its recipient a great deal of trouble. How was he to get it changed? He knew his landlord for a suspicious curmudgeon, and refusal of the favour, with such a look as Mr. Suggs knew how to give, would be a sore humiliation; besides, it was very doubtful whether Mr. Suggs could make any use of the cheque himself. To whom else could he apply? Literally, to no one in London.

'Well, the first thing to do was to answer Mrs. Weare's letter. He lit his lamp and sat down at the crazy little deal table; but his pen dipped several times into the ink before he found himself able to write.

'Dear Mrs. Weare,'—

Then, so long a pause that he seemed to be falling asleep. With a jerk, he bent again to his task.

'With sincere gratitude I acknowledge the receipt of your most kind and generous donation. The money...'

(Again his hand lay idle for several minutes.)

'shall be used as you wish, and I will render to you a detailed account of the benefits conferred by it.'

Never had he found composition so difficult. He felt that he was expressing himself wretchedly; a clog was on his brain. It cost him an exertion of physical strength to conclude the letter. When it was done, he went out, purchased a stamp at a tobacconist's shop, and dropped the envelope into the post.

Little slumber had Mr. Tymperley that night. On lying down, he began to wonder where he should find the poor people worthy of sharing in this benefaction. Of course he had no acquaintance with the class of persons of whom Mrs. Weare was thinking. In a sense, all the families round about were poor, but—he asked himself—had poverty the same meaning for them as for him? Was there a man or woman in this grimy street who, compared with himself, had any right to be called poor at all? An educated man forced to live among the lower classes arrives at many interesting conclusions with regard to them; one conclusion long since fixed in Mr. Tymperley's mind was that the 'suffering' of those classes is very much exaggerated by outsiders using a criterion quite inapplicable. He saw around him a world of coarse jollity, of contented labour, and of brutal apathy. It seemed to him more than probable that the only person in this street conscious of poverty, and suffering under it, was himself.

From nightmarish dozing, he started with a vivid thought, a recollection which seemed to pierce his brain. To whom did he owe his fall from comfort and self-respect, and all his long miseries? To Mrs. Weare's father. And, from this point of view, might the cheque for five pounds be considered as mere restitution? Might it not strictly be applicable to his own necessities?

Another little gap of semi-consciousness led to another strange reflection.

What if Mrs. Weare (a sensible woman) suspected, or even had discovered, the truth about him. What if she secretly *meant* the money for his own use?

Earliest daylight made this suggestion look very insubstantial; on the other hand, it strengthened his memory of Mr. Charman's virtual indebtedness to him. He jumped out of bed to reach the cheque, and for an hour lay with it in his hand. Then he rose and dressed mechanically.

After the day's work he rambled in a street of large shops. A bootmaker's arrested him; he stood before the window for a long time, turning over and over in his pocket a sovereign—no small fraction of the ready coin which had to support him until dividend day. Then he crossed the threshold.

Never did man use less discretion in the purchase of a pair of boots. His business was transacted in a dream; he spoke without hearing what he said; he stared at objects without perceiving them. The result was that not till he had got home, with his easy old footgear under his arm, did he become aware that the new boots pinched him most horribly. They creaked too: heavens! how they creaked! But doubtless all new boots had these faults; he had forgotten; it was so long since he had bought a pair. The fact was, he felt dreadfully tired, utterly worn out. After munching a mouthful of supper he crept into bed.

All night long he warred with his new boots. Footsore, he limped about the streets of a spectral city, where at every corner some one seemed to lie in ambush for him, and each time the lurking enemy proved to be no other than Mrs. Weare, who gazed at him with scornful eyes and let him totter by. The creaking of the boots was an articulate voice, which ever and anon screamed at him a terrible name. He shrank and shivered and groaned; but on he went, for in his hand he held a crossed cheque, which he was bidden to get changed, and no one would change it. What a night!

When he woke his brain was heavy as lead; but his meditations were very lucid. Pray, what did he mean by that insane outlay of money, which he could not possibly afford, on a new (and detestable) pair of boots? The old would have lasted, at all events, till winter began. What was in his mind when he entered the shop? Did he intend...? Merciful powers!

Mr. Tymperley was not much of a psychologist. But all at once he saw with awful perspicacity the moral crisis through which he had been living. And it taught him one more truth on the subject of poverty.

Immediately after his breakfast he went downstairs and tapped at the door of Mr. Suggs' sitting-room.

'What is it?' asked the bookbinder, who was eating his fourth large rasher, and spoke with his mouth full.

'Sir, I beg leave of absence for an hour or two this morning. Business of some moment demands my attention.'

Mr. Suggs answered, with the grace natural to his order, 'I s'pose you can do as you like. I don't pay you nothing.'

The other bowed and withdrew.

Two days later he again penned a letter to Mrs. Weare. It ran thus:—

'The money which you so kindly sent, and which I have already acknowledged, has now been distributed. To ensure a proper use of it, I handed the cheque, with clear instructions, to a clergyman in this neighbourhood, who has been so good as to jot down, on the sheet enclosed, a memorandum of his beneficiaries, which I trust will be satisfactory and gratifying to you.

'But why, you will ask, did I have recourse to a clergyman. Why did I not use my own experience, and give myself the pleasure of helping poor souls in whom I have a personal interest—I who have devoted my life to this mission of mercy?
'The answer is brief and plain. I have lied to you.

'I am *not* living in this place of my free will. I am *not* devoting myself to works of charity. I am—no, no, I was—merely a poor gentleman, who, on a certain day, found that he had wasted his substance in a foolish speculation, and who, ashamed to take his friends into his confidence, fled to a life of miserable obscurity. You see that I have added disgrace to misfortune. I will not tell you how very near I came to something still worse.

'I have been serving an apprenticeship to a certain handicraft which will, I doubt not, enable me so to supplement my own scanty resources that I shall be in better circum than hitherto. I entreat you to forgive me, if you can, and henceforth to forget

Yours unworthily,
'S. V. TYMPERLEY.'

MISS RODNEY'S LEISURE

A young woman of about eight-and-twenty, in tailor-made costume, with unadorned hat of brown felt, and irreproachable umbrella; a young woman who walked faster than any one in Wattleborough, yet never looked hurried; who crossed a muddy street seemingly without a thought for her skirts, yet somehow was never splashed; who held up her head like one thoroughly at home in the world, and frequently smiled at her own thoughts. Those who did not know her asked who she was; those who had already made her acquaintance talked a good deal of the new mistress at the High School, by name Miss Rodney. In less than a week after her arrival in the town, her opinions were cited and discussed by Wattleborough ladies. She brought with her the air of a University; she knew a great number of important people; she had a quiet decision of speech and manner which was found very impressive in Wattleborough drawing-rooms. The headmistress spoke of her in high terms, and the incumbent of St. Luke's, who knew her family, reported that she had always been remarkably clever.

A stranger in the town, Miss Rodney was recommended to the lodgings of Mrs. Ducker, a churchwarden's widow; but there she remained only for a week or two, and it was understood that she left because the rooms 'lacked character.' Some persons understood this as an imputation on Mrs. Ducker, and were astonished; others, who caught a glimpse of Miss Rodney's meaning, thought she must be 'fanciful.' Her final choice of an abode gave general surprise, for though the street was one of those which Wattleborough opinion classed as 'respectable,' the house itself, as Miss Rodney might have learnt from the incumbent of St. Luke's, in whose parish it was situated, had objectionable features. Nothing grave could be alleged against Mrs. Turpin, who regularly attended the Sunday evening service; but her husband, a carpenter, spent far too much time at 'The Swan With Two Necks'; and then there was a lodger, young Mr. Rawcliffe, concerning whom Wattleborough had for some time been too well informed. Of such comments upon her proceeding Miss Rodney made light; in the aspect of the rooms she found a certain 'quaintness' which decidedly pleased her. 'And as for Mrs. Grundy,' she added, *'je m'en fiche?'* which certain ladies of culture declared to be a polite expression of contempt.

Miss Rodney never wasted time, and in matters of business had cultivated a notable brevity. Her interview with Mrs. Turpin, when she engaged the rooms, occupied perhaps a quarter of an hour; in that space of time she had sufficiently surveyed the house, had learnt all that seemed necessary as to its occupants, and had stated in the clearest possible way her present requirements.

'As a matter of course,' was her closing remark, 'the rooms will be thoroughly cleaned before I come in. At present they are filthy.'

The landlady was too much astonished to reply; Miss Rodney's tones and bearing had so impressed her that she was at a loss for her usual loquacity, and could only stammer respectfully broken answers to whatever was asked. Assuredly no one had ever dared to tell her that her lodgings were 'filthy'—any ordinary person who had ventured upon such an insult would have been overwhelmed with clamorous retort. But Miss Rodney, with a pleasant smile and nod, went her way, and Mrs. Turpin stood at the open door gazing after her, bewildered 'twixt satisfaction and resentment.

She was an easy-going, wool-witted creature, not ill-disposed, but sometimes mendacious and very indolent. Her life had always been what it was now—one of slatternly comfort and daylong gossip, for she came of a small tradesman's family, and had married an artisan who was always in well-paid work. Her children were two daughters, who, at seventeen and fifteen, remained in the house with her doing little or nothing, though they were supposed to 'wait upon the lodgers.' For some months only two of the four rooms Mrs. Turpin was able to let had been occupied, one by 'young Mr. Rawcliffe,' always so called, though his age was nearly thirty, but, as was well known, he belonged to the 'real gentry,' and Mrs. Turpin held him in reverence on that account. No matter for his little weaknesses—of which evil tongues, said Mrs. Turpin, of course made the most. He might be irregular in payment; he might come home 'at all hours,' and make unnecessary noise in going upstairs; he might at times grumble when his chop was ill-cooked; and, to tell the truth, he might occasionally be 'a little too free' with the young ladies—that is to say, with Mabel and Lily Turpin; but all these things were forgiven him because he was 'a real gentleman,' and spent just as little time as he liked daily in a solicitor's office.

Miss Rodney arrived early on Saturday afternoon. Smiling and silent, she saw her luggage taken up to the bedroom; she paid the cabman; she beckoned her landlady into the parlour, which was on the ground-floor front.

'You haven't had time yet, Mrs. Turpin, to clean the rooms?'

The landlady stammered a half-indignant surprise. Why, she and her daughters had given the room a thorough turn out. It was done only yesterday, and *hours* had been devoted to it.

'I see,' interrupted Miss Rodney, with quiet decision, 'that our notions of cleanliness differ considerably. I'm going out now, and I shall not be back till six o'clock. You will please to *clean* the bedroom before then. The sitting-room shall be done on Monday.'

And therewith Miss Rodney left the house.

On her return she found the bedroom relatively clean, and, knowing that too much must not be expected at once, she made no comment. That night, as she sat reading at eleven o'clock, a strange sound arose in the back part of the house; it was a man's voice, hilariously mirthful and breaking into rude song. After listening for a few minutes, Miss Rodney rang her bell, and the landlady appeared.

'Whose Voice is that I hear?'

'Voice, miss?'

'Who is shouting and singing?' asked Miss Rodney, in a disinterested tone.

'I'm sorry if it disturbs you, miss. You'll hear no more.'

'Mrs. Turpin, I asked who it was.'

'My 'usband, miss. But—'

'Thank you. Good night, Mrs. Turpin.'

There was quiet for an hour or more. At something after midnight, when Miss Rodney had just finished writing half a dozen letters, there sounded a latch-key in the front door, and some one entered. This person, whoever it was, seemed to stumble about the passage in the dark, and at length banged against the listener's door. Miss Rodney started up and flung the door open. By the light of her lamp she saw a moustachioed face, highly flushed, and grinning.

'Beg pardon,' cried the man, in a voice which harmonised with his look and bearing. 'Infernally dark here; haven't got a match. You're Miss—pardon—forgotten the name—new lodger. Oblige me with a light? Thanks awfully.'

Without a word Miss Rodney took a match-box from her chimney-piece, entered the passage, entered the second parlour—that occupied by Mr. Rawcliffe—and lit a candle which stood on the table.

'You'll be so kind,' she said, looking her fellow-lodger in the eyes, 'as not to set the house on fire.'

'Oh, no fear,' he replied, with a high laugh. 'Quite accustomed. Thanks awfully, Miss—pardon—forgotten the name.'

But Miss Rodney was back in her sitting-room, and had closed the door.

Her breakfast next morning was served by Mabel Turpin, the elder daughter, a stupidly good-natured girl, who would fain have entered into conversation. Miss Rodney replied to a question that she had slept well, and added that, when she rang her bell, she would like to see Mrs. Turpin. Twenty minutes later the landlady entered.

'You wanted me, miss?' she began, in what was meant for a voice of dignity and reserve. 'I don't really wait on lodgers myself.'

'We'll talk about that another time, Mrs. Turpin. I wanted to say, first of all, that you have spoiled a piece of good bacon and two good eggs. I must trouble you to cook better than this.'

'I'm very sorry, miss, that nothing seems to suit you'

'Oh, we shall get right in time!' interrupted Miss Rodney cheerfully. 'You will find that I have patience. Then I wanted to ask you whether your husband and your lodger come home tipsy *every* night, or only on Saturdays?'

The woman opened her eyes as wide as saucers, trying hard to look indignant.

'Tipsy, miss?'

'Well, perhaps I should have said "drunk"; I beg your pardon.'

'All I can say, miss, is that young Mr. Rawcliffe has never behaved himself in *this* house excepting as the gentleman he is. You don't perhaps know that he belongs to a very high-connected family, miss, or I'm sure you wouldn't'

'I see,' interposed Miss Rodney. 'That accounts for it. But your husband. Is *he* highly connected?'

'I'm sure, miss, nobody could ever say that my 'usband took too much—not to say *really* too much. You may have heard him a bit merry, miss, but where's the harm of a Saturday night?'

'Thank you. Then it is only on Saturday nights that Mr. Turpin becomes merry. I'm glad to know that. I shall get used to these little things.'

But Mrs. Turpin did not feel sure that she would get used to her lodger. Sunday was spoilt for her by this beginning. When her husband woke from his prolonged slumbers, and shouted for breakfast (which on this day of rest he always took in bed), the good woman went to him with downcast visage, and spoke querulously of Miss Rodney's behaviour.

'I *won't* wait upon her, so there! The girls may do it, and if she isn't satisfied let her give notice. I'm sure I shan't be sorry. She's given me more trouble in a day than poor Mrs. Brown did all the months she was here. I *won't* be at her beck and call, so there!'

Before night came this declaration was repeated times innumerable, and as it happened that Miss Rodney made no demand for her landlady's attendance, the good woman enjoyed a sense of triumphant self-assertion. On Monday morning Mabel took in the breakfast, and reported that Miss Rodney had made no remark; but, a quarter of an hour later, the bell rang, and Mrs. Turpin was summoned. Very red in the face, she obeyed. Having civilly greeted her, Miss Rodney inquired at what hour Mr. Turpin took his breakfast, and was answered with an air of surprise that he always left the house on week-days at half-past seven.

'In that case,' said Miss Rodney, 'I will ask permission to come into your kitchen at a quarter to eight to-morrow morning, to show you how to fry bacon and boil eggs. You mustn't mind. You know that teaching is my profession.'

Mrs. Turpin, nevertheless, seemed to mind very much. Her generally good-tempered face wore a dogged sullenness, and she began to mutter something about such a thing never having been heard of; but Miss Rodney paid no heed, renewed the appointment for the next morning, and waved a cheerful dismissal.

Talking with a friend that day, the High School mistress gave a humorous description of her lodgings, and when the friend remarked that they must be very uncomfortable, and that surely she would not stay there, Miss Rodney replied that she had the firmest intention of staying, and, what was more, of being comfortable.

'I'm going to take that household in hand,' she added. 'The woman is foolish, but can be managed, I think, with a little patience. I'm going to *tackle* the drunken husband as soon as I see my way. And as for the highly connected gentleman whose candle I had the honour of lighting, I shall turn him out.'

'You have your work set!' exclaimed the friend, laughing.

'Oh, a little employment for my leisure! This kind of thing relieves the monotony of a teacher's life, and prevents one from growing old.'

Very systematically she pursued her purpose of getting Mrs. Turpin 'in hand.' The two points at which she first aimed were the keeping clean of her room and the decent preparation of her meals. Never losing temper, never seeming to notice the landlady's sullen mood, always using a tone of legitimate authority, touched sometimes with humorous compassion, she exacted obedience to her directions, but was well aware that at any moment the burden of a new civilisation might prove too heavy for the Turpin family and cause revolt. A week went by; it was again Saturday, and Miss Rodney devoted a part of the morning (there being no school to-day) to culinary instruction. Mabel and Lily shared the lesson with their mother, but both young ladies wore an air of condescension, and grimaced at Miss Rodney behind her back. Mrs. Turpin was obstinately mute. The pride of ignorance stiffened her backbone and curled her lip.

Miss Rodney's leisure generally had its task; though as a matter of principle she took daily exercise, her walking or cycling was always an opportunity for thinking something out, and this afternoon, as she sped on wheels some ten miles from Wattleborough, her mind was busy with the problem of Mrs. Turpin's husband. From her clerical friend of St. Luke's she had learnt that Turpin was at bottom a decent sort of man, rather intelligent, and that it was only during the last year or two that he had taken to passing his evenings at the public-house. Causes for this decline could be suggested. The carpenter had lost his only son, a lad of whom he was very fond; the boy's death quite broke him down at the time, and perhaps he had begun to drink as a way for forgetting his trouble. Perhaps, too, his foolish, slatternly wife bore part of the blame, for his home had always been comfortless, and such companionship must, in the long-run, tell on a man. Reflecting upon this, Miss Rodney had an idea, and she took no time in putting it into practice. When Mabel brought in her tea, she asked the girl whether her father was at home.

'I think he is, miss,' was the distant reply—for Mabel had been bidden by her mother to 'show a proper spirit' when Miss Rodney addressed her.

'You think so? Will you please make sure, and, if you are right, ask Mr. Turpin to be so kind as to let me have a word with him.'

Startled and puzzled, the girl left the room. Miss Rodney waited, but no one came. When ten minutes had elapsed she rang the bell. A few minutes more and there sounded a heavy foot in the passage; then a heavy knock at the door, and Mr. Turpin presented himself. He was a short, sturdy man, with hair and beard of the hue known as ginger, and a face which told in his favour. Vicious he could assuredly not be, with those honest grey eyes; but one easily imagined him weak in character, and his attitude as he stood just within the room, half respectful, half assertive, betrayed an embarrassment altogether encouraging to Miss Rodney. In her pleasantest tone she begged him to be seated.

'Thank you, miss,' he replied, in a deep voice, which sounded huskily, but had nothing of surliness; 'I suppose you want to complain about something, and I'd rather get it over standing.'

'I was not going to make any complaint, Mr. Turpin.'

'I'm glad to hear it, miss; for my wife wished me to say she'd done about all she could, and if things weren't to your liking, she thought it would be best for all if you suited yourself in somebody else's lodgings.'

It evidently cost the man no little effort to deliver his message; there was a nervous twitching about his person, and he could not look Miss Rodney straight in the face. She, observant of this, kept a very steady eye on him, and spoke with all possible calmness.

'I have not the least desire to change my lodgings, Mr. Turpin. Things are going on quite well. There is an improvement in the cooking, in the cleaning, in everything; and, with a little patience, I am sure we shall all come to understand one another. What I wanted to speak to you about was a little practical matter in which you may be able to help me. I teach mathematics at the High School, and I have an idea that I might make certain points in geometry easier to my younger girls if I could demonstrate them in a mechanical way. Pray look here. You see the shapes I have sketched on this piece of paper; do you think you could make them for me in wood?'

The carpenter was moved to a show of reluctant interest. He took the paper, balanced himself now on one leg, now on the other, and said at length that he thought he saw what was wanted. Miss Rodney, coming to his side, explained in more detail; his interest grew more active.

'That's Euclid, miss?'

'To be sure. Do you remember your Euclid?'

'My own schooling never went as far as that,' he replied, in a muttering voice; 'but my Harry used to do Euclid at the Grammar School, and I got into a sort of way of doing it with him.'

Miss Rodney kept a moment's silence; then quietly and kindly she asked one or two questions about the boy who had died. The father answered in an awkward, confused way, as if speaking only by constraint.

'Well, I'll see what I can do, miss,' he added abruptly, folding the paper to take away. 'You'd like them soon?'

'Yes. I was going to ask you, Mr. Turpin, whether you could do them this evening. Then I should have them for Monday morning.'

Turpin hesitated, shuffled his feet, and seemed to reflect uneasily; but he said at length that he 'would see about it,' and, with a rough bow, got out of the room. That night no hilarious sounds came from the kitchen. On Sunday morning, when Miss Rodney went into her sitting-room, she found on the table the wooden geometrical forms, excellently made, just as she wished. Mabel, who came with breakfast, was bidden to thank her father, and to say that Miss Rodney would like to speak with him again, if his leisure allowed, after tea-time on Monday. At that hour the carpenter did not fail to present himself, distrustful still, but less embarrassed. Miss Rodney praised his work, and desired to pay for it. Oh! that wasn't worth talking about, said Turpin; but the lady insisted, and money changed hands. This piece of business transacted, Miss Rodney produced a Euclid, and asked Turpin to show her how far he had gone in it with his boy Harry. The subject proved fruitful of conversation. It became evident that the carpenter had a mathematical bias, and could be readily interested in such things as geometrical problems. Why should he not take up the subject again?

'Nay, miss,' replied Turpin, speaking at length quite naturally; 'I shouldn't have the heart. If my Harry had lived'

But Miss Rodney stuck to the point, and succeeded in making him promise that he would get out the old Euclid and have a look at it in his leisure time. As he withdrew, the man had a pleasant smile on his honest face.

On the next Saturday evening the house was again quiet.

Meanwhile, relations between Mrs. Turpin and her lodger were becoming less strained. For the first time in her life the flabby, foolish woman had to do with a person of firm will and bright intelligence; not being vicious of temper, she necessarily felt herself submitting to domination, and darkly surmised that the rule might in some way be for her good. All the sluggard and the slattern in her, all the obstinacy of lifelong habits, hung back from the new things which Miss Rodney was forcing upon her acceptance, but she was no longer moved by active resentment. To be told that she cooked badly had long ceased to be an insult, and was becoming merely a worrying truism. That she lived in dirt there seemed no way of denying, and though every muscle groaned, she began to look upon the physical exertion of dusting and scrubbing as part of her lot in life. Why she submitted, Mrs. Turpin could not have told you. And, as was presently to be seen, there were regions of her mind still unconquered, instincts of resistance which yet had to come into play.

For, during all this time, Miss Rodney had had her eye on her fellow-lodger, Mr. Rawcliffe, and the more she observed this gentleman, the more resolute she became to turn him out of the house; but it was plain to her that the undertaking would be no easy one. In the landlady's eyes Mr. Rawcliffe, though not perhaps a faultless specimen of humanity, conferred an honour on her house by residing in it; the idea of giving him notice to quit was inconceivable to her. This came out very clearly in the first frank conversation which Miss Rodney held with her on the topic. It happened that Mr. Rawcliffe had passed an evening at home, in the company of his friends. After supping together, the gentlemen indulged in merriment which, towards midnight, became uproarious. In the morning Mrs. Turpin mumbled a shamefaced apology for this disturbance of Miss Rodney's repose.

'Why don't you take this opportunity and get rid of him?' asked the lodger in her matter-of-fact tone.

'Oh, miss!'

'Yes, it's your plain duty to do so. He gives your house a bad character; he sets a bad example to your husband; he has a bad influence on your daughters.'

'Oh! miss, I don't think'

'Just so, Mrs. Turpin; you *don't* think. If you had, you would long ago have noticed that his behaviour to those girls is not at all such as it should be. More than once I have chanced to hear bits of talk, when either Mabel or Lily was in his sitting-room, and didn't like the tone of it. In plain English, the man is a blackguard.'

Mrs. Turpin gasped.

'But, miss, you forget what family he belongs to.'

'Don't be a simpleton, Mrs. Turpin. The blackguard is found in every rank of life. Now, suppose you go to him as soon as he gets up, and quietly give him notice. You've no idea how much better you would feel after it.'

But Mrs. Turpin trembled at the suggestion. It was evident that no ordinary argument or persuasion would bring her to such a step. Miss Rodney put the matter aside for the moment.

She had found no difficulty in getting information about Mr. Rawcliffe. It was true that he belonged to a family of some esteem in the Wattleborough neighbourhood, but his father had died in embarrassed circumstances, and his mother was now the wife of a prosperous merchant in another town. To his stepfather Rawcliffe owed an expensive education and two or three starts in life. He was in his second year of articles to a Wattle-borough solicitor, but there seemed little probability of his ever earning a living by the law, and reports of his excesses which reached the stepfather's ears had begun to make the young man's position decidedly precarious. The incumbent of St. Luke's, whom Rawcliffe had more than once insulted, took much interest in Miss Rodney's design against this common enemy; he could not himself take active part in the campaign, but he never met the High School mistress without inquiring what progress she had made. The conquest of Turpin, who now for several weeks had kept sober, and spent his evenings in mathematical study, was a most encouraging circumstance; but Miss Rodney had no thought of using her influence over her landlady's husband to assail Rawcliffe's position. She would rely upon herself alone, in this as in all other undertakings.

Only by constant watchfulness and energy did she maintain her control over Mrs. Turpin, who was ready at any moment to relapse into her old slatternly ways. It was not enough to hold the ground that had been gained; there must be progressive conquest; and to this end Miss Rodney one day broached a subject which had already been discussed between her and her clerical ally.

'Why do you keep both your girls at home, Mrs. Turpin?' she asked.

'What should I do with them, miss? I don't hold with sending girls into shops, or else they've an aunt in Birmingham, who's manageress of—'

'That isn't my idea,' interposed Miss Rodney quietly. 'I have been asked if I knew of a girl who would go into a country-house not far from here as second housemaid, and it occurred to me that Lily—'

A sound of indignant protest escaped the landlady, which Miss Rodney, steadily regarding her, purposely misinterpreted.

'No, no, of course, she is not really capable of taking such a position. But the lady of whom I am speaking would not mind an untrained girl, who came from a decent house. Isn't it worth thinking of?'

Mrs. Turpin was red with suppressed indignation, but as usual she could not look her lodger defiantly in the face.

'We're not so poor, miss,' she exclaimed, 'that we need send our daughters into service,'

'Why, of course not, Mrs. Turpin, and that's one of the reasons why Lily might suit this lady.'

But here was another rock of resistance which promised to give Miss Rodney a good deal of trouble. The landlady's pride was outraged, and after the manner of the inarticulate she could think of no adequate reply save that which took the form of personal abuse. Restrained from this by more than one consideration, she stood voiceless, her bosom heaving.

'Well, you shall think it over,' said Miss Rodney, 'and we'll speak of it again in a day or two.'

Mrs. Turpin, without another word, took herself out of the room.

Save for that singular meeting on Miss Rodney's first night in the house, Mr. Rawcliffe and the energetic lady had held no intercourse whatever. Their parlours being opposite each other on the ground floor, they necessarily came face to face now and then, but the High School mistress behaved as though she saw no one, and the solicitor's clerk, after one or two attempts at polite formality, adopted a like demeanour. The man's proximity caused his neighbour a ceaseless irritation; of all objectionable types of humanity, this loafing and boozing degenerate was, to Miss Rodney, perhaps the least endurable; his mere countenance excited her animosity, for feebleness and conceit, things abhorrent to her, were legible in every line of the trivial features; and a full moustache, evidently subjected to training, served only as emphasis of foppish imbecility. 'I could beat him!' she exclaimed more than once within herself, overcome with contemptuous wrath, when she passed Mr. Rawcliffe. And, indeed, had it been possible to settle the matter thus simply, no doubt Mr. Rawcliffe's rooms would very soon have been vacant.

The crisis upon which Miss Rodney had resolved came about, quite unexpectedly, one Sunday evening. Mrs. Turpin and her daughters had gone, as usual, to church, the carpenter had gone to smoke a pipe with a neighbour, and Mr. Rawcliffe believed himself alone in the house. But Miss Rodney was not at church this evening; she had a headache, and after tea lay down in her bedroom for a while. Soon impatient of repose, she got up and went to her parlour. The door, to her surprise, was partly open; entering—the tread of her slippered feet was noiseless—she beheld an astonishing spectacle. Before her writing-table, his back turned to her, stood Mr. Rawcliffe, engaged in the deliberate perusal of a letter which he had found there. For a moment she observed him; then she spoke.

'What business have you here?'

Rawcliffe gave such a start that he almost jumped from the ground. His face, as he put down the letter and turned, was that of a gibbering idiot; his lips moved, but no sound came from them.

'What are you doing in my room?' demanded Miss Rodney, in her severest tones.

'I really beg your pardon—I really beg—'

'I suppose this is not the first visit with which you have honoured me?'

'The first—indeed—I assure you—the very first! A foolish curiosity; I really feel quite ashamed of myself; I throw myself upon your indulgence.'

The man had become voluble; he approached Miss Rodney smiling in a sickly way, his head bobbing forward.

'It's something,' she replied, 'that you have still the grace to feel ashamed. Well, there's no need for us to discuss this matter; it can have, of course, only one result. To-morrow morning you will oblige me by giving notice to Mrs. Turpin—a week's notice.'

'Leave the house?' exclaimed Rawcliffe.

'On Saturday next—or as much sooner as you like.'

'Oh! but really—'

'As you please,' said Miss Rodney, looking him sternly in the face. 'In that case I complain to the landlady of your behaviour, and insist on her getting rid of you. You ought to have been turned out long ago. You are a nuisance, and worse than a nuisance. Be so good as to leave the room.'

Rawcliffe, his shoulders humped, moved towards the door; but before reaching it he stopped and said doggedly—

'I *can't* give notice.'

'Why not?'

'I owe Mrs. Turpin money.'

'Naturally. But you will go, all the same.'

A vicious light flashed into the man's eyes.

'If it comes to that, I shall *not* go!'

'Indeed?' said Miss Rodney calmly and coldly. 'We will see about it. In the meantime, leave the room, sir!'

Rawcliffe nodded, grinned, and withdrew.

Late that evening there was a conversation between Miss Rodney and Mrs. Turpin. The landlady, though declaring herself horrified at what had happened, did her best to plead for Mr. Rawcliffe's forgiveness, and would not be brought to the point of promising to give him notice.

'Very well, Mrs. Turpin,' said Miss Rodney at length, 'either he leaves the house or I do.'

Resolved, as she was, *not* to quit her lodgings, this was a bold declaration. A meeker spirit would have trembled at the possibility that Mrs. Turpin might be only too glad to free herself from a subjection which, again and again, had all but driven her to extremities. But Miss Rodney had the soul of a conqueror; she saw only her will, and the straight way to it.

'To tell you the truth, miss,' said the landlady, sore perplexed, 'he's rather backward with his rent—'

'Very foolish of you to have allowed him to get into your debt. The probability is that he would never pay his arrears; they will only increase, the longer he stays. But I have no more time to spare at present. Please understand that by Saturday next it must be settled which of your lodgers is to go.'

Mrs. Turpin had never been so worried. The more she thought of the possibility of Miss Rodney's leaving the house, the less did she like it. Notwithstanding Mr. Rawcliffe's 'family,' it was growing clear to her that, as a stamp of respectability and a source of credit, the High School mistress was worth more than the solicitor's clerk. Then there was the astonishing change that had come over Turpin, owing, it seemed, to his talk with Miss Rodney; the man spent all his leisure time in 'making shapes and figuring'—just as he used to do when poor Harry was at the Grammar School. If Miss Rodney disappeared, it seemed only too probable that Turpin would be off again to 'The Swan With Two Necks.' On the other hand, the thought of 'giving notice' to Mr. Rawcliffe caused her something like dismay; how could she have the face to turn a real gentleman out of her house? Yes, but was it not true that she had lost money by him—and stood to lose more? She had never dared to tell her husband of Mr. Rawcliffe's frequent shortcomings in the matter of weekly payments. When the easy-going young man smiled and nodded, and said, 'It'll be all right, you know, Mrs. Turpin; you can trust *me*, I hope,' she could do nothing but acquiesce. And Mr. Rawcliffe was more and more disposed to take advantage of this weakness. If she could find courage to go through with the thing, perhaps she would be glad when it was over.

Three days went by. Rawcliffe led an unusually quiet and regular life. There came the day on which his weekly bill was presented. Mrs. Turpin brought it in person at breakfast, and stood with it in her hand, an image of vacillation. Her lodger made one of his familiar jokes; she laughed feebly. No; the words would not come to her lips; she was physically incapable of giving him notice.

'By the bye, Mrs. Turpin,' said Rawcliffe in an offhand way, as he glanced at the bill, 'how much exactly do I owe you?'

Pleasantly agitated, his landlady mentioned the sum.

'Ah! I must settle that. I tell you what, Mrs. Turpin. Let it stand over for another month, and we'll square things up at Christmas. Will that suit you?'

And, by way of encouragement, he paid his week's account on the spot, without a penny of deduction. Mrs. Turpin left the room in greater embarrassment than ever.

Saturday came. At breakfast Miss Rodney sent for the landlady, who made a timid appearance just within the room.

'Good morning, Mrs. Turpin. What news have you for me? You know what I mean?'

The landlady took a step forward, and began babbling excuses, explanations, entreaties. She was coldly and decisively interrupted.

'Thank you, Mrs. Turpin, that will do. A week to-day I leave.'

With a sound which was half a sob and half grunt Mrs. Turpin bounced from the room. It was now inevitable that she should report the state of things to her husband, and that evening half an hour's circumlocution brought her to the point. Which of the two lodgers should go? The carpenter paused, pipe in mouth, before him a geometrical figure over which he had puzzled for a day or two, and about which, if he could find courage, he wished to consult the High School mistress. He reflected for five minutes, and uttered an unhesitating decision. Mr. Rawcliffe must go. Naturally, his wife broke into indignant clamour, and the debate lasted for an hour or two; but Turpin could be firm when he liked, and he had solid reasons for preferring to keep Miss Rodney in the house. At four o'clock Mrs. Turpin crept softly to the sitting-room where her offended lodger was quietly reading.

'I wanted just to say, miss, that I'm willing to give Mr. Rawcliffe notice next Wednesday.'

'Thank you, Mrs. Turpin,' was the cold reply. 'I have already taken other rooms.'

The landlady gasped, and for a moment could say nothing. Then she besought Miss Rodney to change her mind. Mr. Rawcliffe should leave, indeed he should, on Wednesday week. But Miss Rodney had only one reply; she had found other rooms that suited her, and she requested to be left in peace.

At eleven Mr. Rawcliffe came home. He was unnaturally sober, for Saturday night, and found his way into the parlour without difficulty. There in a minute or two he was confronted by his landlady and her husband: they closed the door behind them, and stood in a resolute attitude.

'Mr. Rawcliffe,' began Turpin, 'you must leave these lodgings, sir, on Wednesday next.'

'Hullo! what's all this about?' cried the other. 'What do you mean, Turpin?'

The carpenter made plain his meaning; spoke of Miss Rodney's complaint, of the irregular payment (for his wife, in her stress, had avowed everything), and of other subjects of dissatisfaction; the lodger must go, there was an end of it. Rawcliffe, putting on all his dignity, demanded the legal week's notice; Turpin demanded the sum in arrear. There was an exchange of high words, and the interview ended with mutual defiance. A moment after Turpin and his wife knocked at Miss Rodney's door, for she was still in her parlour. There followed a brief conversation, with the result that Miss Rodney graciously consented to remain, on the understanding that Mr. Rawcliffe left the house not later than Wednesday.

Enraged at the treatment he was receiving, Rawcliffe loudly declared that he would not budge. Turpin warned him that if he had made no preparations for departure on Wednesday he would be forcibly ejected, and the door closed against him.

'You haven't the right to do it,' shouted the lodger. 'I'll sue you for damages.'

'And I,' retorted the carpenter, 'will sue you for the money you owe me!'

The end could not be doubtful. Rawcliffe, besides being a poor creature, knew very well that it was dangerous for him to get involved in a scandal; his stepfather, upon whom he depended, asked but a fair excuse for cutting him adrift, and more than one grave warning had come from his mother during the past few months. But he enjoyed a little blustering, and even at breakfast-time on Wednesday his attitude was that of contemptuous defiance. In vain had Mrs. Turpin tried to coax him with maternal suavity; in vain had Mabel and Lily, when serving his meals, whispered abuse of Miss Rodney, and promised to find some way of getting rid of her, so that Rawcliffe might return. In a voice loud enough to be heard by his enemy in the opposite parlour, he declared that no 'cat of a school teacher should get the better of *him*.' As a matter of fact, however, he arranged on Tuesday evening to take a couple of cheaper rooms just outside the town, and ordered a cab to come for him at eleven next morning.

'You know what the understanding is, Mr. Rawcliffe,' said Turpin, putting his head into the room as the lodger sat at breakfast. 'I'm a man of my word.'

'Don't come bawling here!' cried the other, with a face of scorn.

And at noon the house knew him no more.

Miss Rodney, on that same day, was able to offer her landlady a new lodger. She had not spoken of this before, being resolved to triumph by mere force of will.

'The next thing,' she remarked to a friend, when telling the story, 'is to pack off one of the girls into service. I shall manage it by Christmas,' and she added with humorous complacency, 'it does one good to be making a sort of order in one's own little corner of the world.'

A CHARMING FAMILY

'I must be firm,' said Miss Shepperson to herself, as she poured out her morning tea with tremulous hand. 'I must really be very firm with them.'

Firmness was not the most legible characteristic of Miss Shepperson's physiognomy. A plain woman of something more than thirty, she had gentle eyes, a twitching forehead, and lips ever ready for a sympathetic smile. Her attire, a little shabby, a little disorderly, well became the occupant of furnished lodgings, at twelve and sixpence a week, in the unpretentious suburb of Acton. She was the daughter of a Hammersmith draper, at whose death, a few years ago, she had become possessed of a small house and an income of forty pounds a year; her two elder sisters were comfortably married to London tradesmen, but she did not see very much of them, for their ways were not hers, and Miss Shepperson had always been one of those singular persons who shrink into solitude the moment they feel ill at ease. The house which was her property had, until of late, given her no trouble at all; it stood in a quiet part of Hammersmith, and had long been occupied by good tenants, who paid their rent (fifty pounds) with exemplary punctuality; repairs, of course, would now and then be called for, and to that end Miss Shepperson carefully put aside a few pounds every year. Unhappily, the old tenants were at length obliged to change their abode. The house stood empty for two months; it was then taken on a three years' lease by a family named Rymer—really nice people, said Miss Shepperson to herself after her first interview with them. Mr. Rymer was 'in the City'; Mrs. Rymer, who had two little girls, lived only for domestic peace—she had been in better circumstances, but did not repine, and forgot all worldly ambition in the happy discharge of her wifely and maternal duties. 'A charming family!' was Miss Shepperson's mental comment when, at their invitation, she had called one Sunday afternoon soon after they were settled in the house; and, on the way home to her lodgings, she sighed once or twice, thinking of Mrs. Rymer's blissful smile and the two pretty children.

The first quarter's rent was duly paid, but the second quarter-day brought no cheque; and, after the lapse of a fortnight, Miss Shepperson wrote to make known her ingenuous fear that Mr. Rymer's letter might have miscarried. At once there came the politest and friendliest reply. Mr. Rymer (wrote his wife) was out of town, and had been so overwhelmed with business that the matter of the rent must have altogether escaped his mind; he would be back in a day or two, and the cheque should be sent at the earliest possible moment; a thousand apologies for this unpardonable neglect. Still the cheque did not come; another quarter-day arrived, and again no rent was paid. It was now a month after Christmas, and Miss Shepperson, for the first time in her life, found her accounts in serious disorder. This morning she had a letter from Mrs. Rymer, the latest of a dozen or so, all in the same strain—

'I really feel quite ashamed to take up the pen,' wrote the graceful lady, in her delicate hand. 'What *must* you think of us! I assure you that never, never before did I find myself in such a situation. Indeed, I should not have the courage to write at all, but that the end of our troubles is already in view. It is *absolutely certain* that, in a month's time, Mr. Rymer will be able to send you a cheque in complete discharge of his debt. Meanwhile, I *beg* you to believe, dear Miss Shepperson, how very, *very* grateful I am to you for your most kind forbearance.' Another page of almost affectionate protests closed with the touching subscription, 'ever yours, sincerely and gratefully, Adelaide Rymer.'

But Miss Shepperson had fallen into that state of nervous agitation which impels to a decisive step. She foresaw the horrors of pecuniary embarrassment. Her faith in the Rymers' promises was exhausted. This very morning she would go to see Mrs. Rymer, lay before her the plain facts of the case, and with all firmness—with unmistakable resolve—make known to her that, if the arrears were not paid within a month, notice to quit would be given, and the recovery of the debt be sought by legal process. Fear had made Miss Shepperson indignant; it was wrong and cowardly for people such as the Rymers to behave in this way to a poor woman who had only just enough to live upon. She felt sure that they *could* pay if they liked; but because she had shown herself soft and patient, they took advantage of her. She would be firm, very firm.

So, about ten o'clock, Miss Shepperson put on her best things, and set out for Hammersmith. It was a foggy, drizzly, enervating day. When Miss Shepperson found herself drawing near to the house, her courage sank, her heart throbbed painfully, and for a moment she all but stopped and turned, thinking that it would be much better to put her ultimatum into writing. Yet there was the house in view, and to turn back would be deplorable weakness. By word of mouth she could so much better depict the gravity of her situation. She forced herself onwards. Trembling in every nerve, she rang the bell, and in a scarce audible gasp she asked for Mrs. Rymer. A brief delay, and the servant admitted her.

Mrs. Rymer was in the drawing-room, giving her elder child a piano-lesson, while the younger, sitting in a baby-chair at the table, turned over a picture-book. The room was comfortably and prettily furnished; the children were very becomingly dressed; their mother, a tall woman, of fair complexion and thin, refined face, with wandering eyes and a forehead rather deeply lined, stepped forward as if in delight at the unexpected visit, and took Miss Shepperson's ill-gloved hand in both her own, gazing with tender interest into her eyes.

'How kind of you to have taken this trouble! You guessed that I really wished to see you. I should have come to you, but just at present I find it so difficult to get away from home. I am housekeeper, nursemaid, and governess all in one! Some women would find it rather a strain, but the dear tots are so good—so good! Cissy, you remember Miss Shepperson? Of course you do. They look a little pale, I'm afraid; don't you think so? After the life they were accustomed to—but we won't talk about *that*. Tots, school-time is over for this morning. You can't go out, my poor dears; look at the horrid, horrid weather. Go and sit by the nursery-fire, and sing "Rain, rain, go away!"'

Miss Shepperson followed the children with her look as they silently left the room. She knew not how to enter upon what she had to say. To talk of the law and use threats in this atmosphere of serene domesticity seemed impossibly harsh. But the necessity of broaching the disagreeable subject was spared her.

'My husband and I were talking about you last night,' began Mrs. Rymer, as soon as the door had closed, in a tone of the friendliest confidence. 'I had an idea; it seems to me so good. I wonder whether it will to you? You told me, did you not, that you live in lodgings, and quite alone?'

'Yes,' replied Miss Shepperson, struggling to command her nerves and betraying uneasy wonder.

'Is it by choice?' asked the soft-voiced lady, with sympathetic bending of the head. 'Have you no relations in London? I can't help thinking you must feel very lonely.'

It was not difficult to lead Miss Shepperson to talk of her circumstances—a natural introduction to the announcement which she was still resolved to make with all firmness. She narrated in outline the history of her family, made known exactly how she stood in pecuniary matters, and ended by saying—

'You see, Mrs. Rymer, that I have to live as carefully as I can. This house is really all I have to depend upon, and—and—'

Again she was spared the unpleasant utterance. With an irresistible smile, and laying her soft hand on the visitor's ill-fitting glove, Mrs. Rymer began to reveal the happy thought which had occurred to her. In the house there was a spare room; why should not Miss Shepperson come and live here—live, that is to say, as a member of the family? Nothing simpler than to arrange the details of such a plan, which, of course, must be 'strictly businesslike,' though carried out in a spirit of mutual goodwill. A certain sum of money was due to her for rent; suppose this were repaid in the form of board and lodging, which might be reckoned at—should one say, fifteen shillings a week? At midsummer next an account would be drawn up, 'in a thoroughly businesslike way,' and whatever then remained due to Miss Shepperson would be paid at once; after which, if the arrangement proved agreeable to both sides, it might be continued, cost of board and lodging being deducted from the rent, and the remainder paid 'with regularity' every quarter. Miss Shepperson would thus have a home—a real home—with all family comforts, and Mrs. Rymer, who was too much occupied with house and children to see much society, would have the advantage of a sympathetic friend under her own roof. The good lady's voice trembled with joyous eagerness as she unfolded the project, and her eyes grew large as she waited for the response.

Miss Shepperson felt such astonishment that she could only reply with incoherencies. An idea so novel and so strange threw her thoughts into disorder. She was alarmed by the invitation to live with people who were socially her superiors. On the other hand, the proposal made appeal to her natural inclination for domestic life; it offered the possibility of occupation, of usefulness. Moreover, from the pecuniary point of view, it would be so very advantageous.

'But,' she stammered at length, when Mrs. Rymer had repeated the suggestion in words even more gracious and alluring, 'but fifteen shillings is so very little for board and lodging.'

'Oh, don't let *that* trouble you, dear Miss Shepperson,' cried the other gaily. 'In a family, so little difference is made by an extra person. I assure you it is a perfectly businesslike arrangement; otherwise my husband, who is prudence itself, would never have sanctioned it. As you know, we are suffering a temporary embarrassment. I wrote to you yesterday before my husband's return from business. When he came home, I learnt, to my dismay, that it might be rather *more* than a month before he was able to send you a cheque. I said: "Oh, I must write again to Miss Shepperson. I can't bear to think of misleading her." Then, as we talked, that idea came to me. As I think you will believe, Miss Shepperson, I am not a scheming or a selfish woman; never, never have I wronged any one in my life. This proposal, I cannot help feeling, is as much for your benefit as for ours. Doesn't it really seem so to you? Suppose you come up with me and look at the room. It is not in perfect order, but you will see whether it pleases you.

Curiosity allying itself with the allurement which had begun to work upon her feelings, Miss Shepperson timidly rose and followed her smiling guide upstairs. The little spare room on the second floor was furnished simply enough, but made such a contrast with the bedchamber in the Acton lodging-house that the visitor could scarcely repress an exclamation. Mrs. Rymer was voluble with promise of added comforts. She interested herself in Miss Shepperson's health, and learnt with the utmost satisfaction that it seldom gave trouble. She inquired as to Miss Shepperson's likings in the matter of diet, and strongly approved her preference for a plain, nutritive regimen. From the spare room the visitor was taken into all the others, and before they went downstairs again Mrs. Rymer had begun to talk as though the matter were decided.

'You will stay and have lunch with me,' she said. 'Oh yes, indeed you will; I can't dream of your going out into this weather till after lunch. Suppose we have the tots into the drawing-room again? I want them to make friends with you at once. I *know* you love children.—Oh, I have known that for a long time!'

Miss Shepperson stayed to lunch. She stayed to tea. When at length she took her leave, about six o'clock, the arrangement was complete in every detail. On this day week she would transfer herself to the Rymers' house, and enter upon her new life.

She arrived on Saturday afternoon, and was received by the assembled family like a very dear friend or relative. Mr. Rymer, a well-dressed man, polite, good-natured, with a frequent falsetto laugh, talked over the teacups in the pleasantest way imaginable, not only putting Miss Shepperson at ease, but making her feel as if her position as a member of the household were the most natural thing in the world. His mere pronunciation of her name gave it a dignity, an importance quite new to Miss Shepperson's ears. He had a way of shaping his remarks so as to make it appear that the homely, timid woman was, if anything, rather the superior in rank and education, and that their simple ways might now and then cause her amusement. Even the children seemed to do their best to make the newcomer feel at home. Cissy, whose age was nine, assiduously handed toast and cake with a most engaging smile, and little Minnie, not quite six, deposited her kitten in Miss Shepperson's lap, saying prettily, 'You may stroke it whenever you like.'

Miss Shepperson, to be sure, had personal qualities which could not but appeal to people of discernment. Her plain features expressed a simplicity and gentleness which more than compensated for the lack of conventional grace in her manners; she spoke softly and with obvious frankness, nor was there much fault to find with her phrasing and accent; dressed a little more elegantly, she would in no way have jarred with the tone of average middle-class society. If she had not much education, she was altogether free from pretence, and the possession of property (which always works very decidedly for good or for evil) saved her from that excess of deference which would have accentuated her social shortcomings. Undistinguished as she might seem at the first glance, Miss Shepperson could not altogether be slighted by any one who had been in her presence for a few minutes. And when, in the course of the evening, she found courage to converse more freely, giving her views, for instance, on the great servant question, and on other matters of domestic interest, it became clear to Mr. and Mrs. Rymer that their landlady, though a soft-hearted and simple-minded woman, was by no means to be regarded as a person of no account.

The servant question was to the front just now, as Mrs. Rymer explained in detail. She, 'of course,' kept two domestics, but was temporarily making shift with only one, it being so difficult to replace the cook, who had left a week ago. Did Miss Shepperson know of a cook, a sensible, trustworthy woman? For the present Mrs. Rymer—she confessed it with a pleasant little laugh—had to give an eye to the dinner herself.

'I only hope you won't make yourself ill, dear,' said Mr. Rymer, bending towards his wife with a look of well-bred solicitude. 'Miss Shepperson, I beg you to insist that she lies down a little every afternoon. She has great nervous energy, but isn't really very strong. You can't think what a relief it will be to me all day to know that some one is with her.'

On Sunday morning all went to church together; for, to Mrs. Rymer's great satisfaction, Miss Shepperson was a member of the orthodox community, and particular about observances. Meals were reduced to the simplest terms; a restful quiet prevailed in the little house; in the afternoon, while Mrs. Rymer reposed, Miss Shepperson read to the children. She it was who—the servant being out—prepared tea. After tea, Mr. and Mrs. Rymer, with many apologies, left the home together for a couple of hours, being absolutely obliged to pay a call at some distance, and Miss Shepperson again took care of the children till the domestic returned.

After breakfast the next day—it was a very plain meal, merely a rasher and dry toast—the lady of the house chatted with her friend more confidentially than ever. Their servant, she said, a good girl but not very robust, naturally could not do all the work of the house, and, by way of helping, Mrs. Rymer was accustomed to 'see to' her own bedroom.

'It's really no hardship,' she said, in her graceful, sweet-tempered way, 'when once you're used to it; in fact, I think the exercise is good for my health. But, of course, I couldn't think of asking *you* to do the same. No doubt you will like to have a breath of air, as the sky seems clearing.'

What could Miss Shepperson do but protest that to put her own room in order was such a trifling matter that they need not speak of it another moment. Mrs. Rymer was confused, vexed, and wished she had not said a word; but the other made a joke of these scruples.

'When do the children go out?' asked Miss Shepperson. 'Do you take them yourself?'

'Oh, always! almost always! I shall go out with them for an hour at eleven. And yet'—she checked herself, with a look of worry—'oh, dear me! I must absolutely go shopping, and I do so dislike to take the tots in that direction. Never mind; the walk must be put off till the afternoon. It *may* rain; but—'

Miss Shepperson straightway offered her services; she would either shop or go out with the children, whichever Mrs. Rymer preferred. The lady thought she had better do the shopping—so her friend's morning was pleasantly arranged. In a day or two things got into a happy routine. Miss Shepperson practically became nursemaid, with the privilege of keeping her own bedroom in order and of helping in a good many little ways throughout the domestic day. A fortnight elapsed, and Mrs. Rymer was still unable to 'suit herself' with a cook, though she had visited, or professed to visit, many registry-offices and corresponded with many friends. A week after that the subject of the cook had somehow fallen into forgetfulness; and, indeed, a less charitably disposed observer than Miss Shepperson might have doubted whether Mrs. Rymer had ever seriously meant to engage one at all. The food served on the family table was of the plainest, and not always superabundant in quantity; but the table itself was tastefully ordered, and, indeed, no sort of carelessness appeared in any detail of the household life. Mrs. Rymer was always busy, and without fuss, without irritation. She had a large correspondence; but it was not often that people called. No guest was ever invited to lunch or dinner. All this while the master of the house kept regular hours, leaving home at nine and returning at seven; if he went out after dinner, which happened rarely, he was always back by eleven o'clock. No more respectable man than Mr. Rymer; none more even-tempered, more easily pleased, more consistently polite and amiable. That he and his wife were very fond of each other appeared in all their talk and behaviour; both worshipped the children, and, in spite of that, trained them with a considerable measure of good sense. In the evenings Mr. Rymer sometimes read aloud, or he would talk instructively of the affairs of the day. The more Miss Shepperson saw of her friends the more she liked them. Never had she been the subject of so much kind attention, and in no company had she ever felt so happily at ease.

Time went on, and it was near midsummer. Of late Mrs. Rymer had not been very well, and once or twice Miss Shepperson fancied that her eyes showed traces of tears; it was but natural that the guest, often preoccupied with the thought of the promised settlement, should feel a little uneasy. On June 23 Mrs. Rymer chose a suitable moment, and with her most confidential air, invited Miss

Shepperson to an intimate chat.

'I want to explain to you,' she said, rather cheerfully than otherwise, 'the exact state of our affairs. I'm sure it will interest you. We have become such good friends—as I knew we should. I shall be much easier in mind when you know exactly how we stand.'

Thereupon she spoke of a certain kinsman of her husband, an old and infirm man, whose decease was expected, if not from day to day, at all events from week to week. The event would have great importance for them, as Mr. Rymer was entitled to the reversion of several thousands of pounds, held in use by his lingering relative.

'Now let me ask you a question,' pursued the lady in friendship's undertone. 'My husband is *quite* prepared to settle with you to-morrow. He wishes to do so, for he feels that your patience has been most exemplary. But, as we spoke of it last night, an idea came to me. I can't help thinking it was a happy idea, but I wish to know how it strikes you. On receiving the sum due to you, you will no doubt place it in a bank, or in some way invest it. Suppose, now, you leave the money in Mr. Rymer's hands, receiving his acknowledgment, and allowing him to pay it, with four per cent, interest, when he enters into possession of his capital? Mind, I only suggest this; not for a moment would I put pressure upon you. If you have need of the money, it shall be paid *at once*. But it struck me that, knowing us so well now, you might even be glad of such an investment as this. The event to which we are looking forward may happen very soon; but it *may* be delayed. How would you like to leave this money, and the sums to which you will be entitled under our arrangements, from quarter to quarter, to increase at compound interest? Let us make a little calculation—'

Miss Shepperson listened nervously. She was on the point of saying that, on the whole, she preferred immediate payment; but while she struggled with her moral weakness Mrs. Rymer, anxiously reading her face, struck another note.

'I mustn't disguise from you that the money, though such a small sum, would be useful to my husband. Poor fellow! he has been fighting against adversity for the last year or two, and I'm sure no man ever struggled more bravely. You would never think, would you? that he is often kept awake all night by his anxieties. As I tell him, he need not really be anxious at all, for his troubles will so soon come to an end. But there is no more honourable man living, and he worries at the thought of owing money—you can't imagine how he worries! Then, to tell you a great secret—'

A change came upon the speaker's face; her voice softened to a whisper as she communicated a piece of delicate domestic news.

'My poor husband,' she added, 'cannot bear to think that, when it happens, we may be in really straitened circumstances, and I may suffer for lack of comforts. To tell you the whole truth, dear Miss Shepperson, I have no doubt that, if you like my idea, he would at once put aside that money to be ready for an emergency. So, you see, it is self-interest in me, after all.' Her smile was very sweet. 'But don't judge me too severely. What I propose is, as you see, really a very good investment—is it not?'

Miss Shepperson found it impossible to speak as she wished, and before the conversation came to an end she saw the matter entirely from her friend's point of view. She had, in truth, no immediate need of money, and the more she thought of it, the more content she was to do a kindness to the Rymers, while at the same time benefiting herself. That very evening Mr. Rymer prepared a legal document, promising to pay on demand the sum which became due to Miss Shepperson to-morrow, with compound interest at the rate of four per cent. While signing this, he gravely expressed his conviction that before Michaelmas the time for payment would have arrived.

'But if it were next week,' he added, with a polite movement towards his creditor, 'I should be not a bit the less grateful to our most kind friend.'

'Oh, but it's purely a matter of business,' said Miss Shepperson, who was always abashed by such expressions.

'To be sure,' murmured Mrs. Rymer. 'Let us look at it in that light. But it shan't prevent us from calling Miss Shepperson our dearest friend.'

The homely woman blushed and felt happy.

Towards the end of autumn, when the domestic crisis was very near, the servant declared herself ill, and at twenty-four hours' notice quitted the house. As a matter of fact, she had received no wages for several months; the kindness with which she was otherwise treated had kept her at her post thus long, but she feared the increase of work impending, and preferred to go off unpaid. Now for the first time did Mrs. Rymer's nerves give way. Miss Shepperson found her sobbing by the fireside, the two children lamenting at such an unwonted spectacle. Where was a new servant to be found? In a day or two the monthly nurse would be here, and must, of course, be waited upon. And what was to become of the children? Miss Shepperson, moved by the calamitous situation, entreated her friend to leave everything to her. She would find a servant somehow, and meanwhile would keep the house going with her own hands. Mrs. Rymer sobbed that she was ashamed to allow such a thing; but the other, braced by a crisis, displayed wonderful activity and resource. For two days Miss Shepperson did all the domestic labour; then a maid, of the species known as 'general,' presented herself, and none too soon, for that same night there was born to the Rymers a third daughter. But troubles were by no means over. While Mrs. Rymer was ill—very ill indeed—the new handmaid exhibited a character so eccentric that, after nearly setting fire to the house while in a state of intoxication, she had to be got rid of as speedily as possible. Miss Shepperson resolved that, for the present, there should be no repetition of such disagreeable things. She quietly told Mr. Rymer that she felt quite able to grapple with the situation herself.

'Impossible!' cried the master of the house, who, after many sleepless nights and distracted days, had a haggard, unshorn face, scarcely to be recognised. 'I cannot permit it! I will go myself.'

Then, suddenly turning again to Miss Shepperson, he grasped her hand, called her his dear friend and benefactress, and with breaking voice whispered to her—

'I will help you. I can do the hard work. It's only for a day or two.'

Late that evening he and Miss Shepperson were in the kitchen together: the one was washing crockery, the other, who had been filling coal-scuttles, stood with dirty hands and melancholy visage, his eyes fixed on the floor. Their looks met; Mr. Rymer took a step forward, smiling with confidential sadness.

'I feel that I ought to speak frankly,' he said, in a voice as polite and well-tuned as ever. 'I should like to make known to you the exact state of my affairs.'

'Oh, but Mrs. Rymer has told me everything,' replied Miss Shepperson, as she dried a tea-cup.

'No; not quite everything, I'm afraid.' He had a shovel in his hand, and eyed it curiously. 'She has not told you that I am considerably in debt to various people, and that, not long ago, I was obliged to raise money on our furniture.'

Miss Shepperson laid down the tea-cup and gazed anxiously at him, whereupon he began a detailed story of his misfortunes in business. Mr. Rymer was a commission-agent—that is to say, he was everything and nothing. Struggle with pecuniary embarrassment was his normal condition, but only during the last twelvemonth had he fallen under persistent ill-luck and come to all but the very end of his resources. It would still be possible for him, he explained, to raise money on the reversion for which he was waiting, but of such a step he could not dream.

'It would be dishonesty, Miss Shepperson, and, how unfortunate, I have never yet lost my honour. People have trusted me, knowing that I am an honest man. I belong to a good family—as, no doubt, Mrs. Rymer has told you. A brother of mine holds a respected position in Birmingham, and, if the worst comes to the worst, he will find me employment. But, as you can well understand, I shrink from that extremity. For one thing, I am in debt to my brother, and I am resolved to pay what I owe him before asking for any more assistance. I do not lose courage. You know the proverb: "Lose heart, lose all." I am blest with an admirable wife, who stands by me and supports me under every trial. If my wife were to die, Miss Shepperson—' He faltered; his eyes glistened in the gas 'But no, I won't encourage gloomy fears. She is a little better to-day, they tell me. We shall come out of our troubles, and laugh over them by our cheerful fireside—you with us—you, our dearest and staunchest friend.'

'Yes, we must hope,' said Miss Shepperson, reassured once more as to her own interests; for a moment her heart had sunk very low indeed. 'We are all doing our best.'

'You above all,' said Mr. Rymer, pressing her hand with his coal-blackened fingers. 'I felt obliged to speak frankly, because you must have thought it strange that I allowed things to get so disorderly—our domestic arrangements, I mean. The fact is, Miss Shepperson, I simply don't know how I am going to meet the expenses of this illness, and I dread the thought of engaging servants. I cannot—I will not—raise money on my expectations! When the money comes to me, I must be able to pay all my debts, and have enough left to recommence life with. Don't you approve this resolution, Miss Shepperson?'

'Oh yes, indeed I do,' replied the listener heartily.

'And yet, of course,' he pursued, his eyes wandering, 'we *must* have a servant—'

Miss Shepperson reflected, she too with an uneasy look on her face. There was a long silence, broken by a deep sigh from Mr. Rymer, a sigh which was almost a sob. The other went on drying her plates and dishes, and said at length that perhaps they might manage with quite a young girl, who would come for small wages; she herself was willing to help as much as she could—

'Oh, you shame me, you shame me!' broke in Mr. Rymer, laying a hand on his forehead, and leaving a black mark there. 'There is no end to your kindness; but I feel it as a disgrace to us—to me—that you, a lady of property, should be working here like a servant. It is monstrous—monstrous!'

At the flattering description of herself Miss Shepperson smiled; her soft eyes beamed with the light of contentment.

'Don't you give a thought to that, Mr. Rymer,' she exclaimed. 'Why, it's a pleasure to me, and it gives me something to do—it's good for my health. Don't you worry. Think about your business, and leave me to look after the house. It'll be all right.'

A week later Mrs. Rymer was in the way of recovery, and her husband went to the City as usual. A servant had been engaged—a girl of sixteen, who knew as much of housework as London girls of sixteen generally do; at all events, she could carry coals and wash steps. But the mistress of the house, it was evident, would for a long time be unable to do anything whatever; the real maid-of-all-work was Miss Shepperson, who rose every morning at six o'clock, and toiled in one way or another till weary bedtime. If she left the house, it was to do needful shopping or to take the children for a walk. Her reward was the admiration and gratitude of the family; even little Minnie had been taught to say, at frequent intervals: 'I love Miss Shepperson because she is good!' The invalid behaved to her as to a sister, and kissed her cheek morning and evening. Miss Shepperson's name being Dora, the baby was to be so called, and, as a matter of course, the godmother drew a sovereign from her small savings to buy little Miss Dora a christening present. It would not have been easy to find a house in London in which there reigned so delightful a spirit of harmony and kindliness.

'I was so glad,' said Mrs. Rymer one day to her friend, the day on which she first rose from bed, 'that my husband took you into his confidence about our affairs. Now you know everything, and it is much better. You know that we are very unlucky, but that no one can breathe a word against our honour. This was the thought that held me up through my illness. In a very short time all our debts will be paid—every farthing, and it will be delightful to remember how we struggled, and what we endured, to keep an honest name. Though,' she added tenderly, 'how we should have done without *you*, I really cannot imagine. We might have sunk—gone down!'

For months Mrs. Rymer led the life of a feeble convalescent. She ought to have had change of air, but that was out of the question, for Mr. Rymer's business was as unremunerative as ever, and with difficulty he provided the household with food. One gleam of light kept up the courage of the family: the aged relative was known to be so infirm that he could only leave the house in a bath-chair; every day there might be news even yet more promising. Meanwhile, the girl of sixteen exercised her incompetence in the meaner departments of domestic life, and Miss Shepperson did all the work that required care or common-sense, the duties of nursemaid alone taking a great deal of her time. On the whole, this employment seemed to suit her; she had a look of improved health, enjoyed more equable spirits, and in her manner showed more self-confidence. Once a month she succeeded in getting a few hours' holiday, and paid a visit to one or the other of her sisters; but to neither of them did she tell the truth regarding her position in the house at Hammersmith. Now and then, when every one else under the roof was asleep, she took from a locked drawer in her bedroom a little account-book, and busied herself with figures. This she found an enjoyable moment; it was very pleasant indeed to make the computation of what the Rymers owed to her, a daily-growing debt of which the payment could not now be long delayed. She did not feel quite sure with regard to the interest, but the principal of the debt was very easily reckoned, and it would make a nice little sum to put by. Certainly Miss Shepperson was not unhappy.

Mrs. Rymer was just able to resume her normal habits, to write many letters, teach her children, pay visits in distant parts of London—the care of the baby being still chiefly left to Miss Shepperson—when, on a pleasant day of spring, a little before lunch-time, Mr. Rymer rushed into the house, calling in an agitated voice his wife's name. Miss Shepperson was the only person at home, for Mrs. Rymer had gone out with the children, the servant accompanying her to wheel baby's perambulator; she ran up from the kitchen, aproned, with sleeves rolled to the elbow, and met the excited man as he descended from a vain search in the bedrooms.

'Has it happened?' she cried—for it seemed to her that there could be only one explanation of Mr. Rymer's behaviour.

'Yes! He died this morning—this morning!'

They clasped hands; then, as an afterthought, their eyes fell, and they stood limply embarrassed.

'It seems shocking to take the news in this way,' murmured Mr. Rymer; 'but the relief; oh, the relief! And then, I scarcely knew him; we haven't seen each other for years. I can't help it! I feel as if I had thrown off a load of tons! Where is Adelaide? Which way have they gone?'

He rushed out again, to meet his wife. For several minutes Miss Shepperson stood motionless, in a happy daze, until she suddenly remembered that chops were at the kitchen fire, and sped downstairs.

Throughout that day, and, indeed, for several days to come, Mrs. Rymer behaved very properly indeed; her pleasant, refined face wore a becoming gravity, and when she spoke of the deceased she called him *poor* Mr. So-and-so. She did not attend the funeral, for baby happened to be ailing, but Mr. Rymer, of course, went. He, in spite of conscientious effort to imitate his wife's decorum, frequently betrayed the joy which was in his mind; Miss Shepperson heard him singing as he got up in the morning, and noticed that he ate with unusual appetite. The house brightened. Before the end of a week smiles and cheerful remarks ruled in the family; sorrows were forgotten, and everybody looked forward to the great day of settlement.

It did not come quickly. In two months' time Mr. Rymer still waited upon the pleasure of the executors. But he was not inactive. His brother at Birmingham had suggested 'an opening' in that city (thus did Mrs. Rymer phrase it), and the commission-agent had decided to leave London as soon as his affairs were in order. Towards the end of the third month the family was suffering from hope deferred. Mr. Rymer had once more a troubled face, and his wife no longer talked to Miss Shepperson in happy strain of her projects for the future. At length notice arrived that the executors were prepared to settle with Mr. Rymer; yet, in announcing the fact, he manifested only a sober contentment, while Mrs. Rymer was heard to sigh. Miss Shepperson noted these things, and wondered a little, but Mrs. Rymer's smiling assurance that now at last all was well revived her cheerful expectations.

With a certain solemnity she was summoned, a day or two later, to a morning colloquy in the drawing-room. Mr. Rymer sat in an easy-chair, holding a bundle of papers; Mrs. Rymer sat on the sofa, the dozing baby on her lap; over against them their friend took her seat. With a little cough and a rustle of his papers, the polite man began to speak—

'Miss Shepperson, the day has come when I am able to discharge my debt to you. You will not misunderstand that expression—I speak of my debt in money. What I owe to you—what we all owe to you—in another and a higher sense, can never be repaid. That moral debt must still go on, and be acknowledged by the unfailing gratitude of a lifetime.'

'Of a lifetime,' repeated Mrs. Rymer, sweetly murmuring, and casting towards her friend an eloquent glance.

'Here, however,' resumed her husband, 'is the pecuniary account. Will you do me the kindness, Miss Shepperson, to glance it over and see if you find it correct?'

Miss Shepperson took the paper, which was covered with a very neat array of figures. It was the same calculation which she herself had so often made, but with interest on the money due to her correctly computed. The weekly sum of fifteen shillings for board and lodging had been deducted, throughout the whole time, from the rent due to her as landlady. Mr. Rymer stood her debtor for not quite thirty pounds.

'It's *quite* correct,' said Miss Shepperson, handing back the paper with a pleased smile.

Mr. Rymer turned to his wife.

'And what do *you* say, dear? Do *you* think it correct?'

Mrs. Rymer shook her head.

'No,' she answered gently, 'indeed I do not.'

Miss Shepperson was startled. She looked from one to the other, and saw on their faces only the kindliest expression.

'I really thought it came to about that,' fell from her lips. 'I couldn't quite reckon the interest—'

'Miss Shepperson,' said Mr. Rymer impressively, 'do you really think that we should allow you to pay us for your board and lodging—you, our valued friend—you, who have toiled for us, who have saved us from endless trouble and embarrassment? That indeed would be a little too shameless. This account is a mere joke—as I hope you really thought it. I insist on giving you a cheque for the total amount of the rent due to you from the day when you first entered this house.'

'Oh, Mr. Rymer!' panted the good woman, turning pale with astonishment.

'Why, of course!' exclaimed Mrs. Rymer. 'Do you think it would be *possible* for us to behave in any other way? Surely you know us too well, dear Miss Shepperson!'

'How kind you are!' faltered their friend, unable to decide in herself whether she should accept this generosity or not—sorely tempted by the money, yet longing to show no less generous a spirit on her own side. 'I really don't know—'

Mr. Rymer imposed silence with a wave of the hand, and began talking in a slow, grave way.

'Miss Shepperson, to-day I may account myself a happy man. Listen to a very singular story. You know that I was indebted to others besides you. I have communicated with all those persons; I have drawn up a schedule of everything I owe; and—extraordinary coincidence!—the sum-total of my debts is exactly that of the reversion upon which I have entered, *minus* three pounds fourteen shillings.'

'Strange!' murmured Mrs. Rymer, as if delightedly.

'I did not know, Miss Shepperson, that I owed so much. I had forgotten items. And suppose, after all, the total had *exceeded* my resources! That indeed would have been a blow. As it is, I am a happy man; my wife is happy. We pay our debts to the last farthing, and we begin the world again—with three pounds to the good. Our furniture must go; I cannot redeem it; no matter. I owe nothing; our honour is saved!'

Miss Shepperson was aghast.

'But, Mrs. Rymer,' she began, 'this is dreadful! What are you going to do?'

'Everything is arranged, dear friend,' Mrs. Rymer replied. 'My husband has a little post in Birmingham, which will bring him in just enough to support us in the most modest lodgings. We cannot hope to have a house of our own, for we are determined never again to borrow—and, indeed, I do not know who would lend to us. We are poor people, and must live as poor people do. Miss Shepperson, I ask one favour of you. Will you permit us to leave your house without the customary notice? We should feel very grateful. To-day I pay Susan, and part with her; to-morrow we must travel to Birmingham. The furniture will be removed by the people who take possession of it—'

Miss Shepperson was listening with a bewildered look. She saw Mr. Rymer stand up.

'I will now,' he said, 'pay you the rent from the day—'

'Oh, Mr. Rymer!' cried the agitated woman. 'How *can* I take it? How can I leave you penniless? I should feel it a downright robbery, that I should!'

'Miss Shepperson,' exclaimed Mrs. Rymer in soft reproach, 'don't you understand how much better it is to pay all we owe, even though it does leave us penniless? Why, even darling baby'—she kissed it—'would say so if she could speak, poor little mite. Of course you will accept the money; I insist upon it. You won't forget us. We will send you our address, and you shall hear of your little godchild—'

Her voice broke; she sobbed, and rebuked herself for weakness, and sobbed again. Meanwhile Mr. Rymer stood holding out banknotes and gold. The distracted Miss Shepperson made a wild gesture.

'How *can* I take it? How *can* I? I should be ashamed the longest day I lived!'

'I must insist,' said Mr. Rymer firmly; and his wife, calm again, echoed the words. In that moment Miss Shepperson clutched at the notes and gold, and, with a quick step forward, took hold of the baby's hand, making the little fingers close upon the money.

'There! I give it to little Dora—there!'

Mr. Rymer turned away to hide his emotion. Mrs. Rymer laid baby down on the sofa, and clasped Miss Shepperson in her arms.

* * * * *

A few days later the house at Hammersmith was vacant. The Rymers wrote from Birmingham that they had found sufficient, though humble, lodgings, and were looking for a tiny house, which they would furnish very, very simply with the money given to baby by their ever dear friend. It may be added that they had told the truth regarding their position—save as to one detail: Mr. Rymer thought it needless to acquaint Miss Shepperson with the fact that his brother, a creditor for three hundred pounds, had generously forgiven the debt.

Miss Shepperson, lodging in a little bedroom, with an approving conscience to keep her company, hoped that her house would soon be let again.

A DAUGHTER OF THE LODGE

FOR a score of years the Rocketts had kept the lodge of Brent Hall. In the beginning Rockett was head gardener; his wife, the daughter of a shopkeeper, had never known domestic service, and performed her duties at the Hall gates with a certain modest dignity not displeasing to the stately persons upon whom she depended. During the lifetime of Sir Henry the best possible understanding existed between Hall and lodge. Though Rockett's health broke down, and at length he could work hardly at all, their pleasant home was assured to the family; and at Sir Henry's death the nephew who succeeded him left the Rocketts undisturbed. But, under this new lordship, things were not quite as they had been. Sir Edwin Shale, a middle-aged man, had in his youth made a foolish marriage; his lady ruled him, not with the gentlest of tongues, nor always to the kindest purpose, and their daughter, Hilda, asserted her rights as only child with a force of character which Sir Edwin would perhaps have more sincerely admired had it reminded him less of Lady Shale.

While the Hall, in Sir Henry's time, remained childless, the lodge prided itself on a boy and two girls. Young Rockett, something of a scapegrace, was by the baronet's advice sent to sea, and thenceforth gave his parents no trouble. The second daughter, Betsy, grew up to be her mother's help. But Betsy's elder sister showed from early years that the life of the lodge would afford no adequate scope for *her* ambitions. May Rockett had good looks; what was more, she had an intellect which sharpened itself on everything with which it came in contact. The village school could never have been held responsible for May Rockett's acquirements and views at the age of ten; nor could the High School in the neighbouring town altogether account for her mental development at seventeen. Not without misgivings had the health-broken gardener and his wife consented to May's pursuit of the higher learning; but Sir Henry and the kind old Lady Shale seemed to think it the safer course, and evidently there was little chance of the girl's accepting any humble kind of employment: in one way or another she must depend for a livelihood upon her brains. At the time of Sir Edwin's succession Miss Rockett had already obtained a place as governess, giving her parents to understand that this was only, of course, a temporary expedient—a paving of the way to something vaguely, but superbly, independent. Nor was promotion long in coming. At two-and-twenty May accepted a secretaryship to a lady with a mission—concerning the rights of womanhood. In letters to her father and mother she spoke much of the importance of her work, but did not confess how very modest was her salary. A couple of years went by without her visiting the old home; then, of a sudden, she made known her intention of coming to stay at the lodge 'for a week or ten days.' She explained that her purpose was rest; intellectual strain had begun rather to tell upon her, and a few days of absolute tranquillity, such as she might expect under the elms of Brent Hall, would do her all the good in the world. 'Of course,' she added, 'it's unnecessary to say anything about me to the Shale people. They and I have nothing in common, and it will be better for us to ignore each other's existence.'

These characteristic phrases troubled Mr. and Mrs. Rockett. That the family at the Hall should, if it seemed good to them, ignore the existence of May was, in the Rocketts' view, reasonable enough; but for May to ignore Sir Edwin and Lady Shale, who were just now in residence after six months spent abroad, struck them as a very grave impropriety. Natural respect demanded that, at some fitting moment, and in a suitable manner, their daughter should present herself to her feudal superiors, to whom she was assuredly indebted, though indirectly, for 'the blessings she enjoyed.' This was Mrs. Rockett's phrase, and the rheumatic, wheezy old gardener uttered the same opinion in less conventional language. They had no affection for Sir Edwin or his lady, and Miss Hilda they decidedly disliked; their treatment at the hands of these new people contrasted unpleasantly enough with the memory of old times; but a spirit of loyal subordination ruled their blood, and, to Sir Edwin at all events, they felt gratitude for their retention at the lodge. Mrs. Rockett was a healthy and capable woman of not more than fifty, but no less than her invalid husband would she have dreaded the thought of turning her back on Brent Hall. Rockett had often consoled himself with the thought that here he should die, here amid the fine old trees that he loved, in the ivy-covered house which was his only idea of home. And was it not a reasonable hope that Betsy, good steady girl, should some day marry the promising young gardener whom Sir Edwin had recently taken into his service, and so re-establish the old order of things at the lodge?

'I half wish May wasn't coming,' said Mrs. Rockett after long and anxious thought. 'Last time she was here she quite upset me with her strange talk.'

'She's a funny girl, and that's the truth,' muttered Rockett from his old leather chair, full in the sunshine of the kitchen window. They had a nice little sitting-room; but this, of course, was only used on Sunday, and no particular idea of comfort attached to it. May, to be sure, had always used the sitting-room. It was one of the habits which emphasised most strongly the moral distance between her and her parents.

The subject being full of perplexity, they put it aside, and with very mixed feelings awaited their elder daughter's arrival. Two days later a cab deposited at the lodge Miss May, and her dress-basket, and her travelling-bag, and her holdall, together with certain loose periodicals and a volume or two bearing the yellow label of Mudie. The young lady was well dressed in a severely practical way; nothing unduly feminine marked her appearance, and in the matter of collar and necktie she inclined to the example of the other sex; for all that, her soft complexion and bright eyes, her well-turned figure and light, quick movements, had a picturesque value which Miss May certainly did not ignore. She manifested no excess of feeling when her mother and sister came forth to welcome her; a nod, a smile, an offer of her cheek, and the pleasant exclamation, 'Well, good people!' carried her through this little scene with becoming dignity.

'You will bring these things inside, please,' she said to the driver, in her agreeable head-voice, with the tone and gesture of one who habitually gives orders.

Her father, bent with rheumatism, stood awaiting her just within. She grasped his hand cordially, and cried on a cheery note, 'Well, father, how are you getting on? No worse than usual, I hope?' Then she added, regarding him with her head slightly aside, 'We must have a talk about your case. I've been going in a little for medicine lately. No doubt your country medico is a duffer. Sit down, sit down, and make yourself comfortable. I don't want to disturb any one. About teatime, isn't it, mother? Tea very weak for me, please, and a slice of lemon with it, if you have such a thing, and just a mouthful of dry toast.'

So unwilling was May to disturb the habits of the family that, half an hour after her arrival, the homely three had fallen into a state of nervous agitation, and could neither say nor do anything natural to them. Of a sudden there sounded a sharp rapping at the window. Mrs. Rockett and Betsy started up, and Betsy ran to the door. In a moment or two she came back with glowing cheeks.

'I'm sure I never heard the bell!' she exclaimed with compunction. 'Miss Shale had to get off her bicycle!'

'Was it she who hammered at the window?' asked May coldly.

'Yes—and she was that annoyed.'

'It will do her good. A little anger now and then is excellent for the health.' And Miss Rockett sipped her lemon-tinctured tea with a smile of ineffable contempt.

The others went to bed at ten o'clock, but May, having made herself at ease in the sitting-room, sat there reading until after twelve. Nevertheless, she was up very early next morning, and, before going out for a sharp little walk (in a heavy shower), she gave precise directions about her breakfast. She wanted only the simplest things, prepared in the simplest way, but the tone of her instructions vexed and perturbed Mrs. Rockett sorely. After breakfast the young lady made a searching inquiry into the state of her father's health, and diagnosed his ailments in such learned words that the old gardener began to feel worse than he had done for many a year. May then occupied herself with correspondence, and before midday sent her sister out to post nine letters.

'But I thought you were going to rest yourself?' said her mother, in an irritable voice quite unusual with her.

'Why, so I am resting!' May exclaimed. 'If you saw my ordinary morning's work! I suppose you have a London newspaper? No? How *do* you live without it? I must run into the town for one this afternoon.'

The town was three miles away, but could be reached by train from the village station. On reflection, Miss Rockett announced that she would use this opportunity for calling on a lady whose acquaintance she desired to make, one Mrs. Lindley, who in social position stood on an equality with the family at the Hall, and was often seen there. On her mother's expressing surprise, May smiled indulgently.

'Why shouldn't I know Mrs. Lindley? I have heard she's interested in a movement which occupies me a good deal just now. I know she will be delighted to see me. I can give her a good deal of first-hand information, for which she will be grateful. You *do* amuse me, mother,' she added in her blandest tone. 'When will you come to understand what my position is?'

The Rocketts had put aside all thoughts of what they esteemed May's duty towards the Hall; they earnestly hoped that her stay with them might pass unobserved by Lady and Miss Shale, whom, they felt sure, it would be positively dangerous for the girl to meet. Mrs. Rockett had not slept for anxiety on this score. The father was also a good deal troubled; but his wonder at May's bearing and talk had, on the whole, an agreeable preponderance over the uneasy feeling. He and Betsy shared a secret admiration for the brilliant qualities which were flashed before their eyes; they privately agreed that May was more of a real lady than either the baronet's hard-tongued wife or the disdainful Hilda Shale.

So Miss Rockett took the early afternoon train, and found her way to Mrs. Lindley's, where she sent in her card. At once admitted to the drawing-room, she gave a rapid account of herself, naming persons whose acquaintance sufficiently recommended her. Mrs. Lindley was a good-humoured, chatty woman, who had a lively interest in everything 'progressive'; a new religion or a new cycling-costume stirred her to just the same kind of happy excitement; she had no prejudices, but a decided preference for the society of healthy, high-spirited, well-to-do people. Miss Rockett's talk was exactly what she liked, for it glanced at innumerable topics of the 'advanced' sort, was much concerned with personalities, and avoided all tiresome precision of argument.

'Are you making a stay here?' asked the hostess.

'Oh! I am with my people in the country—not far off,' May answered in an offhand way. 'Only for a day or two.'

Other callers were admitted, but Miss Rockett kept the lead in talk; she glowed with self-satisfaction, feeling that she was really showing to great advantage, and that everybody admired her. When the door again opened the name announced was 'Miss Shale.' Stopping in the middle of a swift sentence, May looked at the newcomer, and saw that it was indeed Hilda Shale, of Brent Hall; but this did not disconcert her. Without lowering her voice she finished what she was saying, and ended in a mirthful key. The baronet's daughter had come into town on her bicycle, as was declared by the short skirt, easy jacket, and brown shoes, which well displayed her athletic person. She was a tall, strongly built girl of six-and-twenty, with a face of hard comeliness and magnificent tawny hair. All her movements suggested vigour; she shook hands with a downward jerk, moved about the room with something of a stride and, in sitting down, crossed her legs abruptly.

From the first her look had turned with surprise to Miss Rockett. When, after a minute or two, the hostess presented that young lady to her, Miss Shale raised her eyebrows a little, smiled in another direction, and gave a just perceptible nod. May's behaviour was as nearly as possible the same.

'Do you cycle, Miss Rockett?' asked Mrs. Lindley.

'No, I don't. The fact is, I have never found time to learn.'

A lady remarked that nowadays there was a certain distinction in not cycling; whereupon Miss Shale's abrupt and rather metallic voice sounded what was meant for gentle irony.

'It's a pity the machines can't be sold cheaper. A great many people who would like to cycle don't feel able to afford it, you know. One often hears of such cases out in the country, and it seems awfully hard lines, doesn't it?'

Miss Rockett felt a warmth ascending to her ears, and made a violent effort to look unconcerned. She wished to say something, but could not find the right words, and did not feel altogether sure of her voice. The hostess, who made no personal application of Miss Shale's remark, began to discuss the prices of bicycles, and others chimed in. May fretted under this turn of the conversation. Seeing that it was not likely to revert to subjects in which she could shine, she rose and offered to take leave.

'Must you really go?' fell with conventional regret from the hostess's lips.

'I'm afraid I must,' Miss Rockett replied, bracing herself under the converging eyes and feeling not quite equal to the occasion. 'My time is so short, and there are so many people I wish to see.'

As she left the house, anger burned in her. It was certain that Hilda Shale would make known her circumstances. She had fancied this revelation a matter of indifference; but, after all, the thought stung her intolerably. The insolence of the creature, with her hint about the prohibitive cost of bicycles! All the harder to bear because hitting the truth. May would have long ago bought a bicycle had she been able to afford it. Straying about the main streets of the town, she looked flushed and wrathful, and could think of nothing but her humiliation.

To make things worse, she lost count of time, and presently found that she had missed the only train by which she could return home. A cab would be too much of an expense; she had no choice but to walk the three or four miles. The evening was close; walking rapidly, and with the accompaniment of vexatious thoughts, she reached the gates of the Hall tired perspiring, irritated. Just as her hand was on the gate a bicycle-bell trilled vigorously behind her, and, from a distance of twenty yards, a voice cried imperatively—

'Open the gate, please!'

Miss Rockett looked round, and saw Hilda Shale slowly wheeling forward, in expectation that way would be made for her. Deliberately May passed through the side entrance, and let the little gate fall to.

Miss Shale dismounted, admitted herself, and spoke to May (now at the lodge door) with angry emphasis.

'Didn't you hear me ask you to open?'

'I couldn't imagine you were speaking to *me*,' answered Miss Rockett, with brisk dignity. 'I supposed some servant of yours was in sight.'

A peculiar smile distorted Miss Shale's full red lips. Without another word she mounted her machine and rode away up the elm avenue.

Now Mrs. Rockett had seen this encounter, and heard the words exchanged: she was lost in consternation.

'What *do* you mean by behaving like that, May? Why, I was running out myself to open, and then I saw you were there, and, of course, I thought you'd do it. There's the second time in two days Miss Shale has had to complain about us. How *could* you forget yourself, to behave and speak like that! Why, you must be crazy, my girl!'

'I don't seem to get on very well here, mother,' was May's reply. 'The fact is, I'm in a false position. I shall go to-morrow morning, and there won't be any more trouble.'

Thus spoke Miss Rockett, as one who shakes off a petty annoyance—she knew not that the serious trouble was just beginning. A few minutes later Mrs. Rockett went up to the Hall, bent on humbly apologising for her daughter's impertinence. After being kept waiting for a quarter of an hour she was admitted to the presence of the housekeeper, who had a rather grave announcement to make.

'Mrs. Rockett, I'm sorry to tell you that you will have to leave the lodge. My lady allows you two months, though, as your wages have always been paid monthly, only a month's notice is really called for. I believe some allowance will be made you, but you will hear about that. The lodge must be ready for its new occupants on the last day of October.'

The poor woman all but sank. She had no voice for protest or entreaty—a sob choked her; and blindly she made her way to the door of the room, then to the exit from the Hall.

'What in the world is the matter?' cried May, hearing from the sitting-room, whither she had retired, a clamour of distressful tongues.

She came into the kitchen, and learnt what had happened.

'And now I hope you're satisfied!' exclaimed her mother, with tearful wrath. 'You've got us turned out of our home—you've lost us the best place a family ever had—and I hope it's a satisfaction to your conceited, overbearing mind! If you'd *tried* for it you couldn't have gone to work better. And much *you* care! We're below you, we are; we're like dirt under your feet! And your father'll go and end his life who knows where miserable as miserable can be; and your sister'll have to go into service; and as for me—'

'Listen, mother!' shouted the girl, her eyes flashing and every nerve of her body strung. 'If the Shales are such contemptible wretches as to turn you out just because they're offended with *me*, I should have thought you'd have spirit enough to tell them what you think of such behaviour, and be glad never more to serve such brutes! Father, what do *you* say? I'll tell you how it was.'

She narrated the events of the afternoon, amid sobs and ejaculations from her mother and Betsy. Rockett, who was just now in anguish of lumbago, tried to straighten himself in his chair before replying, but sank helplessly together with a groan.

'You can't help yourself, May,' he said at length. 'It's your nature, my girl. Don't worry. I'll see Sir Edwin, and perhaps he'll listen to me. It's the women who make all the mischief. I must try to see Sir Edwin—'

A pang across the loins made him end abruptly, groaning, moaning, muttering. Before the renewed attack of her mother May retreated into the sitting-room, and there passed an hour wretchedly enough. A knock at the door without words called her to supper, but she had no appetite, and would not join the family circle. Presently the door opened, and her father looked in.

'Don't worry, my girl,' he whispered. 'I'll see Sir Edwin in the morning.'

May uttered no reply. Vaguely repenting what she had done, she at the same time rejoiced in the recollection of her passage of arms with Miss Shale, and was inclined to despise her family for their pusillanimous attitude. It seemed to her very improbable that the expulsion would really be carried out. Lady Shale and Hilda meant, no doubt, to give the Rocketts a good fright, and then contemptuously pardon them. She, in any case, would return to London without delay, and make no more trouble. A pity she had come to the lodge at all; it was no place for one of her spirit and her attainments.

In the morning she packed. The train which was to take her back to town left at half-past ten, and after breakfast she walked into the village to order a cab. Her mother would scarcely speak to her; Betsy was continually in reproachful tears. On coming back to the lodge she saw her father hobbling down the avenue, and walked towards him to ask the result of his supplication. Rockett had seen Sir Edwin, but only to hear his sentence of exile confirmed. The baronet said he was sorry, but could not interfere; the matter lay in Lady Shale's hands, and Lady Shale absolutely refused to hear any excuses or apologies for the insult which had been offered her daughter.

'It's all up with us,' said the old gardener, who was pale and trembling after his great effort. 'We must go. But don't worry, my girl, don't worry.'

Then fright took hold upon May Rockett. She felt for the first time what she had done. Her heart fluttered in an anguish of self-reproach, and her eyes strayed as if seeking help. A minute's hesitation, then, with all the speed she could make, she set off up the avenue towards the Hall.

Presenting herself at the servants' entrance, she begged to be allowed to see the housekeeper. Of course her story was known to all the domestics, half a dozen of whom quickly collected to stare at her, with more or less malicious smiles. It was a bitter moment for Miss Rockett, but she subdued herself, and at length obtained the interview she sought. With a cold air of superiority and of disapproval the housekeeper listened to her quick, broken sentences. Would it be possible, May asked, for her to see Lady Shale? She desired to—to apologise for—for rudeness of which she had been guilty, rudeness in which her family had no part, which they utterly deplored, but for which they were to suffer severely.

'If you could help me, ma'am, I should be very grateful—indeed I should—'

Her voice all but broke into a sob. That 'ma'am' cost her a terrible effort; the sound of it seemed to smack her on the ears.

'If you will go in-to the servants' hall and wait,' the housekeeper deigned to say, after reflecting, 'I'll see what can be done.'

And Miss Rockett submitted. In the servants' hall she sat for a long, long time, observed, but never addressed. The hour of her train went by. More than once she was on the point of rising and fleeing; more than once her smouldering wrath all but broke into flame. But she thought of her father's pale, pain-stricken face, and sat on.

At something past eleven o'clock a footman approached her, and said curtly,

'You are to go up to my lady; follow me.' May followed, shaking with weakness and apprehension, burning at the same time with pride all but in revolt. Conscious of nothing on the way, she found herself in a large room, where sat the two ladies, who for some moments spoke together about a topic of the day placidly. Then the elder seemed to become aware of the girl who stood before her.

'You are Rockett's elder daughter?'

Oh, the metallic voice of Lady Shale! How gratified she would have been could she have known how it bruised the girl's pride!

'Yes, my lady—'

'And why do you want to see me?'

'I wish to apologise—most sincerely—to your ladyship—for my behaviour of last evening—'

'Oh, indeed!' the listener interrupted contemptuously. 'I am glad you have come to your senses. But your apology must be offered to Miss Shale—if my daughter cares to listen to it.'

May had foreseen this. It was the bitterest moment of her ordeal. Flushing scarlet, she turned towards the younger woman.

'Miss Shale, I beg your pardon for what I said yesterday—I beg you to forgive my rudeness—my impertinence—'

Her voice would go no further; there came a choking sound. Miss Shale allowed her eyes to rest triumphantly for an instant on the troubled face and figure, then remarked to her mother—

'It's really nothing to me, as I told you. I suppose this person may leave the room now?'

It was fated that May Rockett should go through with her purpose and gain her end. But fate alone (which meant in this case the subtlest preponderance of one impulse over another) checked her on the point of a burst of passion which would have startled Lady Shale and Miss Hilda out of their cold-blooded complacency. In the silence May's blood gurgled at her ears, and she tottered with dizziness.

'You may go,' said Lady Shale.

But May could not move. There flashed across her the terrible thought that perhaps she had humiliated herself for nothing.

'My lady—I hope—will your ladyship please to forgive my father and mother? I entreat you not to send them away. We shall all be so grateful to your ladyship if you will overlook—'

'That will do,' said Lady Shale decisively. 'I will merely say that the sooner you leave the lodge the better; and that you will do well never again to pass the gates of the Hall. You may go.'

Miss Rockett withdrew. Outside, the footman was awaiting her. He looked at her with a grin, and asked in an undertone, 'Any good?' But May, to whom this was the last blow, rushed past him, lost herself in corridors, ran wildly hither and thither, tears streaming from her eyes, and was at length guided by a maidservant into the outer air. Fleeing she cared not whither, she came at length into a still corner of the park, and there, hidden amid trees, watched only by birds and rabbits, she wept out the bitterness of her soul.

By an evening train she returned to London, not having confessed to her family what she had done, and suffering still from some uncertainty as to the result. A day or two later Betsy wrote to her the happy news that the sentence of expulsion was withdrawn, and peace reigned once more in the ivy-covered lodge. By that time Miss Rockett had all but recovered her self-respect, and was so busy in her secretaryship that she could only scribble a line of congratulation. She felt that she had done rather a meritorious thing, but, for the first time in her life, did not care to boast of it.

THE RIDING-WHIP

IT was not easy for Mr. Daffy to leave his shop for the whole day, but an urgent affair called him to London, and he breakfasted early in order to catch the 8.30 train. On account of his asthma he had to allow himself plenty of time for the walk to the station; and all would have been well, but that, just as he was polishing his silk hat and giving final directions to his assistant, in stepped a customer, who came to grumble about the fit of a new coat. Ten good minutes were thus consumed, and with a painful glance at his watch the breathless tailor at length started. The walk was uphill; the sun was already powerful; Mr. Daffy reached the station with dripping forehead and panting as if his sides would burst. There stood the train; he had barely time to take his ticket and to rush across the platform. As a porter slammed the carriage-door behind him, he sank upon the seat in a lamentable condition, gasping, coughing, writhing; his eyes all but started from his head, and his respectable top-hat tumbled to the floor, where unconsciously he gave it a kick. A grotesque and distressing sight.

Only one person beheld it, and this, as it happened, a friend of Mr. Daffy's. In the far corner sat a large, ruddy-cheeked man, whose eye rested upon the sufferer with a look of greeting disturbed by compassion. Mr. Lott, a timber-merchant of this town, was in every sense of the word a more flourishing man than the asthmatic tailor; his six-feet-something of sound flesh and muscle, his ripe sunburnt complexion, his attitude of eupeptic and broad-chested ease, left the other, by contrast, scarce his proverbial fraction of manhood. At a year or two short of fifty, Mr. Daffy began to be old; he was shoulder-bent, knee-shaky, and had a pallid, wrinkled visage, with watery, pathetic eye. At fifty turned, Mr. Lott showed a vigour and a toughness such as few men of any age could rival. For a score of years the measure of Mr. Lott's robust person had been taken by Mr. Daffy's professional tape, and, without intimacy, there existed kindly relations between the two men. Neither had ever been in the other's house, but they had long met, once a week or so, at the Liberal Club, where it was their habit to play together a game of draughts. Occasionally they conversed; but it was a rather one-sided dialogue, for whereas the tailor had a sprightly intelligence and—so far as his breath allowed—a ready flow of words, the timber-merchant found himself at a disadvantage when mental activity was called for. The best-natured man in the world, Mr. Lott would sit smiling and content so long as he had only to listen; asked his opinion (on anything but timber), he betrayed by a knitting of the brows, a rolling of the eyes, an inflation of the cheeks, and other signs of discomposure, the serious effort it cost him to shape a thought and to utter it. At times Mr. Daffy got on to the subject of social and political reform, and, after copious exposition, would ask what Mr. Lott thought. He knew the timber-merchant too well to expect an immediate reply. There came a long pause, during which Mr. Lott snorted a little, shuffled in his chair, and stared at vacancy, until at length, with a sudden smile of relief he exclaimed, 'Do you know *my* idea!' And the idea, often rather explosively stated, was generally marked by common-sense of the bull-headed, British kind.

'Bad this morning,' remarked Mr. Lott, abruptly but sympathetically, as soon as the writhing tailor could hear him.

'Rather bad—ugh, ugh!—had to run—ugh!—doesn't suit me, Mr. Lott,' gasped the other, as he took the silk hat which his friend had picked up and stroked for him.

'Hot weather trying.'

'I vary so,' panted Mr. Daffy, wiping his face with a handkerchief. 'Sometimes one things seems to suit me—ugh, ugh—sometimes another. Going to town, Mr. Lott?'

'Yes.'

The blunt affirmative was accompanied by a singular grimace, such as might have been caused by the swallowing of something very unpleasant; and thereupon followed a silence which allowed Mr. Daffy to recover himself. He sat with his eyes half closed and head bent, leaning back.

They had a general acquaintance with each other's domestic affairs. Both were widowers; both lived alone. Mr. Daffy's son was married, and dwelt in London; the same formula applied to Mr. Lott's daughter. And, as it happened, the marriages had both been a subject of parental dissatisfaction. Very rarely had Mr. Lott let fall a word with regard to his daughter, Mrs. Bowles, but the townsfolk were well aware that he thought his son-in-law a fool, if not worse; Mrs. Bowles, in the seven years since her wedding, had only two or three times revisited her father's house, and her husband never came. A like reticence was maintained by Mr. Daffy concerning his son Charles Edward, once the hope of his life. At school the lad had promised well; tailoring could not be thought of for him; he went into a solicitor's office, and remained there just long enough to assure himself that he had no turn for the law. From that day he was nothing but an expense and an anxiety to his father, until—now a couple of years ago—he announced his establishment in a prosperous business in London, of which Mr. Daffy knew nothing more than that it was connected with colonial enterprise. Since that date Charles Edward had made no report of himself, and his father had ceased to write letters which received no reply.

Presently, Mr. Lott moved so as to come nearer to his travelling companion, and said in a muttering, shamefaced way—

'Have you heard any talk about my daughter lately?'

Mr. Daffy showed embarrassment.

'Well, Mr. Lott, I'm sorry to say I *have* heard something—'

'Who from?'

'Well—it was a friend of mine—perhaps I won't mention the name—who came and told me something—something that quite upset me. That's what I'm going to town about, Mr. Lott. I'm—well, the fact is, I was going to call upon Mr. Bowles.'

'Oh, you were!' exclaimed the timber-merchant, with gruffness, which referred not to his friend but to his son-in-law. 'I don't particularly want to see *him*, but I had thought of seeing my daughter. You wouldn't mind saying whether it was John Roper—?'

'Yes, it was.'

'Then we've both heard the same story, no doubt.'

Mr. Lott leaned back and stared out of the window. He kept thrusting out his lips and drawing them in again, at the same time wrinkling his forehead into the frown which signified that he was trying to shape a thought.

'Mr. Lott,' resumed the tailor, with a gravely troubled look, 'may I ask if John Roper made any mention of my son?'

The timber-merchant glared, and Mr. Daffy, interpreting the look as one of anger, trembled under it.

'I feel ashamed and miserable!' burst from his lips.

'It's not your fault, Mr. Daffy,' interrupted the other in a good-natured growl. 'You're not responsible, no more than for any stranger.'

'That's just what I can't feel,' exclaimed the tailor, nervously slapping his knee. 'Anyway, it would be a disgrace to a man to have a son a bookmaker—a blackguard bookmaker. That's bad enough. But when it comes to robbing and ruining the friends of your own family—why, I never heard a more disgraceful thing in my life. How I'm going to stand in my shop, and hold up my head before my customers, I—do—not—know. Of course, it'll be the talk of the town; we know what the Ropers are when they get hold of anything. It'll drive me off my head, Mr. Lott, I'm sure it will.'

The timber-merchant stretched out a great hand, and laid it gently on the excited man's shoulder.

'Don't worry; that never did any good yet. We've got to find out, first of all, how much of Roper's story is true. What did he tell you?'

'He said that Mr. Bowles had been going down the hill for a year or more—that his business was neglected, that he spent his time at racecourses and in public-houses—and that the cause of it all was my son. *My son?* What had my son to do with it? Why, didn't I know that Charles was a racing and betting man, and a notorious bookmaker? You can imagine what sort of a feeling that gave me. Roper couldn't believe it was the first I had heard of it; he said lots of people in the town knew how Charles was living. Did *you* know, Mr. Lott?'

'Not I; I'm not much in the way of gossip.'

'Well, there's what Roper said. It was last night, and what with that and my cough, I didn't get a wink of sleep after it. About three o'clock this morning I made up my mind to go to London at once and see Mr. Bowles. If it's true that he's been robbed and ruined by Charles, I've only one thing to do—my duty's plain enough. I shall ask him how much money Charles has had of him, and, if my means are equal to it, I shall pay every penny back—every penny.'

Mr. Lott's countenance waxed so grim that one would have thought him about to break into wrath against the speaker. But it was merely his way of disguising a pleasant emotion.

'I don't think most men would see it in that way,' he remarked gruffly.

'Whether they would or not,' exclaimed Mr. Daffy, panting and wriggling, 'it's as plain as plain could be that there's no other course for a man who respects himself. I couldn't live a day with such a burden as that on my mind. A bookmaker! A blackguard bookmaker! To think my son should come to that! *You* know very well, Mr. Lott, that there's nothing I hate and despise more than horse-racing. We've often talked about it, and the harm it does, and the sin and shame it is that such doings should be permitted—haven't we?'

'Course we have, course we have,' returned the other, with a nod. But he was absorbed in his own reflections, and gave only half an ear to the gasping vehemences which Mr. Daffy poured forth for the next ten minutes. There followed a short silence, then the strong man shook himself and opened his lips.

'Do you know *my* idea?' he blurted out.

'What's that, Mr. Lott?'

'If I were you I wouldn't go to see Bowles. Better for me to do that. We've only gossip to go upon, and we know what that often amounts to. Leave Bowles to me, and go and see your son.'

'But I don't even know where he's living.'

'You don't? That's awkward. Well then, come along with me to Bowles's place of business; as likely as not, if we find him, he'll be able to give you your son's address. What do you say to my idea, Mr. Daffy?'

The tailor assented to this arrangement, on condition that, if things were found to be as he had heard, he should be left free to obey his conscience. The stopping of the train at an intermediate station, where new passengers entered, put an end to the confidential talk. Mr. Daffy, breathing hard, struggled with his painful thoughts; the timber-merchant, deeply meditative, let his eyes wander about the carriage. As they drew near to the London terminus, Mr. Lott bent forward to his friend.

'I want to buy a present for my eldest nephew,' he remarked, 'but I can't for the life of me think what it had better be.'

'Perhaps you'll see something in a shop-window,' suggested Mr. Daffy.

'Maybe I shall.'

They alighted at Liverpool Street. Mr. Lott hailed a hansom, and they were driven to a street in Southwark, where, at the entrance of a building divided into offices, one perceived the name of Bowles and Perkins. This firm was on the fifth floor, and Mr. Daffy eyed the staircase with misgiving.

'No need for you to go up,' said his companion. 'Wait here, and I'll see if I can get the address.'

Mr. Lott was absent for only a few minutes. He came down again with his lips hard set, knocking each step sharply with his walking-stick.

'I've got it,' he said, and named a southern suburb.

'Have you seen Mr. Bowles?'

'No; he's out of town,' was the reply. 'Saw his partner.'

They walked side by side for a short way, then Mr. Lott stopped.

'Do you know *my* idea? It's a little after eleven. I'm going to see my daughter, and I dare say I shall catch the 3.49 home from Liverpool Street. Suppose we take our chance of meeting there?'

Thus it was agreed. Mr. Daffy turned in the direction of his son's abode; the timber-merchant went northward, and presently reached Finsbury Park, where in a house of unpretentious but decent appearance, dwelt Mr. Bowles. The servant who answered the door wore a strange look, as if something had alarmed her; she professed not to know whether any one was at home, and, on going to inquire, shut the door on the visitor's face. A few minutes elapsed before Mr. Lott was admitted. The hall struck him as rather bare; and at the entrance of the drawing-room he stopped in astonishment, for, excepting the window-curtains and a few ornaments, the room was quite unfurnished. At the far end stood a young woman, her hands behind her, and her head bent—an attitude indicative of distress or shame.

'Are you moving, Jane?' inquired Mr. Lott, eyeing her curiously.

His daughter looked at him. She had a comely face, with no little of the paternal character stamped upon it; her knitted brows and sullen eyes bespoke a perturbed humour, and her voice was only just audible.

'Yes, we are moving, father.'

Mr. Lott's heavy footfall crossed the floor. He planted himself before her, his hands resting on his stick.

'What's the matter, Jane? Where's Bowles?'

'He left town yesterday. He'll be back to-morrow, I think.'

'You've had the brokers in the house—isn't that it, eh?'

Mrs. Bowles made no answer, but her head sank again, and a trembling of her shoulders betrayed the emotion with which she strove. Knowing that Jane would tell of her misfortunes only when and how she chose, the father turned away and stood for a minute or two at the window; then he asked abruptly whether there was not such a thing as a chair in the house. Mrs. Bowles, who had been on the point of speaking, bade him come to another room. It was the dining-room, but all the appropriate furniture had vanished: a couple of bedroom chairs and a deal table served for present necessities. Here, when they had both sat down, Mrs. Bowles found courage to break the silence.

'Arthur doesn't know of it. He went away yesterday morning, and the men came in the afternoon. He had a promise—a distinct promise—that this shouldn't be done before the end of the month. By then he hoped to have money.'

'Who's the creditor?' inquired Mr. Lott, with a searching look at her face.

Mrs. Bowles was mute, her eyes cast down.

'Is it Charles Daffy?'

Still his daughter kept silence.

'I thought so,' said the timber-merchant, and clumped on the floor with his stick. 'You'd better tell me all about it, Jane. I know something already. Better let us talk it over, my girl, and see what can be done.'

He waited a moment. Then his daughter tried to speak, with difficulty overcame a sob, and at length began her story. She would not blame her husband. He had been unlucky in speculations, and was driven to a money-lender—his acquaintance, Charles Daffy. This man, a heartless rascal, had multiplied charges and interest on a small sum originally borrowed, until it became a crushing debt. He held a bill of sale on most of their furniture, and yesterday, as if he knew of Bowles's absence, had made the seizure; he was within his legal rights, but had led the debtor to suppose that he would not exercise them. Thus far did Jane relate, in a hard matter-of-fact voice, but with many nervous movements. Her father listened in grim silence, and, when she ceased, appeared to reflect.

'That's *your* story!' he said of a sudden. 'Now, what about the horse-racing?'

'I know nothing of horse-racing,' was the cold reply.

'Bowles keeps all that to himself, does he? We'd better have our talk out, Jane, now that we've begun. Better tell me all you know, my girl.'

Again there was a long pause; but Mr. Lott had patience, and his dogged persistency at length overcame the wife's pride. Yes, it was true that Bowles had lost money at races; he had been guilty of much selfish folly; but the ruin it had brought upon him would serve as a lesson. He was a wretched and a penitent man; a few days ago he had confessed everything to his wife, and besought her to pardon him; at present he was making desperate efforts to recover an honest footing. The business might still be carried on if some one could be induced to put a little capital into it; with that in view, Bowles had gone to see certain relatives of his in the north. If his hope failed, she did not know what was before them; they had nothing left now but their clothing and the furniture of one or two rooms.

'Would you like to come back home for a while?' asked Mr. Lott abruptly.

'No, father,' was the not less abrupt reply. 'I couldn't do that.'

'I'll give no money to Bowles.'

'He has never asked you, and never will.'

Mr. Lott glared and glowered, but, with all that, had something in his face which hinted softness. The dialogue did not continue much longer; it ended with a promise from Mrs. Bowles to let her father know whether her husband succeeded or not in re-establishing himself. Thereupon they shook hands without a word, and Mr. Lott left the house. He returned to the City, and, it being now nearly two o'clock, made a hearty meal. When he was in the street again, he remembered the birthday present he wished to buy for his nephew, and for half an hour he rambled vaguely, staring into shop-windows. At length something caught his eye; it was a row of riding-whips, mounted in silver; just the thing, he said to himself, to please a lad who would perhaps ride to hounds next winter. He stepped in, chose carefully, and made the purchase. Then, having nothing left to do, he walked at a leisurely pace towards the railway station.

Mr. Daffy was there before him; they met at the entrance to the platform from which their train would start.

'Must you go back by this?' asked the tailor. 'My son wasn't at home, and won't be till about five o'clock. I should be terribly obliged, Mr. Lott, if you could stay and go to Clapham with me. Is it asking too much?'

The timber-merchant gave a friendly nod, and said it was all the same to him. Then, in reply to anxious questions, he made brief report of what he had learnt at Finsbury Park. Mr. Daffy was beside himself with wrath and shame. He would pay every farthing, if he had to sell all he possessed!

'I'm so glad and so thankful you will come with me Mr. Lott. He'd care nothing for what *I* said; but when he sees *you*, and hears your opinion of him, it may have some effect. I beg you to tell him your mind plainly! Let him know what a contemptible wretch, what a dirty blackguard, he is in the eyes of all decent folk—let him know it, I entreat you! Perhaps even yet it isn't too late to make him ashamed of himself.'

They stood amid a rush of people; the panting tailor clung to his big companion's sleeve. Gruffly promising to do what he could, Mr. Lott led the way into the street again, where they planned the rest of their day. By five o'clock they were at Clapham. Charles Daffy occupied the kind of house which is known as eminently respectable; it suggested an income of at least a couple of thousand a year. As they waited for the door to open, Mr. Lott smote gently on his leg with the new riding-whip. He had been silent and meditative all the way hither.

A smart maidservant conducted them to the dining-room, and there, in a minute or two, they were joined by Mr. Charles. No one could have surmised from this gentleman's appearance that he was the son of the little tradesman who stood before him; nature had given the younger Mr. Daffy a tall and shapely person, and experience of life had refined his manners to an easy assurance he would never have learnt from paternal example. His smooth-shaven visage, so long as it remained grave, might have been that of an acute and energetic lawyer; his smile, however, disturbed this impression, for it had a twinkling insolence, a raffish facetiousness, incompatible with any sober quality. He wore the morning dress of a City man, with collar and necktie of the latest fashion; his watchguard was rather demonstrative, and he had two very solid rings on his left hand.

'Ah, dad, how do you do!' he exclaimed, on entering, in an affected head-voice. 'Why, what's the matter?'

Mr. Daffy had drawn back, refusing the offered hand. With an unpleasant smile Charles turned to his other visitor.

'Mr. Lott, isn't it! You're looking well, Mr. Lott; but I suppose you didn't come here just to give me the pleasure of seeing you. I'm rather a busy man; perhaps one or the other of you will be good enough to break this solemn silence, and let me know what your game is.'

He spoke with careless impertinence, and let himself drop on to a chair. The others remained standing, and Mr. Daffy broke into vehement speech.

'I have come here, Charles, to ask what you mean by disgracing yourself and dishonouring my name. Only yesterday, for the first time, I heard of the life you are leading. Is this how you repay me for all the trouble I took to have you well educated, and to make you an honest man? Here I find you living in luxury and extravagance—and how? On stolen money—money as much stolen as if you were a pickpocket or a burglar! A pleasant thing for me to have all my friends talking about Charles Daffy, the bookmaker and the moneylender! What *right* have you to dishonour your father in this way? I ask, what *right* have you,

Charles?'

Here the speaker, who had struggled to gasp his last sentence, was overcome with a violent fit of coughing. He tottered back and sank on to a sofa.

'Are you here to look after him?' asked Charles of Mr. Lott, crossing his legs and nodding towards the sufferer. 'If so, I advise you to take him away before he does himself harm. You're a *lot* bigger than he is and perhaps have more sense.'

The timber-merchant stood with legs slightly apart, holding his stick and the riding-whip horizontally with both hands. His eyes were fixed upon young Mr. Daffy, and his lips moved in rather an ominous way; but he made no reply to Charles's smiling remark.

'Mr. Lott,' said the tailor, in a voice still broken by pants and coughs, 'will you speak or me? Will you say what you think of him?'

'You'll have to be quick about it,' interposed Charles, with a glance at his watch. 'I can give you five minutes; you can say a *lot* in that time, if you're sound of wind.'

The timber-merchant's eyes were very wide, and his cheeks unusually red. Abruptly he turned to Mr. Daffy.

'Do you know *my* idea?'

But just as he spoke there sounded a knock at the door, and the smart maidservant cried out that a gentleman wished to see her master.

'Who is it?' asked Charles.

The answer came from the visitor himself, who, pushing the servant aside, broke into the room. It was a young man of no very distinguished appearance, thin, red-haired, with a pasty complexion and a scrubby moustache; his clothes were approaching shabbiness, and he had an unwashed look, due in part to hasty travel on this hot day. Streaming with sweat, his features distorted with angry excitement, he shouted as he entered, 'You've got to see me, Daffy; I won't be refused!' In the same moment his glance discovered the two visitors, and he stopped short. 'Mr. Lott, you here? I'm glad of it—I'm awfully glad of it. I couldn't have wished anything better. I don't know who this other gentleman is, but it doesn't matter. I'm glad to have witnesses—I'm infernally glad! Mr. Lott, you've been to my house this morning; you know what's happened there. I had to go out of town yesterday, and this Daffy, this cursed liar and swindler, used the opportunity to sell up my furniture. He'll tell you he had a legal right. But he gave me his word not to do anything till the end of the month. And, in any case, I don't really owe him half the sum he has down against me. I've paid that black-hearted scoundrel hundreds of pounds—honourably paid him—debts of honour, and now he has the face to charge me sixty per cent, on money I was fool enough to borrow from him! Sixty per cent.—what do you think of that, Mr. Lott? What do *you* think of it, sir?'

'I'm sorry to say it doesn't at all surprise me,' answered Mr. Daffy, who perceived that the speaker was Mr. Lott's son-in-law. 'But I can't sympathise with you very much. If you have dealings with a book-maker—'

'A blackleg, a blackleg!' shouted Bowles. 'Bookmakers are respectable men in comparison with him. He's bled me, the brute! He tempted me on and on—

Look here, Mr. Lott, I know as well as you do that I've been an infernal fool. I've had my eyes opened—now that it's too late. I hear my wife told you that, and I'm glad she did. I've been a fool, yes; but I fell into the hands of the greatest scoundrel unhung, and he's ruined me. You heard from Jane what I was gone about. It's no good. I came back by the first train this morning without a mouthful of breakfast. It's all up with me; I'm a cursed beggar—and that thief is the cause of it. And he comes into my house no better than a burglar—and lays his hands on everything that'll bring money. Where's the account of that sale, you liar? I'll go to a magistrate about this.'

Charles Daffy sat in a reposeful attitude. The scene amused him; he chuckled inwardly from time to time. But of a sudden his aspect changed; he started up, and spoke with a snarling emphasis.

'I've had just about enough. Look here, clear out, all of you! There's the door—go!'

Mr. Daffy moved towards him.

'Is that how you speak to your father, Charles?' he exclaimed indignantly.

'Yes, it is. Take your hook with the others; I'm sick of your tommy-rot!'

'Then listen to me before I go,' cried Mr. Daffy, his short and awkward figure straining in every muscle for the dignity of righteous wrath. 'I don't know whether you are more a fool or a knave. Perhaps you really think that there's as much to be said for your way of earning a living as for any other. I hope you do, for it's a cruel thing to suppose that my son has turned out a shameless scoundrel. Let me tell you, then, this business of yours is one that moves every honest and sensible man to anger and disgust. It matters nothing whether you keep the rules of the blackguard game, or whether you cheat; the difference between bookmaker and blackleg is so small that it isn't worth talking about. You live by the plunder of people who are foolish and vicious enough to fall into your clutches. You're an enemy of society—that's the plain truth of it; as much an enemy of society as the forger or the burglar. You live—and live in luxury—by the worst vice of our time, the vice which is rotting English life, the vice which will be our national ruin if it goes on much longer. When you were a boy, you've heard me many a time say all I thought about racing and betting; you've heard me speak with scorn of the high-placed people who set so vile an example to the classes below them. If I could have foreseen that *you* would sink to such disgrace!'

Charles was standing in an attitude of contemptuous patience. He looked at his watch and interjected a remark.

'I can only allow your eloquence one minute and a half more.'

'That will be enough,' replied his father sternly. 'The only thing I have to add is, that all the money you have stolen from Mr. Bowles I, as a simple duty, shall repay. You're no longer a boy. In the eye of the law I am not responsible for you; but for very shame I must make good the wrong you have done in this case. I couldn't stand in my shop day by day, and know that every one was saying, "There's the man whose son ruined Mr. Lott's son-in-law and sold up his home," unless I had done all I could to repair the mischief. I shall ask Mr.

Bowles for a full account of what he has lost to you, and if it's in my power, every penny shall be made good. He, thank goodness, seems to have learnt his lesson.'

'That I have, Mr. Daffy; that I have!' cried Bowles.

'There's not much fear that *he*'ll fall into your clutches again. And I hope, I most earnestly hope, that before you can do much more harm, you'll overreach yourself, and the law—stupid as it is—will get hold of you. Remember the father I was, Charles, and think what it means that the best wish I can now form for you is that you may come to public disgrace.'

'Does no one applaud?' asked Charles, looking round the room. 'That's rather unkind, seeing how the speaker has blown himself. Be off, dad, and don't fool any longer. Bowles, take your hook. Mr. Lott—'

Charles met the eye of the timber-merchant, and was unexpectedly mute.

'Well, sir,' said Mr. Lott, regarding him fixedly, 'and what have you to say to *me*?'

'Only that my time is too valuable to be wasted,' continued the other, with an impatient gesture. 'Be good enough to leave my house.'

'Mr. Lott,' said the tailor in an exhausted voice, 'I apologise to you for my son's rudeness. I gave you the trouble of coming here hoping it might shame him, but I'm afraid it's been no good. Let us go.'

Mr. Lott regarded him mildly.

'Mr. Daffy,' he said, 'if *you* don't mind, I should like to have a word in private with your son. Do you and Mr. Bowles go on to the station, and wait for me; perhaps I shall catch you up before you get there.'

'I have told you already, Mr. Lott,' shouted Charles, 'that I can waste no more time on you. I refuse to talk with you at all.'

'And I, Mr. Charles Daffy,' was the resolute answer, 'refuse to leave this room till I have had a word with you.'

'What do you want to say?' asked Charles brutally.

'Just to let you know an idea of mine,' was the reply, 'an idea that's come to me whilst I've stood here listening.'

The tailor and Mr. Bowles moved towards the door. Charles glanced at them fiercely and insolently, then turned his look again upon the man who remained. The other two passed out; the door closed. Mr. Lott, stick and riding-whip still held horizontally, seemed to be lost in meditation.

'Now,' blurted Charles, 'what is it?'

Mr. Lott regarded him steadily, and spoke with his wonted deliberation.

'You heard what your father said about paying that money back?'

'Of course I heard. If he's idiot enough—'

'Do you know *my* idea, young man? You'd better do the honest thing, and repay it yourself.'

Charles stared for a moment, then sputtered a laugh.

'That's *your* idea, is it, Mr. Lott? Well, it isn't mine. So, good morning!'

Again the timber-merchant seemed to meditate; his eyes wandered from Charles to the dining-room table.

'Just a minute more,' he resumed; 'I have another idea—not a new one; an idea that came to me long ago, when your father first began to have trouble about you. I happened to be in the shop one day—it was when you were living idle at your father's expense, young man—and I heard you speak to him in what I call a confoundedly impertinent way. Thinking it over afterwards, I said to myself: If I had a son who spoke to me like that, I'd give him the soundest thrashing he'd be ever likely to get. That was my idea, young man; and as I stood listening to you to-day, it came back into my mind again. Your father can't thrash you; he hasn't the brawn for it. But as it's nothing less than a public duty, somebody *must*, and so—'

Charles, who had been watching every movement of the speaker's face, suddenly sprang forward, making for the door. But Mr. Lott had foreseen this; with astonishing alertness and vigour he intercepted the fugitive seized him by the scruff of the neck, and, after a moment's struggle, pinned him face downwards across the end of the table. His stick he had thrown aside; the riding-whip he held between his teeth. So brief was this conflict that there sounded only a scuffling of feet on the floor, and a growl of fury from Charles as he found himself handled like an infant; then, during some two minutes, one might have thought that a couple of very strenuous carpet-beaters were at work in the room. For the space of a dozen switches Charles strove frantically with wild kicks, which wounded only the air, but all in silence; gripped only the more tightly, he at length uttered a yell of pain, followed by curses hot and swift. Still the carpet-beaters seemed to be at work, and more vigorously than ever. Charles began to roar. As it happened, there were only servants in the house. When the clamour had lasted long enough to be really alarming, knocks sounded at the door, which at length was thrown open, and the startled face of a domestic appeared. At the same moment Mr. Lott, his right arm being weary, brought the castigatory exercise to an end. Charles rolled to his feet, and began to strike out furiously with both fists.

'Just as you like, young man,' said the timber-merchant, as he coolly warded off the blows, 'if you wish to have it this way too. But, I warn you, it isn't a fair match. Sally, shut the door and go about your business.'

'Shall I fetch a p'liceman, sir?' shrilled the servant.

Her master, sufficiently restored to his senses to perceive that he had not the least chance in a pugilistic encounter with Mr. Lott, drew back and seemed to hesitate.

'Answer the girl,' said Mr. Lott, as he picked up his whip and examined its condition. 'Shall we have a policeman in?'

'Shut the door!' Charles shouted fiercely.

The men gazed at each other. Daffy was pale and quivering; his hair in disorder, his waistcoat torn open, collar and necktie twisted into rags, he made a pitiful figure. The timber-merchant was slightly heated, but his countenance wore an expression of calm contentment.

'For the present,' remarked Mr. Lott, as he took up his hat and stick, 'I think our business is at an end. It isn't often that a fellow of your sort gets his deserts, and I'm rather sorry we didn't have the policeman in; a report of the case might do good. I bid you good day, young man. If I were you I'd sit quiet for an hour or two, and just reflect—you've a *lot* to think about.'

So, with a pleasant smile, the visitor took his leave.

As he walked away he again examined the riding-whip. 'It isn't often a thing happens so luckily,' he said to himself. 'First-rate whip; hardly a bit damaged. Harry'll like it none the worse for my having handselled it.'

At the station he found Mr. Daffy and Bowles, who regarded him with questioning looks.

'Nothing to be got out of him,' said Mr. Lott. 'Bowles, I want a talk with you and Jane; it'll be best, perhaps, if I go back home with you. Mr. Daffy, sorry we can't travel down together. You'll catch the eight o'clock.'

'I hope you told him plainly what you thought of him,' said Mr. Daffy, in a voice of indignant shame.

'I did,' answered the timber-merchant, 'and I don't think he's very likely to forget it.'

FATE AND THE APOTHECARY

'FARMILOE. Chemist by Examination.' So did the good man proclaim himself to a suburb of a city in the West of England. It was one of those pretty, clean, fresh-coloured suburbs only to be found in the west; a few dainty little shops, everything about them bright or glistening, scattered among pleasant little houses with gardens eternally green and all but perennially in bloom; every vista ending in foliage, and in one direction a far glimpse of the Cathedral towers, sending forth their music to fall dreamily upon these quiet roads. The neighbourhood seemed to breathe a tranquil prosperity. Red-cheeked emissaries of butcher, baker, and grocer, order-book in hand, knocked cheerily at kitchen doors, and went smiling away; the ponies they drove were well fed and frisky, their carts spick and span. The church of the parish, an imposing edifice, dated only from a few years ago, and had cost its noble founder a sum of money which any church-going parishioner would have named to you with proper awe. The population was largely female, and every shopkeeper who knew his business had become proficient in bowing, smiling, and suave servility.

Mr. Farmiloe, it is to be feared, had no very profound acquaintance with his business from any point of view. True, he was 'chemist by examination,' but it had cost him repeated efforts to reach this unassailable ground and more than one pharmaceutist with whom he abode as assistant had felt it a measure of prudence to dispense with his services. Give him time, and he was generally equal to the demands of suburban customers; hurry or interrupt him, and he showed himself anything but the man for a crisis. Face and demeanour were against him. He had exceedingly plain features, and a persistently sour expression; even his smile suggested sarcasm. He could not tune his voice to the tradesman note, and on the slightest provocation he became, quite unintentionally, offensive. Such a man had no chance whatever in this flowery and bowery little suburb.

Yet he came hither with hopes. One circumstance seemed to him especially favourable: the shop was also a post-office, and no one could fail to see (it was put most impressively by the predecessor who sold him the business) how advantageous was this blending of public service with commercial interest; especially as there was no telegraphic work to make a skilled assistant necessary. As a matter of course, people using the post-office would patronise the chemist; and a provincial chemist can add to his legitimate business sundry pleasant little tradings which benefit himself without provoking the jealousy of neighbour shopmen. 'It will be your own fault, my dear sir, if you do not make a very good thing of it indeed. The sole and sufficient explanation of—of the decline during this last year or two is my shocking health. I really have *not* been able to do justice to the business.'

Necessarily, Mr. Farmiloe entered into negotiation with the postal authorities; and it was with some little disappointment that he learnt how very modest could be his direct remuneration for the responsibilities and labours he undertook. The Post-Office is a very shrewdly managed department of the public service; it has brought to perfection the art of obtaining *maximum* results with a *minimum* expenditure. But Mr. Farmiloe remembered the other aspect of the matter; he would benefit so largely by this ill-paid undertaking that grumbling was foolish. Moreover, the thing carried dignity with it; he served his Majesty, he served the nation. And—ha, ha!—how very odd it would be to post one's letters in one's own post-office. One might really get a good deal of amusement out of the thought, after business hours. His age was eight-and-thirty. For some years he had pondered matrimony, though without fixing his affections on any particular person. It was plain, indeed, that he ought to marry. Every tradesman is made more respectable by wedlock, and a chemist who, in some degree, resembles a medical man, seems especially to stand in need of the matrimonial guarantee. Had it been feasible, Mr. Farmiloe would have brought a wife with him from the town where he had lived for the past few years, but he was in the difficult position of knowing not a single marriageable female to whom he could address himself with hope or with self-respect. Natural shyness had always held him aloof from reputable women; he felt that he could not recommend himself to them—he who had such an unlucky aptitude for saying the wrong word or keeping silence when speech was demanded. With the men of his acquaintance he could relieve his sense of awkwardness and deficiency by becoming aggressive; in fact, he had a reputation for cantankerousness, for pugnacity, which kept most of his equals in some awe of him, and to perceive this was one solace amid many discontents. Nicely dressed and well-spoken and good-looking women above the class of domestic servants he worshipped from afar, and only in vivacious moments pictured himself as the wooer of such a superior being.

It seemed as though fate could do nothing with Mr. Farmiloe. At six-and-thirty he suffered the shock of learning that a relative—an old woman to whom he had occasionally written as a matter of kindness (Farmiloe could do such things)—had left him by will the sum of £600. It was strictly a shock; it upset his health for several days, and not for a week or two could he realise the legacy as a fact. Just when he was beginning to look about him with a new air of confidence, the solicitors who were managing the little affair for him drily acquainted him with the fact that his relative's will was contested by other kinsfolk whom the old woman had passed over, on the ground that she was imbecile and incapable of conducting her affairs. There followed a law-suit, which consumed many months and cost a good deal of money; so that, though he won his case, Mr. Farmiloe lost all satisfaction in his improved circumstances, and was only more embittered against the world at large.

Then, no sooner had he purchased his business, than he learnt from smiling neighbours that he had paid considerably too much for it. His predecessor, beyond a doubt, would have taken very much less; had, indeed, been on the point of doing so just when Mr. Farmiloe appeared. This kind of experience is a trial to any man. It threw Mr. Farmiloe into a silent rage, with the result that two or three customers who chanced to enter his shop declared that they would never have anything more to do with such a surly creature.

And now began his torment—a form of exasperation peculiar to his dual capacity of shopkeeper and manager of a post-office. All day long he stood on the watch for customers—literally stood, now behind the counter, now in front of it, his eager and angry eyes turning to the door whenever the steps of a passer-by sounded without. If the door opened his nerves began to tingle, and he straightened himself like a soldier at attention. For a moment he suffered an agony of doubt. Would the person entering turn to the counter or to the post-office? And seldom was his hope fulfilled; not one in four of the people who came in was a genuine customer; the post-office, always the post-office. A stamp, a card, a newspaper wrapper, a postal-order, a letter to be registered—anything but an honest purchase across the counter or the blessed tendering of a prescription to make up. From vexation he passed to annoyance, to rage, to fury; he cursed the post-office, and committed to eternal perdition the man who had waxed eloquent upon its advantages.

Of course, he had hired an errand-boy, and never had errand-boy so little legitimate occupation. Resolved not to pay him for nothing, Mr. Farmiloe kept him cleaning windows, washing bottles, and the like, until the lad fairly broke into rebellion. If this was the sort of work he was engaged for he must have higher wages; he wasn't over strong and his mother said he must lead an open-air life—that was why he had taken the place. To be bearded thus in his own shop was too much for Mr. Farmiloe, he seized the opportunity of giving his wrath full swing, and burst into a frenzy of vilification. Just as his passion reached its height (he stood with his back to the door) there entered a lady who wished to make a large purchase of disinfectants. Alarmed and scandalised at what was going on, she had no sooner crossed the threshold than she turned again, and hurried away. Her friends were not long in learning from her that the new chemist was a most violent man, a most disagreeable person—the very last man one could think of doing business with.

The home was but poorly furnished, and Mr. Farmiloe had engaged a very cheap general servant, who involved him in dirt and discomfort. It was a matter of talk among the neighbouring tradesmen that the chemist lived in a beggarly fashion. When the dismissed errand-boy spread the story of how he had been used, people jumped to the conclusion that Mr. Farmiloe drank. Before long there was a legend that he had been suffering from an acute attack of delirium tremens.

The post-office, always the post-office. If he sat down at a meal the shop-bell clanged, and hope springing eternal, he hurried forth in readiness to make up a packet or concoct a mixture; but it was an old lady who held him in talk for ten minutes about rates of postage to South America. When, by rare luck, he had a prescription to dispense (the hideous scrawl of that pestilent Dr. Bunker) in came somebody with letters and parcels which he was requested to weigh; and his hand shook so with rage that he could not resume his dispensing for the next quarter of an hour. People asked extraordinary questions, and were surprised, offended, when he declared he could not answer them. When could a letter be delivered at a village on the north-west coast of Ireland? Was it true that the Post-Office contemplated a reduction of rates to Hong-Kong? Would he explain in detail the new system of express delivery? Invariably he betrayed impatience, and occasionally he lost his temper; people went away exclaiming what a *horrid man* he was!

'Mr. What's-your-name,' said a shopkeeper one day, after receiving a short answer, 'I shall make it my business to complain of you to the Postmaster-General. I don't come here to be insulted.'

'Who insulted you?' returned Farmiloe like a sullen schoolboy.

'Why, you did. And you are always doing it.'

'I'm not.'

'You are.'

'If I did'—terror stole upon the chemist's heart—'I didn't mean it, and I— I'm sure I apologise. It's a way I have.'

'A damned bad way, let me tell you. I advise you to get out of it.'

'I'm sorry—'

'So you should be.'

And the tradesman walked off, only half appeased.

Mr. Farmiloe could have shed tears in his mortification, and for some minutes he stood looking at a bottle of laudanum, wishing he had the courage to have done with life. Plainly he could not live very long unless things improved. His ready money was coming to an end, rents and taxes loomed before him. An awful thought of bankruptcy haunted him in the early morning hours.

The most frequent visitor to the post-office was a well-dressed, middle-aged man, who spoke civilly, and did his business in the fewest possible words. Mr. Farmiloe rather liked the look of him, and once or twice made conversational overtures, but with no encouraging result. One day, feeling bolder than usual the chemist ventured to speak what he had in mind. After supplying the grave gentleman with stamps and postal-orders, he said, in a tone meant to be conciliatory—

'I don't know whether you ever have need of mineral waters, sir?'

'Why, yes, sometimes. My ordinary tradesman supplies them.'

'I thought I'd just mention that I keep them in stock.'

'Ah—thank you—'

'I've noticed,' went on the luckless apothecary, his bosom heaving with a sense of his wrongs, 'that you're a pretty large customer of the post-office, and it seems to me'—he meant to speak jocosely—'that it would be only fair if you gave *me* a turn now and then. I get next to nothing out of *this*, you know. I should be much obliged if you—'

The man of few words was looking at him, half in surprise, half in indignation, and when the chemist blundered into silence he spoke:—

'I really have nothing to do with that. As a matter of fact, I was on the point of making a little purchase in your shop, but I decidedly object to this kind of behaviour, and shall make my purchase elsewhere.'

He strode solemnly into the street, and Mr. Farmiloe, unconscious of all about him, glared at vacancy.

Whether from the angry tradesman, or from some lady with whom Mr. Farmiloe had been abrupt, a complaint did presently reach the postal authorities, with the result that an official called at the chemist's shop. The interview was unpleasant. It happened that Mr. Farmiloe (not for the first time) had just then allowed himself to run out of certain things always in demand by the public—halfpenny stamps, for instance. Moreover, his accounts were not in perfect order. This, he had to hear, was emphatically unbusinesslike, and, in brief, would not do.

'It shall not occur again, sir,' mumbled the unhappy man. 'But, if you consider my position—'

'Mr. Farmiloe, allow me to tell you that this is a matter for your *own* consideration, and no one else's.'

'True, sir, quite true. Still, when you come to think of it—I assure you—'

'The only assurance I want is that the business of the post-office will be properly attended to, and that assurance I must have. I shall probably call again before long. Good morning.'

It was always with a savage satisfaction that Mr. Farmiloe heard the clock strike eight on Saturday evening. His shop remained open till ten, but at eight came the end of the post-office business. If, as happened, any one entered five minutes too late, it delighted him to refuse their request. These were the only moments in which he felt himself a free man. After eating his poor supper, he smoked a pipe or two of cheap tobacco, brooding; or he fingered the pages of his menacing account-books; or, very rarely, he walked about the dark country roads, asking himself, with many a tragi-comic gesture and ejaculation, why he could not get on like other men.

One afternoon it seemed that he, at length, had his chance. There entered a maidservant with a prescription to be made up and sent as soon as possible. A glance at the name delighted Mr. Farmiloe; it was that of the richest family in the suburbs. The medicine, to be sure, was only for a governess, but his existence was recognised, and the patronage of such people would do him good. But for the never-sufficiently-to-be-condemned handwriting of Dr. Bunker, the prescription offered no difficulty. Rubbing his palms together, and smiling as he seldom smiled, he told the domestic that the medicine should be delivered in less than half an hour.

Scarcely had he begun upon it, when a lady came in, a lady whom he knew well. Her business was at the post-office side, and she looked a peremptory demand for his attention. Inwardly furious, he crossed the shop.

'Be so good as to tell me what this will cost by book-post.'

It seemed to be a pamphlet. Giving a glance at one of the open ends, Mr. Farmiloe saw handwriting within, and his hostility to the woman found vent in a sharp remark.

'There's a written communication in this. It will be letter rate.'

The lady eyed him with terrible scorn.

'You will oblige me by minding your own business. Your remark is the merest impertinence. That packet consists of MS., and will, therefore, go at book rate. Be so good as to weigh it at once.'

Mr. Farmiloe lost all control of himself, and well-nigh screamed.

'No, madam, I will *not* weigh it. And let me inform you, as you are so ignorant, that to weigh packets is not part of my duty. I do it merely to oblige civil persons, and you, madam, are not one of them.'

The lady instantly turned and withdrew.

'Damn the post-office!' yelled Mr. Farmiloe, alone with his errand-boy, and shaking his fist in the air. 'This very day I write to give it up. I say—*damn* the post-office.'

He returned to his dispensing, completed it, wrapped up the bottle in the customary manner, and despatched the boy to the house.

Five minutes later a thought flashed through his mind which put him in a cold sweat. He happened to glance along the shelf from which he had taken the bottle containing the last ingredient of the mixture, and it struck him, with all the force of a horrible doubt, that he had made a mistake. In the irate confusion of his thoughts, he had done the dispensing almost mechanically. The bottle he ought to have taken down was *that*, but had he not actually poured from that other? Of poisoning there was no fear, but, if indeed he had made a slip, the result would be a very extraordinary mixture; so surprising, in fact, that the patient would be sure to speak to Dr. Bunker about it. Good heavens! He felt sure he had made the mistake.

Any other man would have taken down the two bottles in question, and have examined the mouths of them for traces of moisture. Mr. Farmiloe, a victim of destiny, could do nothing so reasonable. Heedless of the fact that his shop remained unguarded, he seized his hat and rushed after the errand-boy. If he could only have a sniff at the mixture it would either confirm his fear or set his mind at rest. He tore along the road—and was too late. The boy met him, having just completed his errand.

With a wild curse he sped to the house, he rushed to the tradesman's door. The medicine just delivered! He must examine it—he feared there was a mistake—an extraordinary oversight.

The bottle had not yet been upstairs. Mr. Farmiloe tore off the wrapper, wrenched out the cork, sniffed—and smiled feebly.

'Thank you. I'm glad to find there was *no* mistake. I'll take it back, and have it wrapped up again, and send it immediately—immediately. And, by the bye'—he fumbled in his pocket for half-a-crown, still smiling like a detected culprit—'I'm sure you won't mention this little affair. A new assistant of mine—stupid fellow—I am going to get rid of him at once. Thank you, thank you.'

Notwithstanding that half-crown the incident was, of course, talked of through the house before a quarter of an hour had elapsed. Next day it was the gossip of the suburbs; and the day after the city itself heard the story. People were alarmed and scandalised. Why, such a chemist was a public danger! One lady declared that he ought at once to be 'struck off the roll!'

And so in a sense he was. Another month and the flowery, bowery little suburb knew him no more. He hid himself in a great town, living on the wreck of his fortune whilst he sought a place as an assistant. A leaky pair of boots and a bad east wind found the vulnerable spot of his constitution. After all, there was just enough money left to bury him.

TOPHAM'S CHANCE

CHAPTER I

On a summer afternoon two surly men sat together in a London lodging. One of them occupied an easy-chair, smoked a cigarette, and read the newspaper; the other was seated at the table, with a mass of papers before him, on which he laboured as though correcting exercises. They were much of an age, and that about thirty, but whereas the idler was well dressed, his companion had a seedy appearance and looked altogether like a man who neglected himself. For half an hour they had not spoken.

Of a sudden the man in the chair jumped up.

'Well, I have to go into town,' he said gruffly, 'and it's uncertain when I shall be back. Get that stuff cleared off, and reply to the urgent letters—mind you write in the proper tone to Dixon—as soapy as you can make it. Tell Miss Brewer we can't reduce the fees, but that we'll give her credit for a month. Guarantee the Leicestershire fellow a pass if he begins at once.'

The other, who listened, bit the end of his wooden penholder to splinters.

'All right,' he replied. 'But, look here, I want a little money.'

'So do I.'

'Yes, but you're not like me, without a coin in your pocket. Look here, give me half-a-crown. I have absolute need of it. Why, I can't even get my hair cut. I'm sick of this slavery.'

'Then go and do better,' cried the well-dressed man insolently. 'You were glad enough of the job when I offered it to you. It's no good your looking to me for money. I can do no more myself than just live; and as soon as I see a chance, you may be sure I shall clear out of this rotten business.'

He moved towards the door, but before opening it stood hesitating.

'Want to get your hair cut, do you? Well, there's sixpence, and it's all I can spare.'

The door closed. And the man at the table, leaning back, stared gloomily at the sixpenny piece on the table before him.

His name was Topham; he had a university degree and a damaged reputation. Six months ago, when his choice seemed to be between staying in the streets and turning sandwich-man, luck had made him acquainted with Mr. Rudolph Starkey, who wrote himself M.A. of Dublin University and advertised a system of tuition by correspondence. In return for mere board and lodging Topham became Mr. Starkey's assistant; that is to say, he did by far the greater part of Mr. Starkey's work. The tutorial business was but moderately successful; still, it kept its proprietor in cigarettes, and enabled him to pass some hours a day at a club, where he was convinced that before long some better chance in life would offer itself to him. Having always been a lazy dog, Starkey regarded himself as an example of industry unrewarded; being as selfish a fellow as one could meet, he reproached himself with the unworldliness of his nature, which had so hindered him in a basely material age. One of his ventures was a half-moral, half-practical little volume entitled *Success in Life*. Had it been either more moral or more practical, this book would probably have yielded him a modest income, for such works are dear to the British public; but Rudolph Starkey, M.A., was one of those men who do everything by halves and snarl over the ineffectual results.

Topham's fault was that of a man who had followed his instincts but too thoroughly. They brought him to an end of everything, and, as Starkey said, he had been glad enough to take the employment which was offered without any inconvenient inquiries. The work which he undertook he did competently and honestly for some time without a grumble. Beginning with a certain gratitude to his employer, though without any liking, he soon grew to detest the man, and had much ado to keep up a show of decent civility in their intercourse. Of better birth and breeding than Starkey, he burned with resentment at the scant ceremony with which he was treated, and loathed the meanness which could exact so much toil for such poor remuneration. When offering his terms Starkey had talked in that bland way characteristic of him with strangers.

'I'm really ashamed to propose nothing better to a man of your standing. But—well, I'm making a start, you see, and the fact of the matter is that, just at present, I could very well manage to do all the work myself. Still, if you think it worth your while, there's no doubt we shall get on capitally together, and, of course, I need not say, as soon as our progress justifies it, we must come to new arrangements. A matter of six or seven hours a day will be all I shall ask of you at present. For my own part, I work chiefly at night.'

CHAPTER II

By the end of the first month Topham was working, not six or seven, but ten or twelve hours a day, and his spells of labour only lengthened as time went on. Seeing himself victimised, he one day alluded to the promise of better terms, but Starkey turned sour.

'You surprise me, Topham. Here are we, practically partners, doing our best to make this thing a success, and all at once you spring upon me an unreasonable demand. You know how expensive these rooms are—for we must have a decent address. If you are dissatisfied, say so, and give me time to look out for some one else.'

Topham was afraid of the street, and that his employer well knew. The conversation ended in mutual sullenness, which thenceforward became the note of their colloquies. Starkey felt himself a victim of ingratitude, and consequently threw even more work upon his helpless assistant. That the work was so conscientiously done did not at all astonish him. Now and then he gave himself the satisfaction of finding fault: just to remind Topham that his bread depended on another's goodwill. Congenial indolence grew upon him, but he talked only the more of his ceaseless exertions. Sometimes in the evening he would throw up his arms, yawn wearily, and declare that so much toil with such paltry results was a heart-breaking thing.

Topham stared sullenly at the sixpence. This was but the latest of many insults, yet never before had he so tasted the shame of his subjection. Though he was earning a living, and a right to self-respect, more strenuously than Starkey ever had, this fellow made him feel like a mendicant. His nerves quivered, he struck the table fiercely, shouting within himself, 'Brute! Cad!' Then he pocketed the coin and got on with his duties.

It was toil of a peculiarly wearisome and enervating kind. Starkey's advertisements, which were chiefly in the country newspapers, put him in communication with persons of both sexes, and of any age from seventeen onwards, the characteristic common to them all being inexperience and intellectual helplessness. Most of these correspondents desired to pass some examination; a few aimed—or professed to aim—merely at self-improvement, or what they called 'culture.' Starkey, of course, undertook tuition in any subject, to any end, stipulating only that his fees should be paid in advance. Throughout the day his slave had been correcting Latin and Greek exercises, papers in mathematical or physical science, answers to historical questions: all elementary and many grotesquely bad. On completing each set he wrote the expected comment; sometimes briefly, sometimes at considerable length. He now turned to a bundle of so-called essays, and on opening the first could not repress a groan. No! This was beyond his strength. He would make up the parcels for post, write the half-dozen letters that must be sent to-day, and go out. Had he not sixpence in his pocket?

Just as he had taken this resolve some one knocked at the sitting-room door, and with the inattention of a man who expects nothing, Topham bade enter.

'A gen'man asking for Mr. Starkey, sir,' said the servant.

'All right. Send him in.'

And then entered a man whose years seemed to be something short of fifty, a hale, ruddy-cheeked, stoutish man, whose dress and bearing made it probable that he was no Londoner.

'Mr. Starkey, M.A.?' he inquired, rather nervously, though his smile and his upright posture did not lack a certain dignity.

'Quite right,' murmured Topham, who was authorised to represent his principal to any one coming on business. 'Will you take a seat?'

'You will know my name,' began the stranger. 'Wigmore—Abraham Wigmore.'

'Very glad to meet you, Mr. Wigmore. I was on the point of sending your last batch of papers to the post. You will find, this time, I have been able to praise them unreservedly.'

The listener fairly blushed with delight; then he grasped his short beard with his left hand and laughed silently, showing excellent teeth.

'Well, Mr. Starkey,' he replied at length in a moderately subdued voice, 'I did really think I'd managed better than usual. But there's much thanks due to you, sir. You've helped me, Mr. Starkey, you really have. And that's one reason why, happening to come up to London, I wished to have the pleasure of seeing you; I really did want to thank you, sir.'

CHAPTER III

Topham was closely observing this singular visitor. He had always taken 'Abraham Wigmore' for a youth of nineteen or so, some not over-bright, but plodding and earnest clerk or counter-man in the little Gloucestershire town from which the correspondent wrote; it astonished him to see this mature and most respectable person. They talked on. Mr. Wigmore had a slight west-country accent, but otherwise his language differed little from that of the normally educated; in every word he revealed a good and kindly, if simple, nature. At length a slight embarrassment interfered with the flow of his talk, which, having been solely of tuitional matters, began to take a turn more personal. Was he taking too much of Mr. Starkey's time? Reassured on this point, he begged leave to give some account of himself.

'I dare say, Mr. Starkey, you're surprised to see how old I am. It seems strange to you, no doubt, that at my age I should be going to school.' He grasped his beard and laughed. 'Well, it is strange, and I'd like to explain it to you. To begin with, I'll tell you what my age is; I'm seven-and-forty. Only that. But I'm the father of two daughters—both married. Yes, I was married young myself, and my good wife died long ago, more's the pity.'

He paused, looked round the room, stroked his hard-felt hat, Topham murmuring a sympathetic sound.

'Now, as to my business, Mr. Starkey. I'm a fruiterer and greengrocer. I might have said fruiterer alone; it sounds more respectable, but the honest truth is, I do sell vegetables as well, and I want you to know that, Mr. Starkey. Does it make you feel ashamed of me?'

'My dear sir! What business could be more honourable? I heartily wish I had one as good and as lucrative.'

'Well, that's your kindness, sir,' said Wigmore, with a pleased smile. 'The fact is, I have done pretty well, though I'm not by any means a rich man: comfortable, that's all. I gave my girls a good schooling, and what with that and their good looks, they've both made what may be called better marriages than might have been expected. For down in our country, you know, sir, a shopkeeper is one thing, and a gentleman's another. Now my girls have married gentlemen.'

Again he paused, and with emphasis. Again Topham murmured, this time congratulation.

'One of them is wife to a young solicitor; the other to a young gentleman farmer. And they've both gone to live in another part of the country. I dare say you understand that, Mr. Starkey?'

The speaker's eyes had fallen; at the same time a twitching of the brows and hardening of the mouth changed the expression of his face, marking it with an unexpected sadness, all but pain.

'Do you mean, Mr. Wigmore,' asked Topham, 'that your daughters desire to live at a distance from you?'

'Well, I'm sorry to say that's what I do mean, Mr. Starkey. My son-in-law the solicitor had intended practising in the town where he was born; instead of that he went to another a long way off. My son-in-law the gentleman farmer was to have taken a farm close by us; he altered his mind, and went into another county. You see, sir! It's quite natural: I find no fault. There's never been an unkind word between any of us. But—'

He was growing more and more embarrassed. Evidently the man had something he wished to say, something to which he had been leading up by this disclosure of his domestic affairs; but he could not utter his thoughts. Topham tried the commonplaces naturally suggested by the situation; they were received with gratitude, but still Mr. Wigmore hung his head and talked vaguely, with hesitations, pauses.

'I've always been what one may call serious-minded, Mr. Starkey. As a boy I liked reading, and I've always had a book at hand for my leisure time—the kind of book that does one good. Just now I'm reading *The Christian Year*. And since my daughters married—well, as I tell you, Mr. Starkey, I've done pretty well in business—there's really no reason why I should keep on in my shop, if I chose to—to do otherwise.'

'I quite understand,' interrupted Topham, in whom there began to stir a thought which made his brain warm. 'You would like to retire from business. And you would like to—well, to pursue your studies more seriously.'

Again Wigmore looked grateful, but even yet the burden was not off his mind.

'I know,' he resumed presently, turning his hat round and round, 'that it sounds a strange thing to say, but—well, sir, I've always done my best to live as a religious man.'

'Of that I have no doubt whatever, Mr. Wigmore.'

'Well, then, sir, what I should like to ask you is this. Do you think, if I gave up the shop and worked very hard at my studies—with help, of course, with help,—do you think, Mr. Starkey, that I could hope to get on?'

He was red as a peony; his voice choked.

'You mean,' put in Topham, he, too, becoming excited, 'to become a really well-educated man?'

'Yes, sir, yes. But more than that. I want, Mr. Starkey, to make myself—something—so that my daughters and my sons-in-law would never feel ashamed of me—so that their children won't be afraid to talk of their grandfather. I know it's a very bold thought, sir, but if I could—'

'Speak, Mr. Wigmore,' cried Topham, quivering with curiosity, 'speak more plainly. What do you wish to become? With competent help—of course, with competent help—anything is possible.'

'Really?' exclaimed the other. 'You mean that, Mr. Starkey? Then, sir'—he leaned forward, blushing, trembling, gasping—'could I get to be—a curate?'

Topham fell back into his chair. For two or three minutes he was mute with astonishment; then the very soul of him sang jubilee.

'My dear Mr. Wigmore,' he began, restraining himself to an impressive gravity. 'I should be the last man to speak lightly of the profession of a clergyman or to urge any one to enter the Church whom I thought unfitted for the sacred office. But in your case, my good sir, there can be no such misgiving. I entertain no doubt whatever of your fitness—your moral fitness, and I will go so far as to say that with competent aid you might, in no very long time, be prepared for the necessary examination.'

The listener laughed with delight. He began to talk rapidly, all diffidence subdued. He told how the idea had first come to him, how he had brooded upon it, how he had worked at elementary lesson-books, very secretly—then how the sight of Starkey's advertisement had inspired him with hope.

'Just to get to be a curate—that's all. I should never be worthy of being a vicar or a rector. I don't look so high as that, Mr. Starkey. But a curate is a clergyman, and for my daughters to be able to say their father is in the Church— that would be a good thing, sir, a good thing!'

He slapped his knee, and again laughed with joy. Meanwhile Topham seemed to have become pensive, his head was on his hand.

'Oh,' he murmured at length, 'if I had time to work seriously with you, several hours a day.'

Wigmore looked at him, and let his eyes fall: 'You are, of course, very busy, Mr. Starkey!'

'Very busy.'

Topham waved his hand at the paper-covered table, and appeared to sink into despondency. Thereupon Wigmore cautiously and delicately approached the next thought he had in mind, Topham—cunning fellow—at one moment facilitating, at another retarding what he wished to say. It came out at last. Would it be quite impossible for Mr. Starkey to devote himself to one sole pupil.

CHAPTER IV

'Mr. Wigmore, I will be frank with you. If I asked an equivalent for the value of my business as a business, I could not expect you to agree to such a proposal. But, to speak honestly, my health has suffered a good deal from overwork, and I must take into consideration the great probability that in any case, before long, I shall be obliged to find some position where the duties were less exhausting.'

'Good gracious!' exclaimed the listener. 'Why, you'll kill yoursel, sir. And I'm bound to say, you look far from well.'

Topham smiled pathetically, paused a moment as if to reflect, and continued in the same tone of genial confidence. Let us consider the matter in detail. Do you propose, Mr. Wigmore, to withdraw from business at once?'

The fruiterer replied that he could do so at very short notice. Questioned as to his wishes regarding a place of residence, he declared that he was ready to live in any place where, being unknown, he could make, as it were, a new beginning.

'You would not feel impatient,' said Topham, 'if, say, two or three years had to elapse before you could be ordained?'

'Impatient,' said the other cheerily. 'Why, if it took ten years I would go through with it. When I make up my mind about a thing, I'm not easily dismayed. If I could have your help, sir—'

The necessity of making a definite proposal turned Topham pale; he was so afraid of asking too much. Almost in spite of himself, he at length spoke. 'Suppose we say—if I reside with you—that you pay me a salary of, well, £200 a year?'

The next moment he inwardly raged. Wigmore's countenance expressed such contentment, that it was plain the good man would have paid twice that sum.

'Ass!' cried Topham, in his mind. 'I always undervalue myself.'

* * * * *

It was late that evening when Starkey came home; to his surprise he found that Topham was later still. In vain he sat writing until past one o'clock. Topham did not appear, and indeed never came back at all. The overworked corresponding tutor was taking his ease at the seaside on the strength of a quarter's salary in advance, which Mr. Wigmore, tremulously anxious to clinch their bargain, had insisted on paying him. Before leaving London he had written to Starkey, apologising for his abrupt departure, 'The result of unforeseen circumstances.' He enclosed six penny stamps in repayment of a sum lent, and added—

'When I think of my great debt to you I despair of expressing my gratitude. Be assured, however, that the name of Starkey will always be cherished in my remembrance.'

Under that name Topham dwelt with the retired shopkeeper, and assiduously discharged his tutorial duties. A day came when, relying upon the friendship between them, and his pupil's exultation in the progress achieved, the tutor unbosomed himself. Having heard the whole story, Wigmore laughed a great deal, and declared that such a fellow as Starkey was rightly served.

'But,' he inquired, after reflection, 'how was it the man never wrote to ask why I sent no more work?'

'That asks for further confession. While at the seaside I wrote, in a disguised hand, a letter supposed to come from a brother of yours in which I said you were very ill and must cease your correspondence. Starkey hadn't the decency to reply, but if he had done so I should have got his letter at the post-office.'

Mr. Wigmore looked troubled for a moment. However, this too was laughed away, and the pursuit of gentility went on as rigorously as ever.

But Topham, musing over his good luck, thought with a shiver on how small an accident it had depended. Had Starkey been at home when the fruiterer called, he, it was plain, would have had the offer of this engagement.

'With the result that dear old Wigmore would have been bled for who knows how many years by a mere swindler. Whereas he is really being educated, and, for all I know, may some day adorn the Church of England.' Such thoughts are very consoling.

A LODGER IN MAZE POND

HARVEY Munden had settled himself in a corner of the club smoking-room, with a cigar and a review. At eleven o'clock on a Saturday morning in August he might reasonably expect to be undisturbed. But behold, there entered a bore, a long-faced man with a yellow waistcoat, much dreaded by all the members; he stood a while at one of the tables, fingering newspapers and eyeing the solitary. Harvey heard a step, looked up, and shuddered.

The bore began his attack in form; Harvey parried with as much resolution as his kindly nature permitted.

'You know that Dr. Shergold is dying?' fell casually from the imperturbable man.

'Dying?'

Munden was startled into attention, and the full flow of gossip swept about him. Yes, the great Dr. Shergold lay dying; there were bulletins in the morning papers; it seemed unlikely that he would see another dawn.

'Who will benefit by his decease?' inquired the bore. 'His nephew, do you think?'

'Very possibly.'

'A remarkable man, that—a *most* remarkable man. He was at Lady Teasdale's the other evening, and he talked a good deal. Upon my word, it reminded one of Coleridge, or Macaulay,—that kind of thing. Certainly most brilliant talk. I can't remember what it was all about—something literary. A sort of fantasia, don't you know. Wonderful eloquence. By the bye, I believe he is a great friend of yours?'

'Oh, we have known each other for a long time.'

'Somebody was saying that he had gone in for medicine—walking one of the hospitals—that kind of thing.'

'Yes, he's at Guy's.'

To avoid infinite questioning, Harvey flung aside his review and went to glance at the *Times*. He read the news concerning the great physician. Then, as his pursuer drew near again, he hastily departed.

By midday he was at London Bridge. He crossed to the Surrey side, turned immediately to the left, and at a short distance entered one of the vaulted thoroughfares which run beneath London Bridge Station. It was like the mouth of some monstrous cavern. Out of glaring daylight he passed into gloom and chill air; on either side of the way a row of suspended lamps gave a dull, yellow light, revealing entrances to vast storehouses, most of them occupied by wine merchants; an alcoholic smell prevailed over indeterminate odours of dampness. There was great concourse of drays and waggons; wheels and the clang of giant hoofs made roaring echo, and above thundered the trains. The vaults, barely illumined with gas-jets, seemed of infinite extent; dim figures moved near and far, amid huge barrels, cases, packages; in rooms partitioned off by glass framework men sat writing. A curve in the tunnel made it appear much longer than it really was; till midway nothing could be seen ahead but deepening darkness; then of a sudden appeared the issue, and beyond, greatly to the surprise of any one who should have ventured hither for the first time, was a vision of magnificent plane-trees, golden in the August sunshine—one of the abrupt contrasts which are so frequent in London, and which make its charm for those who wander from the beaten tracks; a transition from the clangorous cave of commerce to a sunny leafy quietude, amid old houses—some with quaint tumbling roofs—and byways little frequented.

The planes grow at the back of Guy's Hospital, and close by is a short narrow street which bears the name of Maze Pond. It consists for the most part of homely, flat-fronted dwellings, where lodgings are let to medical students. At one of these houses Harvey Munden plied the knocker.

He was answered by a trim, rather pert-looking girl, who smiled familiarly.

'Mr. Shergold isn't in, sir,' she said at once, anticipating his question. 'But he *will* be very soon. Will you step in and wait?'

'I think I will.'

As one who knew the house, he went upstairs, and entered a sitting-room on the first floor. The girl followed him.

'I haven't had time to clear away the breakfast things,' she said, speaking rapidly and with an air. 'Mr. Shergold was late this mornin'; he didn't get up till nearly ten, an' then he sat writin' letters. Did he know as you was comin', sir?'

'No; I looked in on the chance of finding him, or learning where he was.'

'I'm sure he'll be in about half-past twelve, 'cause he said to me as he was only goin' to get a breath of air. He hasn't nothing to do at the 'ospital just now.'

'Has he talked of going away?'

'Going away?' The girl repeated the words sharply, and examined the speaker's face. 'Oh, he won't be goin' away just yet, I think.'

Munden returned her look with a certain curiosity, and watched her as she began to clink together the things upon the table. Obviously she esteemed herself a person of some importance. Her figure was not bad, and her features had the trivial prettiness so commonly seen in London girls of the lower orders,—the kind of prettiness which ultimately loses itself in fat and chronic perspiration. Her complexion already began to show a tendency to muddiness, and when her lips parted, they showed decay of teeth. In dress she was untidy; her hair exhibited a futile attempt at elaborate arrangement; she had dirty hands.

Disposed to talk, she lingered as long as possible, but Harvey Munden had no leanings to this kind of colloquy; when the girl took herself off, he drew a breath of satisfaction, and smiled the smile of an intellectual man who has outlived youthful follies.

He stepped over to the lodger's bookcase. There were about a hundred volumes, only a handful of them connected with medical study. Seeing a volume of his own Munden took it down and idly turned the pages; it surprised him to discover a great many marginal notes in pencil, and an examination of these showed him that Shergold must have gone carefully through the book with an eye to the correction of its style; adjectives were deleted and inserted, words of common usage removed for others which only a fine literary conscience could supply, and in places even the punctuation was minutely changed. Whilst he still pondered this singular manifestation of critical zeal, the door opened, and Shergold came in.

A man of two-and-thirty, short, ungraceful, ill-dressed, with features as little commonplace as can be imagined. He had somewhat a stern look, and on his brow were furrows of care. Light-blue eyes tended to modify the all but harshness of his lower face; when he smiled, as on recognising his friend, they expressed a wonderful innocence and suavity of nature; overshadowed, in thoughtful or troubled mood, by his heavy eyebrows, they became deeply pathetic. His nose was short and flat, yet somehow not ignoble; his full lips, bare of moustache, tended to suggest a melancholy fretfulness. But for the high forehead, no casual observer would have cared to look at him a second time; but that upper story made the whole countenance vivid with intellect, as though a light beamed upon it from above.

'You hypercritical beggar!' cried Harvey, turning with the volume in his hand. 'Is this how you treat the glorious works of your contemporaries?'

Shergold reddened and was mute.

'I shall take this away with me,' pursued the other, laughing. 'It'll be worth a little study.'

'My dear fellow—you won't take it ill of me—I didn't really mean it as a criticism,' the deep, musical voice stammered in serious embarrassment.

'Why, wasn't it just this kind of thing that caused a quarrel between George Sand and Musset?'

'Yes, yes; but George Sand was such a peremptory fellow, and Musset such a vapourish young person. Look! I'll show you what I meant.'

'Thanks,' said Munden, 'I can find that out for myself.' He thrust the book into his coat-pocket. 'I came to ask you if you are aware of your uncle's condition.'

'Of course I am.

'When did you see him last?'

'See him?' Shergold's eyes wandered vaguely. 'Oh, to talk with him, about a month ago.'

'Did you part friendly?'

'On excellent terms. And last night I went to ask after him. Unfortunately he didn't know any one, but the nurse said he had been mentioning my name, and in a kind way.'

'Capital! Hadn't you better walk in that direction this afternoon?'

'Yes, perhaps I had, and yet, you know, I hate to have it supposed that I am hovering about him.'

'All the same, go.'

Shergold pointed to a chair. 'Sit down a bit. I have been having a talk with Dr. Salmon. He discourages me a good deal. You know it's far from certain that I shall go on with medicine.'

'Far from certain!' the other assented, smiling. 'By the bye, I hear that you have been in the world of late. You were at Lady Teasdale's not long ago.'

'Well—yes—why not?'

Perhaps it was partly his vexation at the book incident,—Shergold seemed unable to fix his thoughts on anything; he shuffled in his seat and kept glancing nervously towards the door.

'I was delighted to hear it,' said his friend. 'That's a symptom of health. Go everywhere; see everybody—that's worth seeing. They got you to talk, I believe?'

'Who has been telling you? I'm afraid I talked a lot of rubbish; I had shivers of shame all through a sleepless night after it. But some one brought up Whistler, and etching, and so on, and I had a few ideas of which I wanted to relieve my mind. And, after all, there's a pleasure in talking to intelligent people. Henry Wilt was there with his daughters. Clever girls, by Jove! And Mrs. Peter Rayne—do you know her?'

'Know of her, that's all.'

'A splendid woman—brains, brains! Upon my soul, I know no such delight as listening to a really intellectual woman, when she's also beautiful. I shake with delight—and what women one does meet, nowadays! Of course the world never saw their like. I have my idea of Aspasia—but there are lots of grander women in London to-day. One ought to live among the rich. What a wretched mistake, when one can help it, to herd with narrow foreheads, however laudable your motive! Since I got back among the better people my life has been trebled—oh, centupled—in value!'

'My boy,' remarked Munden quietly, 'didn't I say something to this effect on a certain day nine years ago?'

'Don't talk of it,' the other replied, waving his hand in agitation. 'We'll never look back at that.'

'Your room is stuffy,' said Munden, rising. 'Let us go and have lunch somewhere.'

'Yes, we will! Just a moment to wash my hands—I've been in the dissecting-room.'

The friends went downstairs. At the foot they passed the landlady's daughter: she drew back, but, as Shergold allowed his companion to pass into the street, her voice made itself heard behind him.

'Shall you want tea, Mr. Shergold?'

Munden turned sharply and looked at the girl. Shergold did not look at her, but he delayed for a moment and appeared to balance the question. Then, in a friendly voice, he said—

'No, thank you. I may not be back till late in the evening.' And he went on hurriedly.

'Cheeky little beggar that,' Munden observed, with a glance at his friend.

'Oh, not a bad girl in her way. They've made me very comfortable. All the same, I shan't grieve when the day of departure comes.'

It was not cheerful, the life-story of Henry Shergold. At two-and-twenty he found himself launched upon the world, with a university education incomplete and about forty pounds in his pocket. A little management, a little less of boyish pride, and he might have found the means to go forward to his degree, with pleasant hopes in the background; but Henry was a Radical, a scorner of privilege, a believer in human perfectibility. He got a place in an office, and he began to write poetry—some of which was published and duly left unpaid for. A year later there came one fateful day when he announced to his friend Harvey Munden that he was going to be married. His chosen bride was the daughter of a journeyman tailor—a tall, pale, unhealthy girl of eighteen, whose acquaintance he had made at a tobacconist's shop, where she served. He was going to marry her on principle—principle informed with callow passion, the passion of a youth who has lived demurely, more among books than men. Harvey Munden flew into a rage, and called upon the gods in protest. But Shergold was not to be shaken. The girl, he declared, had fallen in love with him during conversations across the counter; her happiness was in his hands, and he would not betray it. She had excellent dispositions; he would educate her. The friends quarrelled about it, and Shergold led home his bride.

With the results which any sane person could have foretold. The marriage was a hideous disaster; in three years it brought Shergold to an attempted suicide, for which he had to appear at the police-court. His relative, the distinguished doctor, who had hitherto done nothing for him, now came forward with counsel and assistance. Happily the only child of the union had died at a few weeks old, and the wife, though making noisy proclamation of rights, was so weary of her husband that she consented to a separation.

But in less than a year the two were living together again; Mrs. Shergold had been led by her relatives to believe that some day the poor fellow would have his uncle's money, and her wiles ultimately overcame Shergold's resistance. He, now studying law at the doctor's expense, found himself once more abandoned, and reduced to get his living as a solicitor's clerk. His uncle had bidden him good-bye on a postcard, whereon was illegibly scribbled something about 'damned fools.'

He bore the burden for three more years, then his wife died. One night, after screaming herself speechless in fury at Shergold's refusal to go with her to a music-hall, she had a fit on the stairs, and in falling received fatal injuries.

The man was free, but terribly shattered. Only after a long sojourn abroad, at his kinsman's expense, did he begin to recover health. He came back and entered himself as a student at Guy's, greatly to Dr. Shergold's satisfaction. His fees were paid and a small sum was allowed him to live upon—a very small sum. By degrees some old acquaintances began to see him, but it was only quite of late that he had accepted invitations from people of social standing, whom he met at the doctor's house. The hints of his story that got about made him an interesting figure, especially to women, and his remarkable gifts were recognised as soon as circumstances began to give him fair play. All modern things were of interest to him, and his knowledge, acquired with astonishing facility, formed the fund of talk which had singular charm alike for those who did and those who did not understand it. Undeniably shy, he yet, when warmed to a subject, spoke with nerve and confidence. In days of jabber, more or less impolite, this appearance of an articulate mortal, with soft manners and totally unaffected, could not but excite curiosity. Lady Teasdale, eager for the uncommon, chanced to observe him one evening as he conversed with his neighbour at the dinner-table; later, in the drawing-room, she encouraged him with flattery of rapt attention to a display of his powers; she resolved to make him a feature of her evenings. Fortunately, his kindred with Dr. Shergold made a respectable introduction, and Lady Teasdale whispered it among matrons that he would inherit from the wealthy doctor, who had neither wife nor child. He might not be fair to look upon, but handsome is that handsome has.

And now the doctor lay sick unto death. Society was out of town, but Lady Teasdale, with a house full of friends about her down in Hampshire, did not forget her *protégé*; she waited with pleasant expectation for the young man's release from poverty.

It came in a day or two. Dr. Shergold was dead, and an enterprising newspaper announced simultaneously that the bulk of his estate would pass to Mr. Henry Shergold, a gentleman at present studying for his uncle's profession. This paragraph caught the eye of Harvey Munden, who sent a line to his friend, to ask if it was true. In reply he received a mere postcard: 'Yes. Will see you before long.' But Harvey wanted to be off to Como, and as business took him into the city, he crossed the river and sought Maze Pond. Again the door was opened to him by the landlady's daughter; she stood looking keenly in his face, her eyes smiling and yet suspicious.

'Mr. Shergold in?' he asked carelessly.

'No, he isn't.' There was a strange bluntness about this answer. The girl stood forward, as if to bar the entrance, and kept searching his face.

'When is he likely to be?'

'I don't know. He didn't say when he went out.'

A woman's figure appeared in the background. The girl turned and said sharply, 'All right, mother, it's only somebody for Mr. Shergold.'

'I'll go upstairs and write a note,' said Munden, in a rather peremptory voice.

The other drew back and allowed him to pass, but with evident disinclination. As he entered the room, he saw that she had followed. He went up to a side-table, on which lay a blotting-book, with other requisites for writing, and then he stood for a moment as if in meditation.

'Your name is Emma, isn't it?' he inquired, looking at the girl with a smile.

'Yes, it is.'

'Well then, Emma, shut the door, and let's have a talk. Your mother won't mind, will she?' he added slyly.

The girl tossed her head.

'I don't see what it's got to do with mother.' She closed the door, but did not latch it. 'What do you want to talk about?'

'You're a very nice girl to look at, Emma, and I've always admired you when you opened the door to me. I've always liked your nice, respectful way of speaking, but somehow you don't speak quite so nicely to-day. What has put you out?'

Her eyes did not quit his face for a moment; her attitude betokened the utmost keenness of suspicious observation.

'Nothing's put me out, that I know of.'

'Yet you don't speak very nicely—not very respectfully. Perhaps'—he paused—'perhaps Mr. Shergold is going to leave?'

'P'r'aps he may be.'

'And you're vexed at losing a lodger.'

He saw her lip curl and then she laughed.

'You're wrong there.'

'Then *what* is it?'

He drew near and made as though he would advance a familiar arm. Emma started back.

'All right,' she exclaimed, with an insolent nod. 'I'll tell Mr. Shergold.'

'Tell Mr. Shergold? Why? What has it to do with him?'

'A good deal.'

'Indeed? For shame, Emma! I never expected *that*!'

'What do you mean?' she retorted hotly. 'You keep your impudence to yourself. If you want to know, Mr. Shergold is going to *marry* me—so there!'

The stroke was effectual. Harvey Munden stood as if transfixed, but he recovered himself before a word escaped his lips.

'Ah, that alters the case. I beg your pardon. You won't make trouble between old friends?'

Vanity disarmed the girl's misgiving. She grinned with satisfaction.

'That depends how you behave.'

'Oh, you don't know me. But promise, now; not a word to Shergold.'

She gave a conditional promise, and stood radiant with her triumph.

'Thanks, that's very good of you. Well, I won't trouble to leave a note. You shall just tell Shergold that I am leaving England to-morrow for a holiday. I should *like* to see him, of course, and I may possibly look round this evening. If I can't manage it, just tell him that I think he ought to have given me a chance of congratulating him. May I ask when it is to be?'

Emma resumed an air of prudery, 'Before very long, I dessay.'

'I wish you joy. Well, I mustn't talk longer now, but I'll do my best to look in this evening, and then we can all chat together.'

He laughed and she laughed back; and thereupon they parted.

A little after nine that evening, when only a grey reflex of daylight lingered upon a cloudy sky, Munden stood beneath the plane-trees by Guy's Hospital waiting. He had walked the length of Maze Pond and had ascertained that his friend's window as yet showed no light; Shergold was probably still from home. In the afternoon he had made inquiry at the house of the deceased doctor, but of Henry nothing was known there; he left a message for delivery if possible, to the effect that he would call in at Maze Pond between nine and ten.

At a quarter past the hour there appeared from the direction of London Bridge a well-known figure, walking slowly, head bent. Munden moved forward, and, on seeing him, Shergold grasped his hand feverishly.

'Ha! how glad I am to meet you, Munden! Come; let us walk this way.' He turned from Maze Pond. 'I got your message up yonder an hour or two ago. So glad I have met you here, old fellow.'

'Well, your day has come,' said Harvey, trying to read his friend's features in the gloom.

'He has left me about eighty thousand pounds,' Shergold replied, in a low, shaken voice. 'I'm told there are big legacies to hospitals as well. Heavens! how rich he was!'

'When is the funeral?'

'Friday.'

'Where shall you live in the meantime?'

'I don't know—I haven't thought about it.'

'I should go to some hotel, if I were you,' said Munden, 'and I have a proposal to make. If I wait till Saturday, will you come with me to Como?'

Shergold did not at once reply. He was walking hurriedly, and making rather strange movements with his head and arms. They came into the shadow of the vaulted way beneath London Bridge Station. At this hour the great tunnel was quiet, save when a train roared above; the warehouses were closed; one or two idlers, of forbidding aspect, hung about in the murky gaslight, and from the far end came a sound of children at play.

'You won't be wanted here?' Munden added.

'No—no—I think not.' There was agitation in the voice.

'Then you will come?'

'Yes, I will come.' Shergold spoke with unnecessary vehemence and laughed oddly.

'What's the matter with you?' his friend asked.

'Nothing—the change of circumstances, I suppose. Let's get on. Let us go somewhere—I can't help reproaching myself; I ought to feel or show a decent sobriety; but what was the old fellow to me? I'm grateful to him.'

'There's nothing else on your mind?'

Shergold looked up, startled.

'What do you mean? Why do you ask?'

They stood together in the black shadow of an interval between two lamps. After reflecting for a moment, Munden decided to speak.

'I called at your lodgings early to-day, and somehow I got into talk with the girl. She was cheeky, and her behaviour puzzled me. Finally she made an incredible announcement—that you had asked her to marry you. Of course it's a lie?'

'To marry her?' exclaimed the listener hoarsely, with an attempt at laughter. 'Do you think that likely—after all I have gone through?'

'No, I certainly don't. It staggered me. But what I want to know is, can she cause trouble?'

'How do I know?—a girl will lie so boldly. She might make a scandal, I suppose; or threaten it, in hope of getting money out of me.'

'But is there any ground for a scandal?' demanded Harvey.

'Not the slightest, as you mean it.'

'I'm glad to hear that. But she may give you trouble. I see the thing doesn't astonish you very much; no doubt you were aware of her character.'

'Yes, yes; I know it pretty well. Come, let us get out of this squalid inferno; how I hate it! Have you had dinner? I don't want any. Let us go to your rooms, shall we? There'll be a hansom passing the bridge.'

They walked on in silence, and when they had found a cab they drove westward, talking only of Dr. Shergold's affairs. Munden lived in the region of the Squares, hard by the British Museum; he took his friend into a comfortably furnished room, the walls hidden with books and prints, and there they sat down to smoke, a bottle of whisky within easy reach of both. It was plain to Harvey that some mystery lay in his friend's reserve on the subject of the girl Emma; he was still anxious, but would not lead the talk to unpleasant things. Shergold drank like a thirsty man, and the whisky seemed to make him silent. Presently he fell into absolute muteness, and lay wearily back in his chair.

'The excitement has been too much for you,' Munden remarked.

Shergold looked at him, with a painful embarrassment in his features; then suddenly he bent forward.

'Munden, it's I who have lied. I *did* ask that girl to marry me.'

'When?'

'Last night.'

'Why?'

'Because for a moment I was insane.' They stared at each other.

'Has she any hold upon you?' Munden asked slowly.

'None whatever, except this frantic offer of mine.'

'Into which she inveigled you?'

'I can't honestly say she did; it was entirely my own fault. She has never behaved loosely, or even like a schemer. I doubt whether she knew anything about my uncle, until I told her last night.'

He spoke rapidly, in a thick voice, moving his arms in helpless protestation. His look was one of unutterable misery.

'Well,' observed Munden, 'the frenzy has at all events passed. You have the common-sense to treat it as if it had never been; and really I am tempted to believe that it was literal lunacy. Last night were you drunk?'

'I had drunk nothing. Listen, and I will tell you all about it. I am a fool about women. I don't know what it is—certainly not a sensual or passionate nature; mine is nothing of the sort. It's sheer sentimentality, I suppose. I can't be friendly with a woman without drifting into mawkish tenderness—there's the simple truth. If I had married happily, I don't think I should have been tempted to go about philandering. The society of a wife I loved and respected would be sufficient. But there's that need in me—the incessant hunger for a woman's sympathy and affection. Such a hideous mistake as mine when I married would have made a cynic of most men; upon me the lesson has been utterly thrown away. I mean that, though I can talk of women rationally enough with a friend, I am at their mercy when alone with them—at the mercy of the silliest, vulgarest creature. After all, isn't it very much the same with men in general? The average man—how does he come to marry? Do you think he deliberately selects? Does he fall in love, in the strict sense of the phrase, with that one particular girl? No; it comes about by chance—by the drifting force of circumstances. Not one man in ten thousand, when he thinks of marriage, waits for the ideal wife—for the woman who makes capture of his soul or even of his senses. Men marry without passion. Most of us have a very small circle for choice; the hazard of everyday life throws us into contact with this girl or that, and presently we begin to feel either that we have compromised ourselves, or that we might as well save trouble and settle down as soon as possible, and the girl at hand will do as well as another. More often than not it is the girl who decides for us. In more than half the marriages it's the woman who has practically proposed. She puts herself in a man's way. With her it rests almost entirely whether a man shall think of her as a possible wife or not. She has endless ways of putting herself forward without seeming to do so. As often as not, it's mere passivity that effects the end. She has only to remain seated instead of moving away; to listen with a smile instead of looking bored; to be at home instead of being out,—and she is making love to a man. In a Palace of Truth how many husbands would have to confess that it decidedly surprised them when they found themselves engaged to be married? The will comes into play only for a moment or two now and then. Of course it is made to seem responsible, and in a sense it *is* responsible, but, in the vast majority of cases, purely as an animal instinct, confirming the suggestion of circumstances.'

'There's something in all this,' granted the listener, 'but it doesn't explain the behaviour of a man who, after frightful experience in marriage—after recovering his freedom—after finding himself welcomed by congenial society—after inheriting a fortune to use as he likes—goes and offers himself to an artful hussy in a lodging-house.'

'That's the special case. Look how it came to pass. Months ago I knew I was drifting into dangerous relations with that girl. Unfortunately I am not a rascal: I can't think of girls as playthings; a fatal conscientiousness in an unmarried man of no means. Day after day we grew more familiar. She used to come up and ask me if I wanted anything; and of course I knew that she began to come more often than necessary. When she laid a meal for me, we talked—half an hour at a time. The mother, doubtless, looked on with approval; Emma had to find a husband, and why not me as well as another? They knew I was a soft creature— that I never made a row about anything—was grateful for anything that looked like kindness—and so on. Just the kind of man to be captured. But no—I don't want to make out that I am their victim; that's a feeble excuse, and a worthless one. The average man would either have treated the girl as a servant, and so kept her at her distance, or else he would have alarmed her by behaviour which suggested anything you like but marriage. As for me, I hadn't the common-sense to take either of these courses. I made a friend of the girl; talked to her more and more confidentially; and at last—fatal moment—told her my history. Yes, I was ass enough to tell that girl the whole story of my life. Can you conceive such folly?

'Yet the easiest thing in the world to understand. We were alone in the house one evening. After trying to work for about an hour I gave it up. I knew that the mother was out, and I heard Emma moving downstairs. I was lonely and dispirited—wanted to talk—to talk about myself to some one who would give a kind ear. So I went down, and made some excuse for beginning a conversation in the parlour. It lasted a couple of hours; we were still talking when the mother came back. I didn't persuade myself that I cared for Emma, even then. Her vulgarisms of speech and feeling jarred upon me. But she was feminine; she spoke and looked gently, with sympathy. I enjoyed that evening—and you must bear in mind what I have told you before, that I stand in awe of refined women. I am their equal, I know; I can talk with them; their society is an exquisite delight to me;—but when it comes to thinking of intimacy with one of them—! Perhaps it is my long years of squalid existence. Perhaps I have come to regard myself as doomed to life on a lower level. I find it an impossible thing to imagine myself offering marriage—making love—to a girl such as those I meet in the big houses.'

'You will outgrow that,' said Munden.

'Yes, yes,—I hope and believe so. And wouldn't it be criminal to deny myself even the chance, now that I have money? All to-day I have been tortured like a soul that beholds its salvation lost by a moment's weakness of the flesh. You can imagine what my suffering has been; it drove me into sheer lying. I had resolved to deny utterly that I had asked Emma to marry me—to deny it with a savage boldness, and take the consequences.'

'A most rational resolve, my dear fellow. Pray stick to it. But you haven't told me yet how the dizzy culmination of your madness was reached. You say that you proposed *last night?*'

'Yes—and simply for the pleasure of telling Emma, when she had accepted me, that I had eighty thousand pounds! You can't understand that? I suppose the change of fortune has made me a little light-headed; I have been going about with a sense of exaltation which has prompted me to endless follies. I have felt a desire to be kind to people—to bestow happiness—to share my joy with others. If I had some of the doctor's money in my pocket, I should have given away five-pound notes.'

'You contented yourself,' said Munden, laughing, 'with giving a promissory-note for the whole legacy.'

'Yes; but try to understand. Emma came up to my room at supper-time, and as usual we talked. I didn't say anything about my uncle's death—yet I felt the necessity of telling her creep fatally upon me. There was a conflict in my mind, between common-sense and that awful sentimentality which is my curse. When Emma came up again after supper, she mentioned that her mother was gone with a friend to a theatre. "Why don't you go?" I said. "Oh, I don't go anywhere." "But after all," I urged consolingly, "August isn't exactly the time for enjoying the theatre." She admitted it wasn't; but there was the Exhibition at Earl's Court, she had heard so much of it, and wanted to go. "Then suppose we go together one of these evenings?"

'You see? Idiot!—and I couldn't help it. My tongue spoke these imbecile words in spite of my brain. All very well, if I had meant what another man would; but I didn't, and the girl knew I didn't. And she looked at me—and then—why, mere brute instinct did the rest—no, not mere instinct, for it was complicated with that idiot desire to see how the girl would look, hear what she would say, when she knew that I had given her eighty thousand pounds. You can't understand?'

'As a bit of morbid psychology—yes.'

'And the frantic proceeding made me happy! For an hour or two I behaved as if I loved the girl with all my soul. And afterwards I was still happy. I walked up and down my bedroom, making plans for the future—for her education, and so on. I saw all sorts of admirable womanly qualities in her. I *was* in love with her, and there's an end of it!'

Munden mused for a while, then laid down his pipe.

'Remarkably suggestive, Shergold, the name of the street in which you have been living. Well, you don't go back there?'

'No. I have come to my senses. I shall go to an hotel for to-night, and send presently for all my things.'

'To be sure, and on Saturday—or on Friday evening, if you like, we leave England.'

It was evident that Shergold rejoiced with trembling.

'But I can't stick to the lie.' he said. 'I shall compensate the girl. You see, by running away I make confession that there's something wrong. I shall see a solicitor and put the matter into his hands.'

'As you please. But let the solicitor exercise his own discretion as to damages.'

'Damages!' Shergold pondered the word. 'I suppose she won't drag me into court—make a public ridicule of me? If so, there's an end of my hopes. I couldn't go among people after that.'

'I don't see why not. But your solicitor will probably manage the affair. They have their methods,' Munden added drily.

Early the next morning Shergold despatched a telegram to Maze Pond, addressed to his landlady. It said that he would be kept away by business for a day or two. On Friday he attended his uncle's funeral, and that evening he left Charing Cross with Harvey Munden, *en route* for Como.

There, a fortnight later, Shergold received from his solicitor a communication which put an end to his feigning of repose and hopefulness. That he did but feign, Harvey Munden felt assured; signs of a troubled conscience, or at all events of restless nerves, were evident in all his doing and conversing; now he once more made frank revelation of his weakness.

'There's the devil to pay. She won't take money. She's got a lawyer, and is going to bring me into court. I've authorised Reckitt to offer as much as five thousand pounds,—it's no good. He says her lawyer has evidently encouraged her to hope for enormous damages, and then she'll have the satisfaction of making me the town-talk. It's all up with me, Munden. My hopes are vanished like—what is it in Dante?—*il fumo in aere ed in aqua la schiuma*!'

Smoking a Cavour, Munden lay back in the shadow of the pergola, and seemed to disdain reply.

'Your advice?'

'What's the good of advising a man born to be fooled? Why, let the —— do her worst!'

Shergold winced.

'We mustn't forget that it's all my fault.'

'Yes, just as it's your own fault you didn't die on the day of your birth!'

'I must raise the offer—'

'By all means; offer ten thousand. I suppose a jury would give her two hundred and fifty.'

'But the scandal—the ridicule—'

'Face it. Very likely it's the only thing that would teach you wisdom and save your life.'

'That's one way of looking at it. I half believe it might be effectual.'

He kept alone for most of the day. In the evening, from nine to ten, he went upon the lake with Harvey, but could not talk; his blue eyes were sunk in a restless melancholy, his brows were furrowed, he kept making short, nervous movements, as though in silent remonstrance with himself. And when the next morning came, and Harvey Munden rang the bell for his coffee, a waiter brought him a note addressed in Shergold's hand. 'I have started for London,' ran the hurriedly written lines. 'Don't be uneasy; all I mean to do is to stop the danger of a degrading publicity; the fear of *that* is too much for me. I have an idea, and you shall hear how I get on in a few days.'

The nature of that promising idea Munden never learnt. His next letter from Shergold came in about ten days; it informed him very briefly that the writer was 'about to be married,' and that in less than a week he would have started with his wife on a voyage round the world. Harvey did not reply; indeed, the letter contained no address.

One day in November he was accosted at the club by his familiar bore.

'So your friend Shergold is dead?'

'Dead? I know nothing of it.'

'Really? They talked of it last night at Lady Teasdale's. He died a few days ago, at Calcutta. Dysentery, or something of that kind. His wife cabled to some one or other.'

THE SALT OF THE EARTH

STRONG and silent the tide of Thames flowed upward, and over it swept the morning tide of humanity. Through white autumnal mist yellow sunbeams flitted from shore to shore. The dome, the spires, the river frontages slowly unveiled and brightened: there was hope of a fair day.

Not that it much concerned this throng of men and women hastening to their labour. From near and far, by the league-long highways of South London, hither they converged each morning, and joined the procession across the bridge; their task was the same to-day as yesterday, regardless of gleam or gloom. Many had walked such a distance that they plodded wearily, looking neither to right nor left. The more vigorous strode briskly on, elbowing their way, or nimbly skipping into the road to gain advance; yet these also had a fixed gaze, preoccupied or vacant, seldom cheerful. Here and there a couple of friends conversed; girls, with bag or parcel and a book for the dinner hour, chattered and laughed; but for the most part lips were mute amid the clang and roar of heavy-laden wheels.

It was the march of those who combat hunger with delicate hands: at the pen's point, or from behind the breastwork of a counter, or trusting to bare wits pressed daily on the grindstone. Their chief advantage over the sinewy class beneath them lay in the privilege of spending more than they could afford on house and clothing; with rare exceptions they had no hope, no chance, of reaching independence; enough if they upheld the threadbare standard of respectability, and bequeathed it to their children as a solitary heirloom. The oldest looked the poorest, and naturally so; amid the tramp of multiplying feet, their steps had begun to lag when speed was more than ever necessary; they saw newcomers outstrip them, and trudged under an increasing load.

No eye surveying this procession would have paused for a moment on Thomas Bird. In costume there was nothing to distinguish him from hundreds of rather shabby clerks who passed along with their out-of-fashion chimney-pot and badly rolled umbrella; his gait was that of a man who takes no exercise beyond the daily walk to and from his desk; the casual glance could see nothing in his features but patient dullness tending to good humour. He might be thirty, he might be forty—impossible to decide. Yet when a ray of sunshine fell upon him, and he lifted his eyes to the eastward promise, there shone in his countenance something one might vainly have sought through the streaming concourse of which Thomas Bird was an unregarded atom. For him, it appeared, the struggling sunlight had a message of hope. Trouble cleared from his face; he smiled unconsciously and quickened his steps.

For fifteen years he had walked to and fro over Blackfriars Bridge, leaving his home in Camberwell at eight o'clock and reaching it again at seven. Fate made him a commercial clerk as his father before him; he earned more than enough for his necessities, but seemed to have reached the limit of promotion, for he had no influential friends, and he lacked the capacity to rise by his own efforts. There may have been some calling for which Thomas was exactly suited, but he did not know of it; in the office he proved himself a trustworthy machine, with no opportunity of becoming anything else. His parents were dead, his kindred scattered, he lived, as for several years past, in lodgings. But it never occurred to him to think of his lot as mournful. A man of sociable instincts, he had many acquaintances, some of whom he cherished. An extreme simplicity marked his tastes, and the same characteristic appeared in his conversation; an easy man to deceive, easy to make fun of, yet impossible to dislike, or despise—unless by the despicable. He delighted in stories of adventure, of bravery by flood or field, and might have posed—had he ever posed at all—as something of an authority on North Pole expeditions and the geography of Polynesia.

He received his salary once a month, and to-day was pay-day: the consciousness of having earned a certain number of sovereigns always set his thoughts on possible purchases, and at present he was revolving the subject of his wardrobe. Certainly it needed renewal, but Thomas could not decide at which end to begin, head or feet. His position in a leading house demanded a good hat, the bad weather called for new boots. Living economically as he did, it should have been a simple matter to resolve the doubt by purchasing both articles, but, for one reason and another, Thomas seldom had a surplus over the expenses of his lodgings; in practice he found it very difficult to save a sovereign for other needs.

When evening released him he walked away in a cheerful frame of mind, grasping the money in his trousers' pocket, and all but decided to make some acquisition on the way home. Near Ludgate Circus some one addressed him over his shoulder.

'Good evening, Tom; pleasant for the time of year.'

The speaker was a man of fifty, stout and florid—the latter peculiarity especially marked in his nose; he looked like a substantial merchant, and spoke with rather pompous geniality. Thrusting his arm through the clerk's, he walked with him over Blackfriars Bridge, talking in the friendliest strain of things impersonal. Beyond the bridge—

'Do you tram it?' he asked, glancing upwards.

'I think so, Mr. Warbeck,' answered the other, whose tone to his acquaintance was very respectful.

'Ah! I'm afraid it would make me late.—Oh, by the bye, Tom, I'm really ashamed—most awkward that this kind of thing happens so often, but—could you, do you think?—No, no; one sovereign only. Let me make a note of it by the light of this shop-window. Really, the total is getting quite considerable. Tut, tut! You shall have a cheque in a day or two. Oh, it can't run on any longer; I'm completely ashamed of myself. Entirely temporary—as I explained. A cheque on Wednesday at latest. Good-bye, Tom.'

They shook hands cordially, and Mr. Warbeck went off in a hansom. Thomas Bird, changing his mind about the tram, walked all the way home, and with bent head. One would have thought that he had just done something discreditable.

He was wondering, not for the first time, whether Mrs. Warbeck knew or suspected that her husband was in debt to him. Miss Warbeck—Alma Warbeck—assuredly had never dreamed of such a thing. The system of casual loans dated from nearly twelve months ago, and the total was now not much less than thirty pounds. Mr. Warbeck never failed to declare that he was ashamed of himself, but probably the creditor experienced more discomfort of that kind. At the first playful demand Thomas felt a shock. He had known the Warbecks since he was a lad, had always respected them as somewhat his social superiors, and, as time went on, had recognised that the difference of position grew wider: he remaining stationary, while his friends progressed to a larger way of living. But they were, he thought, no less kind to him; Mrs. Warbeck invited him to the house about once a month, and Alma—Alma talked with him in such a pleasant, homely way. Did their expenditure outrun their means? He would never have supposed it, but for the City man's singular behaviour. About the cheque so often promised he cared little, but with all his heart he hoped Mrs. Warbeck did not know.

Somewhere near Camberwell Green, just as he had resumed the debate about his purchases, a middle-aged woman met him with friendly greeting. Her appearance was that of a decent shopkeeper's wife.

'I'm so glad I've met you, Mr. Bird. I know you'll be anxious to hear how our poor friend is getting on.'

She spoke of the daughter of a decayed tradesman, a weak and overworked girl, who had lain for some weeks in St. Thomas's Hospital. Mrs. Pritchard, a gadabout infected with philanthropy, was fond of discovering such cases, and in everyday conversation made the most of her charitable efforts.

'They'll allow her out in another week,' she pursued. 'But, of course, she can't expect to be fit for anything for a time. And I very much doubt whether she'll ever get the right use of her limbs again. But what we have to think of now is to get her some decent clothing. The poor thing has positively nothing. I'm going to speak to Mrs. Doubleday, and a few other people. Really, Mr. Bird, if it weren't that I've presumed on your good nature so often lately—'

She paused and smiled unctuously at him.

'I'm afraid I can't do much,' faltered Thomas, reddening at the vision of a new 'chimney-pot.'

'No, no; of course not. I'm sure I should never expect—it's only that every little—however little—does help, you know.'

Thomas thrust a hand into his pocket and brought out a florin, which Mrs. Pritchard pursed with effusive thanks.

Certain of this good woman's critics doubted her competence as a trustee, but Thomas Bird had no such misgiving. He talked with kindly interest of the unfortunate girl, and wished her well in a voice that carried conviction.

His lodgings were a pair of very small, mouldy, and ill-furnished rooms; he took them unwillingly, overcome by the landlady's doleful story of their long lodgerless condition, and, in the exercise of a heavenly forbearance, remained year after year. The woman did not cheat him, and Thomas knew enough of life to respect her for this remarkable honesty; she was simply an ailing, lachrymose slut, incapable of effort. Her son, a lad who had failed in several employments from sheer feebleness of mind and body, practically owed his subsistence to Thomas Bird, whose good offices had at length established the poor fellow at a hairdresser's. To sit frequently for an hour at a time, as Thomas did, listening with attention to Mrs. Batty's talk of her own and her son's ailments, was in itself a marvel of charity. This evening she met him as he entered, and lighted him into his room.

'There's a letter come for you, Mr. Bird. I put it down somewheres—why, now, where *did* I—? Oh, 'ere it is. You'll be glad to 'ear as Sam did his first shave to-day, an' his 'and didn't tremble much neither.'

Burning with desire to open the letter, which he saw was from Mrs. Warbeck, Thomas stood patiently until the flow of words began to gurgle away amid groans and pantings.

'Well,' he cried gaily, 'didn't I promise Sam a shilling when he'd done his first shave? If I didn't I ought to have done, and here it is for him.'

Then he hurried into the bedroom, and read his letter by candle-light. It was a short scrawl on thin, scented, pink-hued notepaper. Would he do Mrs. Warbeck the 'favour' of looking in before ten to-night? No explanation of this unusually worded request; and Thomas fell at once into a tremor of anxiety. With a hurried glance at his watch, he began to make ready for the visit, struggling with drawers which would neither open nor shut, and driven to despair by the damp condition of his clean linen.

In this room, locked away from all eyes but his own, lay certain relics which Thomas worshipped. One was a photograph of a girl of fifteen. At that age Alma Warbeck promised little charm, and the photograph allowed her less; but it was then that Thomas Bird became her bondman, as he had ever since remained. There was also a letter, the only one that he had ever received from her—'Dear Mr. Bird,—Mamma says will you buy her some more of those *jewjewbs* at the shop in the city, and bring them on Sunday.—Yours sincerely, Alma Warbeck'—written when she was sixteen, seven years ago. Moreover, there was a playbill, used by Alma on the single occasion when he accompanied the family to a theatre.

Never had he dared to breathe a syllable of what he thought—'hoped' would misrepresent him, for Thomas in this matter had always stifled hope. Indeed, hope would have been irrational. In the course of her teens Alma grew tall and well proportioned; not beautiful of feature, but pleasing; not brilliant in personality, but good-natured; fairly intelligent and moderately ambitious. She was the only daughter of a dubiously active commission-agent, and must deem it good fortune if she married a man with three or four hundred a year; but Thomas Bird had no more than his twelve pounds a month, and did not venture to call himself a gentleman. In Alma he found the essentials of true ladyhood— perhaps with reason; he had never heard her say an ill-natured thing, nor seen upon her face a look which pained his acute sensibilities; she was unpretentious, of equal temper, nothing of a gossip, kindly disposed. Never for a moment had he flattered himself that Alma perceived his devotion or cared for him otherwise than as for an old friend. But thought is free, and so is love. The modest clerk had made this girl the light of his life, and whether far or near the rays of that ideal would guide him on his unworldly path.

New shaven and freshly clad, he set out for the Warbecks' house, which was in a near part of Brixton. Not an imposing house by any means, but an object of reverence to Thomas Bird. A servant whom he did not recognise—servants came and went at the Warbecks'—admitted him to the drawing-room, which was vacant; there, his eyes wandering about the gimcrack furniture, which he never found in the same arrangement at two successive visits, he waited till his hostess came in.

Mrs. Warbeck was very stout, very plain, and rather untidy, yet her countenance made an impression not on the whole disagreeable; with her wide eyes, slightly parted lips, her homely smile, and unadorned speech, she counteracted in some measure the effect, upon a critical observer, of the pretentious ugliness with which she was surrounded. Thomas thought her a straightforward woman, and perhaps was not misled by his partiality. Certainly the tone in which she now began, and the tenor of her remarks, repelled suspicion of duplicity.

'Well, now, Mr. Thomas, I wish to have a talk.' She had thus styled him since he grew too old to be called Tom; that is to say, since he was seventeen. He was now thirty-one. 'And I'm going to talk to you just like the old friends we are. You see? No nonsense; no beating about the bush. You'd rather have it so, wouldn't you?' Scarce able to articulate, the visitor showed a cheery assent. 'Yes, I was sure of that. Now—better come to the point at once—my daughter is— well, no, she isn't yet, but the fact is I feel sure she'll very soon be engaged.'

The blow was softened by Thomas's relief at discovering that money would not be the subject of their talk, yet it fell upon him, and he winced.

'You've expected it,' pursued the lady, with bluff good-humour. 'Yes, of course you have.' She said "ave,' a weakness happily unshared by her daughter. 'We don't want it talked about, but I know you can hold your tongue. Well, it's young Mr. Fisher, of Nokes, Fisher and Co. We haven't known him long, but he took from the first to Alma, and I have my reasons for believing that the feeling is *mutial*, though I wouldn't for the world let Alma hear me say so.'

Young Mr. Fisher. Thomas knew of him; a capable business man, and son of a worthy father. He kept his teeth close, his eyes down.

'And now,' pursued Mrs. Warbeck, becoming still more genial, 'I'm getting round to the unpleasant side of the talk, though I don't see that it *need* be unpleasant. We're old friends, and where's the use of being friendly if you can't speak your mind, when speak you must? It comes to this: I just want to ask you quite straightforward, not to be offended or take it ill if we don't ask you to come here till this business is over and settled. You see? The fact is, we've told Mr. Fisher he can look in whenever he likes, and it might happen, you know, that he'd meet you here, and, speaking like old friends—I think it better not.'

A fire burned in the listener's cheeks, a noise buzzed in his ears. He understood the motive of this frank request; humble as ever—never humbler than when beneath this roof—he was ready to avow himself Mr. Fisher's inferior; but with all his heart he wished that Mrs. Warbeck had found some other way of holding him aloof from her prospective son-in-law.

'Of course,' continued the woman stolidly, 'Alma doesn't know I'm saying this. It's just between our two selves. I haven't even spoken of it to Mr. Warbeck. I'm quite sure that you'll understand that we're obliged to make a few changes in the way we've lived. It's all very well for you and me to be comfortable together, and laugh and talk about all sorts of things, but with one like Alma in the 'ouse, and the friends she's making and the company that's likely to come here—now you *do* see what I mean, *don't* you, now? And you won't take it the wrong way? No, I was sure you wouldn't. There, now, we'll shake 'ands over it, and be as good friends as ever.' The handshaking was metaphorical merely. Thomas smiled, and was endeavouring to shape a sentence, when he heard voices out in the hall.

'There's Alma and her father back,' said Mrs. Warbeck. 'I didn't think they'd come back so soon; they've been with some new friends of ours.' Thomas jumped up.

'I can't—I'd rather not see them, please, Mrs. Warbeck. Can you prevent it?' His voice startled her somewhat, and she hesitated. A gesture of entreaty sent her from the room. As the door opened Alma was heard laughing merrily; then came silence. In a minute or two the hostess returned and the visitor, faltering, 'Thank you. I quite understand,' quietly left the house.

For three weeks he crossed and recrossed Blackfriars Bridge without meeting Mr. Warbeck. His look was perhaps graver, his movements less alert, but he had not noticeably changed; his life kept its wonted tenor. The florid-nosed gentleman at length came face to face with him on Ludgate Hill in the dinner-hour—an embarrassment to both. Speedily recovering self-possession Mr. Warbeck pressed the clerk's hand with fervour and drew him aside.

'I've been wanting to see you, Tom. So you keep away from us, do you? I understand. The old lady has given me a quiet hint. Well, well, you're quite right, and I honour you for it, Tom. Nothing selfish about *you*; you keep it all to yourself; I honour you for it, my dear boy. And perhaps I had better tell you, Alma is to be married in January. After that, same as before, won't it be?—Have a glass of wine with me? No time? We must have a quiet dinner together some evening; one of the old chop houses.—There was something else I wanted to speak about, but I see you're in a hurry. All right, it'll do next time.'

He waved his hand and was gone. When next they encountered Mr. Warbeck made bold to borrow ten shillings, without the most distant allusion to his outstanding debt.

Thomas Bird found comfort in the assurance that Mrs. Warbeck had kept *her* secret as the borrower kept *his*.

Alma's father was not utterly dishonoured in his sight.

One day in January, Thomas, pleading indisposition, left work at twelve. He had a cold and a headache, and felt more miserable than at any time since his school-days. As he rode home in an omnibus Mr. and Mrs. Warbeck were entertaining friends at the wedding-breakfast, and Thomas knew it. For an hour or two in the afternoon he sat patiently under his landlady's talk, but a fit of nervous exasperation at length drove him forth, and he did not return till supper-time. Just as he sat down to a basin of gruel, Mrs. Batty admitted a boy who brought him a message. 'Mother sent me round, Mr. Bird,' said the messenger, 'and she wants to know if you could just come and see her; it's something about father. He had some work to do, but he hasn't come home to do it.'

Without speaking Thomas equipped himself and walked a quarter of a mile to the lodgings of a married friend of his—a clerk chronically out of work, and too often in liquor. The wife received him with tears. After eight weeks without earning a penny, her husband had obtained the job of addressing five hundred envelopes, to be done at home and speedily. Tempted forth by an acquaintance 'for half a minute' as he sat down to the task, he had been absent for three hours, and would certainly return unfit for work.

'It isn't only the money,' sobbed his wife, 'but it might have got him more work, and now, of course, he's lost the chance, and we haven't nothing more than a crust of bread left. And—'

Thomas slipped half-a-crown into her hand and whispered, 'Send Jack before the shops close.' Then, to escape thanks, he shouted out, 'Where's these blessed envelopes, and where's the addresses? All right, just leave me this corner of the table and don't speak to me as long as I sit here.'

Between half-past nine and half-past twelve, at the rate of eighty an hour, he addressed all but half the five hundred envelopes. Then his friend appeared, dolefully drunk. Thomas would not look at him.

'He'll finish the rest by dinner to-morrow,' said the miserable wife, 'and that's in time.'

So Thomas Bird went home. He felt better at heart, and blamed himself for his weakness during the day. He blamed himself often enough for this or that, knowing not that such as he are the salt of the earth.

THE PIG AND WHISTLE

'I possess a capital of thirty thousand pounds. One-third of this is invested in railway shares, which bear interest at three and a half per cent.; another third is in Government stock, and produces two and three-quarters per cent.; the rest is lent on mortgages, at three per cent. Calculate my income for the present year.'

This kind of problem was constantly being given out by Mr. Ruddiman, assistant master at Longmeadows School. Mr. Ruddiman, who had reached the age of five-and-forty, and who never in his life had possessed five-and-forty pounds, used his arithmetic lesson as an opportunity for flight of imagination. When dictating a sum in which he attributed to himself enormous wealth, his eyes twinkled, his slender body struck a dignified attitude, and he smiled over the class with a certain genial condescension. When the calculation proposed did not refer to personal income it generally illustrated the wealth of the nation, in which Mr. Ruddiman had a proud delight. He would bid his youngsters compute the proceeds of some familiar tax, and the vast sum it represented rolled from his lips on a note of extraordinary satisfaction, as if he gloried in this evidence of national prosperity. His salary at Longmeadows just sufficed to keep him decently clad and to support him during the holidays. He had been a master here for seven years, and earnestly hoped that his services might be retained for at least seven more; there was very little chance of his ever obtaining a better position, and the thought of being cast adrift, of having to betake himself to the school agencies and enter upon new engagements, gave Mr. Ruddiman a very unpleasant sensation. In his time he had gone through hardships such as naturally befall a teacher without diplomas and possessed of no remarkable gifts; that he had never broken down in health was the result of an admirable constitution and of much native cheerfulness. Only at such an establishment as Longmeadows—an old-fashioned commercial 'academy,' recommended to parents by the healthiness of its rural situation—could he have hoped to hold his ground against modern educational tendencies, which aim at obliterating Mr. Ruddiman and all his kind. Every one liked him; impossible not to like a man so abounding in kindliness and good humour; but his knowledge was anything but extensive, and his methods in instruction had a fine flavour of antiquity. Now and then Mr. Ruddiman asked himself what was to become of him when sickness or old age forbade his earning even the modest income upon which he could at present count, but his happy temper dismissed the troublesome reflection. One thing, however, he had decided; in future he would find some more economical way of spending his holidays. Hitherto he had been guilty of the extravagance of taking long journeys to see members of his scattered family, or of going to the seaside, or of amusing himself (oh, how innocently!) in London. This kind of thing must really stop. In the coming summer vacation he had determined to save at least five sovereigns, and he fancied he had discovered a simple way of doing it.

On pleasant afternoons, when he was 'off duty,' Mr. Ruddiman liked to have a long ramble by himself about the fields and lanes. In solitude he was never dull; had you met him during one of these afternoon walks, more likely than not you would have seen a gentle smile on his visage as he walked with head bent. Not that his thoughts were definitely of agreeable things; consciously he thought perhaps of nothing at all; but he liked the sunshine and country quiet, and the sense of momentary independence. Every one would have known him for what he was. His dress, his gait, his countenance, declared the under-master. Mr. Ruddiman never carried a walking-stick; that would have seemed to him to be arrogating a social position to which he had no claim. Generally he held his hands together behind him; if not so, one of them would dip its fingers into a waistcoat pocket and the other grasp the lapel of his coat. If anything he looked rather less than his age, a result, perhaps, of having always lived with the young. His features were agreeably insignificant; his body, though slight of build, had something of athletic outline, due to long practice at cricket, football, and hockey.

If he had rather more time than usual at his disposal he walked as far as the Pig and Whistle, a picturesque little wayside inn, which stood alone, at more than a mile from the nearest village. To reach the Pig and Whistle one climbed a long, slow ascent, and in warm weather few pedestrians, or, for the matter of that, folks driving or riding, could resist the suggestion of the ivy-shadowed porch which admitted to the quaint parlour. So long was it since the swinging sign had been painted that neither of Pig nor of Whistle was any trace now discoverable; but over the porch one read clearly enough the landlord's name: William Fouracres. Only three years ago had Mr. Fouracres established himself here; Ruddiman remembered his predecessor, with whom he had often chatted whilst drinking his modest bottle of ginger beer. The present landlord was a very different sort of man, less affable, not disposed to show himself to every comer. Customers were generally served by the landlord's daughter, and with her Mr. Ruddiman had come to be on very pleasant terms.

But as this remark may easily convey a false impression, it must be added that Miss Fouracres was a very discreet, well-spoken, deliberate person, of at least two-and-thirty. Mr. Ruddiman had known her for more than a year before anything save brief civilities passed between them. In the second twelvemonth of their acquaintance they reached the point of exchanging reminiscences as to the weather, discussing the agricultural prospects of the county, and remarking on the advantage to rural innkeepers of the fashion of bicycling. In the third year they were quite intimate; so intimate, indeed, that when Mr. Fouracres chanced to be absent they spoke of his remarkable history. For the landlord of the Pig and Whistle had a history worth talking about, and Mr. Ruddiman had learnt it from the landlord's own lips. Miss Fouracres would never have touched upon the subject with any one in whom she did not feel confidence; to her it was far from agreeable, and Mr. Ruddiman established himself in her esteem by taking the same view of the matter.

Well, one July afternoon, when the summer vacation drew near, the under-master perspired up the sunny road with another object than that of refreshing himself at the familiar little inn. He entered by the ivied porch, and within, as usual, found Miss Fouracres, who sat behind the bar sewing. Miss Fouracres wore a long white apron, which protected her dress from neck to feet, and gave her an appearance of great neatness and coolness. She had a fresh complexion, and features which made no disagreeable impression. At sight of the visitor she rose, and, as her habit was, stood with one hand touching her chin, whilst she smiled the discreetest of modest welcomes.

'Good day, Miss Fouracres,' said the under-master, after his usual little cough.

'Good day, sir,' was the reply, in a country voice which had a peculiar note of honesty. Miss Fouracres had never yet learnt her acquaintance's name.

'Splendid weather for the crops. I'll take a ginger-beer, if you please.'

'Indeed, that it is, sir. Ginger-beer; yes, sir.'

Then followed two or three minutes of silence. Miss Fouracres had resumed her sewing, though not her seat. Mr. Ruddiman sipped his beverage more gravely than usual.

'How is Mr. Fouracres?' he asked at length.

'I'm sorry to say, sir,' was the subdued reply, 'that he's thinking about the Prince.'

'Oh, dear!' sighed Mr. Ruddiman, as one for whom this mysterious answer had distressing significance. 'That's a great pity.'

'Yes, sir. And I'm sorry to say,' went on Miss Fouracres, in the same confidential tone, 'that the Prince is coming here. I don't mean *here*, sir, to the Pig and Whistle, but to Woodbury Manor. Father saw it in the newspaper, and since then he's had no rest, day or night. He's sitting out in the garden. I don't know whether you'd like to go and speak to him, sir?'

'I will. Yes, I certainly will. But there's something I should like to ask you about first, Miss Fouracres. I'm thinking of staying in this part of the country through the holidays'—long ago he had made known his position—'and it has struck me that perhaps I could lodge here. Could you let me have a room? Just a bedroom would be enough.'

'Why, yes, sir,' replied the landlord's daughter. 'We have two bedrooms, you know, and I've no doubt my father would be willing to arrange with you.'

'Ah, then I'll mention it to him. Is he in very low spirits?'

'He's unusual low to-day, sir. I shouldn't wonder if it did him good to see you, and talk a bit.'

Having finished his ginger-beer, Mr. Ruddiman walked through the house and passed out into the garden, where he at once became aware of Mr. Fouracres. The landlord, a man of sixty, with grizzled hair and large, heavy countenance, sat in a rustic chair under an apple-tree; beside him was a little table, on which stood a bottle of whisky and a glass. Approaching, Mr. Ruddiman saw reason to suspect that the landlord had partaken too freely of the refreshment ready to his hand. Mr. Fouracres' person was in a limp state; his cheeks were very highly coloured, and his head kept nodding as he muttered to himself. At the visitor's greeting he looked up with a sudden surprise, as though he resented an intrusion on his privacy.

'It's very hot, Mr. Fouracres,' the under-master went on to remark with cordiality.

'Hot? I dare say it is,' replied the landlord severely. 'And what else do you expect at this time of the year, sir?'

'Just so, Mr. Fouracres, just so!' said the other, as good-humouredly as possible. 'You don't find it unpleasant?'

'Why should I, sir? It was a good deal hotter day than this when His Royal Highness called upon me; a good deal hotter. The Prince didn't complain; not he. He said to me—I'm speaking of His Royal Highness, you understand; I hope you understand that, sir?'

'Oh, perfectly!'

'His words were—"Very seasonable weather, Mr. Fouracres." I'm not likely to forget what he said; so it's no use you or any one else trying to make out that he didn't say that. I tell you he *did!* "Very season weather, Mr. Fouracres"— calling me by name, just like that. And it's no good you nor anybody else—'

The effort of repeating the Prince's utterance with what was meant to be a princely accent proved so exhausting to Mr. Fouracres that he sank together in his chair and lost all power of coherent speech. In a moment he seemed to be sleeping. Having watched him a little while, Mr. Ruddiman spoke his name, and tried to attract his attention; finding it useless he went back into the inn.

'I'm afraid I shall have to put it off to another day,' was his remark to the landlord's daughter. 'Mr. Four-acres is—rather drowsy.'

'Ah, sir!' sighed the young woman. 'I'm sorry to say he's often been like that lately.'

Their eyes met, but only for an instant. Mr. Ruddiman looked and felt uncomfortable.

'I'll come again very soon, Miss Fouracres,' he said. 'You might just speak to your father about the room.'

'Thank you, sir. I will, sir.'

And, with another uneasy glance, which was not returned, the under-master went his way. Descending towards Longmeadows, he thought over the innkeeper's story, which may be briefly related. Some ten years before this Mr. Fouracres occupied a very comfortable position; he was landlord of a flourishing inn—called an hotel—in a little town of some importance as an agricultural centre, and seemed perfectly content with the life and the society natural to a man so circumstanced. His manners were marked by a certain touch of pompousness, and he liked to dwell upon the excellence of the entertainment which his house afforded, but these were innocent characteristics which did not interfere with his reputation as a sensible and sound man of business. It happened one day that two gentlemen on horseback, evidently riding for their pleasure, stopped at the inn door, and, after a few inquiries, announced that they would alight and have lunch. Mr. Fouracres—who himself received these gentlemen—regarded one of them with much curiosity, and presently came to the startling conclusion that he was about to entertain no less a person than the Heir Apparent. He knew that the Prince was then staying at a great house some ten miles away, and there could be no doubt that one of his guests had a strong resemblance to the familiar portraits of His Royal Highness. In his excitement at the supposed discovery, Mr. Fouracres at once communicated it to those about him, and in a very few minutes half the town had heard the news. Of course the host would allow no one but himself to wait at the royal table—which was spread in the inn's best room, guarded against all intrusion. In vain, however, did he listen for a word from either of the gentlemen which might confirm his belief; in their conversation no name or title was used, and no mention made of anything significant. They remained for an hour. When their horses were brought round for them a considerable crowd had gathered before the hotel, and the visitors departed amid a demonstration of exuberant loyalty. On the following day, one or two persons who had been present at this scene declared that the two gentlemen showed surprise, and that, though both raised their hats in acknowledgment of the attention they received, they rode away laughing.

For the morrow brought doubts. People began to say that the Prince had never been near the town at all, and that evidence could be produced of his having passed the whole day at the house where he was a visitor. Mr. Fouracres smiled disdainfully; no assertion or argument availed to shake his proud assurance that he had entertained the Heir to the Throne. From that day he knew no peace. Fired with an extraordinary arrogance, he viewed as his enemy every one who refused to believe in the Prince's visit; he quarrelled violently with many of his best friends; he brought insulting accusations against all manner of persons. Before long the man was honestly convinced that there existed a conspiracy to rob him of a distinction that was his due. Political animus had, perhaps, something to do with it, for the Liberal newspaper (Mr. Fouracres was a stout Conservative) made more than one malicious joke on the subject. A few townsmen stood by the landlord's side and used their ingenuity in discovering plausible reasons why the Prince did not care to have it publicly proclaimed that he had visited the town and lunched at the hotel. These partisans scorned the suggestion that Mr. Fouracres had made a mistake, but they were unable to deny that a letter, addressed to the Prince himself, with a view to putting an end to the debate, had elicited (in a secretarial hand) a brief denial of the landlord's story. Evidently something very mysterious underlay the whole affair, and there was much shaking of heads for a long time.

To Mr. Fouracres the result of the honour he so strenuously vindicated was serious indeed. By way of defiance to all mockers he wished to change the time-honoured sign of the inn, and to substitute for it the Prince of Wales's Feathers. On this point he came into conflict with the owner of the property, and, having behaved very violently, received notice that his lease, just expiring, would not be renewed. Whereupon what should Mr. Fouracres do but purchase land and begin to build for himself an hotel twice as large as that he must shortly quit. On this venture he used all, and more than all, his means, and, as every one had prophesied, he was soon a ruined man. In less than three years from the fatal day he turned his back upon the town where he had known respect and prosperity, and went forth to earn his living as best he could. After troublous wanderings, on which he was accompanied by his daughter, faithful and devoted, though she had her doubts on a certain subject, the decayed publican at length found a place of rest. A small legacy from a relative had put it in his power to make a new, though humble, beginning in business; he established himself at the Pig and Whistle.

The condition in which he had to-day been discovered by Mr. Ruddiman was not habitual with him. Once a month, perhaps, his melancholy thoughts drove him to the bottle; for the most part he led a sullen, brooding life, indifferent to the state of his affairs, and only animated when he found a new and appreciative listener to the story of his wrongs. That he had been grievously wronged was Mr. Fouracres' immutable conviction. Not by His Royal Highness; the Prince knew nothing of the strange conspiracy which had resulted in Fouracres' ruin; letters addressed to His Royal Highness were evidently intercepted by underlings, and never came before the royal eyes. Again and again had Mr. Fouracres written long statements of his case, and petitioned for an audience. He was now resolved to adopt other methods; he would use the first opportunity of approaching the Prince's person, and lifting up his voice where he could not but be heard. He sought no vulgar gain; his only desire was to have this fact recognised, that he had, indeed, entertained the Prince, and so put to shame all his scornful enemies. And now the desired occasion offered itself. In the month of September His Royal Highness would be a guest at Woodbury Manor, distant only some couple of miles from the Pig and Whistle. It was the excitement of such a prospect which had led Mr. Fouracres to undue indulgence under the apple-tree this afternoon.

A week later Mr. Ruddiman again ascended the hill, and, after listening patiently to the narrative which he had heard fifty times, came to an arrangement with Mr. Fouracres about the room he wished to rent for the holidays. The terms were very moderate, and the under-master congratulated himself on this prudent step. He felt sure that a couple of months at the Pig and Whistle would be anything but disagreeable. The situation was high and healthy; the surroundings were picturesque. And for society, well, there was Miss Fouracres, whom Mr. Ruddiman regarded as a very sensible and pleasant person.

Of course, no one at Longmeadows had an inkling of the under-master's intention. On the day of 'breaking up' he sent his luggage, as usual, to the nearest railway station, and that same evening had it conveyed by carrier to the little wayside inn, where, much at ease in mind and body, he passed his first night.

He had a few books with him, but Mr. Ruddiman was not much of a reader. In the garden of the inn, or somewhere near by, he found a spot of shade, and there, pipe in mouth, was content to fleet the hours as they did in the golden age. Now and then he tried to awaken his host's interest in questions of national finance. It was one of Mr. Ruddiman's favourite amusements to sketch Budgets in anticipation of that to be presented by the Chancellor of the Exchequer, and he always convinced himself that his own financial expedients were much superior to those laid before Parliament. All sorts of ingenious little imposts were constantly occurring to him, and his mouth watered with delight at the sound of millions which might thus be added to the national wealth. But to Mr. Fouracres such matters seemed trivial. A churchwarden between his lips, he appeared to listen, sometimes giving a nod or a grunt; in reality his thoughts were wandering amid bygone glories, or picturing a day of brilliant revenge.

Much more satisfactory were the conversations between Mr. Ruddiman and his host's daughter; they were generally concerned with the budget, not of the nation, but of the Pig and Whistle. Miss Fouracres was a woman of much domestic ability; she knew how to get the maximum of comfort out of small resources. But for her the inn would have been a wretched little place—as, indeed, it was before her time. Miss Fouracres worked hard and prudently. She had no help; the garden, the poultry, all the cares of house and inn were looked after by her alone—except, indeed, a few tasks beyond her physical strength, which were disdainfully performed by the landlord. A pony and cart served chiefly to give Mr. Fouracres an airing when his life of sedentary dignity grew burdensome. One afternoon, when he had driven to the market town, his daughter and her guest were in the garden together, gathering broad beans and gossiping with much contentment.

'I wish I could always live here!' exclaimed Mr. Ruddiman, after standing for a moment with eyes fixed meditatively upon a very large pod which he had just picked.

Miss Fouracres looked at him as if in surprise, her left hand clasping her chin.

'Ah, you'd soon get tired of it, sir.'

'I shouldn't! No, I'm sure I shouldn't. I like this life. It suits me. I like it a thousand times better than teaching in a school.'

'That's your fancy, sir.'

As Miss Fouracres spoke a sound from the house drew her attention; some one had entered the inn.

'A customer?' said Mr. Ruddiman. 'Let me go and serve him—do let me!'

'But you wouldn't know how, sir.'

'If it's beer, and that's most likely, I know well enough. I've watched you so often. I'll go and see.'

With the face of a schoolboy he ran into the house, and was absent about ten minutes. Then he reappeared, chinking coppers in his hand and laughing gleefully.

'A cyclist! Pint of half-and-half! I served him as if I'd done nothing else all my life.'

Miss Fouracres looked at him with wonder and admiration. She did not laugh; demonstrative mirth was not one of her characteristics; but for a long time there dwelt upon her good, plain countenance a half-smile of placid contentment. When they went in together, Mr. Ruddiman begged her to teach him all the mysteries of the bar, and his request was willingly granted. In this way they amused themselves until the return of the landlord, who, as soon as he had stabled his pony, called Mr. Ruddiman aside, and said in a hoarse whisper—

'The Prince comes to-morrow!'

'Ha! does he?' was the answer, in a tone of feigned interest.

'I shall see him. It's all settled. I've made friends with one of the gardeners at Woodbury Manor, and he's promised to put me in the way of meeting His Royal Highness. I shall have to go over there for a day or two, and stay in Woodbury, to be on the spot when the chance offers.'

Mr. Fouracres had evidently been making his compact with the aid of strong liquor; he walked unsteadily, and in other ways betrayed imperfect command of himself. Presently, at the tea-table, he revealed to his daughter the great opportunity which lay before him, and spoke of the absence from home it would necessitate.

'Of course you'll do as you like, father,' replied Miss Fouracres, with her usual deliberation, and quite good-humouredly, 'but I think you're going on a fool's errand, and that I tell you plain. If you'd just forget all about the Prince, and settle down quiet at the Pig and Whistle, it 'ud be a good deal better for you.'

The landlord regarded her with surprise and scorn. It was the first time that his daughter had ventured to express herself so unmistakably.

'The Pig and Whistle!' he exclaimed. 'A pothouse! I who have kept an hotel and entertained His Royal Highness. You speak like an ignorant woman. Hold your tongue, and don't dare to let me hear your voice again until to-morrow morning!'

Miss Fouracres obeyed him. She was absolutely mute for the rest of the evening, save when obliged to exchange a word or two with rustic company or in the taproom. Her features expressed uneasiness rather than mortification.

The next day, after an early breakfast, Mr. Fouracres set forth to the town of Woodbury. He had the face of a man with a fixed idea, and looked more obstinate, more unintelligent than ever. To his daughter he had spoken only a few cold words, and his last bidding to her was 'Take care of the pothouse!' This treatment gave Miss Fouracres much pain, for she was a softhearted woman, and had never been anything but loyal and affectionate to her father all through his disastrous years. Moreover, she liked the Pig and Whistle, and could not bear to hear it spoken of disdainfully. Before the sound of the cart had died away she had to wipe moisture from her eyes, and at the moment when she was doing so Mr. Ruddiman came into the parlour.

'Has Mr. Fouracres gone?' asked the guest, with embarrassment.

'Just gone, sir,' replied the young woman, half turned away, and nervously fingering her chin.

'I shouldn't trouble about it if I were you, Miss Fouracres,' said Mr. Ruddiman in a tone of friendly encouragement. 'He'll soon be back, he'll soon be back, and you may depend upon it there'll be no harm done.'

'I hope so, sir, but I've an uneasy sort of feeling; I have indeed.'

'Don't you worry, Miss Fouracres. When the Prince has gone away he'll be better.'

Miss Fouracres stood for a moment with eyes cast down, then, looking gravely at Mr. Ruddiman, said in a sorrowful voice—

'He calls the Pig and Whistle a pothouse.'

'Ah, that was wrong of him!' protested the other, no less earnestly. 'A pothouse, indeed! Why, it's one of the nicest little inns you could find anywhere. I'm getting fond of the Pig and Whistle. A pothouse, indeed! No, I call that shameful.'

The listener's eyes shone with gratification.

'Of course we've got to remember,' she said more softly, 'that father has known very different things.'

'I don't care what he has known!' cried Mr. Ruddiman. 'I hope I may never have a worse home than the Pig and Whistle. And I only wish I could live here all the rest of my life, instead of going back to that beastly school!'

'Don't you like the school, Mr. Ruddiman?'

'Oh, I can't say I dislike it. But since I've been living here—well, it's no use thinking of impossibilities.'

Towards midday the pony and trap came back, driven by a lad from Woodbury, who had business in this direction. Miss Fouracres asked him to unharness and stable the pony, and whilst this was being done Mr. Ruddiman stood by, studiously observant. He had pleasure in every detail of the inn life. To-day he several times waited upon passing guests, and laughed exultantly at the perfection he was attaining. Miss Fouracres seemed hardly less pleased, but when alone she still wore an anxious look, and occasionally heaved a sigh of trouble.

Mr. Ruddiman, as usual, took an early supper, and soon after went up to his room. By ten o'clock the house was closed, and all through the night no sound disturbed the peace of the Pig and Whistle.

The morrow passed without news of Mr. Fouracres. On the morning after, just as Mr. Ruddiman was finishing his breakfast, alone in the parlour, he heard a loud cry of distress from the front part of the inn. Rushing out to see what was the matter, he found Miss Fouracres in agitated talk with a man on horseback.

'Ah, what did I say!' she cried at sight of the guest. 'Didn't I *know* something was going to happen? I must go at once—I must put in the pony—'

'I'll do that for you,' said Mr. Ruddiman. 'But what has happened?'

The horseman, a messenger from Woodbury, told a strange tale. Very early this morning, a gardener walking through the grounds at Woodbury Manor, and passing by a little lake or fishpond, saw the body of a man lying in the water, which at this point was not three feet in depth. He drew the corpse to the bank, and, in so doing, recognised his acquaintance, Mr. Fouracres, with whom he had spent an hour or two at a public-house in Woodbury on the evening before. How the landlord of the Pig and Whistle had come to this tragic end neither the gardener nor any one else in the neighbourhood could conjecture.

Mr. Ruddiman set to work at once on harnessing the pony, while Miss Fouracres, now quietly weeping, went to prepare herself for the journey. In a very few minutes the vehicle was ready at the door. The messenger had already ridden away.

'Can you drive yourself, Miss Fouracres?' asked Ruddiman, looking and speaking with genuine sympathy.

'Oh yes, sir. But I don't know what to do about the house. I may be away all day. And what about you, sir?'

'Leave me to look after myself, Miss Fouracres. And trust me to look after the house too, will you? You know I can do it. Will you trust me?'

'It's only that I'm ashamed, sir—'

'Not a bit of it. I'm very glad, indeed, to be useful; I assure you I am.'

'But your dinner, sir?'

'Why, there's cold meat. Don't you worry, Miss Fouracres. I'll look after myself, and the house too; see if I don't. Go at once, and keep your mind at ease on my account, pray do!'

'It's very good of you, sir, I'm sure it is. Oh, I *knew* something was going to happen! Didn't I *say* so?'

Mr. Ruddiman helped her into the trap; they shook hands silently, and Miss Fouracres drove away. Before the turn of the road she looked back. Ruddiman was still watching her; he waved his hand, and the young woman waved to him in reply.

Left alone, the under-master took off his coat and put on an apron, then addressed himself to the task of washing up his breakfast things. Afterwards he put his bedroom in order. About ten o'clock the first customer came in, and, as luck had it, the day proved a busier one than usual. No less than four cyclists stopped to make a meal. Mr. Ruddiman was able to supply them with cold beef and ham; moreover, he cooked eggs, he made tea—and all this with a skill and expedition which could hardly have been expected of him. None the less did he think constantly of Miss Fouracres. About five in the afternoon wheels sounded; aproned and in his shirt-sleeves, he ran to the door—as he had already done several times at the sound of a vehicle—and with great satisfaction saw the face of his hostess. She, too, though her eyes showed she had been weeping long, smiled with gladness; the next moment she exclaimed distressfully.

'Oh, sir! To think you've been here alone all day! And in an apron!'

'Don't think about me, Miss Fouracres. You look worn out, and no wonder. I'll get you some tea at once. Let the pony stand here a little; he's not so tired as you are. Come in and have some tea, Miss Fouracres.'

Mr. Ruddiman would not be denied; he waited upon his hostess, got her a very comfortable tea, and sat near her whilst she was enjoying it. Miss Fouracres' story of the day's events still left her father's death most mysterious. All that could be certainly known was that the landlord of the Pig and Whistle had drunk rather freely with his friend the gardener at an inn at Woodbury, and towards nine o'clock in the evening had gone out, as he said, for a stroll before bedtime. Why he entered the grounds of Woodbury Manor, and how he got into the pond there, no one could say. People talked of suicide, but Miss Fouracres would not entertain that suggestion. Of course there was to be an inquest, and one could only await the result of such evidence as might be forthcoming. During the day Miss Fouracres had telegraphed to the only relatives of whom she knew anything, two sisters of her father, who kept a shop in London. Possibly one of them might come to the funeral.

'Well,' said Mr. Ruddiman, in a comforting tone, 'all you have to do is to keep quiet. Don't trouble about anything. I'll look after the business.'

Miss Fouracres smiled at him through her tears.

'It's very good of you, sir, but you make me feel ashamed. What sort of a day have you had?'

'Splendid! Look here!'

He exhibited the day's receipts, a handful of cash, and, with delight decently subdued, gave an account of all that had happened.

'I like this business!' he exclaimed. 'Don't you trouble about anything. Leave it all to me, Miss Fouracres.'

One of the London aunts came down, and passed several days at the Pig and Whistle. She was a dry, keen, elderly woman, chiefly interested in the question of her deceased brother's property, which proved to be insignificant enough. Meanwhile the inquest was held, and all the countryside talked of Mr. Fouracres, whose story, of course, was published in full detail by the newspapers. Once more opinions were divided as to whether the hapless landlord really had or had not entertained His Royal Highness. Plainly, Mr. Fouracres' presence in the grounds of Woodbury Manor was due to the fact that the Prince happened to be staying there. In a state of irresponsibility, partly to be explained by intoxication, partly by the impulse of his fixed idea, he must have gone rambling in the dark round the Manor, and there, by accident, have fallen into the water. No clearer hypothesis resulted from the legal inquiry, and with this all concerned had perforce to be satisfied. Mr. Fouracres was buried, and, on the day after the funeral, his sister returned to London. She showed no interest whatever in her niece, who, equally independent, asked neither counsel nor help.

Mr. Ruddiman and his hostess were alone together at the Pig and Whistle. The situation had a certain awkwardness. Familiars of the inn—country-folk of the immediate neighbourhood—of course began to comment on the state of things, joking among themselves about Mr. Ruddiman's activity behind the bar. The under-master himself was in an uneasy frame of mind. When Miss Fouracres' aunt had gone, he paced for an hour or two about the garden; the hostess was serving cyclists. At length the familiar voice called to him.

'Will you have your dinner, Mr. Ruddiman?'

He went in, and, before entering the parlour, stood looking at a cask of ale which had been tilted forward.

'We must tap the new cask,' he remarked.

'Yes, sir, I suppose we must,' replied his hostess, half absently.

'I'll do it at once. Some more cyclists might come.'

For the rest of the day they saw very little of each other. Mr. Ruddiman rambled musing. When he came at the usual hour to supper, guests were occupying the hostess. Having eaten, he went out to smoke his pipe in the garden, and lingered there—it being a fine, warm night—till after ten o'clock.

Miss Fouracres' voice aroused him from a fit of abstraction.

'I've just locked up, sir.'

'Ah! Yes. It's late.'

They stood a few paces apart. Mr. Ruddiman had one hand in his waistcoat pocket, the other behind his back; Miss Fouracres was fingering her chin.

'I've been wondering,' said the under-master in a diffident voice, 'how you'll manage all alone, Miss Fouracres.'

'Well, sir,' was the equally diffident reply, 'I've been wondering too.'

'It won't be easy to manage the Pig and Whistle all alone.'

'I'm afraid not, sir.'

'Besides, you couldn't live here in absolute solitude. It wouldn't be safe.'

'I shouldn't quite like it, sir.'

'But I'm sure you wouldn't like to leave the Pig and Whistle, Miss Fouracres?'

'I'd much rather stay, sir, if I could any way manage it.'

Mr. Ruddiman drew a step nearer.

'Do you know, Miss Fouracres, I've been thinking just the same. The fact is, I don't like the thought of leaving the Pig and Whistle; I don't like it at all. This life suits me. Could you'—he gave a little laugh—'engage me as your assistant, Miss Fouracres?'

'Oh, sir!'

'You couldn't?'

'How can you think of such a thing, sir.'

'Well, then, there's only one way out of the difficulty that I can see. Do you think—'

Had it not been dark Mr. Ruddiman would hardly have ventured to make the suggestion which fell from him in a whisper. Had it not been dark Miss Fouracres would assuredly have hesitated much longer before giving her definite reply. As it was, five minutes of conversation solved what had seemed a harder problem than any the under-master set to his class at Longmeadows, and when these two turned to enter the Pig and Whistle, they went hand in hand.

Lightning Source UK Ltd.
Milton Keynes UK
07 December 2010

163993UK00001B/223/A